Fiona McCallum has enjoyed a life of contrasts. She was raised on a cereal and wool farm in rural South Australia and then moved to inner-city Melbourne to study at university as a mature age student. Becoming involved with an executive high-flyer and accidently starting a writing and editing consultancy saw her mixing in corporate circles in Melbourne and then Sydney. She returned to Adelaide for a slower paced life and to chase her dream of becoming an author – which took nearly a decade full of rejections from agents and publishers to achieve. Fiona now works as a full-time novelist and really is proof dreams can come true. Having survived many ups and downs and heartbreaks, a constant has been the support of a handful of very dear friends for which she will be eternally grateful.

Fiona writes heart-warming journey of self-discovery stories that draw on her life experiences, love of animals and fascination with the power and support that comes from strong friendships. She is the author of eight Australian bestsellers: *Paycheque*, *Nowhere Else*, *Wattle Creek*, *Saving Grace*, *Time Will Tell*, *Meant To Be*, *Leap of Faith* and *Standing Strong*. *Finding Hannah* is her ninth novel.

More information about Fiona and her books can be found on her website at www.fionamccallum.com and she can be followed on Facebook at www.facebook.com/fionamccallum.author.

Also by Fiona McCallum

Paycheque
Nowhere Else
Leap of Faith

The Wattle Creek series
Wattle Creek
Standing Strong

The Button Jar series
Saving Grace
Time Will Tell
Meant To Be

FIONA McCALLUM

Finding Hannah

First Published 2017
Second Australian Paperback Edition 2018
ISBN 978 1 489 24692 9

FINDING HANNAH
© 2017 by Fiona McCallum
Australian Copyright 2017
New Zealand Copyright 2017

This is a work of fiction. Names, characters, places, and incidents are either the product of the author's imagination or are used fictitiously, and any resemblance to actual persons, living or dead, business establishments, events, or locales is entirely coincidental.

Published by
HQ Fiction
An imprint of Harlequin Enterprises (Australia) Pty Ltd.
Level 13, 201 Elizabeth St
SYDNEY NSW 2000
AUSTRALIA

® and TM (apart from those relating to FSC) are trademarks of Harlequin Enterprises Limited or its corporate affiliates. Trademarks indicated with ® are registered in Australia, New Zealand, and in other countries.

Cataloguing-in-Publication details are available from the National Library of Australia www.librariesaustralia.nla.gov.au

Printed and bound in Australia by McPherson's Printing Group

MIX
Paper from
responsible sources
FSC
www.fsc.org   FSC® C001695

In memory of my dad, to whom I owe so much.
Gone for many years, remembered every day.

Chapter One

Hannah stirred and rolled over to face her husband. She returned his beaming smile and snuggled up against him as he held his arms out wide, then hugged her tight.

'Merry Christmas, darling wife,' Tristan said, kissing Hannah on the top of her head.

'Merry Christmas, darling husband,' she said, kissing his chest. Her heart glowed. She loved Christmas, just loved it! Always had.

The Whites had never been keen on spending huge amounts on presents, nor the religious side of it, but they had put on a big feast every year and opened up their house and welcomed everyone who didn't have family or anywhere else to go on Christmas Day. It was always a wonderfully joyful and raucous affair, even with the majority of guests being around Hannah's parents' age. Sadly some were no longer with them – like dear old Pat who was apparently a teetotaller on every day except Christmas, and tended to get mischievous after just a few sips of champagne. Hannah and Tristan still laughed at the shock he'd got the first year when the old lady had caressed his bottom while he carried a tray of drinks.

Tristan and Hannah had only been going out for a few months and Hannah had been afraid he'd be frightened off. Instead, he'd put down the tray and drawn Pat into a haphazard waltz, and had instantly become a firm favourite with all. One of the things Hannah loved about Tristan from the get go was his ability to think quickly on his feet. No doubt that was one of the reasons he'd progressed so quickly up the career ladder. She figured the extra six years of life experience he had on her helped too. And his charm and broad, disarming smile and the twinkle in his big brown eyes.

Giving up the all-day, open-house Christmas extravaganza the Whites were well-known for had been one of the biggest things that had bothered Daphne and Daniel about downsizing and moving into the retirement village. But for the past five years Hannah and Tristan had more than capably kept up the tradition, with Hannah's parents always declaring each year's celebrations were better than the last. Not that they would say anything else.

Hannah was lucky. In her view, she had the best parents in the world. They were generous with praise, encouragement and their love, were never controlling, and only gave opinions when asked. She knew how fortunate she was. So many of her friends had mother issues or father issues. Sometimes she even felt a little guilty when her friends quizzed her in tones of disbelief – did she really get on so well with her parents? 'Yep, afraid so,' she'd say with a laugh.

Hannah felt comforted by knowing that whatever happened she could talk to her parents and they would help her to put everything into perspective and sort through any problems. Not that much had ever gone wrong so far in Hannah's thirty-one years of life, except the common angst that came with teenage hormones and discovering that boys and girls really were very different. But both parents had equally helped steer her through, and after a few bruises to her heart she'd found Tristan.

Dear sweet Tris, who was kind and gentle and encouraging and strong and capable – all the best qualities of her parents rolled into one. Except Hannah thought he was a little obsessed with playing golf and computer games. Both complete time wasters in her opinion. But at least when he was out on a Saturday she could do things around the house in peace or go shopping with friends. She understood how important networking on the golf course was in the business world. And if pretending to be some kind of fictitious character and shoot or hide from aliens in some pretend, online world was how Tristan unwound after a long day, then who was she to argue? He worked hard and was doing well in his career. So, each to their own, she told herself regularly – to the point that it was almost a mantra. Though she didn't like that sometimes she was forced into the role of nagging wife in order to get him to help her with something or other.

The only other major criticism she had of Tristan was that he initially really wasn't much into Christmas. But she'd managed to change that. When they met, Hannah knew that Tristan had thought she was nuts loving Christmas so much. Thankfully he was now almost as nutty about it all as she was.

Hannah still sometimes found herself mentally shaking her head at their first discussion about Christmas. They were out for a casual cafe meal and she'd been completely stunned – rendered speechless several times.

'So, what does your family do for Christmas?' she'd asked.

'Nothing really.'

'Don't be silly. Nobody does *nothing* for Christmas!' she'd cried.

'We don't. Not anymore,' he'd said with a shrug.

'But you at least put up a Christmas tree and exchange presents, right?'

'I don't even know if Mum still has any decorations. I can't remember the last time I saw a Christmas tree up at the farm.'

Hannah had stared open mouthed. *No way!*

'So you used to celebrate, then?'

'Of course.'

Hannah had let out a slight sigh of relief. There was hope for him yet.

'I guess Mum and Dad didn't think there was much to celebrate after Scott died,' he'd added with another nonchalant shrug.

'Scott who?'

'My brother. He was fifteen – two years older than me. He got drunk, took the family car and crashed it.'

'Oh god. I'm so sorry.'

'Thanks.'

'How come he knew how to drive at fifteen?' Hannah said, frowning.

'Oh, we were both driving from the age of eight – it's normal when you grow up on a farm.'

'You poor thing. How awful. And your parents, how sad for them.'

'Thanks, but it was ages ago. Luckily no one else was involved. It certainly put me off drink driving, I can tell you. But please don't mention it to Mum and Dad when you get around to meeting them. They blame themselves.'

'Right. Okay.' The last thing Hannah wanted was to upset anyone.

'Anyway, I guess that was the end of Christmas as I knew it. Not that it was a really big deal in our house before then, anyway. Well, not that I remember.'

With wide eyes Hannah had watched him take a sip of beer. She could tell that Tristan found it hard – almost impossible – to talk about his brother, even though he tried to sound as if he'd got over the accident.

'So, for Christmas Day,' Tristan began, changing the subject, 'do your parents prefer white or red wine – or should I take one of each?' She was still too stunned to speak.

'Hannah?'

'Sorry? What?'

'What wine should I take on Christmas Day?'

'Oh. Bring both. Dad will want you to have any bottles we don't open.'

In the years since, she'd learnt that when a member of the Ainsley family didn't want to discuss something there was no making them. Tristan had inherited a clever ability to carefully deflect a conversation without appearing rude or even particularly defensive. The few times she'd tried to discuss Scott's death Tristan had answered politely then carefully shut down the conversation.

'Yes, we were close and we got on well. Of course I miss him. But there's no point dwelling and being morbid about it. He made a stupid decision and now he's not here. End of story. There's really nothing more to tell, Hann. Honest. I'm fine about it. Really.' He'd sealed the conversation with a kiss and Hannah was left feeling sad, right to the pit of her stomach – as much so in empathy for his loss, but also for his burden in holding it all inside. She couldn't help feeling that if he really was okay with it then he'd be able to talk about his brother, sharing happy memories of him, laughing about their little boy antics. But she also knew that not talking about it, closing the door on it, was another way of dealing with something. If that was Tristan's way – and it clearly was – then it was not for her to judge. She was only a bystander to his grief – which she hadn't even realised until then he was carrying – and not actually living it. She might do it all differently in his shoes, but then again, she might not. But what she did know was that she'd be there if at some point he did want to open up to her or if it did all catch up with him and he fell apart. Hannah was also left to silently wonder if the Ainsley family had really never been much into celebrating Christmas or if they had been and stopped the year of Scott's death. She just couldn't get her head around Christmas not being a huge deal – for anyone.

These days, since retiring, Tristan's parents were rarely home for Christmas, anyway. In fact, they were away more often than they were at their Adelaide property.

They were currently making their way around Australia in their caravan – right now they were in Tasmania. Perhaps they did celebrate in their own way. She liked to think so. But it didn't matter, Tristan had been welcomed into Hannah's family as the son Daphne and Daniel had longed for but never been blessed with. And he had fully embraced the Christmas spirit. While Hannah was grateful, she sometimes felt a little guilty that it meant she got Tristan to herself every year rather than doing miles to visit with both families or having to miss out on spending time with her own parents due to distance, like some of her friends did.

Ah, Christmas, Hannah thought, enjoying the feel of Tristan's strong arms around her and the smell of him. Even though she loved Christmas Day and all it entailed, Hannah also loved these precious moments of just *being* before they got up and set everything in motion.

'Well, no rest for the wicked, it's Christmas!' Hannah said, giving her husband another kiss, and then a gentle, good-natured shove.

She leaned over to where the phone handset sat on its charger on the small bedside table.

'Happy Christmas!' she bellowed as soon as the call was answered.

'And a happy Christmas to you.' It was her mum, Daphne. 'Dad's here. I'll put him on then we can have a longer chat.'

'Good morning, darling heart. Merry Christmas.'

'Hi, Dad, and a merry Christmas to you. Can't wait to see you.'

'What time will Tris be here?'

'No changes. Eight-fifty, on the dot.'

'Great. Well, we'll see you soon. I'll put your mother back on. No doubt you have things to discuss.'

'Okay. Catch ya later.'

'Now darling, should I pop in a few extra oven mitts too?' Daphne White said.

'No, I have plenty here, Mum.' *As always.*

'What about the vegetable peeler. You have one of the special ones, don't you? You know my fingers don't work like they used to.'

'Yes. I know, Mum. I have two of the peelers – remember, you gave them to me.'

'I wouldn't remember my head if it wasn't screwed on these days, dear. Anyway, that's good. Peelers. And what about tea towels?' Hannah heard what sounded like a pen scratching paper – Daphne ticking items off on a list – and smiled. As much as the Whites loved Christmas, they loved lists – making them and following them, Daniel not quite to the same extent as the women.

'Good idea. Thanks, Mum. We can never have enough tea towels. And did you remember to get out a couple of aprons?'

'I did. They're right here. Oh, I know! What about sheer covers – it's going to be warm so the flies will be out and driving us madder than usual.'

'I've got yours already, remember? Everything is under control, Mum. We went through the lists together last week. It will all be fine and you don't need to worry about a thing.' As her mum grew older, the more long-winded and frustrating these conversations became. But Hannah didn't mind. She loved her mother and found her growing frailty and recently acquired slight ditziness quite sweet and endearing.

'I know, dear, sorry, I don't mean to sound like I don't think you can cope, I just …'

'You just like to help. I know. And just having you here to peel all the veggies and be my slave will help heaps.'

'Yes, well, you just sit me at the bench and I won't be any trouble at all.'

'You're never any trouble, Mum.'

'I'd like to at least feel useful and helpful.'

'You're *very* useful and helpful, Mum. And you always will be.'

'Well I would be if it weren't for this damned arthritis and forgetfulness. You know, last night I put your father's coffee in the fridge instead of the microwave. Dear, oh dear, some days I'm as silly as a wheel.'

'I'm sure you were just distracted for a moment. Anyway, Mum, we'll have nothing less than happy – it's Christmas.'

'Yes, golly, listen to me feeling all sorry for myself. I'm just being a nincompoop. So, that's all, then?'

'And the presents.'

'Don't worry, they're in a box beside the front door all ready to go. We can't leave the house without tripping over them.'

'Good one, Mum. I'll see you soon. Get ready to cook up a storm.'

'Right you are. Ready and willing.'

'Brilliant. See you soon. Love you.'

'Love you too. Bye for now.'

'How are they? All ready to go?' Tristan asked, as Hannah wandered into the kitchen.

'Yes. They're well. Looking forward to the day. Did you call your parents?'

'I did.'

'How are they?'

'Good. They send their love.'

Tristan made coffee while Hannah sat at the bench and read through her extensive to-do list, that was timed to the quarter hour and which she'd almost completely memorised. All Tristan had to do now that he had phoned his parents, was to collect her parents twenty minutes' drive away.

Then, when they arrived, Tristan and her father would sit and chew the fat whilst eating their way through the nibbles Hannah had put out for them, and she and Daphne would retreat to the kitchen to get the cooking underway.

After Daphne and Hannah had done the vegetables and organised the meal so it could be left to cook largely unattended for an hour or so, Tristan and her parents would sit around the tree with Hannah on her knees beside it handing out presents. They did it early, before anyone outside the family arrived. There had always been an unwritten convention about three presents being exchanged — nothing too expensive, but three gifts. Daniel, who hated shopping, regularly separated one present into three in order to make his quota. The year Hannah was twelve she'd received a remote-control car, batteries and the remote — all wrapped separately. She loved surprises and unwrapping a remote-control car sure had been a surprise!

'Right, so it's true, you really wanted a son,' Hannah had ribbed.

'No dear, he just wants someone to race with,' Daphne had said.

'Guilty as charged!' Daniel had grinned as he'd proceeded to unwrap a present from his wife — his own remote-control car.

Father and daughter had had a ball racing each other on the concrete paths around the house for the next few months. Hannah loved that she had so many fond memories. She really had enjoyed a happy childhood and blessed life.

'How's it all looking? Anything you need me to get?' Tristan asked as he picked up the car keys.

'No, thanks, I think we're good.'

'Well, if you change your mind ...'

'Yes, I know, there's always the Chans.'

This was another ritual – Hannah was meticulous in her planning and rarely forgot anything. She would start buying supplies weeks out from Christmas and only left the perishables until last thing – like a squirrel gathering its nuts and preparing for the winter. It was all part of the fun for her. She couldn't understand anyone who moaned that Christmas was stressful. As far as she was concerned, with a bit – or a lot – of planning, it didn't need to be.

The Whites hadn't joined the seafood craze so thankfully she didn't have to be out queuing early at the fish markets. No matter the weather, they always had the full cooked shebang – stuffed roast turkey and a leg of lamb, mountains of roast vegetables. Their cool offering was a leg of ham, which Hannah – and her mother before her – prepared on Christmas Eve.

Everything was closed on Christmas Day, anyway. Well, everything except the little corner shop at the end of their road run by the Chan family. Hannah wasn't sure what religion they were or if they were just industrious and clever enough to cash in on the frenzy that was Christmas Day.

'Good on them,' Tristan had declared the first year he'd driven past and seen the queue outside the shop. 'Successful business is all about demand and supply – supplying a demand.'

'Okay, so how long do you think the line-up to buy forgotten batteries and last-minute vegetables will be this year?' Tristan asked with a cheeky grin. After her parents arrived they would discuss the size of the crowd waiting for the Chans' store to open at nine forty-five. They had even started taking bets on the length of the queue, which had been known to stretch right around the corner.

'Just to the corner – no further,' Hannah said. 'Surely people will have learnt by now.'

'Come on, no one will ever be as organised as you, my darling,' he said. 'Look, we even have a list of the lists we have,' he said, picking up a piece of paper.

'Cheeky devil,' she said, dragging a tea towel from the bench and throwing it at him. 'Be grateful, mister.'

'I am. And I wouldn't have you any other way, my love,' he said, wrapping his arms around her and planting a kiss on her neck before nuzzling it. 'I *love* your list-making obsession.'

'Just as well. And there's nothing wrong with being organised. Anyway, it's not my fault – it's in my genes. Blame my mother,' Hannah said, pouting.

'Oh no, she has my eternal gratitude,' he said with a theatrical wave of the tea towel in his hand.

'As it should be,' Hannah said, catching the tea towel and putting it back on the bench.

'Okay, so is that your final bet? I'm writing it down,' he said, going to the fridge and holding up the whiteboard marker. 'Last chance.'

'Yep, to the corner. So, what say you, smarty pants?'

'To the post box.'

'Ooh, we have a bold prediction from Mr Ainsley this year,' Hannah said, picking up a serving spoon and using it as a pretend microphone. 'No worries, that'll just be another ten bucks you'll owe me.'

'I wouldn't be too quick to call it, Mrs Ainsley.'

'Well, we shall see, Mr Ainsley.'

'Yes, we shall!'

'Okay, I'd better be off. See you in a bit,' Tristan said, kissing Hannah.

'Drive carefully.'

'Always. You be careful with the knives. And no peeking at the presents,' he said, grinning.

*

As she carried sprigs of rosemary for flavouring the leg of lamb in from the garden, Hannah glanced at the Weber kettle with its lid off and loaded up with heat beads all ready to be lit to cook the Christmas lunch. Where was Tristan? He needed to light it. She shook her annoyance aside. He'd be here. Tris was nothing if not reliable. Though, he did have her parents to contend with.

No doubt Daphne had put the house keys somewhere and forgotten where or lost her lipstick, or something. Hannah checked her watch, compared it to the schedule, grabbed the extra-long matches from the bench top and raced back outside to light the kettle.

Back inside, she sat for a moment at the bench to double-check her list. She frowned and tapped her fingers on the bench. They were meant to be opening presents by now. She thought about phoning Tristan, but then remembered she'd seen his phone beside the fruit basket earlier. She frowned. So much for being able to phone him to get something from the Chans'. Should she phone her parents? No, they'd be along any minute. *They've just got caught up in the Christmas festivities*, she told herself. Anyway, both her parents' mobiles usually lived in the bottom of her mother's handbag and were rarely heard. And, if they were, it's unlikely her mother would pick one up in time.

Hannah found herself becoming tense at the thought that just being half an hour late would put her carefully planned schedule out completely. *Oh well, in the scheme of things, no one would die if the meal was dished up at one o'clock and not twelve-thirty and people turned up while the lounge room floor was still strewn with discarded wrapping paper and ribbon*, she decided. It wouldn't be ideal, but it wouldn't be the end of the world, either. She tried to relax but the feeling that something was wrong, something more than her precious schedule being disrupted, was creeping into her mind.

In an effort to keep herself busy and the unease at bay, Hannah took the vegetables out of the fridge. She missed her mother's chatter beside her. The house felt strangely empty and echoing, even with the Christmas carols playing in the background.

Finishing the vegetables, she was shocked to find Tristan and her parents were now almost an hour late. Shit, she'd better get the meat on.

She shifted between worry and annoyance at struggling to hold the large, heavy tray whilst getting the meat safely onto the racks above the white ash-covered coals.

There had been a spate of burst water mains across some nearby suburbs recently. Perhaps that was the hold up. She hoped they weren't stuck on a road the other side of a major incident, though a burst water main or malfunctioning traffic lights were more preferable to think about than the obvious …

Hopefully her best friend Sam would be here soon with her husband Rob and boisterous four-year-old boys Oliver and Ethan. The distraction would be good and depending on what mood the kids were in the three adults might even get to relax over a glass of bubbly. Better yet, Tristan and her parents would come bursting in, her father making his usual 'dad joke' about it being a 'White Christmas' despite it being the middle of summer. And then, after they'd all stopped groaning and rolling their eyes at him they'd explain about whatever had held them up whilst apologising profusely – her mother giggling from a bit too much egg nog. Hannah smiled. She really was very lucky to have family and friends she adored so much.

Samantha had been Hannah's best friend since they'd met on their first day at university, standing in the quadrangle turning their maps around trying to figure out where their first classes were on the huge campus. Sam was also an only child, but one who had serious mother issues. Thank goodness Sam had such a lovely, supportive husband in Rob – who also happened to have become one of Tristan's best friends. The two men hadn't really had much of a choice when Sam and Hannah spent so much time together.

A sense of relief washed over Hannah as a triple honk of a car horn sounded. She rushed to see if it was Tristan and her parents or Sam and Rob and the boys. She tried to keep the disappoint-ment and concern at bay upon seeing Sam and Rob's red wagon at the kerb. Hannah raced outside and across the lawn to meet them.

'Merry Christmas!' they all shouted. The twins, dressed in Superman outfits, tumbled out and began racing around the lawn with their arms spread out. It was hard to tell if they were pretend-ing to fly or chasing each other.

'Boys! Stop! You need to take that noise out into the back garden. If it's okay with Auntie Hannah.'

'Off you go,' Hannah said.

'Quietly through the house,' Rob called after them as they took off up the steps towards the front door.

'Give me strength,' Sam said, handing Hannah a large fruit and cheese platter before stepping out of the car. 'Sorry, the boys are a little ratty this morning. They stripped the tree of candy canes,' she added as they made their way inside. 'I thought I'd managed to put them up high enough, but apparently not. I'm about ready to give them away if you're interested,' she said wearily.

'Not exactly a great sales job there, Sammy. So, thanks, but no thanks,' Hannah said with a laugh.

She liked kids, especially Oliver and Ethan. They were dear, sweet, well-brought-up little boys, if a bit rowdy at times. She wanted kids – she and Tristan were trying, well, not seriously trying; they'd simply stopped taking precautions to not get pregnant. Hannah loved the idea of being a parent, having someone else to love, a small person to raise, but she also quite liked the freedom of not having that responsibility yet. She saw far too often how frazzled Sam and Rob were.

At first she'd thought Sam being laid back about cleaning and domestic matters generally would have helped, but later she wondered whether being ordered and organised might hold the key. On one hand she was keen to put it to the test – not to compete with Sam and prove a point – but on the other she was terrified of parenting bringing her undone, not to mention changing her and Tristan's relationship.

It was clear from watching Sam and Rob that despite them still being clearly devoted to each other, the twins required – and received – the most attention.

'I'll just go and check on the boys. I can't hear them – and that's never a good sign,' Rob said after dumping an esky in the kitchen.

'That's the trouble,' Sam said. 'You finally get some peace, but then you have to go check and disturb them because, as Rob said, silence is never a good sign. Oh, I tell you ...'

'And you wouldn't change it for the world,' Hannah said.

'No, I probably wouldn't. They are dear little things most of the time,' Sam said, smiling. 'Now, enough about me,' she said, suddenly serious. 'What's going on with you? Where's your cheer and sparkle on this fine Christmas morning? A White Christmas, no less!'

'Oh, ha-ha,' Hannah said, rolling her eyes at the tired old joke, but smiling despite herself.

'So, why so glum?' Sam said, holding her friend away and scrutinising her. 'And don't say you're not, because I can read you like a book. Has something happened to Daphne and Daniel – where are they? Daphne's usually installed here at the bench. And Tristan should be out standing over the Weber.'

'No. I don't know where they are. They should have been here over an hour ago.'

'Ah, they've probably got caught up sampling all the egg nog. You know what those retirement village residents are like – mob of soaks, all of them. Tris would be overruled in a second.'

'Yeah. I hope you're right. You didn't hear about any accidents or anything on the radio, did you?' Hannah suddenly wondered why she hadn't turned the radio on herself or logged onto the computer. But she'd been too busy trying to convince herself they were just a bit late, and trying to keep everything else on schedule.

'Sorry, we had to have the Wiggles on at full blast.'

'No worries. Lunch might be late, but it'll be fine.'

'So says the queen of impeccable timing.'

'Yes, well, I'm trying to convince myself it'll be fine. So don't you go bursting my bubble.'

'Don't worry. I'm sure they'll come bustling in here soon enough complaining about the traffic, or whatever.'

'I hope so.'

'Is there anything I can do to help? Perhaps I can be Daphne and peel the veggies until she arrives?' Sam said, settling herself on a stool and looking around.

'Thanks, but everything's done.'

'It's okay,' Rob said, coming into the kitchen, 'they're flat out on the lawn pretending to fly and pretending they're not plum tuckered out.'

They shared a chuckle.

'So what can I help with?' he asked, looking around. 'And where's Tristan and your parents, anyway?'

'We don't know. You can pour us a drink, darling. God knows, we need one. Champagne, Hann?'

'Yes, thanks, that would be lovely. I think I'm all done here for now,' she said, casting her eye over her list.

They had just got settled with drinks in hand when Oliver and Ethan appeared.

'Can we please have a drink?' they said, both speaking at once.

'Of course you can,' Sam said, but stayed put.

'It's okay, darling, you sit there. I'll deal with it,' Rob said, getting up and putting a hand to his wife's shoulder and a kiss on her forehead as he passed.

'You're the best,' Sam said, and raised her glass to him.

A few minutes later Sam and Hannah cocked their heads at hearing the sound of car doors closing. Hannah took another sip of champagne as she resisted going out to give Tristan a small piece of her mind. But the last thing she needed was an argument on Christmas Day. They had a dozen more guests arriving in less than an hour.

They looked at each other quizzically when the doorbell sounded.

'I'll get it,' Rob called.

'Thanks,' Hannah replied. She'd better ease up on the champagne if she wanted lunch to be perfect. The few sips she'd had had gone right to her head and she felt a little too relaxed to be bothered getting up. If Tristan and her parents had their hands full of gifts Rob would help them, equally if it was someone who'd turned up early. The Ainsley house, which had been the White house before them, was known to be open and welcoming all day at Christmas. People often dropped in for a drink on their way to or from somewhere else.

Hannah was distracted from her thoughts by Oliver and Ethan sidling up to the Christmas tree.

'Can we please have a candy cane, Auntie Hann?' Oliver asked.

'If it's okay with your mum.'

'Don't you think you had enough at home?' Sam said.

'But, *Muuuum*, it's Christmas,' Ethan whined.

'Just one,' Sam said with a resigned sigh. 'And then sit quietly on the floor to eat them.'

They carefully plucked a brightly striped piece of hooked candy from the tree and sat down.

'You've got to pick your battles,' Sam said as she and Hannah watched them in silence.

Chapter Two

'Um, Hann, these officers need a word.'

Hannah turned with a frown already set on her face. She'd almost forgotten the doorbell had rung. Two uniformed policemen now stood in her lounge room beside Rob.

'Mrs Ainsley?' the taller, younger of the two men asked.

Hannah stared at them as if seeing them but not quite comprehending who they were. She felt strange, suddenly weak, and was thankful she was sitting down. She should get up, but didn't think she could; she was glued to the chair and her legs felt like jelly. Her heart was starting to pound extra hard, and extra slowly, too. It was as if time had stopped still. Hannah continued to stare, frowning, struggling to find the dots to connect, let alone connect them.

'Darling, perhaps you'd better take the boys outside,' Sam said to Rob, nodding at the two boys who were staring with a mixture of awe and bewilderment at the officers.

'Boys, come with me please.'

'But, Daaaad,' Oliver whined.

'Now, boys.'

Ethan's bottom lip drooped but the twins climbed to their feet and reluctantly stomped out, clutching their sweets.

'Mrs Ainsley?' The younger of the two men asked, looking from Hannah to Sam and back again. Hannah swallowed, tried to find her voice. Failed. Nodded.

'Yes. I'm Mrs Ainsley – Hannah,' she finally managed to croak out. She felt the champagne in her stomach bite and she had to consciously swallow back the rising bile. She felt her hands begin to shake. Gradually her heart started to pick up pace. Tears began to prickle. There were only two reasons why the police would come knocking on your door on Christmas morning – someone was badly injured or someone was dead – or *someones*.

She felt Sam sit down beside her and pick up her hand.

'I'm Sergeant Patrick O'Brien,' the younger policeman said. 'And this is Sergeant Barry Dwyer. We're from the Major Collision Investigation Unit.'

'We're sorry to have to inform you that a vehicle registered to this address has been involved in an accident.' Again it was the younger man who spoke. What was his name again? Had they given their names? She blinked and frowned.

'Tristan? My parents?' Hannah asked in barely a whisper, despite knowing the answer. They were dead. She knew it. Otherwise the police officers would have bundled her into the car and whisked her off to the hospital, lights and sirens blaring. This was too calm, too measured. Too final.

'I'm really sorry,' the older policeman said, shaking his head slowly. 'They died at the scene.'

'But they can't be, they're only an hour late.' Hannah felt all she'd known escape her and disappear down her face along with the streaming tears. She so badly wanted to turn back time, stop the clock, for this not to be happening.

She sobbed while Sam held her. It seemed to take forever, but gradually the tears subsided. For a moment she felt self-conscious and bad for the officers having to see her break down, but then there probably wasn't much they hadn't seen or dealt with. A box of tissues appeared in front of her. She looked up. Rob stood over her, his face drawn, his eyes red, and his hand holding the tissues was shaking.

'Thanks,' she said, trying to offer him a consoling smile. She sniffled as she plucked a few out. She had to be strong. Tristan and her parents would want her to be strong. It would be expected. And falling apart wouldn't bring them back.

'What happened?' she heard Sam ask quietly.

'At least Tristan wasn't using his phone while driving – not that he ever does, um, did – it's here on the kitchen bench,' Hannah said, feeling the need to defend her husband.

'At this stage it appears a truck may have failed to stop at a red light. We won't know exactly until a full investigation has been carried out.'

God, Hannah thought, *if only I'd let Tristan buy a four-by-four last year and not said that only wankers drive them and they never go off-road.*

'Um, do you need us to come and identify them or, um, anything?' Sam asked.

Thank god for Sam, Hannah thought.

'Not right now. Autopsies will have to be performed. That will take a couple of days. And …'

'How, um, badly, um. Will they, um, be, um, recognisable?' Sam asked.

'We're not sure at this stage, but it is a very grim scene.'

'Do I have to go and see them?' Hannah asked in a whisper. 'I don't think I want to.' She remembered Tristan telling her how he'd seen his brother in an open coffin at his funeral and never been able to get that last image out of his mind. One of the rare occasions he'd opened up about his brother. Hannah didn't think she could bear to remember Tris and her parents like that.

'They'll need to be identified, but there are several ways we can do it. And while we'd prefer a close relative, someone who knows them well can do a visual identification – depending if this is possible, of course.'

'Can't you just check Tristan's driver's licence – he would have had it with him, wouldn't he?' Sam said.

'There are a number of ways to confirm identification. But we have to be absolutely sure.'

'Of course,' Sam said.

'Mum and Dad's fingerprints will be on record because of their volunteer police checks. Would that help?' Hannah said.

'Thank you. It might.'

'I could do it,' Rob said quietly. 'If it would help. I've known Tristan and Mr and Mrs White for quite a few years. I'll give you my card,' he added, fumbling before extracting his wallet from his back pocket. He dragged a business card out. As he handed it over, it dropped from between his forefinger and thumb.

'God. I'm so sorry.'

'It's okay. I'll get it,' the younger of the officers said kindly, and reached down. Rob stood back, running his hands through his hair, over and over, and biting his lip.

'Thank you, Mr Barrow. We'll let you know. Is there anyone you'd like us to call for you, Mrs Ainsley?'

'I'm fine, thanks,' Hannah said, feeling anything but fine. The truth was, she had no idea what to do. Her brain felt like it had dropped into neutral. Her words were just coming out on their own.

'I'll get us some tea,' Sam said, though made no show of getting up.

'No, I'll get it,' Rob said. He was still standing nearby.

'Can you please just check on the vegetables in the oven, make sure they're not overcooked. Pull them out if they look done,' Hannah said. She stared at her watch while trying to remember what time she had marked down to take them out. 'Actually, I'd better check on the meat too,' she said, starting to get up.

'Hann, you don't need to worry about lunch,' Sam said gently.

'Well I can't let it all burn,' Hannah said. 'And a stack of people will start arriving in half an hour,' she added, frowning at her watch again. Her brain really wasn't working correctly. Though if she could just get up she could cook – she might muddle up the timing, but the actual cooking of Christmas lunch she could do, practically with her eyes closed and one hand tied behind her back. She pictured her to-do list – consulting it was a mere formality; it never changed from year to year.

'Do you have everyone's numbers, I'll start phoning them.'

'Oh. Well. But I …'

'Hannah, sweetie, you can't go on with Christmas lunch,' Sam said, gripping Hannah's hand tightly and staring imploringly into her friend's eyes.

'People will understand,' Rob said from the doorway to the kitchen, the kettle hissing to life loudly behind him.

'But …'

'Hannah, Tris and your parents would understand,' Sam said, squeezing her hand.

Hannah looked back at her friend, feeling stricken. Finally she nodded. She wasn't sure she could even stand up. She was kidding herself if she thought Christmas could go on. Hell, she wasn't sure she could go on. If only she'd gone with Tristan to collect her parents … She felt a couple of fresh tears squeeze out of her eyes, drop and roll down her face, and wiped them away with the ball of soggy tissues.

Rob brought in five mugs of tea on the chopping board and put it on the coffee table, and began handing them out. His hands seemed a little steadier, though the tide was out – as her father would say. *Oh god*.

Looking around for a distraction, the presents on the floor caught Hannah's attention. Christmas would never be the same again. Ever. She suddenly felt childlike, and as if she was actually shrinking back inside herself and becoming an infant again. If only. If only she could not have all these adult responsibilities to deal with, face up to.

Her whole being started to ache as the reality returned: Tristan and Mum and Dad are dead. They won't be coming back. She looked up at the twinkling, cheery tree. Oh. My. God. Her throat caught, her chin wobbled, and then big fat tears began to fall. She brushed them away, over and over, but they continued to fall. First one after the other, then in a torrent down her cheeks.

'I'm sorry,' she said, sniffling.

'Don't be. It's a terrible time,' the policeman closest to her said, handing her the tissue box again.

'Thank you,' Hannah croaked. She'd dabbed the tears away and was calm again when a mug of milky tea appeared in front of her.

'Have some tea,' Rob said.

'Thanks.' She hoped tea really did make everything feel better like the movies and television shows would have you believe. Though nothing was going to bring her family back, was it?

She wished the tears would stop. The wads of tissues she held were doing nothing to stem the flow and her face was beginning to burn from all the salt. They were silently sipping their tea when the doorbell sounded again.

'I'll get it,' Rob said.

Hannah strained to hear the hushed voices. Poor Rob was clearly having trouble getting rid of whoever it was. Moments later Elizabeth Potts, a dear old family friend Hannah had always called Auntie Beth, was in the room and rushing to Hannah's side.

'Oh, darling, I'm so sorry. I saw the police car. I hope I'm not intruding ...' she said. Sam vacated her seat for the old lady to sit down.

'Never. Oh, Auntie Beth, I'm so glad you're here,' Hannah said, clutching the old lady as her chin wobbled again and a new flood of tears started. *I really need to go and put some face cream on to stop the burning. Oh, what does it matter, three – maybe more people are dead?* Hannah realised she hadn't thought to ask if the truck driver had survived. She couldn't bring herself to ask now. It wasn't that she didn't care, she just didn't have the energy to ask.

'What can I do?' Auntie Beth asked, looking around the small group.

'We were about to start calling people to tell them not to come for lunch,' Sam said.

'We'll leave you to your family and friends,' the younger policeman said, getting up and putting his almost full mug back on the chopping board that Rob had used as a tray. The second policeman followed suit.

'I'm sorry,' Hannah said, 'do I need to do anything for you?'

'We'll need a statement from you at some point – sooner would be better, but when you're up to it.'

'A statement about what? Obviously I didn't see anything – I was here.'

'It will be useful for us if you can provide details such as what your husband was wearing, when he left home, et cetera – as you might have been the last to see him.'

'Darling, why don't you do that now while we deal with the food and letting the guests know?' Beth said, patting Hannah's hand. 'Then it will be out of the way and one less horrible thing to deal with down the track. I'm sure it will be helpful to these nice fellows.'

Hannah nodded. As dreadful as all this was, she felt a glimmer of relief at having her kind but no-nonsense Auntie Beth helping to take charge. Not to dismiss Sam and Rob, of course.

'Only if you feel up to it,' both policemen said at once.

'I'll try. I'm really sorry, but I've forgotten your names,' Hannah said, frowning and blinking. *Did they even tell me?*

'That's quite all right.'

'Completely understandable, Mrs Ainsley. I'm Sergeant Patrick O'Brien,' the younger policeman said, 'and this is Sergeant Barry Dwyer.'

'Please, call me Hannah.'

'Darling, Sam and Rob and I will go and sort things out in the kitchen,' Auntie Beth said, releasing Hannah's hands and getting up. 'Will you be okay for a bit?'

'I'm fine.' *Why are two policemen in my house again?*

Hannah looked blankly at the uniformed men sitting on the couch opposite her, suddenly wondering why they were still there. Didn't they have criminals to catch, crimes to be off fighting instead of sitting here with her drinking cups of tea? Oh, but that's right, she was a victim. They were providing victim liaison services, or whatever they were called.

Oh, that's right, they're waiting for me to make a statement. They're very patient.

Chapter Three

Hannah wasn't exactly sure what the sergeants wanted to know, so she started at when she and Tristan had woken up. She told them everything she could think of in minute detail, right through to when they knocked on her door.

She was exhausted, completely spent, when she finally said quietly, 'And then you arrived with the terrible news.'

'Thank you for being so brave. And so thorough,' Sergeant O'Brien said.

'Yes, we appreciate it. It'll be a real help,' Sergeant Dwyer added.

Now she'd stopped speaking and concentrating so hard on what she said, the voices from the kitchen became clear.

'But, Mum, I'm hungry,' she heard one of the twins say.

'Me too,' the other said.

'Soon, darling,' she heard Sam reply.

'We'll leave you to your friends now. Here are our contact details if you need anything,' Sergeant Dwyer said, placing a business card on the coffee table before standing up. Sergeant

O'Brien got up too and Hannah tried to follow suit. But her legs refused to obey.

'Please don't get up. We can see ourselves out,' Sergeant O'Brien said.

'Thank you. You've been really kind. I'm so sorry you had to knock on my door and deliver such news. Especially on Christmas Day. It must be terrible for you to have to do that ...'

Hannah realised she was babbling and stopped abruptly. She felt weird, like she was losing her grip on a life preserver that was slowly being eased away from her as the two men were making their way from her lounge room. While she'd been a mess of tears and sadness, she'd felt a certain comfort in having them there; their uniforms, their calm manner. She didn't like the feeling that their leaving was casting her adrift to deal with it all alone. Having Sam and Rob and Auntie Beth there was different somehow. Hannah almost cried after them, 'No, don't go. Please,' but the tightness in her chest and the lump in her throat stopped her.

She sat staring into space, not seeing. She knew she should get up and check on what was happening in the kitchen, but she couldn't make herself care or move.

The pain in her chest and throat seeped away and left behind a numb emptiness. She felt as if her heart and soul hadn't just been shattered, but that they had been taken from her completely, along with her whole family.

She noticed some movement and looked over to find Beth hovering nearby, wringing her hands and nibbling her bottom lip as if undecided about something. She frowned. *What now?*

Beth sat beside her on the couch and gently clasped Hannah's hands.

'What's wrong?' *Well, apart from the obvious.*

'Lunch is ready and ...'

'Thanks, but I can't ...' *There's no way I can eat, I can barely breathe.*

'I know. It's just ...'

'What?'

'The boys, the dear little things, they ... Oh, sweetheart ...' Beth started to cry. Hannah wanted to do something, but couldn't do anything but stare like an unfeeling, expressionless pillar of stone. Beth swallowed hard and visibly tried to pull herself together.

Suddenly Hannah felt something – a sharp pain somewhere deep within her. The boys, her darling, innocent little de-facto nephews needed her. They must be so worried, confused, bewildered.

She wasn't sure where the strength came from, but she struggled to her feet. And then on legs she wasn't sure were even connected to her and with Beth's help she managed to make her way slowly to the dining room.

The mingling scents of Christmas lunch greeted her and she felt the bile rise in her throat. Putting both her hands over her mouth, she tried to swallow the burning acid, but it kept coming.

'Sorry,' she gasped, and stumbled from the room. Halfway down the hall to the bathroom she erupted, macerated nuts and champagne spewing down her front and onto the carpet. Her legs collapsed and she sank down to her knees. She couldn't make herself care that she was in the mess. She moaned and began to sob. And then she heard an unrecognisable, unearthly wail bounce off the walls. Had that come from her?

Arms came around her from behind and held her close. She gagged again and her stomach heaved over and over. There was nothing left.

'It's okay. It's okay. Let it out.' It was Sam.

She clutched at Sam's arms across her chest and pulled her friend closer and began sobbing so hard she thought she might actually cough up her lungs. She thought her bowels might have let go too, but she couldn't make herself care about that either.

After what seemed like hours huddled on the floor with Sam, Hannah felt herself slowly coming back to the present.

'Oh god,' she said, looking around her.

'Don't worry about it.' Sam rubbed her back.

Out of the corner of her eye she noticed one of the twins curled around the doorframe to the dining room, watching on – a terrified look on his face.

'The boys,' she croaked, nodding her head in the direction of the little boy.

'Don't worry about it,' Sam said. But in the next breath she called out, 'Olly, darling, go back to Daddy. Rob!'

As Hannah stared at the little boy, a whole new worry washed over her: This could traumatise them for life. It took all of her strength, but she forced herself onto her knees and then onto her feet. She made her way to the bathroom and stood in front of the mirror, unsure of what to do next and unsure if she could do anything beyond just standing there. And then she remembered the little boy's face blinking at her in the hall. She dragged at her dress covered in vomit, struggled, gave up and let her hands drop.

'Come on, let's get you cleaned up,' Sam said, pushing the door closed behind them, her tone suddenly all commanding and full of purpose. Hannah stood and lifted her arms for her dress to be removed, and then her bra. Hannah knew she should be embarrassed but she couldn't feel or do anything. She continued to stand while Sam washed her chest all over with a damp flannel and then dried her off with a towel.

'Back in a sec,' Sam said, and disappeared. Moments later she returned with a bra, t-shirt and track pants. Hannah watched and stood and behaved every bit the obedient child as Sam re-dressed her.

'Thanks.'

'Your hair's probably a bit rank, so we'd better tie it back.' The words and tone caused Hannah to smile. It was the one normal thing – Sam being Sam – in this whole sorry mess that had become Christmas. When her thick, dark hair was tied back with the band that Sam had found on the vanity top, Hannah rinsed her mouth out and having done so thought she might even feel ever so slightly better – more stable.

'Come on, I've held up lunch long enough,' she said.

'You don't have to,' Sam told her friend.

'I know. But I'm going to try.'

'Okay. Good girl,' Sam said, patting her shoulder.

Hannah steeled herself before entering the dining room where Rob and Beth and the twins were seated at one end of the long table. Plates of food were laid out in front of them. Thankfully she was done with throwing up. Now she just felt empty and a strange mix of pain and numbness. She sat and looked away from the plate of food in front of her. She was relieved to see that instead of the customary bottles of wine there was a large pitcher of water with slices of lemon and mint leaves floating in it and each place had a glass of water in front of it. She probably really would throw up if she added more alcohol to the mix. Her stomach was already beginning to turn again. But there was nothing there so she would just swallow it down and keep breathing. She must, if not for her, then for the two little boys sitting there as good as can be. She owed it to them to make an effort to salvage a little of the Christmas spirit and not have the twins completely scarred for life.

The adults at the table exchanged sympathetic tight smiles that were more grimaces. The Whites weren't religious so didn't say grace, but every year they did raise their glasses to make a toast. Tristan had done it since they'd moved into what had been Hannah's parents' house. Now she supposed that fell to her, like everything else would from now on. She felt suddenly weighed down with the burden of that thought. She stared down at her plate with revulsion. She couldn't do it. A few tense moments passed.

Hearing Rob clear his throat gently, she looked up. He raised his glass.

'Um. To Tris, Daph and Dan,' he said quietly and awkwardly. 'We're here for you, Hann, anything you need – you only have to ask,' he added with a snuffle.

Hannah's chin wobbled as she looked at his red, tear-filled eyes and streaked face. Her heart went out to him. Bless him for having the strength to say it – someone had needed to say something. For the first time she realised the magnitude of the loss for everyone sitting at this table – not only her. They were a close-knit group – had spent many years together navigating various ups and downs. Though, of course, nothing like this. Still, Hannah felt the slightest glimmer of comfort that she wasn't completely alone.

'Thank you for being my friends and for being here. You mean the world to me and I love you all very much.' She choked back a sob when Oliver and Ethan solemnly raised their plastic cups and mumbled unintelligibly to mimic the adults' murmurs of agreement.

'You're the best ever sort-of-auntie,' Oliver said as he put his cup back down.

'Yes. You really are,' Ethan said, his lips pursed.

Sam reached across the corner of the table and clasped her friend's hand and Auntie Beth did the same from the other side. Hannah bit her lip to stop herself from crying, and squeezed back.

She pulled back after a moment and stared down at the table, until a slight commotion between Rob and Sam and the boys made her look up with a start.

'Shh, just eat,' Sam hissed.

'But, Mum, it's not …'

'What's up, boys?' Hannah asked.

The twins pursed their lips, their little arms folded tightly across their chests in defiance.

'Come on, you can tell me.'

'There are no crackers,' Oliver said finally.

'Oh. Well, that's no good. We can't eat Christmas lunch without silly hats on,' Hannah said, making a huge effort to sound jovial. She was actually a little relieved to turn her attention to the small boys; she'd been struggling to even look at food, let alone eat anything.

'See, Mum,' Oliver and Ethan said. 'Auntie Hann understands.'

'It's okay, boys, things are a little different this year. But we can do crackers,' Hannah said, looking around, frowning. Last night the table had been set with sixteen places, festive table centre, candles and two crackers on each placemat.

'I'll get them,' Sam said, standing up and going to the sideboard.

Soon they were all wearing colourful tissue-paper hats and the boys had a collection of small useless plastic trinkets beside them. To anyone looking in through the window it might have seemed like an ordinary Australian suburban Christmas, although it was anything but that. For one, the slips of paper with stupid, corny jokes lay unread on the table. For another, what little of the meal that was consumed was largely done in silence, the only sounds the clink and scrape of cutlery on fine bone china.

Hannah cut up all her meat and pushed her meal around her plate, backwards and forwards, from one side to the other and back again. She took a deep breath and picked up a tiny piece of pumpkin with her fork. And then put it down again. No matter how hard she tried, she just couldn't eat.

Thankfully her plate was gathered quickly along with the others – all except the boys' meals were largely untouched – and no comment passed. A few new tears trickled down Hannah's cheeks at the thought of how devastated Daphne would have been seeing such wastefulness. Ordinarily Hannah would have been too, but she was only just managing to sit upright and keep herself together a little for the boys.

The process was repeated with the fruit pudding, custard and cream – a bowl was placed in front of her, and again she feigned interest while the others ate sparingly. Then the food she'd mangled into a mess was collected along with the others' bowls of partially eaten desserts. Again, all without a word. Thankfully the boys seemed too engrossed in their food to take much notice.

Finally they were all pushing back from the table and packing everything up. Rob took the boys into the backyard, out of the way while Hannah sat, as instructed, at the kitchen bench and vacantly watched on while Sam and Auntie Beth rinsed the pans and loaded the dishwasher.

'God, all this leftover food,' Hannah said, her stomach turning again at seeing the platters on the bench in front of her.

'We'll pack it up and freeze it for you. It won't go to waste.'

Hannah nodded. It was well-known how much Hannah Ainsley loved her Christmas-lunch leftovers – just as they were or turned into shepherd's pie or curry. Well, not any more. She really wanted to tell them that the last thing she needed was to be reminded of this terrible day every time she opened her freezer or ate a meal of leftovers, which, looking at how much food there was, might take her three months to get through. And she couldn't imagine finding the energy or inclination to cook up a storm. What would be the point when there was no one to cook for?

They'd just finished when Rob came back in. 'I think I'd better take the boys home,' he said, 'they're starting to get overtired.' He looked a wreck and was running his hands through his dark blond hair over and over again.

'Yes, it's been a big day,' Sam said, looking a little stricken too.

'Darling, it's fine, you stay with Hannah,' Rob said, laying a hand on his wife's shoulder. 'If Hannah wants you to, that is.'

'That'd be good, thanks. If it's okay with you,' Hannah said, not sure what she wanted other than to curl up and go to sleep and then wake up sometime later to find out her life was still just as it had been on Christmas Eve. But as much as she wished for it, she knew it wasn't going to happen. The next best thing was to have her dear friend Sam beside her. Perhaps it was selfish – Sam's little family needed her, but Hannah couldn't make herself say it was okay for Sam to go. She did have Auntie Beth who she knew would be a brick, but still …

'I'll be off,' Auntie Beth said.

'Oh, don't go on my account,' Sam said, clearly concerned.

'It's fine, Sam, honestly. I'm a little worn out, actually. Hannah, darling, I'll be right across the road. Call or come over if you need anything. Anything at all. Either of you. Anytime.'

Hannah nodded. 'Thanks, Auntie Beth. For everything. I'll speak to you tomorrow.'

'I'll help you strap these ragamuffins in,' Sam said, ruffling the hair of the twins now standing on either side of her chair. 'Quick hug and thank you to Auntie Hannah, boys.'

'Thanks for Christmas, Auntie Hann,' Oliver and Ethan mumbled into Hannah's chest as they both hugged her.

'Sorry it was a bit weird, boys.'

'That's okay,' they both said, and wandered towards the hall where Sam stood with Beth.

'I'm so sorry, Hann,' Rob said, sitting beside Hannah and wrapping his arms around her. 'I'll see you tomorrow. But call if I can do anything at all.'

'Thanks Rob.' *And thanks for letting Sam stay.*

Chapter Four

Hannah sat in the lounge room desperately trying not to look towards the corner that was filled with the Christmas tree and the piles of presents covering the floor around it. The tree was still beautiful with its ornaments and brightly coloured lights, but if she had the energy she'd pull it down – and give into the disappointment she now felt for Christmas and all it entailed. *Bloody Christmas, I hate you!* She wanted to scream. But instead she sat there staring dumbly and feeling everything but nothing.

'How are you doing?' Sam said, breaking the silence as she came back into the room and handed her another mug of milky tea.

'Thanks. Honestly, I don't really know. I feel numb. And sad, Sammy, so, so sad,' Hannah said. She had her hands wrapped around the mug. It probably should have been too hot to hold like this, but she couldn't feel anything except its weight.

'Of course you do, darling. You've had a huge shock. You'll feel sad for a very long time. And you might get angry and afraid and overwhelmed, and everything in between.'

'The police arriving and everything since then is a bit of a blur. I know I spoke to them and sat down to lunch and everything, but … We did crackers, didn't we?'

'Yes, and the boys were so grateful. Thank you for doing that for them. You don't know how much …' Sam choked back a sob.

'It's as if it was someone else doing all those things. Or I dreamt it, or something. You know, like it wasn't real and not really me.'

Sam nodded.

'God, what am I going to do without them?'

'You're strong, Hann, you will be okay. You have to believe that. It'll take time.'

'I feel like I'm a completely different person from the one who woke up this morning.'

'You *are* a completely different person, Hannah. Nothing will ever be exactly the same again. You don't get *over* something like this,' Sam said. 'You get through it. One step at a time.'

'I know they're gone, but it doesn't make sense, it's like my brain won't truly believe it. I only saw Tristan and spoke to Mum and Dad this morning. I keep half-expecting them to turn up and announce there's been a huge mistake. But that's not going to happen, is it?'

'I'm afraid not, sweetie.'

'God, I really don't want to go and see them in the morgue all, you know, *damaged*.' *And dead*.

'I couldn't do it. Rob has said he will. Or perhaps Auntie Beth – she's known them longer. And maybe Tristan's parents could …'

'Oh no!' Hannah said.

'What?'

'Tristan's parents haven't been told. Or would the police have rung them?'

'I don't think so. They came here because this is where the car was registered to – and the address on Tristan's licence.'

'God, how could I have forgotten? Here I am sitting around drinking cups of tea and chatting when …'

'Don't beat yourself up, it's only been a few hours. Where are they at the moment?'

'Tasmania. I'm not sure exactly where. And I thought lightning wasn't meant to strike twice,' Hannah added, suddenly remembering their previous loss.

'Shit, I'd forgotten about that. The poor, poor things.'

'God, it's really not the sort of news you should hear over the phone, is it?' said Hannah.

'No, but I don't think you have much choice. Do you want me to call them for you?'

'Thanks, but I'd better do it. And right now.' She placed her mug on the coffee table and made her way through to the kitchen where the phone sat on its charger. It was blinking with messages. She hadn't heard it ring. Someone must have turned the volume down to silent on both the handset and the base station earlier. Thank goodness for that. Hannah sighed.

She and Tristan tended to keep their mobiles on silent while they were at home. Right now she was grateful for that too. The thought of calling people back and saying the same thing dozens of times and answering the same questions over and over made her feel exhausted and overwhelmed. If only she could leave it like that and ignore all the messages and calls forever.

She tried unsuccessfully to steady her nerves with some deep breathing and then, with shaking fingers, she scrolled through the saved numbers until she found *Raelene and Adrian Ainsley Mobile*. She took several more deep breaths to try to steady her racing heart and pressed the green call button. The ringing seemed to go on forever. She was deliberating over whether to hang up or leave a simple please call me message if the voicemail ever cut in when a breathless female voice answered. 'Hello?'

'Raelene, it's Hannah.'

'Hannah, happy Christmas. Lovely to hear from you. Tristan rang early this morning, but I think you were in the shower or busy putting together your gorgeous big lunch. I hope you've had a wonderful ...'

'Raelene, are you driving or in the van? It's ...'

'Of course we're in the van. You know we're off travelling in Tasmania,' she said with a laugh.

'Yes, but are you driving or stopped and inside your van right now, sitting down? And is Adrian there with you?'

'What is it, Hannah? What's going on? You're worrying me. Yes, we're parked and in the van.'

'Please just get Adrian and sit down.'

'He's here beside me.'

Hannah took a deep breath. 'There's been an accident, a car accident. Tristan's been killed.' She hoped the words weren't too harsh, but how else did you say it? There was no way to carefully step around the truth. She was grateful to feel Sam's comforting arm come around her shoulder.

'What? No. He can't be. We spoke to him this morning,' Raelene said.

'What's going on?' Adrian asked gruffly.

'Adrian, I'm really sorry to have to tell you this – especially over the phone – but Tristan was killed in a car accident a couple of hours ago.'

'Where? What was he doing out on the road on Christmas Day?'

'He was picking my parents up from the retirement village to bring them over for lunch. I think a truck might have run a red light or something. That's all I know right now.'

'Oh. Are your parents okay?'

'No, they're, um, they're gone too.' Hannah barely managed to get the words out. She bit her bottom lip to try to stop the new wave of tears.

Hannah heard a loud exhale of breath. 'Oh god. I'm so sorry. We'll be there just as soon as we can. We'll start packing up right now. But I'm afraid it's going to take us a couple of days to get there.'

'Thanks very much. That would be good. Please drive safely, though.' It was a useless thing to say, but it had come out automatically. Tristan was a careful driver, just like his father, and look where that had got him.

After hanging up Hannah stared at the phone in her hand, trying to figure out what she felt, if anything.

'They're on their way, then?' Sam said.

'Yes. Oh, Sammy, that was the hardest phone call I've ever had to make,' Hannah said, sagging into her friend. 'They were so nice. I half expected them to be angry at me – I don't know why, just because of the shock I suppose. I still feel awful for having to tell them over the phone.'

'You were very brave to do it. And at least they have each other for support.'

'God, I'd better tell Steve at Tristan's work so he can let everyone know. Oh, and the retirement village. And *my* boss to arrange to take some time off work … I don't know how long I'll need. Oh, god, what a mess.'

'Just breathe, sweetie. Slow, deep breaths. There's no rush. People will understand. And I'm pretty sure Rob called Steve as soon as we found out – when he was outside with the boys. I'll text him to make sure.'

'Right. Of course,' Hannah said, nodding. In her haze, Hannah had completely forgotten that Tristan's boss, Steve, was an old friend of Rob's – that's how Tristan had got the job.

'And if you give me your Facebook login I'll do a post on your behalf.'

'God, what would I do without you?'

'I'm here, Hann, and I will be, for whatever and for however long you need me,' Sam said, smiling warmly at her friend and trying to hold back her own tears. 'We'll just take it one step at a time.'

'All the phones are blinking with messages. I can't face them, but I can't just delete them, can I?'

'People will understand if it takes you a while to get back to them – and I'm sure even if you don't answer them at all, for that matter. For the mobile ones we can do a group text message.'

'Yes, let's do that now. Then I'll feel like I've at least done something useful.'

'Okay, and we'll write a to-do list. That might help you stop feeling so overwhelmed,' Sam said, getting up and leading the way to the study.

Hannah trailed slowly behind, feeling the slightest sense of relief at having someone else making the decisions.

After turning on the computer, Hannah sat in silence while Sam typed. Thankfully she always left Facebook logged in because there was no way she could have remembered the password or where she'd written it down. She was barely functioning. She even had to keep reminding herself to breathe.

'Right, what about this for a Facebook post, or is it too blunt?' Sam said, fingers paused above the keypad of Hannah's laptop. 'Today my world was shattered when my husband Tristan and parents Daphne and Daniel were killed in a car crash. I will provide further updates and details of funerals when I am able, but until then I will be off Facebook while I try to deal with this tragedy.'

'Um.' Hannah struggled to focus on what she'd heard and if it was what she wanted to say. 'Good, I think,' she said, frowning.

'We don't have to do this at all, you know. It's entirely up to you.'

'What do you think? Honestly.'

'I think it's a good idea. People will soon know about the accident. This way you can tell everyone at once.'

'Okay. But can you say it's from you on my behalf, though?'

'Got it. I'll add, "This is Hannah's friend, Sam" and change it to third person,' she said, tapping. 'We've got that you'll be off Facebook, do you want to make that stronger?'

'I can't bear the thought of talking to anyone, but I can't really say that, can I?'

'We can say whatever you want. And technically it's me saying it, not you, remember? So I can be a little blunt. How's this? "Hannah understands many of you will want to pass on your best wishes personally, but please don't contact her direct – right now she needs her space. Please be assured she is being taken care of and we will let you know if there's any way you can help". How about that?'

'Oh, Sammy, what would I do without you?' Hannah said.

'That, my darling, you don't have to think about, because I am right here,' Sam said, gently stroking Hannah's hair. 'Now, before we both collapse, do you think we can manage a group text message? I think it really will help to get it out of the way.'

'Okay. But I can't bear to look at Tris's phone. I just can't.'

'You don't need to. I think Rob's already done a message with Tristan's phone. I hope that's okay.'

Hannah nodded.

'There's a heap of Christmas messages from early this morning. Shall I just group those people and let them know? I'll just say pretty much what we said for Facebook, okay?'

Hannah nodded again. She could barely hold her head up and struggled to see the screen, let alone the words on it. But she trusted Sam with all her being. Whatever she said would be fine.

'So Rob's telling some people, Beth will be too and we've covered Facebook and both your mobiles. We've done well.'

'There's still all the messages on the landline,' Hannah said.

'They can wait. We've done enough for now.' Sam shut the laptop, startling Hannah slightly. It was as if she was coming out of a trance. She peered at her watch, and frowned. Over two hours had passed without her realising. She felt so numb.

'You must be exhausted,' Sam said.

'I am a bit.' And suddenly she was. It was only coming up to seven o'clock, but Hannah felt as if she'd struggle to walk to the bedroom, let alone get changed into her pyjamas. But at the same time, she didn't feel sleepy tired and wasn't sure she'd be able to sleep. How could she? She couldn't imagine doing any of the normal things again. Putting on a front and eating Christmas lunch had been a real struggle. But she'd have to try, wouldn't she?

'Come on, then, let's get you into bed,' Sam said. 'You probably won't actually sleep, but you need to try and at least get some rest.'

'I know. I'll try,' Hannah said, easing herself slowly to her feet.

'Do you want me to call one of those medical clinics that do house-calls? They could prescribe you something.'

'Thanks, but I'm okay.' *Well, I'm not, and some sleeping tablets might be good, but I can't think about or deal with anything else or speak to another person right now. I don't even have the energy to say the words.*

'You can always let me know if you change your mind. Meanwhile, I'll get us some milk with brandy. That might help.'

'All right.'

Chapter Five

Hannah stood at the doorway to the bedroom staring in while listening to Sam preparing their drinks in the kitchen. She couldn't make herself step over the threshold where everything was exactly the same as it had been that morning. Tristan's track pants, t-shirt and fleece top were still laid over the chair and she knew his scent would still be on his clothes and pillow. She couldn't bear to smell him, but couldn't bear not to. Swallowing the lump forming in her throat, she made her way across to their bed and pulled back the covers on Tristan's side and climbed in. She buried her head in his pillow and took a deep whiff. And then the floodgates opened again.

The next thing she knew was the sound of a glass being put on the side table and the bed shifting as Sam settled against her.

'Oh Hann,' Sam cooed, drawing Hannah to her and wrapping her arms around her friend.

'He's everywhere,' Hannah sobbed, clinging to her friend.

'I know, sweetie, I know. Let it out.'

After a few minutes Hannah sat up and dried her eyes. She picked up her glass and sipped.

'Do you feel a little better?' Sam asked, clearly feeling the need to say something, but not sure what that should be.

'Yes and no. I feel both numb and aching inside. I know that doesn't really make sense. I don't feel right and, worse than that, I have this awful feeling that I'll never feel quite right again.'

'I feel so helpless,' Sam said. 'I just wish there was something I could do or say to take the pain away. If only I could wave a magic wand and make this not have happened at all.' Tears were flowing freely, streaking her face. She reached over and gripped Hannah's hand and offered her a sad smile.

Hannah returned her friend's gaze and squeezed her hand. 'I know. Me too. But I'm so lucky to have you,' she said. 'Thank you for being here.'

'I always will be, just like you would be for me. Now drink your brandy, it feels good and I'm sure it will help.'

Hannah did as she was told.

'Do you mind if I have the TV on quietly? Would that bother you? It's too early for me to go to bed.'

'No, that's okay. I doubt I'll fall asleep anyway. Here,' she added, handing over the remote that Tristan always commandeered.

'At least close your eyes and try and rest,' Sam said.

'I don't think I'll have a choice. I feel absolutely wrung out.'

Sam turned on the TV and they sat up side by side sipping on their drinks. An old Christmas movie was just starting. Hannah stared at it whilst concentrating on getting her mind to still. Slowly she started to feel the relaxing effects of the brandy.

Having put her empty glass aside, she snuggled down. God, she wished she couldn't smell Tristan's scent, but buried her face deeper into it anyway. It made her feel so much sadder, but it was also kind of nice. Or was it? Was it making her feel worse? She didn't know, but she couldn't drag herself away from it. Everything was so confusing and she was too exhausted to think any more ...

*

The next thing Hannah knew there was a gasp from Sam and the sound of fumbling. She sat up and looked over at her friend – who was clearly trying to pick something up off the bedside table – and then turn off the TV. She let out a gasp of her own and brought her hands to her face. There on the screen was the chaotic scene of a vehicle accident. Uniformed emergency service personnel moved quickly and methodically around a barely recognisable green sedan with a truck lodged deeply in its distorted side. What affected Hannah the most was seeing the several blankets or sheets draped about. She knew their placement was strategic, deliberate. That meant the bodies were still there during filming. The ticker tape running across the bottom of the screen told her that three people had died in the accident and that the truck driver was in a critical condition.

She felt the bile making its way up into her throat, dragged back the covers and stumbled out of bed. In the bathroom she threw up curdled milk and brandy into the toilet. And then it was over and Sam was beside her rubbing her back and stroking her hair.

'Oh my god. I am so, so sorry. I didn't think,' Sam said, remote still in hand.

Hannah stared at her friend, seeing but not really seeing her.

'Hann, I'm really sorry. Please forgive me.' She looked more stricken, worse than she'd looked since, since ...

Hannah couldn't find any words. She swiped away the tears.

'What can I do?' Sam said. Hannah held out her hand to be helped up and then allowed herself to be led back to the bedroom.

She crawled back into bed and curled into the foetal position, trying to climb into herself and find some comfort, anything. A moment later she realised Tristan's scent was now all around her, and stronger. Her darling Tris.

The wail of an injured wild animal made its way around the room. And then she felt Sam's body covering her from behind, her arms wrapping around her, drawing her close.

'Oh, Sam, it hurts. It hurts so, so much.'

'I know, sweetie,' Sam said, rubbing Hannah's back.

Hannah's chest heaved, the lump in her throat exploded and she sobbed like she'd never sobbed before. She took huge gasping, gulping breaths and fought for air when all she wanted to do was die, drown, choke on her tears and for this pain to end. She felt Sam's body shaking as she sobbed along with her.

After what seemed forever, the episode subsided and Sam slowly eased her grip and drew away. Hannah was spent, but wide awake. She closed her eyes, but she could still see the mangled wreckage draped with blankets and the line of text making its way across the bottom of the screen. She opened her eyes and stared at the carpet, but it was there too. She was so tired, but she'd never sleep now. And couldn't imagine ever being able to again. Her whole body ached with sadness.

'Please don't leave me,' she whispered.

'Never,' Sam whispered back.

*

Hannah woke with a start, unsure of where she was. What had woken her? A bad dream? She stayed still, trying to remember and trying to get her bearings. Her heart began to race. She was in her bedroom, but she was on the wrong side of her bed. But Tristan was there beside her, she could hear quiet breathing. Thank god. It had just been a dream – well, nightmare, more like. Fragments came back to her. She took a few deep breaths and rolled over towards him. Why was he on the wrong side? Oh well. She desperately needed to be enveloped in his strong arms, drawn into his warm chest and be reassured everything was all right. But the breathing wasn't quite right, was it?

Suddenly she was wide awake. It wasn't Tristan at all. A mass of dark hair fanned out across the pillow beside her. Sam. The truth hit her like a bolt of lightning. And then she felt her heart and soul leave her for the second time that day.

Hannah slipped out of bed, careful not to wake Sam. At least someone was getting some sleep. In the kitchen she got a glass of water and stood at the bench sipping it while wondering what she could do to pass the hours until daylight. She wasn't going to turn on the television and risk seeing the news highlights again. She sighed at thinking how if her mum were here she'd say everything would seem better in the morning. Hannah felt terribly sad to think that this time Daphne would be very, very wrong.

She went through into the lounge and sat down in front of the Christmas tree. Part of her wanted to take all the ornaments off and pack it away. It was too joyful. But at the same time she welcomed its bright, twinkling cheer. Didn't she?

But taking away the reminders that it was Christmas might help her start to move on, mightn't it? Hannah didn't know what she should do. Anyway, she might make too much noise and wake Sam, she realised. She looked at the presents underneath. She knew what was contained in all but three – Tristan's to her. The others were from her, and them.

She reached forward to retrieve the smallest, which was sitting on top. Placing it there would have been almost the last thing Tris would have done before he'd left, before he'd left the house and then left her forever, she thought with a renewed pang of sadness and heartache. She knew what the parcel contained – well, sort of. She always knew the general *theme* of what she was being given, just not the actual form.

Hannah turned the small package over, unsure if she really wanted to open it or not, as she thought fondly but sadly about how his gift-giving tradition – which had ended today – had started.

For their first Christmas as a couple, Tristan had given Hannah a gorgeous bracelet with a heart charm dangling from it. Excited that she loved it so much, and not one to enjoy traipsing to shop after shop looking for the perfect gift, he'd seized the opportunity to make things easier for himself and begun a new tradition.

That first year Hannah had given Tristan a beautiful silk tie after seeing him admire it but dismiss it as too expensive. While it hadn't become such an entrenched habit as his gifts to her had, Hannah often gave him a really smart tie or another carefully selected piece of clothing. They tended to give each other one special gift and then two that were more along the lines of useful or practical – items like books, DVDs, vouchers or golf balls for Tristan. Things they'd usually asked for. From day one Tristan had wholeheartedly adopted the Whites's gift-giving quirk. He'd fitted in well straight away, full stop, she thought sadly.

She slowly and carefully prised the tightly tied ribbon off and then the sticky tape, and eased the small jewellers' box out of its paper wrapping. She paused. Did she really want to know what her last gift from Tristan was? But the need to have something of him, something he'd have considered carefully and chosen just for her saw her prise open the box.

She gasped. Inside, sitting on a small white cushion, was a stunning red-and-black enamel ladybird charm.

'Oh, Tris,' she whispered.

She sat with the box on her lap staring up at the Christmas tree, feeling engulfed with another layer of sadness added to what had already settled within her. Where was the luck this charm was meant to bring?

At that moment she realised you really could possibly die of a broken heart. She certainly felt as if she were dying. The tears made their way down her face and she struggled to find the energy to lift her hand to wipe them away. Her numbness was so strong she almost felt paralysed. As she stared at the brightly lit tree, she realised she now knew with certainty when Tristan's parents had last put up a Christmas tree and why they no longer bothered.

Tristan had always shrugged off their lack of Christmas participation, but now she wondered if that was because he didn't want to dwell on it, and his brother's death. To celebrate as they had before would be too stark a reminder of who was missing. Hannah could see that now. She felt bad for the judgemental thoughts she'd had – which, thankfully, she'd always kept to herself. She'd thought they didn't care, now she realised they'd actually cared too much.

God, how would they cope with losing another son – their only other child? Parents weren't meant to outlive their children, but she was reminded of how her own parents hadn't. That was right, but still so, so wrong.

'Here you are.'

Hannah looked up through sodden lashes to see Sam standing in the doorway.

'What are you doing? Are you okay?'

Hannah silently held up the small box containing the charm.

'It's beautiful.'

'But why this?' Hannah said. 'Why now?'

'Oh, Hann, I don't know.' Sam sighed heavily as she settled herself cross-legged beside her friend, put an arm around her shoulders, and pulled her close.

'But you're always saying everything is connected, everything means something,' said Hannah.

'I don't know, Hann. To be honest, I don't know what to believe anymore – after yesterday. Maybe I've had it wrong all these years,' she added quietly.

Hannah stared at the charm in the box, deliberating over whether to add it to her bracelet or not. It seemed somehow disrespectful to Tristan not to, but it clearly wasn't lucky. It hadn't stopped the accident, her whole life being ruined. But perhaps that was because it had been locked away in its box. Perhaps if they'd unwrapped their presents over breakfast no one would have died. Hannah's mind was starting to race.

'Maybe it will bring you good luck for the future,' Sam whispered, her voice shaky, drawing Hannah away from her thoughts.

Maybe it will. Hopefully it will, because I'm certainly going to need it. Hannah nodded in reply and took the charm out of the box and started to add it to her chain. She liked to keep the charms in order because, until now, she'd felt they'd been telling a story: love heart, 'H', '&', 'T' and the infinity symbol. She smiled sadly at remembering how she'd jokingly ribbed Tristan about how he shouldn't have kept the 'H' separated from 'T' for a whole year – it might prove bad luck. He'd told her to be patient and not be greedy. And now the real H and T had been separated forever.

And now she had a ladybug, a well-known symbol for good luck. It was beautiful, but didn't really seem to fit the pattern. And had come too late …

'Come on, let's go and try to get some more sleep,' Sam said.

Again Hannah nodded, and allowed herself to be helped up from the floor. She felt like she was a child again, and being taken back to bed by her dad after falling asleep in front of the television. *Oh, if only …*

Chapter Six

Hannah had been lightly dozing for ages. She didn't want to wake Sam, who was sleeping soundly beside her. The light filtering through the blinds and curtains told Hannah it was quite late in the morning – maybe even as late as nine, although she could be wrong. She was usually good at reading the level of light and guessing the time, but she didn't think she could be sure of anything anymore. Ordinarily she was an early riser, too, but she didn't want to get up and face the day. She heard rustling and turned over to find Sam looking at her.

'How are you doing this morning?' her friend asked.

'Same. Pretty shit,' Hannah said quietly. 'I guess that's to be expected, right?'

'I'm afraid so. Did you manage to get any sleep?'

'Bits here and there.'

'I probably should have insisted on getting a doctor in to give you something. Sorry.'

'It's okay. I could have asked. Anyway, I don't want to get hooked on prescription drugs – I've got enough problems already to deal with.'

'I think you'd be okay with one or two, just a couple of nights, but I suppose it's good to be cautious. Well, at least keep it in mind. It's an option. You're going to need your wits about you so you'll need a decent sleep sometime soon. And plenty of food. Could you eat? I'm starving.'

'I don't know.'

'How about I do a fry-up and we'll see?'

'Okay.'

'Do you mind if I have a quick shower?' Sam said.

'Of course. You don't need to ask.'

'And could I borrow some clothes? These probably reek.'

'Sure, help yourself.' Hannah snuggled back down. She didn't want to leave the closest thing she had to a safe cocoon. Sam had bought her some time by wanting to use the shower first.

Hannah sighed at hearing the doorbell. She toyed with ignoring it, but good manners saw her throw back the covers and get out of bed. At least she was already dressed, albeit in yesterday's clothes …

Auntie Beth stood on the threshold, carrying a carton of eggs and a parcel wrapped in butcher's paper.

'Oh, I'm so sorry, I've woken you up, haven't I?'

'No, I was just lying in bed.' *Trying not to face reality.* 'Sam's in the shower. Come in.'

'I thought you could do with a decent breakfast,' Beth said, hurrying past Hannah and through to the kitchen. 'I know you probably won't feel like eating, but it is important you at least try.'

'You're a gem. Sam had the same idea. But thank goodness you're here. Just between you and me, Sam's not quite the cook she thinks she is,' Hannah whispered and smiled weakly.

'It'll be our little secret,' Auntie Beth said, offering a strained smile and tapping her nose with her index finger.

Hannah was surprised to see that according to the kitchen clock it was nearly ten o'clock. She'd spent a lot of the hours of darkness lying in bed staring into the night, thinking of Tristan and her parents, missing them, remembering them, trying not to think about them, and trying to banish the images she'd seen on the television. Several times Sam had rolled over and held her and they'd cried together. Her eyes and cheeks still felt red raw and burnt.

'Bathroom's free if you want it,' Sam said, wandering into the kitchen. 'Oh, hello Auntie Beth,' she said.

'I hope you don't mind me taking over breakfast duties.'

'Not at all. I'm a little relieved to be honest. I've become quite good at toast soldiers, but I still sometimes fail at bacon. So, you've saved my bacon. Pun intended,' she said, smiling warmly at Auntie Beth. 'Hann, Rob sends his love. He rang while I was getting dressed. He's on his way over.'

'Well, there's plenty of food,' Auntie Beth said.

'Thanks, but I think they'll have already eaten.'

Hannah was surprised to find herself unable to resist the lure of bacon and eggs on toast, and immediately tucked into the plateful put in front of her. Perhaps if she could focus on that she might not be so sad for a few minutes.

'Can I help you do anything today, Hannah?' Auntie Beth asked during the meal.

'Oh, I hadn't even given today any thought at all. But I really don't think I want to be alone. Sam, you can go to the sales. I'm sure Auntie Beth can keep me company.'

'Hann, the last thing I'm interested in is going shopping. I'll do whatever you want me to. I can help with anything or just keep you company. Whatever you want.'

The last few Boxing Days Tristan and Rob had spent playing golf with Sam off with the kids shopping for bargain clothes and shoes. Once it had been Sam and Hannah shopping together till they dropped, but that had changed when the twins came along. Now Hannah tended to watch the start of the Sydney to Hobart yacht race on TV with her parents, often joined by Beth. But of course everything now was far from usual. Sitting quietly watching TV might be okay, but could she bear the reminder of who wasn't there beside her? Could she bear to sit still and have the quietness plagued with all the awful thoughts constantly churning through her brain? But she couldn't think of what else to do and wasn't sure she'd have any energy to do anything anyway.

'Darling, how about we just take it one minute at a time and see how we go?' Beth said. 'Okay?'

Hannah nodded. It was a relief to have someone else doing the thinking for her. She was having enough trouble remembering to breathe and trying not to cry. Every damn thing was a reminder of what was different or missing. Her coffee hadn't even tasted the same as yesterday morning when Tristan had made it, despite coming out of the same machine in the same way.

They finished breakfast and packed up the dishwasher, then went through to the lounge room with mugs of coffee. The longer Hannah stared at the Christmas tree, the more she itched to take it down and remove the reminder of the festive season. She didn't care if it was the wrong thing to do. She hated Christmas and wanted all trace of it removed from her house. Now.

She got up and retrieved the box for the decorations from the sideboard and began removing each ornament and strand of tinsel. Beth and Sam silently joined her and then Sam disappeared and returned with the step stool from behind the kitchen door. Before long the artificial tree was almost bare.

'Where's the box for the tree?' Sam asked.

'In the wardrobe in the study.'

Slowly the tree was taken apart and carefully packed into the box, and then Sam put it away in the wardrobe. Hannah briefly considered telling Sam to take it out to the rubbish bin instead, but didn't want to appear unhinged and behaving irrationally. It was certainly what she felt like doing.

'Can you get the boxes marked "Christmas lights" and a couple of pairs of pliers from the garage, please, Sammy?'

'Sure,' she said, and disappeared.

Auntie Beth silently followed her outside, where she stood surveying the display of Christmas lights that Tristan had put up across the front of the house. Hannah was pretending to look at where to start taking them down, but instead she was trying to swallow back the tears and breathe through the painful thudding of her shattered heart.

They beavered away, carefully snipping all the cable ties and releasing the strands of lights. Before long they had reached the point where they would need a ladder to keep going. Sam silently fetched it and the three of them stood around it, no one willing to go any further.

They turned as one at hearing a male voice. 'Can I be of some assistance?' Rob was striding up the path.

'Yes, please,' Hannah said, handing over her pliers. She let out a sigh of relief not just because she wouldn't have to climb the ladder, but since Sam had said Rob was on his way she'd been bracing herself for the hurricane-like arrival of the twins. She adored them, but wasn't sure she could cope with their energy this morning. Thankfully Rob was alone.

'Perfect timing, as usual, darling,' Sam said, giving her husband a quick peck. 'Where are the boys?'

'I left them with Joan across the road. I figured the last thing Hann needed was those two tearaways in her face, especially if she hasn't slept,' he said, hugging Hannah. 'It's okay, we know you love them.'

'Thanks,' Hannah said.

It didn't take Rob long to finish and for all signs of Tristan's handiwork to be removed from the house and packed away out of sight in the garage. Again Hannah wanted to ask them to throw the lights away and remove all traces of Christmas, but again stopped herself.

*

They were drinking coffee in the kitchen – Hannah staring at the digital clock on the oven and barely aware of what she was doing – when the doorbell rang.

'Shall I answer it, since I'm nearest?' Auntie Beth said, getting up. 'I imagine that's going to be ringing a lot in the coming days.'

Chapter Seven

'Thank you, and we're so sorry for your loss too. I know Daniel and Daphne were very dear friends for many years. They'll leave a big void.'

Hannah recognised the voice at once, but was a little confused. It couldn't be. Could it? She rushed out of the kitchen to see, her eyes already brimming.

'Oh, Hannah,' Tristan's parents, Raelene and Adrian, cried as they gathered her into a three-way hug.

'I'm so sorry,' Hannah said, melting into them. They stayed fused together, crying almost silently.

Slowly they peeled apart and made their way into the kitchen where Rob and Sam and Auntie Beth were standing waiting for them. Beth filled the kettle again while Rob and Sam in turn hugged Raelene and Adrian and offered their condolences. Hannah stood back, feeling a surge of gratitude and relief so great that she thought a few pieces of her shattered heart may have joined back together. She felt a huge weight had lifted off her shoulders with them walking through the door. They were loving, methodical, capable people, not that Rob, Sam and Auntie Beth weren't, but Hannah saw the slightest glimmer of a light at the end of the tunnel with regards to the arrangements in particular.

For a start, with Raelene and Adrian here she was definitely released from the burden of identifying Tristan, something that had been worrying her much more than she'd realised. She knew it was selfish and weak, but she really didn't want to remember her dear, sweet husband as being in whatever state he was. When she could think fondly of him again without being consumed by grief and sadness — and she desperately hoped one day she would — she wanted to draw on memories of places they'd been, things they'd done together and picture him in his prime as he was, not a broken, lacerated, roughly sewn back together body.

Sam and Rob knew Hannah inside out, Beth, having lost her husband, knew about grief, but Raelene and Adrian had been through almost exactly this before. Did that make it harder or easier? Would they feel more comfortable or more heartbroken in knowing what to expect? Did going through more than one experience of a traumatic death in the family ease the grief or compound it? Hannah had always got along well with Tristan's parents, but right then her renewed respect for them and all they'd been through settled inside her as a second sharp pain to her heart. Bless them. They were so calm, so composed. Hannah felt hugely comforted having them here. They'd know the questions to answer, the order things went in, what was expected of Hannah by whom and when.

'And how are your gorgeous little boys?' Raelene asked.

'Growing like mushrooms and causing havoc,' Sam said. 'Speaking of which, we'd better go and pick them up and leave you to catch up with Hannah.'

'Yes. Joan will be wondering where I've got to,' Rob said.

Hannah knew they were simply making a polite exit, and was grateful. She was starting to feel a little crowded and desperately wanted to welcome her parents-in-law at her own pace.

Hannah's best friend and her husband hugged her warmly.

'Thanks so much for your help,' she said.

'We'll see ourselves out. Call if you need anything,' Sam said.

'Yes, anything, Hann,' Rob reiterated.

'Thanks. I really appreciate it.'

'We'll call or see you soon. Take care,' Sam said.

'You must be exhausted,' Beth said to Raelene and Adrian. 'Can I get you a tea or coffee? Or perhaps something to eat?'

'Tea would be great, thanks,' Raelene said.

'Hannah?'

'Tea, please.'

'I'll make a pot, then. You go through to the lounge and catch up properly, I'll be in in a minute.'

'Thanks, Auntie Beth, you're too good to me. There's a tea pot in the left-hand cupboard under the bench.' *Thank goodness for you keeping up the social etiquette and keeping me organised*, Hannah thought as she led the way through to the lounge room.

'You've no idea how good it is to see you. I really appreciate you getting here so quickly,' Hannah said.

'It's the least we could do. It's a terrible time.'

'How *did* you get here so quickly? Even driving all night you couldn't have ... And, anyway, there's the ...'

'We flew. After we got off the phone we realised it was much more sensible to leave the van where it was and fly over. We drove to Launceston last night and got an early flight out this morning,' Adrian explained.

'So, honestly, how are you doing?' Raelene asked.

'I really don't know. I feel just so sad and empty. And the tears won't stop,' she said. 'I don't know how you did it,' she sniffed as she pulled a wad of fresh tissues from the box still on the coffee table.

'It does get easier,' Adrian said kindly.

'With time,' Raelene said, tugging a handkerchief from her sleeve as her own tears began to fall again.

'It's not an easy road by any means,' Adrian agreed, gripping his wife's hand briefly then pulling a neatly folded, ironed handkerchief out of his trouser pocket and dabbing at his eyes.

'I'm so sorry,' Hannah said, feeling the need to say something, but not sure what.

'But at least we've had each other.' The words 'you've lost your entire family' hung unspoken in the air.

'I don't know how I'll survive without him. I loved him so much. We were so happy,' Hannah sobbed.

'We know. But you will survive. It probably won't feel like it for a very long time, but you will get through this. You're a strong young woman, Hannah, just you remember that,' Raelene said.

Hannah was relieved that Beth's arrival meant she didn't have to reply. Strong was the last thing she felt. And she really didn't feel she could go on without Tristan by her side. They'd had so many plans.

'Aren't you having one, Auntie Beth?' Hannah asked when she realised Beth had only brought in three cups on the tray with the teapot and plate of sliced fruit cake.

'No, I'll leave you to catch up.'

'Please don't feel you have to go,' Hannah said.

'It's fine, I'm sure you have plenty of arrangements to discuss. Just please let me know if I can do anything to help – flowers, food, anything. And the offer still stands, Hannah, if you'd like me to go to the morgue on your behalf, or with you, you only have to ask. I'll see you soon. Raelene and Adrian, please accept my sincere condolences again.'

'Thank you,' Raelene said.

'Yes. Thank you. It's good to see you. If only it were under better circumstances,' Adrian said.

Hannah eased herself to her feet and followed Beth out. 'You're the best, Auntie Beth. Thank you for everything,' she said as she tightly hugged the old lady.

'Well, promise me you won't be shy if you think of anything at all I can do for you,' Beth said, smiling sadly at Hannah.

'I promise. You're amazing,' Hannah said, giving her dear old friend another quick hug.

'Nonsense, but thank you, dear. You take good care. I'll be in touch.'

'Bless her,' Hannah said as she went back into the lounge room.

'Yes, she certainly is a brick. And when she must be hurting so much too,' Raelene added.

'So, where are your suitcases?' Hannah asked.

'In the car,' Adrian said.

'Why?'

'Oh. Well, we don't want to impose. We're fine in a motel. You have enough on your plate without dealing with guests,' Raelene said.

'You're very welcome to stay here. Please. I'd really like it if you would, actually. But it's entirely up to you. If you'd prefer your own space …'

'All right, if you're absolutely sure. Thank you, that's very generous. Just until after the funeral,' Adrian said.

'And if we get in your way, you have to tell us. This is the time for you to take care of your own needs first, dear,' Raelene said kindly.

'Is this the card for the policemen who were here?' Adrian said, picking up the business card.

'Yes. I'll have to call them because I can't remember what they said about the, um, the um, bodies – if they or the coroner will let me know or if I have to call the coroner or the police,' Hannah said, becoming flustered. She rubbed her forehead. *Please, no more tears.* But they kept coming and again she was trying to stem the flow with a sodden, useless ball of tissues.

'Why don't I go and call them now and see where things stand?' Adrian asked.

'Oh, would you? That would be a huge weight off me. I can't remember much at all of what they said yesterday.'

'That's entirely understandable. You don't need to worry about anything. We'll work through all these things bit by bit together.'

'Thank you. You've no idea what a relief it is to have you here,' Hannah said, sniffling. 'Sorry, I just can't stop crying.'

'There's no need to apologise. And, I'm afraid you might be like this for quite a while yet,' Raelene said. 'But it's good for you to let them out.'

'Do you feel up to discussing a few things while there's no one else here?'

'Yes, good idea, Adrian. Hannah, if your experience is anything like ours when we lost Scott,' Raelene explained, 'you'll soon be inundated with visitors dropping in to offer their condolences and deliver food. In fact, I'm surprised they haven't already. Perhaps that's because of it being Christmas. Anyway, it would be good to sort a few details out now while we have the chance. Or perhaps later,' she added, as the doorbell rang.

Chapter Eight

Hannah stared out the window of Raelene and Adrian's hire car and looked back at the house. It was the first time she had left it since her world had been turned upside down. And she didn't want to. While she was in there, she felt safe. Miserable, but safe. Now she felt terrified, like going to the dentist. No, she knew what to expect at her dentist's – this was more like when she was a teenager and had gone to meet the headmistress of the private girls only high school before she started there. She shook the thought aside – this had no comparison. And what was the point of thinking like that anyway?

She wished Beth or Sam were sitting beside her – she badly needed someone's hand to hold. But they had both declined, saying ever so gently while they each held one of her hands that what she was about to do couldn't be delegated. Only she and Raelene and Adrian could take care of the funeral arrangements.

'Sweetheart, one day you'll understand,' Beth said, clearly wretched that she couldn't take this pain away.

The only sound inside the car came from the GPS unit Adrian had programmed and attached to the windscreen. Hannah was grateful no one was talking, trying to make anyone feel better with useless chatter. Perhaps she was already realising that it was right for just the three of them to do this. She concentrated on taking deep breaths and listening to the sounds of cars whizzing by.

At the end of the street, her heart began to race. *God, we don't have to go near the crash scene, do we?* She couldn't bear that. She couldn't bear any of this, but that would completely do her in. Adrian had contacted the funeral home to make the appointment. It was the same firm they'd used for Scott – apparently it had branches right across the country. Hannah didn't know where their office was located or where she was going. She didn't care. She released her breath when they turned to go in the opposite direction to her parents' retirement village.

A couple was having wedding photos taken in the park. They seemed to be laughing and playing up for the camera. Having fun. *They think they have a lifetime to spend together*, she thought sadly. *I hope you will have many years of happiness.* When they were out of sight Hannah realised that she was sobbing. She'd seemed to barely feel the tears on her numb red-raw face anymore. She'd grown used to having red, puffy eyes and now dabbed at them out of habit. She'd stopped looking at herself in the mirror. She didn't even care how she looked. Her hair would be a tangled mess and she'd be in track pants and be braless under an oversized t-shirt right now if Sam and Beth hadn't intervened. Bless Raelene and Adrian, they hadn't had the heart to comment on her attire when she'd appeared in the kitchen.

It had taken both Sam and Beth to dress her. She was limp and couldn't seem to find any balance – in her head and literally. When she sat down she kept folding into herself, as if everything inside her had actually been scooped out, not just that it felt like it. She'd always easily balanced on one leg and then the other to put her socks on. Now she had to sit to do it. And she couldn't find any inclination to try to reach behind her to brush her hair or do up a bra. She couldn't even find enough shame to feel embarrassed at being practically naked in front of Beth and Sam. Thank goodness she had such dear friends.

Hannah had no idea how long they'd been driving for or where they were, but suddenly they were parking in front of a modern building that looked like any other commercial premises. She felt slightly relieved that it looked so benign, but at the same time she was a little disappointed that they would make such important decisions at somewhere so ... so, *ordinary*. What they were going through was so far from ordinary.

'Okay,' Raelene said after a deep breath and she opened her door. They all got out and together silently regrouped by taking another deep breath before walking forward, and again as they pushed open the glass door. Hannah felt queasy. She shook all over from the inside out and her heart was hammering. She took note that the women's toilets were just a couple of steps to her right.

Hannah knew that Adrian, who was standing at the front desk, had given the receptionist their names, but she could barely hear anything over the sound of blood pounding in her ears. She nodded and murmured, 'Hello,' as she shook an older man's hand. He had a kind, open, smiling but not smiling face. Hannah felt bad for not being friendlier, more polite.

He ushered them into a large lounge area with two leather chesterfields and a coffee table with neatly stacked brochures and a tray holding a teapot, cups and saucers and a small plate with three slices of cake. On the far side of the room was an open door. Through it Hannah could see a coffin. She'd never been to a funeral before and had never seen a coffin or casket in real life, so while she was a little repulsed, she was also curious. The room was filled with a wide selection of them, carefully arranged – some on metal legs with wheels and others on plain plinths. Some were made from dark glossy timber, like Hannah had seen in movies, but there were also some in lighter coloured timbers. But what she was shocked to see were the coloured ones – as shiny as cars and in pink, white, green and … oh god … Bermuda blue – Tristan's favourite colour.

'I'm sorry,' she cried, and turned and bolted from the room, a hand clasped over her mouth.

Hannah made it to the basin just as she vomited. She fought to breathe. She began panting uncontrollably – short, gasping, ragged breaths – and was starting to lose her balance as Raelene appeared beside her.

'Here, come and sit down,' Raelene said, wrapping her arms around Hannah and easing her back out and over to a small couch.

'I'm so sorry. I can't …' she gasped.

'Breathe, Hannah, slow, deep breaths – in and out. Come on, there's a good girl,' Raelene said, rubbing her back.

Gradually Hannah brought her breathing under control. She wiped her mouth, snotty nose and dabbed at the streams of tears on her face. She relinquished the wet tissues when Raelene held up a small bin and then plucked several fresh ones from the box her mother-in-law silently held up to her.

'I'm sorry, Raelene, but I really can't do it.'

'Yes, you can. And you have to, Hannah. I know it's hard, but you have to do this. This is your last chance to honour them. I'm not saying this to be cruel, but, darling, as much as we loved your parents, we didn't know them well enough at all to plan their funerals.' Right then Hannah wished she'd insisted on Beth and Sam being there. They'd know.

'But what if I get it wrong?'

'You can't get it wrong if you do your best and follow your heart. Just think about how they'd like to be remembered.'

They wouldn't want me to be doing any of this and be in so much pain at all. They shouldn't have fucking left me! She wanted to scream and shout, but didn't have the energy.

'It's just so hard.'

'I know it is,' Raelene said. 'But you can do it. You just have to believe you can.'

'But I don't want to say goodbye. They should still be here. Tristan and I didn't even get to ...' *Have children.*

'I know. This is horrible, but we have to say goodbye. We don't have a choice. So we need to do it carefully. I don't want you having regrets later.'

It was the different tone in her voice that made Hannah look up and search her mother-in-law's face.

'What do you regret about, um, Scott's, um, funeral?' She ventured carefully.

'Well, not having a coloured casket, for one,' she said with a knowing smile. 'He loved all colours, but his favourite was green – deep emerald green. I like to think he might have become an artist. Or something to do with cars. Or both – like a panel beater. He loved cars right from when day one,' she said wistfully, and then let out a deep sigh.

Hannah hugged her and wished Tristan had talked about his brother like this – shared him and his memories with her. She wanted to tell Raelene, but how could she without letting on that Tristan had only really spoken of his brother two or three times – and never about what Scott was like or with any real affection.

Perhaps she and Adrian had known. Perhaps he'd talked about Scott with them. She really hoped so.

'Even if I knew they existed, it wasn't what one did back then – a coloured casket, that is. Not in the country. And certainly not under the circumstances. You had your service in the local church or at the local cemetery, or both, in the typical way. All very stock standard. You didn't cause a fuss or do anything outlandish. It just wasn't done,' she added.

'What else would you have done differently?' Hannah asked quietly.

'Bunches of streamers instead of flowers, pop music instead of hymns – no church. Definitely no church. And balloons. I think I would've liked to have let go of a bunch of helium-filled balloons. Though, back then I didn't know how terrible they were for the planet and animals. Dreadful things. Sorry, I've got a bit of a bee in my bonnet about them.'

Hannah found herself smiling faintly. Raelene should have a conversation with Sam about the planet and saving the animals.

'Anyway,' Raelene said. 'Scott was a child. Tristan was a … a… Oh god, Hannah, what are we going to do without him?' Raelene dissolved and they clung together, their chests heaving in unison.

The two women sobbed uncontrollably until they were spent. It could have been hours or mere moments later, for all Hannah knew.

'Tristan's favourite colour was blue – the same blue as …' she suddenly found herself saying.

'Yes, I know.'

'Do you want to …?'

'It's up to you, Hannah. He was your husband. We loved him dearly, but he's belonged to you for the past five years.'

'I think we should have the blue one. If Adrian agrees, that is,' Hannah said.

'Oh, that would be nice. Are you sure?' Raelene said.

'Absolutely.' As they hugged again, Hannah thought it was the most definite she'd felt about anything since Christmas Day. And she even felt the slightest glimmer of strength at having made one decision.

'Come on, we've left Adrian out there on his own for ages. I can do this,' she added, more to herself than Raelene.

'Good girl,' Raelene said, and they got up.

Adrian was waiting for them by the reception desk. He offered a gentle smile and held out his arms to them both.

'Sorry,' Hannah said into his chest.

'It's quite okay. We have all the time in the world,' he said, stroking the top of her head.

'We're feeling a little better. At least ready to tackle this, aren't we, Hannah?' Raelene said.

Hannah nodded whilst biting down on her quivering bottom lip.

'Sorry,' Hannah said to the funeral director, who stood up as they entered the room again.

'You don't need to be sorry, dear. It's a very difficult time for you. Please understand, there's really no rush to decide on anything. You just take your time.' He seemed even kinder than before – almost like an old family friend.

Hannah deliberately sat with her back to the caskets. Her head was feeling a little clearer. Suddenly she remembered the man's name was Graeme. She felt good about that, it was bothering her that she'd forgotten it as soon as he'd introduced himself.

'Would you like a cup of tea?'

'No, thank you, Graeme, I think we should get started, if that's okay,' Hannah said. She looked at Adrian and Raelene, who nodded their agreement.

'Of course,' Graeme said. 'Now, I see you're looking at Wednesday.'

'Yes. Is it too short notice?' Raelene asked.

'I think we can manage it. It's more about giving family and friends enough time to travel.'

'I just want ...' *It over with.* Hannah couldn't say that. It sounded terrible. What she really wanted was to have it over before the New Year – it felt terribly important to her to not taint the next year with the funeral. She'd told Raelene and Adrian and they seemed to have understood.

'I don't foresee any problems there.'

'Thank you. Right, well, now we're looking to have a simple, pleasant, non-religious service,' Adrian said. 'Oh, and we'd like for it to be a joint service.'

Last night Hannah, Raelene, Adrian, Beth, Sam and Rob had looked at the funeral home's website and discussed some options. It had felt so wrong to be using the everyday tools of tablet and Google – essentially putting it in the same category as online banking and shopping for shoes and books. Hannah had found it all hideous, but at least they'd agreed to some arrangements, which they'd listed on the piece of paper Adrian now held. It was crumpled and limp – no doubt his hands were sweaty like Hannah's.

'I couldn't bear to go through it all twice,' Hannah felt the need to explain. It was probably considered strange for a couple and their son-in-law to have a joint service. But if that was the case, Graeme didn't let on.

'That's really not a problem at all. Are you considering burial or cremation?' Hannah didn't like the idea of her parents or Tristan in the ground or being burnt. She didn't like the idea of them being dead, full stop, but that wasn't an option.

'Cremation for our son, Tristan, Hannah's husband. We'll take his ashes home to our farm in South Australia,' Adrian explained.

Hannah had agreed to this as Adrian and Raelene were very clear on wanting to scatter Tristan's ashes under his favourite gum tree on the farm. She didn't feel she could argue. They'd offered for her to have half to scatter in their garden or another favourite place. She hoped she'd managed to successfully hide her horror. How ghoulish to have your loved one sitting on the mantel until their ashes were scattered. She knew people did it. But still ...

'Burial is the expensive option, though, isn't it?' Raelene said.

'Here in the city it is because space is so limited. Leases in some cemeteries are now tens of thousands of dollars,' Graeme said, 'and that's in addition to all the other funeral costs.'

'I think I'd like to have Mum and Dad somewhere I can visit, though.'

'Perhaps a niche wall would suit,' Graeme suggested.

'Yes. Perhaps.' She thought it a bit undignified to put her parents, who had given her so much, in a hole in a brick wall with a tiny brass plaque over the top. She was beginning to see that these decisions couldn't be made lightly or quickly. And she was becoming very tired.

'Darling, you don't need to rush into a decision. You can always decide on a niche wall later, can't she, Graeme?' Raelene said.

'Of course.'

'Okay. Let's do that. Could I leave Mum and Dad's ashes here and decide later?' She wasn't sure why, but she couldn't bear the thought of having them in the house.

'Yes, that's fine.'

Hannah felt relieved. Deferring part of the decision wasn't ideal, but going around in circles and making a snap decision just to save time wasn't either. Like Raelene said, she didn't want to have regrets. She was starting to think that funerals out in the country, with only a few options, sounded better, not at all a curse like Raelene was suggesting.

Her head began to spin again. There was so much to take care of. If only her parents had discussed all this at some point, but most people tended not to if they were still healthy. Death was too depressing to discuss in a casual chat over a cup of tea. If only they'd stated their wishes in their wills. She wouldn't have even thought to check this with the solicitor if it hadn't been for Raelene and Adrian.

'Do you have a particular venue in mind for the service? The chapel here is available on Wednesday at two p.m. I've made a tentative booking, but it's entirely up to you.'

'Where we have it doesn't matter if we're not interring the ashes right away, does it?' Adrian said.

'It doesn't matter anyway because the ashes won't be ready for collection for several days after the service.'

'Oh, I hadn't thought of that, but, yes, it makes sense,' Adrian said. 'Shall we have it here?' he asked Hannah and Raelene.

'Is the chapel nice?' Raelene asked.

'Very. I can take you to see it before you decide. Here are some photos.'

'Oh, yes, it looks lovely. Nice and new and peaceful,' Raelene said, flipping through the pages of images. 'Okay, Hannah?'

Hannah nodded.

'All right, we'll have it here. So that side of things is decided. Now onto the details of the service,' Adrian said.

'You're doing really well,' Raelene whispered to Hannah.

'Yes you are,' Graeme said. 'You all are.'

'Thank you,' Adrian said. He wiped a few tears away, took a deep breath and cleared his throat. 'Right, moving on. We'd like some background music played at appropriate times, but definitely no hymns and no one singing.'

'I couldn't bear to hear people singing hymns – it's too much like wailing,' Hannah blurted. Or had she? Had she said the words aloud? Yes, she had. Graeme looked like he was trying not to smile too broadly.

'I completely understand. It's your service to be held in any way you wish.'

'They would hate that,' Hannah added. Raelene put her arm around her and squeezed briefly before letting her go and putting her hand over Hannah's that was clutching yet another ball of sodden tissues. They were necessary because she cried all the time, but the mess had also become a strange sort of security blanket to her. She'd begun to feel slightly unsettled each time she gave up a mass of the damp, macerated paper. She got used to the uncomfortable, yet also sort of comfortable feeling she got from holding them and fresh, dry tissues felt strange in her hand. Pretty much everything felt strange. She kept analysing odd, random things and how she felt about them and wondered if she was going mad.

Finally they'd run through their list and were double-checking between themselves and with Graeme that they hadn't missed anything. Hannah felt as if she'd been there for most of the day, but the clock on the far wall showed that only a little over an hour had passed. She had to stare at it for a few beats of the second hand to convince herself it was still working.

She felt completely wiped out – hollow and empty but aching deep inside. *Tired, so, so tired.* So tired that when she heard what the funerals were going to cost she couldn't express her surprise out loud. *Christ!* But she just stared at the number on the bottom of the brochure Graeme had pointed out. No wonder people took out funeral insurance. If only her parents had.

Apparently all their requests fitted neatly into the basic cremation package. Hannah was relieved they hadn't wanted anything more elaborate – like tea and biscuits afterwards. Or two separate services. Adrian had already insisted he and Raelene were paying for Tristan's share, so that was something. Did she have a plastic card or two with that much available credit? Her heart started racing and her mind started closing in on itself.

'It's all right, Hannah, we don't need to worry about paying for this today,' Adrian said.

'Yes, you've got enough on your plate right now, and you've been very brave,' Raelene said.

'We do have several payment options available that we can discuss,' Graeme offered.

Hannah nodded and muttered, 'Thanks.' She was starting to feel ill again. While Graeme was a very nice man, she didn't want to discuss finances in front of him. She'd been raised to consider discussions about finances with anyone other than close relatives and friends to be crass. Of course she'd find a way to pay it. She'd also been raised to be careful with money too, and always paid her bills in full and on time. It was part of being well organised. She would find a way. But she didn't want to talk about it here. Or now. *One bloody thing at a time, for Christ's sake!* She wanted to snap that everyone should damn well be happy she'd managed this much today – it was more than she'd managed in all the days since …

'Thank you for being so understanding, Graeme,' Raelene said, getting up. 'And now I think I'd like a quick look at the chapel before we go, if that's possible.'

'Yes, of course,' Graeme said.

Hannah stood up and they trailed outside, where Hannah noticed the sign post for the chapel and parking. It turned out the office only took up a small portion of a large block. Behind it was plenty of parking and a lovely cream rendered building, the only giveaway that it might be a chapel was that it was long and narrow and had brightly coloured stained-glass windows. Inside, the walls were painted cream and there was a pleasant carpet runner down the aisle, but other than that everything was timber – the rows of polished pews, the lectern up front and two occasional tables to its left and right, and several tall pedestals standing empty, waiting for floral arrangements to be placed upon them.

'Oh, yes, this is lovely,' Raelene said, looking around. 'Nicely understated,' she added, nodding approvingly.

'Yes. Beautiful,' Adrian said, wrapping his arms around his wife and Hannah, who stood trying to take it in.

'Hannah?' Adrian asked, squeezing her closer to him.

She murmured her agreement and nodded.

Yes it is beautiful, but don't forget why we're here, she wanted to say.

'I think your parents would have approved, don't you?' Raelene said.

Have you lost your minds? We're looking at a funeral place, not a bloody wedding venue. As she stood there she was shocked at her overwhelming urge to pick up a pedestal and throw it through one of the beautiful windows.

Hannah bolted from the room.

Outside, tears poured down her face. She crumpled onto a bench and began sobbing.

'Let's get you home,' Raelene said, easing her up. 'Yes. Thank you for everything, Graeme.'

'You're welcome. You have my number, so do call anytime if you have any questions,' he said, shaking Adrian's hand.

Hannah stood dumbly while he took both her hands in his and peered sympathetically into her face. 'We'll take good care of Tristan, Daphne and Daniel, and give you a beautiful service to honour them, my dear. Take care and I'll see you Wednesday.'

Hannah nodded and sniffled in response.

★

Hannah sat at the front of the chapel staring ahead at the three caskets – one shiny blue with stainless-steel handles and two in polished mahogany with gold handles.

Raelene was to her left and Adrian next to her. Beside Hannah to her right was Beth, Sam and then Rob. An hour earlier, back at the house, Beth had pressed a pill in her hand.

'It's Valium. From a friend. We need something to get us through today.'

Hannah had taken it, but wasn't sure she should have. She was calm, but woozy – a different woozy from the numb, empty feeling she'd been growing used to. This was kind of out-of-body and she felt completely vacant in the head. She thought she could hear the music of a string quartet coming from the speakers, but the sound was muffled. She could hear the chapel filling up behind her, but those sounds seemed amplified, as if she were in a tunnel. She stared down, feeling a little perplexed as Beth took hold of her right hand and Raelene her left. Her hands didn't really feel part of her. It was as if they belonged to someone else.

'Are you ready to begin?' Graeme asked, appearing in front of them and looking from Hannah to Raelene and then Adrian.

Hannah blinked a few times before nodding. Her heart was pounding heavily in her chest, but otherwise she was calm – weird.

She looked up at Graeme, who was now standing behind the lectern. Her stomach flipped. She just had to sit there and not do anything, so why was she suddenly nervous? Rob stood up and walked to the front to give his eulogy for Tristan. He cleared his throat. Hannah's heart went out to him. Between her fuzzy cocooned state and being so intent on trying to stifle the sound of her sobbing, she barely heard what he said. Thankfully the Valium stopped her from panicking about that, which she might have done. That and the fact Adrian and Raelene had warned her that she probably wouldn't remember many of the details of the day. She had the order of service on her lap with the quotes they'd selected, and Rob and Beth had said they'd give her copies of their eulogies. The main thing was to get through it without collapsing and embarrassing herself.

There was a moment when the whole room chuckled. Something about golf, but Hannah had missed the punch line.

Suddenly Rob was sitting down again and being consoled by Sam as tears poured from his face.

Why did you have to die and put everyone through this? Look at us. How could there be a god who people say is so wonderful and takes care of everyone, if he was okay with this? It's too cruel, Hannah thought as she offered Rob a sympathetic smile of thanks.

It was now Beth's turn to get up and give her speech. Hannah tried to force herself to concentrate, but her mind kept wandering. Suddenly she wondered which casket held her mum and which held her dad. The longer she stared, the more important it felt for her to know. She found herself wringing her hands until Raelene put a hand over them. And then more tears fell as Hannah realised Tristan and her parents were right there in those boxes. She hadn't really thought about it. And now she was, she found it quite shocking.

What did you think? That they'd be empty? Yes, I probably did, actually, Hannah conceded to herself. And a whole new level of sadness came over her. She turned her attention back to Beth.

At least Hannah felt she was able to breathe today without too much conscious effort. Beth had said that would be the best thing about the Valium – it would keep the overwhelming jitters at bay. It had, but Hannah was like a zombie. Even through her foggy mind, she was impressed with how together Beth was as she spoke of what good friends Daniel and Daphne had been to her and her late husband.

'Daph was the epitome of welcoming. She was a very good cook and host, and it was my honour to have been able to call Daphne and Daniel my best friends for over thirty-five years. I remember the day they arrived in our street as if it were yesterday. While the boxes were still being unloaded, Daph was in the kitchen busy cooking cupcakes to bribe her new neighbours with. She soon had the entire street eating out of her hand – literally. We were all devastated when they went to live in a retirement village, but soon realised they had left us in very capable hands with Hannah and Tristan.' She paused and smiled at Hannah, who tried to smile back, but just burst into a new flood of tears.

Hannah didn't hear any more and was shocked when just moments later – it seemed – the music was back on and Graeme was indicating for her to rise. She allowed Graeme to take her hand and, with Raelene and Adrian following, lead her to the caskets. Hannah wanted to run, escape to some fresh air, but funerals were sedate, decorous occasions.

Goodbye, Mum, Dad, I'll love you always, she silently told the dark wooden boxes. She stood in front of the beautiful blue box. 'Oh, Tris,' she blurted. She couldn't make herself move, didn't want to leave him. *It isn't right.* Her legs buckled and she had to put a hand on the casket to stop herself falling. She was barely aware of being held up and helped away, but she was. The next moment she was going out a side door and into bright sunshine.

'You've done very well, my dear,' Graeme said.

Hannah, Adrian and Raelene hugged tightly and wordlessly. They broke apart when Beth, Sam and Rob appeared.

'Thank you for such kind, generous words, Rob,' Adrian said. 'And, you, Beth. You spoke so beautifully.'

Hannah nodded dumbly. She should be saying these things, but she just wanted to escape. A part of her now wished they weren't all going back to the house for a wake. She wanted to curl up somewhere dark and be alone.

'You're being so brave, darling,' Beth said. 'Isn't she, Sam?'

'Oh, Hann,' Sam said, bursting into tears and clinging to Hannah.

'Thank god you're here,' Hannah said.

Suddenly people were milling around them, offering various words of condolences and snippets of memories and stories of how they knew Tristan, Daphne and Daniel. Hannah nodded over and over, accepted each hand limply before letting it go and allowed herself to be drawn into and released from dozens of hugs. There were so many people, it was becoming overwhelming. Suddenly she was gasping for breath. She felt as if she'd been standing out here for hours. She probably had. Time was regularly playing tricks on her these days.

'Come on, you've seen enough people and most of them you're going to see again at the house. It's time we were going, anyway,' Beth said, taking her by the elbow.

'Oh, yes, look at the time,' Raelene said, checking her watch. 'We should have left twenty minutes ago.'

Hannah couldn't remember which car she'd come in and who'd been driving. She wished her brain would clear a little, though she was getting used to the dull, doughy feeling consuming her, and quite liked it.

Just as she climbed into the back of Rob's car, she realised she'd come with Raelene and Adrian. She hesitated and looked back.

'It's fine, Hannah, we're all going to the same place,' Raelene said, reading her mind. Seeing Beth getting into the back seat of their hire car made her feel better – they hadn't been totally abandoned.

'Is that the two policemen who came to the house?' Hannah asked, pointing, as they made their way slowly through the car park and the throng of people.

'Yes. I nearly didn't recognise them out of uniform,' Rob said.

'Very good of them to come when they're clearly on their days off,' Sam said. 'That's unusual, don't you think?'

'Well, Adrian has had a bit to do with them this past week,' Rob said.

'I feel bad now I didn't talk to them,' Hannah said.

'But you did, darling,' Sam said, turning and smiling at Hannah. She frowned, trying to remember. 'It's okay, you were very polite and even remembered to thank them for being so wonderful about delivering the news.'

'Really?'

'Really,' Rob said. 'You were great, Hann, really great.'

'There were heaps of people there from work – mine and, um, Tris's. I hope I thanked them all for coming.'

'I'm pretty sure you did. And you'll see most of them again at the house.'

'God, I'm losing the plot,' she muttered. 'Thank goodness you were all there. And Graeme was directing me on what to do and when. He was so nice. It must be hard dealing with sad people day in day out.'

'I think they'd find it rewarding, being so helpful at such a difficult but important time in people's lives,' Sam said.

'Please don't worry about what you might or might not have said or done, Hannah,' said Rob. 'It was a lovely service. And it's okay that you're a little out of it.'

'That'll be the drugs,' said Sam.

'Oh,' said Rob. 'Really?'

Hannah nodded sheepishly to his reflection.

'Say no to drugs, kids,' Sam said, smiling.

'How do you know, anyway?'

'Nothing escapes me, missy. Beth told me. She was worried she'd done the wrong thing.'

'I don't think I should have taken it.'

'No, I think it's the brandy on top that you probably shouldn't have had.'

'Yes, you're probably right.'

'Well, you got through the service, so it's fine. You can relax now. This next bit should be a little easier. And you can go and hide out in your bedroom if you feel so inclined,' Sam said. Hannah clasped the hand she held back between the seats. She leaned forward and put her hand briefly on Rob's shoulder. He put his own over it and squeezed before returning it to the wheel. Hannah sat back and tried to swallow the lump forming again in her throat.

★

Beth herded Hannah, Adrian and Raelene into the lounge room as soon as they arrived back at the house.

'Okay, now, you sit and have a rest in here for a bit and enjoy a cup of tea before the hordes arrive. I'm sure you must be exhausted,' she said, handing them each a cup of tea. 'You can stay here for the duration if you like and that way people can come to you. Unless of course you want to mingle. Entirely up to you. Listen to me being all bossy.'

They all sat. Hannah smiled up at Auntie Beth who was still able to play the part of gracious hostess despite the circumstances.

'Thanks, Beth, that's a good idea. I'm not sure I can move, I'm suddenly exhausted,' Raelene said.

'No, me neither,' said Adrian. 'Why don't you join us, Beth, you must be nearly done in too.'

'Yes, please, Auntie Beth,' Hannah said, patting the couch beside her. 'You were here early this morning getting things ready and you had all the stress of standing up and speaking.'

'Do, please,' Raelene said, holding a hand up to take hold of one of Beth's. 'You've done so much for us. Please sit for a moment and rest.'

'You know, I think I will sit. But I'll just get myself a cuppa first.'

'No you won't. Here, take mine. I'll go and get another one,' Adrian said. 'I'm feeling the need to stretch my legs, anyway.'

'Thank you, Adrian. I'm suddenly not sure I could move another step,' Beth said.

'I'm not surprised. The food looks amazing, Auntie Beth,' Hannah said. 'I peered into the kitchen on my way past. Thank you so much for everything. I don't know what I would have done without …'

'Ach, that's enough,' Beth said. 'You've got to stop thanking me. I'm pleased to take care of you and do my bit.'

'Much more than your bit, I'd say,' Raelene said as she sipped on her tea.

'I think I've seized up,' Hannah said. 'I really shouldn't have taken that Valium. I'm sure it did help me to stay calm but I feel so spaced-out.'

'Just don't make the mistake of getting hooked on the stuff like I did,' Raelene said. 'After Scott died I was spaced-out for years. It was nice to not feel anything, but you miss out on the good things in life too. And there will be good things again, Hannah. You have to believe me.'

'Did you have any counselling?' Hannah asked.

'No. There wasn't a counselling service where we were. I'm not sure it would have been for me anyway. Counselling wasn't as accepted then as it is now. Times have changed,' Raelene said. 'A support group might be more helpful than sitting talking to someone who might not have actually experienced it. But only you can know what you need.'

'The best tonic for me after losing Elliott was a cup of tea and a chat with a dear friend,' Beth said wistfully. 'It doesn't have to be someone who's suffered loss, just someone who cares enough.'

'Exercise and getting out in the fresh air also helped me,' said Raelene. 'Oh, and keeping busy – especially keeping the brain occupied.'

Beth nodded.

Their conversation ended as the first of the guests began trickling in to offer condolences and share their individual memories of Tristan and Daphne and Daniel White.

Chapter Nine

Hannah stood on the lawn next to Raelene as Adrian packed the hire car at the kerb. To say she was grateful for having had them stay for the past week, helping her organise the funeral, keeping her going through the wake yesterday, which had been so hard for her, and generally saving her from disappearing into her grief, was a massive understatement. Without them she might not have answered the door so many times. People were kind, but it was hard to thank them over and over and keep it together. And it was exhausting. Raelene had been able to offer such good advice – like urging Hannah to stay off the Valium. Last night she'd taken another one. While it was the first time Hannah had had anything like a decent night's sleep since the accident, she'd felt terrible this morning. On top of everything else now, she felt hungover, and she hadn't drunk any alcohol beyond some brandy in milk.

'That's how I felt for years,' Raelene had said over breakfast when Hannah had mentioned her discomfort. 'It's the Valium.'

Hannah wondered why the drug was popular if it made you feel so bad. And it seemed to be widely used judging by how much the name was bandied about. She'd often heard it referred to yet in her family they'd rarely even taken paracetamol.

She wrapped her arm around Raelene as she thought about all they'd done for her. Without them she mightn't have thought to check with her parents' financial adviser to see if he'd handled life insurance policies for them, either. In doing so she'd also found out she could put in a claim straight away and not wait for probate, which apparently could take months. It might have occurred to her later when the fog in her mind cleared, but finding out now had put her mind at ease about paying for the funeral, as awful as it was to be in the situation of putting in a claim at all. She'd known Tristan was insured. When they'd bought the house he'd insisted they take out policies to cover the mortgage at least, just in case something happened to one of them. She'd cried a whole new bucket of tears at being grateful for his foresight. He really had been a great provider. It was so heartbreaking that he hadn't had the chance to prove it as a father.

Between Tristan's and her parents' insurance policies, Hannah had been stunned to learn how much she would end up with. It was a strange feeling to gain so much financially, materially, when she'd lost so much personally. She'd rather be penniless if she could have them back. The reality was she wouldn't have to go back to work if she didn't want to – at least for the next six months to a year. But she would. Raelene had made it clear that keeping busy had helped her after losing Scott. And Hannah agreed that it probably wasn't a good idea to make any major decisions for the time being. Raelene had said a minimum of twelve months, but that seemed a very long time. She'd go back to work as planned. Having something normal to do among all this mess might help, as would being around people who cared.

People were so nice. She had to remember that in the coming days, weeks, months.

Reaching out to friends and not hiding away at home alone was another piece of advice Raelene had given her, though in the next breath she'd said travelling had also helped her.

Hannah was really going to miss them. They were flying to Adelaide and staying at their farm for a week or so to scatter Tristan's ashes before flying back to Tasmania to continue their trip.

Hannah still wasn't sure what she was to do with her parents' remains. A few times she wondered if she'd done the right thing having them cremated, then she found herself getting annoyed with them for not sharing their wishes with her and leaving her with such a burden. And then she felt guilty – it wasn't her parents' fault they'd been killed. And she'd cry all over again.

'Now, it's not too late to change your mind and come with us, you know,' Adrian said, putting an arm around her shoulder.

'I know, and I really appreciate it, but I feel I need to stay here.' She shrugged helplessly.

'You have to do what feels right,' Raelene said.

Hannah also had a feeling that they were really just being polite and deep down they wanted to say goodbye to their son on their own.

'We know that you've got plenty of wonderful people taking care of you,' Raelene added, 'but if you decide you want us to come back, you only have to ask.'

'God, I'm going to miss you both so much.' Hannah's eyes filled.

'Oh, darling,' Raelene and Adrian said in unison and they pulled her to them.

'We'll only be a phone call away if you need us,' Raelene said. 'And you're welcome to join us anytime, wherever we are if you need to get away.'

'Go on, or you'll miss your flight,' Hannah croaked, extracting herself and gently pushing them away.

'You will be okay, you know,' Raelene said for the umpteenth time that week. 'You're a lot stronger than you realise – you'll see.' She was holding Hannah by the arms and looking at her intently.

'Thank you so much for everything.'

'And thank you,' Adrian said. 'It's been good to spend the time together. If only it weren't ...'

'I know.'

Adrian hugged her tightly again. They each gave her a final kiss on the forehead and got in the car.

Hannah stood waving as they drove off, tears running down her face. When they were out of sight she felt completely bereft and lost. Now what?

'I see Raelene and Adrian have just left. Are you all right, dear?' Hannah looked up to find Beth hurrying across the road.

'I'll be okay,' she said, smiling warmly at her dear friend and neighbour. 'I'm going to keep busy.' *With what, I don't yet know.*

'Shouldn't you be packing?'

'All done. I have time for a quick cuppa before I go. I feel terrible leaving you at a time like this.'

'Don't worry, Auntie Beth. I have Sam and Rob and no doubt you've organised a roster of people to drop in and keep an eye on me.'

Beth had the good grace to look a little sheepish, which made Hannah smile. 'Just a few. But only until you're back at work. I'm still not sure that's a good idea, but only you can know.'

'I'll see how I go. It might help to get back into a routine and do something that feels a bit more normal. I hope so.'

'Well, remember, take it hour by hour and then when you're stronger, day by day. Now, come over and have a quick farewell cuppa with me. You can tell me what to take out so I can get my suitcase to close,' Beth said, linking her arm through Hannah's and leading her across the street.

★

After tearfully seeing Beth off, Hannah slowly walked back across to her house. She stood in the hallway for a moment, taking stock. For the first time since the accident, she was completely alone. It was so quiet. Too quiet. Her heart began to ache again. The ache was there all the time, but sometimes when she was distracted it wasn't quite so painful. Now she felt like everything within her chest cavity was being wound tighter and tighter, and she found it difficult to breathe.

Hannah sank to the floor, wrapped her arms around her knees. *I want my family back. I don't want to be a widow or an orphan.*

Finally the sobbing stopped and she struggled to her feet. Feeling sorry for herself wouldn't help. Raelene was right, she had to keep her mind occupied.

She went into the laundry where Raelene had left a bundle of sheets and towels they had used. She loaded the washing machine, added detergent, turned it on, and stood listening to the hiss of water for a moment wondering how she could keep herself busy for the next two hours that the machine would take. Then she would have the distraction of hanging the washing on the line to occupy her for ten minutes and then later to bring everything in when it was dry.

She really should do her own sheets too, but couldn't bear the thought of giving up the last faint traces of Tristan's scent.

Chapter Ten

Hannah got the fright of her life when she looked up and saw Sam's face in the window. After taking a few fortifying deep breaths with her hand to her chest, she turned the vacuum cleaner off and went to answer the door.

'God, you scared the shit out of me!' she said.

'Sorry. I did ring the bell. When you didn't answer, I was worried,' Sam said. 'Golly, you're keen. Didn't you only just clean before Christmas?'

Sam was never shy in saying she put off cleaning until the fluff bunnies turned into tumble weeds and started making their way down the hall. Hannah wasn't a clean freak by any stretch, but she didn't have the same level of hatred for the task that her friend did. Sam had often gently ribbed Hannah about being a cardboard cut-out of her mother, Daphne, who kept a spotless house. Hannah didn't mind the comparison at all, in fact, took it as a compliment. The White house had always been a welcoming home, and Daphne always kept it clean and tidy.

'There are crumbs all over the place from yesterday,' Hannah said.

'Fair enough. I just came to check on you now Raelene and Adrian have left. Has Beth left for her cruise yet?'

'Yes, an hour or so ago.'

'How are you feeling?'

'I'm fine.'

'You're allowed to be honest, you know,' Sam told her. 'This is me, your best friend, remember?'

'I'm sad – it's what I am all the time. It was great having them here and I'm really going to miss them. But, you know, I think I'm going to miss Auntie Beth even more.'

'I hope you're not regretting us talking you out of going with her.'

'No, you were right, I might have got bored and I think I would have felt out of place. At least while I'm at home there are things I can do. And there'd be nothing worse than sitting around feeling gloomy and bursting into tears all the time in public.'

'People understand, you know.'

'Maybe. But it still brings the mood down. And I didn't want to ruin her holiday,' said Hannah. 'It's her first cruise – she's probably been saving for it for the last twenty years. I would hate to have put a dampener on it for her – or her friends.'

'You're always so thoughtful.'

Hannah shrugged. 'I really need to start standing on my own two feet, anyway.'

'Sweetie, now is not the time for giving yourself a dose of tough love or being a martyr. It's only been a week.'

'I'm just trying to get on as best I can.'

'I know, and you're doing really well,' Sam said, wrapping her arms around her friend.

'Do you want to come with me while I hang the washing out?'

'Sure, but I really hope you're not overdoing it,' Sam said as they went out to the clothesline.

'I'm fine. I'm not sick, just heartbroken, Sammy. Anyway, it's good to feel a bit useful. I've been sitting around being taken care of and waited on all week. So, enough about me. Why aren't you home getting ready for Bianca's party?'

'Are you sure you won't change your mind and come? You can't stay home on your own on New Year's Eve.'

'Well, I certainly don't feel up to partying. And I don't want to ruin the whole vibe with the black cloud hanging around me. I couldn't do that to Bianca, especially when she's finally starting to get it together after being down for so long.'

'Yes, that bloody rat, Alastair. I still can't believe he ran off with his PA – how bloody clichéd is that! Stupid man!' said Sam. 'She's better off without him. Oh, god, I'm sorry,' she added, putting her hands over her mouth.

'It's okay. But, see, you're already feeling that you have to censor yourself around me. Not that you need to. See how awkward it would be for everyone if I went along tonight?'

'You're too sweet for your own good. For the record, I don't think you staying home alone is a good idea, but you have to do what's right for you. And only you can know what that is.'

'I don't know about that,' Hannah said with a tight laugh. She wasn't sure about anything anymore. Nothing felt right. But she was muddling along the best she could.

'Well, it certainly won't be the same without you,' Sam said later as she was leaving. 'You take good care. And if you change your mind you know where we'll be. Remember, Hann, there's no shame in admitting you don't want to be on your own – not just tonight, any time.'

'I know. Thanks. Now off you go and get your sparkles on,' she said, giving her friend a quick hug and sending her out before the lump in her throat had a chance to burst.

★

Hannah was determined to go to bed feeling exhausted in the hope of getting a full night's sleep – without the help of medication. She longed for a bone-aching weariness to replace the tiredness of shattered nerves and holding her emotions together that had become a part of her life in the last week.

She'd remade the spare bed and dusted, vacuumed and scrubbed the bathroom and kitchen like a maniac. It was almost nine o'clock when she took off her rubber gloves and laid them on the drainer of the kitchen sink.

She forced herself to heat up a portion of casserole – she'd promised Auntie Beth she'd eat regularly. And, anyway, she didn't like waste. A lot of people had gone to so much effort to cook for her, the least she could do was make herself eat.

At ten o'clock she took a glass of milk laced with brandy to bed, as had become her habit, and turned on the TV. She'd watch the fireworks and hopefully fall asleep.

She wondered about seeing a doctor for something – something perhaps not as strong as the pills she'd tried, but better than the over-the-counter tablets that Sam had brought her. She was trying to be careful – those drugs also made her feel sluggish the next day if she took too many. The instructions said to not take them for more than ten days straight. While it had only been a few days, she could see she was at the top of a slippery slope. Even if the substance wasn't considered addictive, the mere act of using something to help her sleep could be. She'd better be careful with the brandy too. She'd never been a big drinker, but she could see herself becoming addicted to the drink she'd come to enjoy and rely on each evening.

As if on autopilot, Hannah cleaned her teeth and then slathered moisturiser on. As she did, she thought about all the times she'd stood here at the mirror with Tristan talking to her from the bedroom. As she had done most nights that week, she tried to tell herself to think of it as if Tristan was just away for work, despite the fact they'd only ever spent two nights apart in their five years of marriage. It never worked. She hated having the whole bed to herself and couldn't imagine getting used to it, didn't want to get used to it. But she had to start to accept that this was her new normal. With a sigh she snuggled down to watch the early fireworks from around the country. At least the accident would be well and truly old news by now and wouldn't surprise her on one of the late night bulletins, and maybe the hum of the TV turned low might lull her to sleep.

*

Hannah woke with a start. Her heart was racing. She'd had a nightmare. She was on her side of the bed. She rolled over to snuggle up to Tris. And suddenly, like all the other nights since Christmas Day, she remembered there was no Tris. This was her life, reality, not a nightmare. Tristan was gone.

She dragged herself out to have the wee she now realised she desperately needed. She'd really have to stop with all the tea. And while in the bathroom she reluctantly took one of the antihistamine pills. One good thing about them was that they seemed to stop her dreaming.

She climbed back into bed, glancing at the clock as she did. It was twelve-thirty. It was the New Year. There was no point hoping this one would be better than the last, it couldn't get any worse. She rolled onto her side and tried to talk herself into going back to sleep. But then she suddenly realised that without Tristan's dad there no one had double-checked that the windows and doors were locked. Tris had always done a patrol of the house before bed, as her father had before him. Adrian had done it too, while he'd been staying there over the last week.

She lay with her eyes open in the darkness, trying to listen for any sounds in the house. She thought it was silent, but the harder she listened, the more noises she thought she heard. She told herself it was the house stretching and yawning, getting settled for the night as the cooler weather came in. But suddenly she was scared. She knew it was silly – no one was there. Still, she wasn't going out there alone to check. If someone was silently ransacking the house, let them. She hoped they'd take all the remnants of Christmas from the garage so she'd never be faced with it again. She wished she'd asked Rob to take it all to the op shop. And if an axe murderer was making his way carefully up the hall to do her in, even better. She didn't care.

Then she started feeling guilty. Tristan and his parents had survived losing Scott. Auntie Beth had survived losing her husband, Elliott. Her parents had suffered the loss of their parents. Plenty of people died and plenty of people who'd loved them coped. She'd just have to learn to as well.

After tossing and turning for another hour, she turned on the TV again.

At four Hannah gave up. She must have nodded off, but the gritty feeling in her eyes told her she couldn't have slept much. Exhausted but too exasperated to try for any more sleep, she threw the covers off and got up. She needed to do *something*.

She looked around and her gaze settled on Tristan's side of the built-in wardrobe covering one wall. That's what she would do. She made her way down to the kitchen. Even with the lights on it was still scary. Her heart began to race. She knew her fear was irrational, but she couldn't help it. She grabbed the roll of garbage bags from the drawer, slammed it shut and raced back to the bedroom. She opened the wardrobe door, took a deep breath and began pulling Tristan's clothes out.

It was only when she paused to ponder what to actually do with the large pile that she realised the ache she'd almost become accustomed to had turned into a knife, stabbing into her side. And then her brain started up:

There's no point keeping his things.

No, it's too soon.

He's not coming back.

Someone else could use them.

Is it too soon?

What will people think?

It doesn't matter what people think, only you know what's right for you.

Well I don't fucking know what's right for me, do I? It all feels wrong, so so wrong!

'Tristan how can you leave me!' Hannah cried out, and sat back against the wall and banged hard on her legs until it hurt too much. And then she curled around the clothes and began to cry — large wracking sobs that shook her whole body.

*

As if coming out of a trance, she looked around and wondered what had happened. Why was she sitting on the floor surrounded by clothes? Oh, that's right. She got up. She couldn't look at the pile now, let alone bag them up. It was too soon. But she had to do something with the clothes. They couldn't stay there like that. She crawled over and began dragging and stuffing everything into the bottom of the wardrobe. She became frantic, desperate to have them out of sight and the room returned to order. But as a jumbled mass, they wouldn't all fit. Tears still poured down her wet, burning face. Overwhelmed and angry she slammed the door shut, but it popped open again. She got up and kicked it.

'Ouch!' she cried, rubbing her foot. She climbed back into bed, but she couldn't stop looking at the wardrobe. It annoyed her to think of how messy it was in there. She couldn't leave it like that.

She got back up and slowly and carefully put each item back in the wardrobe as it had been before – shirts and suits back on hangers, t-shirts, jumpers, socks and jocks all back in their drawers.

When she closed the wardrobe door, she was exhausted but felt a little better. And now light was peering from behind the curtains so it was safe to go into the kitchen.

Hannah leapt up and bounded to the door when she heard the bell.

'God, it's so good to see you,' she said to Sam and wrapped her arms around her.

'Happy New Year,' Sam said.

'Thanks. You too. Hey, you didn't have to come all this way. You could have just called or texted.'

'I did. Both. I was getting worried.'

'Oh. Sorry. I didn't hear the phone.'

'Doesn't matter. We're off to join the hordes at St Kilda Beach and wondered if you'd like to come along, since it's going to be a scorcher.'

'Is it? I can't remember when I last saw a weather report.' Hannah knew it was last night, but with most things these days, she'd watched but not taken anything in.

'So, do you fancy walking miles from where we finally find a park after driving round and around for half an hour and then wrestling for a towel-sized piece of sand?'

'Oh, you sell it so well,' Hannah said, smiling.

'What if I said it was the boys who insisted we come by and invite you? It's true.'

'Really?'

'Really.'

'Oh, bless them, that's so sweet.'

'They love you, Hann. And they're worried about you. As are we,' Sam said.

'I can't exactly say no to them, now can I?'

'Welcome to my world,' Sam said, rolling her eyes. 'So, are you coming?'

'Okay, count me in. Er,' she added, looking down at herself and seeing pyjamas. She felt vague, couldn't quite process how to get herself ready, what she'd need to stuff in a bag. Her brain really was addled these days.

'Put your togs on and then shorts and a top, grab a towel and hat and your handbag, and we're good to go. We've got plenty of sunscreen and snacks.'

'Thanks, Sam.'

'I'll just tell Rob we'll be a few minutes. He was worried too. Oh, and one thing, don't mention the absence of the dogs.'

'Shit, has something happened to them?'

'No, I just wasn't keen on spending the day dealing with two yappy dogs and constantly telling them they're not allowed to run riot while keeping two small boys from drowning at the same time. It's too much.'

'But you've got Rob.'

'You know what men are like – useless at multi-tasking. And a hundred times worse at the beach – they only have to get distracted by the first nice set of silicon sitting in a bikini top and everything goes pear shaped,' Sam said, joking. 'Anyway, we've had tears – thankfully not from me for once, though, nearly – the dogs are at home, and we have two slightly unhappy four-year-olds. So, please, just don't mention the dogs.'

'Got it.'

A few minutes later Hannah pulled the front door closed and got a shock as a blast of warm air hit her face.

'Happy New Year,' Rob said as he got out of the car to give her a hug.

'Thanks, you too. I didn't realise it was going to be so hot today.'

'The air-con's on full blast. Here, you sit in the front,' Sam said, opening the back door.

'Come on,' Hannah said, 'you hate the back.'

'I know, but ...'

'It's fine. Really. I don't mind at all.'

She squeezed into the back of the car beside Ethan, thankful the twins insisted on being seated right next to each other and she was prevented from having to clamber over one to get to the middle.

'Hi guys,' Hannah said.

'We're so glad you're coming!' Oliver said.

'Yes, goody, goody gumdrops,' Ethan said, clapping his hands.

'Thanks very much for the invite. Happy New Year. Are you excited about going to the beach?' she asked the boys.

'Well it won't be as fun without Oofy and Inky,' Oliver said, pouting.

'Oh. Well it will be very hot and there will be lots of people – you don't want them burning their feet or getting trampled. It's best they stay home where it's cool,' Hannah said.

'I suppose. And we might have to walk a long way if we can't find a close park. Mum says we all have to ask the parking angels really nicely,' Oliver said.

'Yes. She says it's all about positive blinking,' Ethan said.

'Okay. Got it. Positive blinking,' Hannah said, smiling. Perhaps this was just the tonic she needed, she thought as she snapped her seatbelt into place.

'So, how are the New Year resolutions holding up?' Hannah asked when they were on their way.

'Oh, I completely forgot this year,' Sam said.

'What's a New Year's resolution?' Oliver asked.

'Sort of like making a wish for the coming year,' Sam said.

'Oh. Then I wish for Uncle Tris and Granny Daph and Grandad Dan to come back,' Oliver said.

'Me too,' said Ethan.

Hannah's heart lurched.

'Thanks, boys. That's lovely. But you know they can't come back, don't you?' she said.

'They're dead. But Mum says if you want something bad enough you can make it happen. What is it, Mum, bill power?'

'*Will power.* And remember we talked about this?' Sam said to her sons. 'Some wishes can't come true, no matter how much you want them to. Uncle Tristan and Granny Daph and Grandad Dan can't come back, sweeties.'

'But that's not fair,' Oliver said.

'No, it's not,' Ethan said. Both boys folded their arms across their chests.

Oh, God, let me out now. Hannah stared out the window holding back the tears until she felt something touch her. She glanced over to find Oliver looking earnestly up at her with his big brown innocent eyes, his hand reaching for hers.

'You can help us make sandcastles if you want. Building sandcastles won't make everything better, but it'll be fun,' Oliver said.

'It might stop you feeling sad for a little while,' Ethan said sagely from his place by the window.

'That would be lovely,' Hannah said as her heart lurched painfully again. 'Though I don't think I'm anywhere near as good at it or as clever as your mother.'

'That's okay. We don't mind,' Oliver said.

'No, it'll still be fun,' said Ethan.

Chapter Eleven

'I'm really sorry about the boys back there in the car. They don't understand,' Sam said, putting her arm around Hannah. They trailed along behind Rob, who was trying to keep up with the boys who'd rushed ahead. They'd managed to easily find a great parking spot. Now, thrilled by their success, the boys were off blinking furiously in the hope of securing a good place on the crowded beach to build sandcastles. Thankfully they both had sunglasses on, so they didn't look as silly or crazy as they might have.

'I know. It's okay,' said Hannah. 'It's sweet that they thought so highly of them and miss them so much.'

'We all do. It's left a huge gap in all of our lives. Poor Rob's putting on a brave front in public – being manly and all – but he's a wreck, like the rest of us.'

'Speaking of being a wreck. I tried to go through Tris's things.'

'Oh, sweetie. It's way too early to even think about doing that.'

'It was horrible. I felt torn apart all over again.'

'Of course you would. So why did you do it?'

'I couldn't sleep. And I just thought getting it done would ...'

'Sweetie, I don't think grief is something you can simply organise your way out of,' Sam said. 'It doesn't work like that.'

'I just want it to stop. I want to feel better.'

'I know you do. And I so badly wish I could help. Maybe you should think about seeing someone – a professional.'

'Maybe. But there wouldn't be much point at the moment, when all I do is cry. That would be a waste, wouldn't it?' she said, smiling weakly at Sam.

'Well, you can talk to me whenever you want,' Sam said, smiling sadly back before pulling Hannah tighter to her. They walked on in thoughtful silence for a few paces.

'How was last night?' Hannah asked.

'Nice and sedate. You were missed, but everyone understood.'

'How's this?' Rob called, looking around.

'Perfect. Well done,' Sam said, dumping her armful of towels and starting to unfold them. Rob put up the first of two sunshade dome tents.

'One for us and one for them,' he explained to Hannah's slightly confused expression.

'There'll be no getting fried on my watch. Hann, you'll be in the boys' tent for sandcastle supervision,' Sam said lightly. 'But don't forget, nothing's compulsory. You can say no to them any time you like and ignore their cute little pleading faces.'

Hannah smiled faintly in reply.

'Here, I brought a book for you if you fancy reading,' Sam said, reaching into her bag and handing Hannah a battered paperback.

'Thanks. I can't remember the last time I read a book.'

'These days I tend to only read when we all come to the beach and Rob can watch the kids,' Sam said. 'But I think I'm going to doodle today instead,' she added, taking out a small sketchbook.

'Are the creative juices finally starting to flow again?'

'Kind of. Not really. It's more an annoying drip, like a tap with a bung washer,' she said with a laugh.

'Oh, Sammy, that's great. Good for you.'

'Well, don't go getting too excited. It's just scribbling at the beach.'

'Yes, but you've got to start somewhere.' Hannah was pleased for her friend who didn't believe enough in her enormous talent. As far as Hannah knew, Sam hadn't worked on anything major since having the boys.

When Hannah and Sam had finished university, Sam had achieved so much – honours in fine art and great marks. She had fierce determination, plenty of talent and a lot of passion. But she had never pursued art as a career. The need to earn money had gradually pushed her dreams out of sight. Hannah thought Sam had forgotten what she'd yearned for all those years ago. Even Rob's encouragement hadn't done enough to reignite her interest. She did a little dabbling occasionally, but that seemed to be all these days.

Hannah had often wished she had some creative talent. She'd done a general arts degree and chosen subjects because they interested her – sociology, psychology, history, communications, gender studies. While she'd got so much from her course, she hadn't found anything she wanted to study in enough depth to try to turn it into a career. Being a romantic at heart she'd loved to have set herself up in a gorgeous studio at the back of the garden and toiled away. Instead she encouraged Sam, who usually laughed or simply shrugged her words away. Sam's lack of confidence in her abilities really bothered Hannah, but until her friend could learn to believe in herself there was nothing she could do.

'We have plenty of time,' Sam said to the boys. 'Why don't you guys have a swim before it gets too hot, then you can build a sandcastle. Mum wants to talk quietly with Auntie Hannah for a bit.'

'Okay,' both boys said.

'But not without sunscreen,' Sam said, diving into the large floral beach bag beside her.

The boys sat dutifully while Sam and Hannah rubbed sunscreen down the parts of their arms and legs not covered by their UV tops and shorts.

As she tended to Oliver, Hannah thought how nice it was to feel useful. But then her thoughts turned to how she wished it was her own little boy she was taking care of. And to have Tristan beside her. She closed her eyes briefly and willed the tears behind her sunglasses to stop and thankfully they did.

'Actually, I'm going to go in for a dip. Want to join me?' Sam asked when the boys had been released and were bounding down to the water's edge with their floaties.

'I'm game if you are.'

'Rob, darling, can you keep an eye on everything here? We're going to have a swim.'

'Huh? Yep, of course,' he said, without taking his eyes off the two boys.

The girls peeled off their tops and shorts and proceeded to slather on sunscreen.

Despite complaining about the warm breeze brushing the beach, Sam sucked in her breath sharply when the water touched her toes.

'No wonder the boys squealed,' she said. 'Brrr, too cold for me. I'm heading back.'

'Mummy's a chicken,' called Ethan. The boys were sitting nearby on their inflatable rings with small waves lapping at them.

'Yes, she is,' Sam called.

'Come on, Auntie Hann,' Oliver said. She wasn't finding the water too cold, but she was treading carefully in case of creepy crawlies. Even strips of seaweed touching her legs startled her. Inch by inch she made it to her knees, then her thighs. The boys got up, pulled their inflated rings up over their bottoms and followed her. Now waist-deep she sank down to coat herself up to her neck. What was Sam on about, the water was fine?

She longed to go out of her depth, lie back and float away. But she couldn't put the boys in danger. And they had no sense of fear. They'd just follow her out, no matter how far she went. Hannah headed back towards the beach, sat down in the shallow water and let the tiny waves lap at her while she watched the twins.

It felt good, though she longed to swim, really swim, like those out there making their way back and forth across the horizon. Sitting here surrounded by people, she could almost believe everything was normal. Well, everything *was* normal, it was just a different, horrible sort of normal.

Suddenly she had the thought that if she were free to swim, she might just keep going until she got tired and the sea claimed her. The thought was both calming and terrifying. *Jesus, where did that come from?* She ached with a sadness that went to the depths of her soul, but she didn't think she was depressed, well, not that sort of depressed. She couldn't start thinking like that. Her parents and Tristan would be so disappointed in her having such negative thoughts. *But, they're not here, are they?*

She sensed movement close by and looked around to see the twins settling themselves back on their tubes beside her. Her heart lurched painfully. She wished it would stop doing that – it hurt. No matter how she felt, she couldn't put the dear little boys through more heartache. They were already clearly affected if their wish for the year was to have their Uncle Tristan and Granny Daph and Grandad Dan back. She'd often thought they were both quite old souls and seeing them sitting quietly beside her, keeping her company when they should have been busy being raucous little boys, splashing and squealing, confirmed it. And made her sad. The world was a cruel place. And it was a pity they had to learn that at such a young age. She'd at least got to thirty-one without any major trauma in her life. But perhaps that meant she wasn't equipped to deal with it. Perhaps if she'd suffered more hardship along the way, like having a cruel mother who bullied – like Sam did – she'd be tougher and coping better now.

She felt the boys leaning into her.

'I love you, Auntie Hann,' Oliver said, looking up at her with big, wide eyes.

'Thanks, sweetie. I love you both too – oh so much,' she said, swallowing back the lump forming in her throat as she put an arm around each twin and squeezed them to her.

'Would you like to make a sandcastle with us now?' Ethan asked a few moments later.

'Don't you want to swim some more?'

'Not really.'

'No, thank you,' Oliver said.

'Okay. Come on then,' Hannah said, getting up and holding out her hands to the boys.

Hannah settled herself in the dome tent as the boys proceeded to tell her they wanted to build a sand turtle and instructed her to start filling the small buckets with sand and to help build up the mound they would need. Hannah did as she was told and then watched while the boys worked diligently, helping how and when instructed. Doing something but not really having to concentrate was quite relaxing, mesmerising even, especially when it came to laying shells on the mound to resemble the turtle's lumpy skin.

She was surprised and a little disappointed when the boys sat back and declared their creation finished and demanded their parents come and inspect their handiwork. After basking in Sam and Rob's praise for a few moments, they promptly lay down and fell asleep, curled around their turtle.

Hannah eased herself out of the dome and reclaimed her chair. She peered over at Sam's lap where a sketch of the scene stretching out before them was taking shape in charcoal.

'That's amazing,' she said.

'It's only rough. But I'm enjoying it, and that's the main thing, right?'

'So, you survived the turtle building?' Rob said, looking up from the paper. 'Thanks for indulging them. It means a lot.'

'You don't have to thank me. I really enjoyed it.'

'A much less stressful affair than the last time we came to the beach when there were two small dogs jumping on everything and digging up the sand everywhere,' Rob said. 'It was chaos, I can tell you.'

'I can imagine. Anything interesting in the paper, Rob?'

'Not really.'

'Can I have the real-estate section when you've finished?'

'There isn't one. It's only Friday, remember?' he said.

'Oh. Oops. So it is.'

'Not thinking of selling up are you?' Sam said.

'Just curious. Anyway, isn't real estate ogling practically compulsory on weekends, being Melbournians?' she added with a laugh and picked up the novel Sam had lent her.

'Just don't do anything rash,' Sam warned.

'I love the house, I always have, but, god, I hate being there on my own,' Hannah said with a sigh, and was shocked to realise she'd actually uttered the words aloud.

'If you want to come and stay with us or have one of us stay,' Rob said, 'you only have to say.'

'Thanks, but I think I really have to start getting used to things being different.'

'Fair enough.'

'How about getting a dog or two for company?' Sam said.

'No, I'm not …'

'Yes, okay, you're not willing to pick up poo in public. I remember,' Sam said, smiling. Hannah had never had pets when she was growing up and didn't even like the idea of them. Tristan had mentioned it a couple of times, but she'd shut him down with the same arguments her mother had made to her as a child: I don't want the garden dug up, hair everywhere, having to walk it come rain, hail, or shine, bath it, et cetera. And these days there was the whole picking up poo in public thing. Ugh! Just the thought of it nearly made Hannah gag. She didn't know how Sam did it day after day, although she'd also dealt with nappies, so perhaps that helped. The truth was, Hannah just wasn't an animal person. She was barely all right with Sam and Rob's dogs, which thankfully tended to give her a wide berth.

'They are great company though,' Sam persisted.

'I might want to travel and then it would be a tie.' *Where the hell did that come from?*

'We'd look after it,' Sam said.

Rob cleared his throat.

'Oh come on, what's one more rowdy beast?' Sam said, scratching away busily with her charcoal.

'I suppose.'

'Where are you planning to go, anyway? Anywhere exciting?' Sam asked.

'I don't know. I might start by visiting Raelene and Adrian and see if the bug bites.'

'Hey, what about a boarder? Then they could look after everything if you went away. There's probably plenty of uni students looking for cheap accommodation. The extra money might be handy, too,' Sam said.

'I think I'll be fine.' Hannah knew she'd be a whole lot better than fine, but she didn't want to say anything to her friend until the insurance came through. Also, she felt weird about becoming rich as a result of such tragic circumstances.

'I couldn't think of anything worse than living in a share house now,' Rob said. 'It's not bad when you're twenty-something, but just imagine at our age. I couldn't deal with the mess for starters.'

'Probably not a whole lot different from sharing with a scatty wife, two small dogs, and a pair of four-year-olds,' Sam pointed out with a grin.

'Hmm, yes,' Rob said.

'But it wouldn't have to be a uni student,' Sam added. 'What about someone older, like a pensioner?'

'A pensioner might be a bit intrusive,' Rob chimed in. 'Different if you had a separate, self-contained wing or a flat set up, but at Hannah's place they'd be in your face all the time.'

'I'm sure I'll be fine. It'll just take some getting used to,' Hannah told them and herself firmly. *I sure hope so.* They meant well, but she now wished she hadn't said anything.

'Yes, it's only been a week,' Sam said.

'You know you can call us at any time of the day or night,' Rob said.

'I do. Thanks.'

They lapsed into silence and Hannah stared at the blurb on the back of the book, unable to focus. She wondered if she should sell up – if she could bring herself to – and maybe move into the city, closer to her work. Perhaps a clean break and a total change might be just what she needed. She was always stunned at what inner-city apartments were listed for – even those with just the one bedroom. Tristan had often shared his daydreams with her about living in a city warehouse conversion, but that was before they'd been given the opportunity to buy Hannah's parents' place.

Hannah opened the book and struggled to get into the story, rereading the first two lines over and over before finally being able to move onto the next. Her mind drifted and she kept getting lost and having to go back.

It was nice to appear to the outside world – the crowded beach full of laughter and energy – as a normal, anonymous person, rather than the recently widowed woman engulfed in sadness, which she was. Here she could hide behind her sunglasses and pretend for now that everything was okay. Perhaps she might even be lucky enough to fall asleep.

Gradually Hannah found the story and characters in the novel becoming more and more interesting and staying in her mind. She settled back in the low beach chair and concentrated, and slowly became lost in her book, which, according to the blurb, was a story of family betrayal and infighting over a will.

*

She was startled from her reading by the two boys appearing beside her and loudly telling their parents they were hungry. Plastic containers filled with carrot and celery sticks, cubes of cheese and crackers were handed out and promises made that if they ate something healthy they could have ice-creams.

In what seemed like seconds, the boys devoured the food and insisted it was time for their dessert. Hannah's mouth started watering too. She loved ice-cream so much that she couldn't keep it in the house or she'd devour a whole tub in one sitting.

'My treat,' she announced. 'Why don't I take them to get the ice-creams and you guys keep an eye on everything here?'

'Okay. Great. I'll have chocolate,' Sam said.

'Strawberry for me, thanks,' Rob said.

'Are you sure you both just want the one flavour? I'm being greedy and going for two scoops,' Hannah said.

'If you insist, two scoops it is, but still just chocolate for me,' Sam said.

'You've twisted my arm. Two scoops of strawberry, please.'

'Okay, coming right up. Come on boys.'

Hannah stood up and swung her handbag over her shoulder. She accepted two small, warm, sandy hands and soon they were walking down the asphalt path. Thankfully there was an ice-cream van parked only about a hundred metres away and they didn't have to walk all the way to the end of the pier. Nevertheless, it was quite hot so they'd better hurry back or have melted ice-cream dripping down their arms.

'Any idea what you'd like, boys,' Hannah asked as they stood waiting to be served.

'Cookies and cream and toffee, please, just like Uncle Tristan,' Oliver announced.

'And me too,' Ethan said.

'Okay. Are you sure?' Hannah asked, slightly staggered that they'd remembered.

'Yes, I am.'

'Me too.'

Thank god Tristan's favourites hadn't been boysenberry and rum and raisin like hers were. She couldn't help but find it a little amusing. As laid back as Sam was as a mother at times, she'd almost certainly have a fit if Hannah gave her four-year-olds a dose of rum. Though it might help them sleep …

They walked back quickly and when they reached their parents the boys loudly announced their choice and why, as only innocent little boys could. At least Hannah found it didn't hurt quite as much the second time and it was nowhere near as hard as their comment about Tristan and New Year's resolutions. Maybe she would be okay in time.

Chapter Twelve

Carrying Ethan across the hot sand, Hannah was a little disappointed at her poor level of fitness. She'd better get back to doing some daily exercise. Going to work again would help re-establish her routine.

Once Rob had pulled up at the kerb outside the house, Hannah kissed the sleeping boys gently on their heads, gave their weary parents a rub on the shoulder each, thanked them for a lovely day, and slowly and quietly got out of the car. She cringed at the noise as she closed the door, and then waited and waved as they pulled away before making her way up the path to her front door.

★

Having showered, Hannah defrosted one of the many packs of food Beth had prepared and left in her freezer, silently thanking and blessing the old lady as she watched it turning under its spotlight in the microwave.

She couldn't bear sitting at the table alone, so she opted for dinner on her lap in front of the TV. She tried to remember when she'd last done this, and couldn't. It would be a bad habit to get into, but the kitchen was too quiet and empty to sit in by herself. Anyway, it wasn't as if there was anyone here to frown at her. As that thought crossed her mind, Hannah tried not to let it bring her mood down. She wondered if the stickler for etiquette had been her or Tristan. Probably both, she decided. They'd been on the same page about most things. But most things were different now.

One of the good things about a day at the beach is the particular weariness you feel when you slip into bed, Hannah thought as she did just that. She let out a sigh. Perhaps this would be the night when she would return to sleeping well.

*

She woke and looked around the room, trying to judge the amount of light coming in between the curtains. Was it the middle of the night or time to consider getting up? She felt rested, really rested – a feeling she hadn't experienced for what seemed so long and wasn't sure she would again. She was so comfortable she didn't want to move. No matter what time it was, she didn't have to get up if she didn't want to. Work was still another couple of days away. But curiosity got the better of her and she shuffled towards the clock radio. Please let it be morning, she silently prayed as she turned the clock around to read. What? She blinked, barely able to believe what she was seeing. It was eight-forty. Even before her life had been turned upside down – for that was how she'd begun to refer to it, rather than dwell on the fact people had died – she'd been a morning person and had only ever slept beyond seven a.m. if she were ill.

Her mum would have said she needed the sleep. And, boy had she! Now she felt ready to tackle the day head-on – not reluctantly and cautiously like every other morning. She actually felt a little more like her old self. She knew she'd never completely be that person again – too much had happened and her whole soul had been decimated – but she felt that this was going to be a good day and a step towards recovery.

Under the shower, she ignored the little voice that warned that grief was a slow process and often it was one step forward and two steps back. She'd read that somewhere. But it didn't have to apply to her, now did it?

Hannah took her coffee and the paper out to sit at the table on the back verandah, like she and Tristan had often done on weekends. But this, like so many things she'd loved doing and had taken for granted, no longer felt right. She couldn't settle. She even shifted places and took the chair Tristan – and her father before him – had always occupied, but that didn't work either. She moved down to the step. That felt better. Perhaps she'd have to create her own new, different everything.

A thought struck her and she looked up and across the expanse of lawn, which was flanked by screening poplar trees. What about putting in a pool? She'd enjoyed the water yesterday. She needed more exercise. But then decided it was a question for another day. She had things to deal with – important things – before getting caught up in daydreams. She finished her coffee and resisted a refill. Most likely Mrs Hobbes at her parents' retirement village would invite her to sit down for a cuppa to discuss things. Would Mrs Hobbes even be in at work on a Saturday? Oh, well, she shouldn't overdo the caffeine, anyway.

But first she had to face driving past the accident scene, which would probably still be highlighted in yellow markings for all to see. Hannah toyed with looking up another way to go, but resisted. She had to face this, and right now.

Her heart raced as she drove towards what she referred to in her mind as The Intersection. As she slowed she tried to see any sign of the devastation that had occurred there a little over a week ago. Thankfully there was nothing more than the splotches and lines of yellow spray paint the investigators used, which she'd prepared herself for.

There were cars all around her and the light ahead was green so she couldn't slow down too much without risking the ire of the driver behind her. He had already shown his impatience by honking at the previous set of lights when she'd missed taking off immediately when the signal had turned green. With the accident in her mind, Hannah now found driving confronting and nerve-racking. Previously she'd been a good, confident driver. Today she felt like a learner – nervous, apprehensive, slow, and struggling to concentrate.

By the time she pulled up in front of the single roller door beside her parents' villa, she felt a nervous wreck and was wishing she'd brought Sam with her or waited until Beth was back and could have come along.

In a daze she made her way out of her parents' mini street, past the communal barbeques and recreational areas to the main office. She'd tried to talk her parents out of giving up their driver's licences – they were only in their late sixties, for goodness sake. Who willingly gave up their driver's licence and independence? Her parents, as it turned out. They said they had everything they needed right here and if not they would catch a taxi or bus. They had decided that they didn't want to one day be the cause of an accident. The irony of this kept running through Hannah's head as she waited while the receptionist phoned to tell the administrator, Mrs Joanne Hobbes, that she'd arrived.

'Hannah, how lovely to see you,' Mrs Hobbes said, and when she wrapped Hannah in a warm hug, Hannah almost crumpled into her.

'I've come to start going through Mum and Dad's things so ...' Hannah blurted despite being suddenly very uneasy about doing it today, after all. She wasn't sure she could unlock the door and walk into her parents' empty home, never mind sorting through their things.

'There's no rush. You take as long as you need,' Mrs Hobbes said, putting a hand on Hannah's arm.

'Thank you.' Hannah swallowed hard. 'And thank you so much again for coming to the funeral, and to the house afterwards. It meant a lot and would have really meant a lot to Mum and Dad to know you and so many of the residents were there.'

'Well, they were very special to us. We're missing them terribly. Come in and sit down. Can I get you a tea or coffee?'

'Coffee would be lovely, thank you.'

'Can you ask Daisy to bring coffee for two to my office please, Tilly?' she said.

'Of course,' the receptionist said, and picked up the phone.

'Come through.' Mrs Hobbes ushered Hannah down the hall and into the first open door. Hannah had been in here that first day with her mother, who had started looking for accommodation before telling her husband what she was up to. Hannah suddenly felt a wave of sadness and nostalgia bubble up. Maybe if she hadn't come here with her mother that day her husband and parents would still be alive. She tried to wipe the few stray tears away while Mrs Hobbes wasn't looking. But when she glanced up, she found a box of tissues being slid across the desk towards her.

'Thanks. I thought I was okay. I was when I left the house,' she added with a tense smile.

'Dear, it hasn't been long. They've left a big void here. I can only imagine how you're feeling. And with it being such a shock. I'm not sure if it's easier knowing they're going to go or not,' she said wistfully. 'You've had an incredible loss – your husband as well. Practically your whole family, is that right?'

Hannah nodded, wiping her dripping nose. She was pleased to have the distraction of the door opening and a young woman walking in with a tray of steaming mugs, a jug of milk and bowl of sugar and plate of biscuits.

'That looks lovely, thank you, Daisy,' Mrs Hobbes said, smiling at the young woman who nodded before leaving. They both added milk and sugar to their coffee in silence.

'Oh, that's good,' Mrs Hobbes said, with clear satisfaction, after a long sip. 'It always tastes so much better when someone else has made it, don't you think?'

'Mmm, it is very nice coffee,' Hannah agreed.

'It's from one of those pod machines. So, tell me, how are you doing?'

'I'm okay, I suppose. Sad, can't stop crying most of the time, as you can see,' she said with an attempt at a smile.

'That's normal, dear, don't be embarrassed about it.'

'Thankfully I've got good friends around me. I'm really lucky in that way. But people have their own lives. I've just got to get used to being alone. At the moment that's what I'm finding the hardest to deal with.'

'Yes. I think there's an art to learning to enjoy your own company and space, especially if you've never had that before. And with your parents being so warm and gregarious and hospitable … Mine were the same, as was my husband. I lost him four years ago …'

'I'm so sorry.'

'Thank you, I've come to terms with it. But what I'm trying to say is that being alone wasn't something I'd ever had to do. We had a big circle of friends and entertained a lot. Learning to be all right with being on my own took some getting used to, I can tell you.'

'But what about your friends?'

'Oh, they were wonderful, and still are, but I was living in Adelaide. I left to take this job.'

'Oh. Wow. That was a big move. And very courageous.'

'Yes, I don't think I quite realised how big or how courageous. You see, like you, I was trying to keep my mind occupied. I don't garden or have any hobbies, really, so for me it was work. As much as I loved my job in Adelaide I needed a new challenge. I stopped wanting to host dinner parties because it wasn't the same without Ted and I found people tend to look at you differently – trying to treat you normally, as before, and not pity you, but failing miserably. And of course no one knows what to say. There is nothing anyone can say, but still people try, don't they? Then the whole evening inevitably becomes awkward and tense. Well, that's what I found, anyway. But I've had the benefit of four years,' she said.

'I avoided a New Year's Eve dinner so as not to ruin it for anyone.'

'Very thoughtful of you. And wise.'

'Thanks. It means a lot to have you say that. I wasn't sure what was the right thing to do. As it turned out I was just too tired and couldn't have found the energy to get dressed up anyway.'

'Oh, I can relate to that. Don't tell anyone, but the moment I get home I'm into my jammies,' she said with a laugh. 'That's a legacy of my period of grief. But, seriously, you have to do what's right for you. If you feel you're being selfish and it goes against your well-mannered upbringing, put that aside.'

'I'm finding replying to all the cards that have come really hard, but I feel like it's something I should do.'

'Doing it might help, but it's entirely up to you if you do it or not. Now is the time for you to do whatever you can to get through this terribly sad time while also accepting that nothing will ever truly be the same again. And, remember, what everyone feels and experiences is different.'

'No one will truly understand what I'm going through, will they?'

'No, not completely. It's your journey and no one else's. People will always analyse, judge and have opinions, offer advice – it's what humans do. But when it comes down to it, the only opinion that matters is your own. Sometimes you'll feel like you're damned if you do and damned if you don't, but my advice – from someone who's been there – is to stay true to yourself and your own feelings. Don't do things because you think it's what's expected.'

'I can see why you're so good at your job,' Hannah said, smiling weakly.

'Oh, that's very kind. I've just been around the block a couple of times. I may be older and a bit fatter, but I'm also a hell of a lot wiser. You will be too – not fat, of course,' she said.

'I know what you meant,' Hannah said, smiling more broadly. 'But, seriously, it really means a lot to hear it from someone who's been through it but doesn't know me personally. My friends are wonderful, but, I don't know, it's just …' she said.

'Different. I know. I'm so sorry you have to go through it.'

'Thanks.'

They both lapsed into silence and finished their coffees.

'Thank you for the coffee and chat,' Hannah said, at last. 'It's been really good.'

'I'm glad. Here are the forms you'll need when you're ready. And take my card. If you have any questions or there's anything I can do, please don't hesitate to ask. And if you'd like another chat, do feel free to call or drop in anytime.'

'Thank you. Now, I've taken up enough of your time, I'd better go and at least see what I'm in for.'

'I'm happy to come with you if you'd like. Equally, if you'd prefer to be alone …'

'I've taken up enough of your time. But, oh, I've just realised, I forgot to bring a key.'

'No problem. We keep spares in the safe. Just wait here and I'll get it.'

'Thanks,' Hannah said, painfully aware she was sounding like a broken record. But what else was there to say? She was grateful to Mrs Hobbes for making her feel so comfortable. As she sat and waited she thought she really would prefer to be alone to start formulating a plan for clearing out her parents' villa.

'I'm sorry, I've just been reminded I have a meeting with some prospective residents now,' Mrs Hobbes said, walking back in. 'Here you are, here's the key. Would you mind finding your own way? Or I could send Tilly with you …'

'No, that's fine. I'll be fine,' Hannah said, standing up on now shaky legs. 'Thanks so much for this morning, Mrs Hobbes. I'll be in touch to sort out all the details when I'm ready. I shouldn't be long – maybe a week or so?'

'Please, call me Joanne. And, as I said, there's no rush.'

Hannah nodded and smiled and resisted uttering the words 'Thanks' or 'Thank you' again – she was beginning to sound like someone with a limited grasp of the English language. She was also starting to feel pretty jittery, so perhaps had lost some of her grasp on it.

Chapter Thirteen

Hannah made her way slowly back to her parents' villa, number eighty-three Lavender Lane, the key she clutched tightly cutting into her hand. She found herself enjoying the pain. She didn't seem to feel much of anything beyond the strange hollow ache deep within her these days.

She stared at her mother's trademark welcoming red Christmas ribbons tied in big bows around each of the terracotta pots full of pansies on either side of the door. Her heart ached at seeing that the pavers underneath the pots were damp. If only it had been her mother out first thing in the morning doing the watering. She sighed heavily, and put the key into the lock.

She carefully wiped her feet before stepping onto the plush cream carpet and, ignoring the closed bedroom doors, walked down the hall to the small but comfortable open-plan lounge, dining and kitchen area. She pictured her mother when she came in here for the first time and declared it quaint. 'Manageable,' her father had always called it.

Bloody Christmas, she silently cursed, and glared at the small Christmas tree in the corner and the strands of coloured foil decorations looped between the windows and large glass sliding door. Other than that, the place was just as it had always been – impeccably neat and ordered, yet homely and lived-in. But as Hannah stood there it struck her just how quiet it was – to the point of eeriness. *Deathly*, she found herself thinking without irony.

Daniel and Daphne weren't raucous, except occasionally when entertaining, but the house seemed to have stopped breathing, as well as her parents. There weren't even any birds to be heard in the tiny back garden. Hannah felt the urge to sit on one of the leather recliners and give into the weeping that was only just being contained beneath the surface.

'Get busy, stay busy,' she told herself. It was starting to become a mantra for her, she realised.

She carefully packed away every remnant of Christmas.

Now what, she wondered, looking around.

Feeling overwhelmed, she wished she'd just stayed home and continued replying to the stack of sympathy cards. While that was confronting, it was at least contained and manageable.

Perhaps this wasn't the right day to be packing up her parents' home. Perhaps it *was* too soon.

About to turn and walk back down the hall and shut the door, she stopped herself. Putting it off wouldn't help, would it? Best to get it over with. And no one else could do it. Joanne could probably organise someone to do any heavy lifting and cleaning, but no one else could decide what to keep and what to discard. Perhaps Auntie Beth could, but it wouldn't be fair to put that on the old lady. Again she wished Sam was here with her. What would her advice be? After a moment, she was sure Sam would say to do it in baby steps – start small and with the less personal and build up.

Perhaps some music for company would help. She turned on the radio that was always set to the ABC. Ignoring the nostalgic feeling that told her she shouldn't change it, she tuned it to MIX — her preferred station in the car. Concentrating on the music, a cheery tune from the eighties she could sing along to perhaps, she felt a little better.

'Right, let's do this,' she said aloud, gritted her teeth, and went into the kitchen area. The fridge — that was the most logical place to start. The milk would be rank by now.

She opened the door and stared inside. And then she began to frown. *That's weird.* There was no milk in the door, or cheese in the dairy keeper, and no eggs on the top shelf where her mother always kept the carton. And they were big milk drinkers so there was always plenty on hand. She opened the fruit and vegetable drawer, even though she could see that it was empty.

Someone had already been in and made sure nothing would go off. Hannah checked the rubbish bin. That was empty too, and someone had put in a clean bin liner. She felt a surge of gratitude towards Joanne, who must have been responsible for the clean up. But she was a little disappointed that it meant she'd have to get straight on to tackling the more personal. She'd hoped to put that off for a bit longer, eased towards it. *Small things*, she reminded herself, and went over to the groups of framed photographs on the sideboard, china cabinet and occasional tables.

Her mother had carefully selected the frames with this modern decor in mind, but they were not to Hannah's taste. She started taking the photos out of them, being careful not to dwell on the smiling faces, and put the frames aside in a pile for the nearest op shop. She'd work her way back down the house towards her parents' bedroom. A part of her wondered if she should do that first and get it over with — rip the Band-Aid off — but she was here now. She looked around, wondering if there was anything she wanted or needed. It was more a question of practicality than sentimentality.

Her parents had been excited to start afresh. Having never splurged on much before, they had gone on a small shopping spree to furnish this place. Everything was bought new, not that there was room for too much. Hannah had been pleased for them, and had enjoyed shopping for new pieces of furniture and a few knick-knacks with her mother, despite nothing being to her taste. She liked things with character and stories to tell; antiques or soon-to-be antiques – just what she'd grown up with and her parents had happily left behind when they moved. Daniel and Daphne had always been more sentimental about people and their relationships with them than about things.

She bagged up the small items – books, DVDs, photo frames, etc – for the op shop, working her way back down the hall.

Finally she stood at the closed door to her parents' bedroom. She'd been coping so well. But with a sigh she realised she'd done the easy bit and couldn't put off opening this door if she was going to finish the task. She was feeling pretty weary. Checking her watch she realised it was a little after one. Perhaps she should come back fresh tomorrow. Indecision gripped. If she could make herself do this, it would be done and she could start moving on. *But it's going to be hard and confronting. You've had it easy up until now*, she heard her inner voice say.

She was standing there deliberating when there was a gentle knock on the front door. *Saved by the bell*, she thought, with slight relief.

She opened the door to find Joanne Hobbes standing there holding a tray with plates of sandwiches covered in cling wrap and bottles of juice.

'Joanne, hi. Come in.'

'I've brought some lunch in case you haven't eaten.'

'Thank you so much. I haven't even given food a thought,' she said, standing aside.

'I thought you might need a break and some sustenance. If you're anything like me, you get bogged down and forget to eat. And, of course, you might have been banking on there being something in the fridge,' she added as she put the tray on the kitchen bench.

'This is so lovely of you. And, you're right on all counts,' she added with a little laugh. 'These sandwiches look fantastic. And thank you for cleaning out the fridge.'

'Honestly, if you'd rather be alone, just say,' Joanne said, hesitating.

'No, please stay. I'd much rather have your company.'

'Great. There's plenty for two. Tuck in.'

They unwrapped the plate of assorted sandwiches and undid the caps on the juice bottles and began to eat.

'So, how's it going?' Joanne asked, looking around. 'You've clearly made some headway.'

'I've done the easy areas. Out here everything is so new it doesn't really feel like it was theirs, if you know what I mean. You saved me, actually. I was just trying to work up the nerve to go into Mum and Dad's room when you knocked. I've been putting it off by starting back here.'

'Ah. Well, perhaps after some nourishment it won't feel so confronting. I could stay and help if you'd like.'

'Oh, I couldn't ask you to do that.'

'You're not. I'm offering. My afternoon is clear, and I wouldn't mind at all. If it would help.'

'I did want to ask you something. Do you think someone would be interested in the place being fully furnished, or do I need to completely clear it out? You see, I already have a fully furnished house and I'm not interested in anything that's here.'

'Well, that's actually the second reason I'm here. Ulterior motive, I'm afraid.'

'Oh?'

'The people I saw this morning asked if there were any villas available fully furnished. I hope it wasn't too presumptuous of me to tell them that there might be one coming up soon – this one.'

'Not at all. Oh, that would be a huge weight off my mind.'

'Hannah, you don't need to worry unnecessarily about all of this – we're, *I'm*, here to help. You're not alone. Sadly, being a retirement facility, we have to deal with this sort of situation regularly. You just choose what you want to take for yourself and then together we can decide what happens to everything else. How does that sound?'

Tears welled in Hannah's eyes at the relief of how good it felt to not be alone in this.

After what seemed to be just a few minutes, they were wiping their mouths and placing crumpled-up paper napkins on their empty plates.

'Right, shall we see what we're dealing with in the bedroom and bathroom, or would you rather do it yourself?' Joanne said, clapping her hands together and getting up.

'I'd really appreciate the company, if you don't mind staying.'

Hannah followed Joanne down the hall. She paused with her hand on the door handle to Hannah's parents' bedroom and looked back with raised, questioning eyebrows.

'Okay?'

'Okay,' Hannah said, nodding, before taking a deep breath.

The room was just as she'd expected – bed neatly made and everything in its place. It was all so normal and, as with the rest of the house, gave no hint of the tragedy that had struck its occupants. And again she couldn't even detect their scents. Hannah was a bit confused at feeling disappointed. What else she'd been expecting she didn't know.

'Are you okay?' Joanne asked.

'Yes. I think so. It's just weird that everything has changed with them being gone, yet nothing has changed here. It's messing with me a bit.'

'I know what you mean. I think that's the hardest thing about losing someone – that life just carries on as if nothing has happened, but almost nothing is as it was. It's hard to come to terms with. I think that's why grief often feels like you're constantly taking one step forwards and two steps back.'

'I'm finding that.'

'I learnt to console myself that at least I cared enough to be sad. Just imagine being the sort of person who could pick up and carry on as if nothing had changed. I wouldn't want to be like that and I doubt you would either – no matter how much it all hurts.'

Hannah nodded. What Joanne said made a lot of sense. 'So, what you're saying is, "no pain, no gain", right?'

'Yes, I guess I am. I know you wish it didn't hurt, but try to be grateful for it, because it means you're kind and loving – the sort of person I know your parents were very proud of.'

'Thanks, Joanne, that's lovely of you to say.'

'You're welcome. I sometimes think I had to go through losing my Teddy in order to help others. I hope I don't sound trite or holier-than-thou.'

'Not at all.'

'I'd just hate for it all to have been in vain. I guess we must hold onto comfort wherever we find it, no matter how tenuous,' she said with a shrug, and smiled. 'Right, how about I start by taking everything out of the wardrobes and checking the pockets and you see if there's anything you want to keep?'

Hannah appreciated Joanne's no-nonsense direction as much as she appreciated her advice on surviving grief. The woman was incredible. Left to her own devices she might have still been standing there feeling weird and overwhelmed in four hours' time. Instead she snapped to attention.

*

It was after five o'clock when Hannah hugged Joanne goodbye and backed out of her parents' driveway. She was so grateful to Joanne for offering to take the bags to the op shop for her – even though she went right by one on her way home. She was struggling with the awful fact that the lives of her parents, and at some point her husband, were being relegated to black plastic garbage bags and pushed into a large bin to be picked through by strangers and then priced up ready to be picked through by another lot of strangers. To stand there and stuff them into the bins might completely do her in. Seeing all the bags in the hallway had been bad enough.

At least someone less fortunate would make good use of her parents' things, she told herself. It was exactly what her mother would have said, and had said, every year when they'd gone through their wardrobes. Daphne would have appreciated this act of practicality.

As she drove out of the main gate and joined the traffic, Hannah felt a wave of sadness hit her that was so strong she gasped. It was all so final, so real. They were never coming back. She'd never visit them here again. And she might not see Joanne Hobbes, who had been so good to her, again either. Of course, Joanne was probably only doing her job, but still Hannah had really appreciated the support. From here on, all her dealings with the retirement village would most likely be done via phone, email or post.

The now-familiar knot of sadness she'd come to accept was back with all its ferocity and caused her whole being to ache. She concentrated on the Melbourne traffic – still manic even on the weekend – while refusing to give into the tears. Actually, she realised, there were none. Hannah wasn't sure what was worse, this ball of emotion sapping her energy or an exhausting bout of tears. She felt so weighed down by it all.

As she drove the rest of the way home, barely aware of the heavy traffic around her, Hannah vowed that tomorrow she would finish writing to everyone who had sent sympathy cards. Then, with these things out of the way, she might be able to start healing. She didn't think Joanne, and her friends for that matter, were wrong about grief being a long, slow process. But she hoped she was stronger and would deal with it better. There were always exceptions to everything, weren't there? She liked to keep busy, was methodical, and thrived on being organised and getting things done – ticking items off the to-do list. Surely that would hold her in good stead. Settling back into work was another hurdle she was looking forward to ticking off.

Chapter Fourteen

Hannah boarded the tram and pressed her Myki card to the reader and waited for the *ding* to sound. It was good to be amongst other commuters again – though thankfully at eight in the morning not too many – and feel normal in that sense. No one around her knew her or her story. Of course, there were those she recognised who caught the same tram at the same time day after day, and who acknowledged each other with a smile or nod or even a brief greeting or goodbye. Someone would occasionally comment on the weather or their frustration over the card reader not working, or say thanks for shuffling over that extra bit or getting up to let them off. But that was all about being polite, not personal.

In her company's building, while the lift was filled with familiar faces she smiled and nodded to, no one else got off on floor twenty-eight. Hannah was pleased to find she was the first to arrive at her side of the floor too.

Good. So far, so normal, she thought as she put her handbag in the cupboard beside her desk and took her lunchbox to the fridge in the kitchen. If all went well, her boss, Craig, would be at his desk.

She thought about how thoughtful he'd been to phone last night and found herself smiling at remembering their conversation:

'Hannah, it's Craig, I just want to check you're absolutely sure you still want to come in tomorrow.'

'I'll be there.'

'Because I can easily get a temp in. You can take as long as you need.'

'I know, and I appreciate it, Craig, but I feel I need to do this.'

'It's very soon, Hannah.'

'Please, Craig. I need some normal.'

'Okay. On one condition.'

'Yes?'

'You don't try to be tough – you tell me if it all gets too much and you need to take off.'

'I'll be okay,' Hannah said, trying to convince herself as much as Craig.

'Hannah …' Craig persisted.

'Okay, I promise.'

'Well, if you're sure, I'll see you when I see you, then.'

'Thanks for this. I won't let you down.' Hannah crossed her fingers behind her back as she said it.

'Hannah, it's not a matter of letting me or anyone else down. It's a matter of doing what's right for you. And if you wake up tomorrow morning and can't do it, then call or text me.'

'All right. Thanks. And can you make me a promise too?'

'Of course. Whatever you need.'

'Don't go easy on my account. I need to do this.'

'Right, gotya, I'll be mean, bad boss Craig, just as always.'

'I doubt you're capable of that, but thanks.' He'd always been a kind, considerate boss and she couldn't imagine him being mean.

'And thanks very much for the call. But I will see you in the morning.'

'Righteo. Goodnight, Hannah.'

And there he was, hunched over his computer, tapping on his keyboard with two fingers.

'Good morning,' Hannah called, stopping in the doorway of the glass cubicle.

'Good morning. How are you doing?'

'Good, thanks. Well, okay,' she added, her resolve slipping a bit.

She could see he was about to say something, but then seemed to think better of it.

'Can I help you with that?' she asked, nodding towards his screen.

Craig Pearson, the lead partner in a large accounting firm, and Hannah had been working together for eight years. Now they knew each other so well that Craig could give her a vague idea of what he was thinking and she'd formulate the rest. She'd started out as an inexperienced temp almost ten years ago and had been asked to stay on. Now she was a highly prized executive PA – worth her weight in gold, according to Craig – and several rival firms and head-hunters had approached her. But she liked where she was – she enjoyed working for Craig, the people were nice, and she was adequately paid. And she was a loyal person through and through. While she was treated well, there was no reason to leave. As far as Hannah could see, most people changed jobs simply to satisfy their egos – they liked the idea of being poached, not necessarily the new job. Anyway, she figured once you'd progressed to the top of your game as an executive PA, it was pretty much the same wherever you worked.

'Um.' He looked a little stricken. And then she understood.

'Craig, we talked about this. You're not to treat me with kid gloves. Please.' She was almost whining, wasn't far off begging. 'I'm fine. I can't promise I won't fall apart at some point, but I haven't lost my skills – I'm sure I can still type ninety words a minute and keep you organised,' she added, and offered a weak smile.

'Okay. But promise you'll tell me if it all gets too much.'

'I already did. Last night. I'll be fine.'

'Well, promise me again.'

'Okay. I promise.'

The office filled as one by one people trickled in. And one by one they stopped at Hannah's desk and said they were sorry for her loss and then hovered awkwardly, not knowing what to say or how to leave. Hannah asked about each person's Christmas and time off, but no one seemed willing to own up to having had any enjoyment. Gradually everyone made the excuse of getting back to work and left.

Normally in the mornings, the office was a hive of activity and animated conversations, with the occasional eruption of raucous laughter as stories were told. Not today. Perhaps she should have stayed away for the good of everyone else. Perhaps that was what Craig had been subtly trying to tell her.

As Hannah tried to focus on the screen that was now swimming in front of her tear-filled eyes, she wondered what she should do. She wanted to stay.

She looked at her mobile that had just *pinged* beside her, signalling a text message. It was from Sam:

Good luck on your first day back. Remember, people won't know what to say or how to act, so don't take any weirdness to heart. People are weird, full stop! ☺ *Just go with it and hang in there. They'll come around. Here if you need me. Thinking of you and sending hugs and lots and lots of love. Xxx*

Hannah smiled and the lump in her throat melted. Bless Sam for knowing her − and *people* − so well and finding exactly the right words to say. She sent a couple of smiley faces and a row of hugs and kisses in reply, then took a deep breath and got back to work.

★

At ten minutes past five, Hannah turned off her computer, took her bag from the cupboard and looked into her boss's office.

'I'm heading off, Craig, have a lovely evening.'

'Thanks. You too. Well done today,' he added quietly, and then as if as an afterthought and as more of a question, he said, 'See you tomorrow?'

'You certainly will,' Hannah said overly brightly. She fought the urge to throw herself at his feet and thank him profusely. He would have no idea just how grateful she was to have her tiny bit of normal, her job, and to him for not sending her home that morning and insisting she take some of her copious amounts of leave.

There had been three times when things had got to her and each time she'd managed to hold on and only shed her tears in the privacy of the ladies toilet, out of sight.

She was putting her coffee mug in the dishwasher when Caitlin, one of the PAs from the other side of the floor, walked in. As one of the senior personal assistants in the firm, Hannah had helped with the selection process for Caitlin two years ago, and then her induction. The PAs tended to hang out together, the younger accountants with each other, and the senior management and partners in another group – although they seemed to do their socialising over long lunches disguised as strategy sessions and networking. Hannah knew because she made many of the bookings and sorted through the corporate credit card statements.

'Hey, a few of us are going out for a drink to celebrate the New Year, would you like to come?' Caitlin said, a little shyly.

'That would be lovely, thanks.' Hannah smiled in an effort to put the clearly uncomfortable young woman at ease.

'Cool. Come on then,' Caitlin said. Hannah was pleased to see the ice seemed to have been broken and was grateful for yet another small win that day.

'So, how are you doing? Really?' Caitlin asked as they walked to the lift together.

'Okay, thanks. I've got some great friends and had a lot of support.'

'That's good.'

When their lift reached the ground floor there was a small group waiting for them. Hannah cringed as she noticed the animated group seemed to suddenly fall silent when they saw her and Caitlin walking towards them. She offered a general 'Hi' and a reassuring smile, and they set off for their current favourite bar – a moody basement venue in Flinders Lane, just a few blocks from the office.

As they walked out into the warm evening sunshine, Hannah wondered what would be worse: going home to be alone or being the wet blanket at her colleagues's evening out. She wanted neither, but she was already regretting agreeing to this. Who was she kidding? Nothing was normal. But more strongly she didn't feel like going home and being alone.

Just then her phone rang. She stopped walking while she dug into her handbag to retrieve it. The small group paused but she waved them on. Only Caitlin remained beside her. She wished she'd left too and then Hannah might have snuck down one of the many lanes and off to catch her tram home.

'Hey, Sam, how are you?' she said.

'Good. I'm just ringing to see how your day was.'

'Okay. Fine. Thanks.'

'Really?'

'Yes, really. I survived.' She snuck a covert look at Caitlin who thankfully was busy with her own phone.

'What's all that noise? Are you on your way to the tram?'

'No, a group of us are going to a bar to celebrate New Year.'

'Really?'

'Yup, it's going to be fun.'

Sam at once seized on her tone. 'Do you need rescuing?'

'Probably. Actually, yes, that would be great.'

'Rob is still in town. I'm just texting him to pick you up. You can have dinner with us. Though, I'm warning you, it's eggs with spaghetti on toast.'

'Can I have my toast as soldiers?'

'Yes, you can.'

'Sounds good to me. Are you sure, though?'

'Of course. You are not going out and getting drunk and having fun if I'm stuck home with the twins. Okay, Rob's just leaving. He'll be at the corner of Collins and Queen by the ANZ bank in around three minutes.'

'Perfect. Thanks. See you soon.'

'Had a better offer, eh?' Caitlin said, after Hannah had hung up.

'Sort of. I'm not sure I'm up for a bar, after all. Sorry.'

'No worries. I'm thinking of bailing myself.' They both looked ahead at the group that was waiting at the next intersection, held up by the traffic lights.

'I'll go let them know for you. See ya. Take care,' Caitlin said, giving Hannah a quick hug.

'Thanks. You too.'

Hannah reached the corner just as Rob's silver sedan pulled into the loading zone. She leapt in and gave him a quick kiss.

'Thanks for this.'

'Sam was a bit vague. So what am I rescuing you from?'

'Myself.'

'Right,' he said, giving her a sideways glance. 'Okay then. Well, it must be bad for you to be willingly signing up for eggs and tinned spaghetti on toast.'

Hannah smiled. If only he knew just how much she was looking forward to the comfort of such a meal. Sam was a great mum and Hannah was looking forward to being welcomed into her little nest and gathered under her wing. On account of the boys they ate early, so there would still be a good chance Hannah could make it home before dark. If she could drag herself away from the comfort of Sam and Rob's chaotic but warm and loving home.

'So, how was the first day back?'

'All right. You've no idea how nice doing something normal can feel when you're …'

'So, it wasn't too weird?'

'Not really. A bit. To start with. But everyone was okay once they got over worrying about what to say and how to act and just got on with things. Actually, it was so good that I got lured into a false sense of security and found myself on the way to the bar with the group of PAs. But then I realised how awful it is to be around people having fun when you feel like shit. I didn't want to be a dampener on their evening either.'

'Fair enough. Don't be too hard on yourself, but it's probably not a good idea to get sozzled. It won't help.'

'I know. But it just felt so good to be a part of things like, um, before.'

'Yes, I can imagine.'

They lapsed into silence. Hannah doubted Rob could understand. How could anyone unless they'd been in the same situation? She'd just have to accept that things had changed and that it would take time to really become a comfortable part of the fold at work again. She didn't want her colleagues to feel sorry for her, and invite her along out of politeness. Especially if they didn't really want her there and thought they had to be on their guard all night in case they made her cry with some unintentionally insensitive or off-hand comment.

★

'Hi, honey, we're home,' Rob called as he dumped his laptop bag in the hall.

'Daddy! Auntie Hann!' cried the two small boys as they thundered down the bare floorboards of the hall, closely followed by two cocker spaniels. Hannah was prepared when Oliver launched himself at her stomach; she'd visited the Barrow household enough times to know what was coming. She pitied Rob as Ethan launched himself at his father, his head right at groin level, and Rob let out a groan.

'What's this? I thought we were having soldiers and tinned spaghetti,' Hannah said, standing in the kitchen after giving Sam a hug. She pointed to a bowl on the bench.

'We are. I just took pity on you and tossed together a salad.'

'You didn't need to.'

'Well, I can't have you getting scurvy or constipated, or whatever.'

'Can I do anything to help?'

'No, I'm almost done. Just have to retrieve the eggs when the timer goes off. Your timing is perfect, by the way, darling husband,' she said, wrapping her arms around Rob when he walked in.

'Sit down. Boys, come in and sit down too. Actually, Hann, can you just pop that pile on the sideboard in the other room?'

'Sure. Wow, you're creating again,' Hannah said, sneaking a peek through the pile of papers and sketchpad she held. 'That's fantastic. I was hoping New Year's Day wasn't just a one off.'

'Yeah, I'm really enjoying it.'

'Mummy's going to be a famous artist one day,' Oliver declared as he settled himself at the table.

'And we're going to go to an expedition,' Ethan added.

'Exhibition,' Rob corrected.

'Yes, well, thanks for the vote of confidence, but we're a long way off that.'

'Yes, first Mummy needs a lallery,' Oliver said, full of authority.

'And maybe a gent,' Ethan said.

'What am I, chopped liver?' Rob asked, feigning offence.

'An *agent* and a *gallery*, darlings,' Hannah corrected, leaning over and giving them each a kiss on the head. 'Or maybe just one or the other,' she added.

'We can help you find one,' Oliver said.

'Yes, Mummy, we'll help.'

'Thank you. That would be lovely.'

*

There was still plenty of daylight when Rob dropped Hannah home.

'Would you like me to come in and make sure everything is okay?' he asked.

'Thanks, but I'll be fine.' *I have to toughen up.* Rob wouldn't be here every evening when she arrived home from work.

'Well, I'll wait until you're inside and I see the lights go on.'

'Okay, thanks. And thanks again for the ride – times two. And dinner. You guys are too wonderful for words,' she added, throwing her arms around him and pecking him on the cheek.

'We love you, Hann. You'll get through this,' he added.

Hannah raced up the path and unlocked the front door. Inside she turned on the hall light – even though there was still plenty of light outside – and waved to Rob from the open front door.

He gave a friendly honk as he drove off.

Hannah stood in the hall feeling unsure what to do with herself. It was too early to go to bed with the television for company and she no longer had any thank-you cards to occupy her at the kitchen table. She still had Tristan's clothes to go through, but she couldn't bear the thought of being brought undone again after such a positive day. Right then she envied Sam her creativity. Perhaps she should buy one of the adult colouring-in books a few people at work had been raving about, not that she thought that was being creative by any stretch.

She'd been amused to find several colleagues sitting at the tables in the staff kitchen quietly and intently colouring instead of the usual gossiping. She'd wanted to discuss it with Sam, but thought that a real artist might be offended by these colourers who thought they were being creative as those at her work seemed to. They were taking it very seriously. Hannah thought it was a waste of time. And what did you do with the pictures afterwards?

Until a few years ago, Daphne had done tapestry in front of the television of an evening. And there had been periods when she'd crocheted or knitted. She said it was relaxing. Hannah supposed this colouring-in craze did the same thing – except doing something relaxing was now apparently called 'mindfulness' and considered 'new age'.

Hannah felt sadness grip her. If only Daphne was here to laugh about it with her. She'd think it was a hoot and would no doubt say the same as Hannah was thinking: why not at least make something, and something that was useful?

Hannah forced her mind back to the here and now. Daphne wasn't here to talk to so she shouldn't dwell on it. She couldn't. She'd had a good day – one step forward – she didn't want to ruin that. But she couldn't let herself get bored – that would be her undoing.

She looked around for inspiration and spied her runners under the small hall table. Without giving herself time to change her mind, she raced through to the bedroom and changed into track pants, sports bra, t-shirt and socks. She and Tristan had often taken an evening jog or brisk walk after dinner. She enjoyed burning off some energy and it came as a bit of a shock to realise she hadn't been out once since losing him.

She loved her work and there was only the odd day when she needed to blow off steam with some exercise. Tristan, being in finance, had had a much more stressful job and had needed a run or their walks to relax before bed. When it was a particularly stressful period, he'd go for a quick run in the mornings as well. Maybe it would help her, too.

The darkness was creeping in much quicker than she realised and once outside Hannah almost turned back around. The streetlights were coming on. But she was in her running gear now, so she may as well take a quick jog around the neighbourhood. Tomorrow she'd leave earlier and get back to the park and have a better workout. Right now, though, she felt a little panicky, as if someone, not just the darkness, was chasing her. Her heart raced and leapt at every little sound, every shadow.

Hannah found herself running, faster and faster to escape the demons that she felt lurking around her.

In ten minutes she was back at her front door fighting for breath, her knuckles white and palms dented from clutching her keys so tightly. She let herself back into the house and nearly melted to the floor. God, she was unfit! She took her shoes off, quickly checked the doors were locked, and made her way through to the bathroom.

As she stood under the streaming shower, she realised she felt good from her quick burst of exercise. But how she yearned for Tristan to be there so she could say, 'I ran, actually ran, and for nearly ten minutes.' God, she missed him.

Chapter Fifteen

Hannah sat at the kitchen bench with her coffee. It was nine o'clock on Saturday morning and she was already bored. No, not bored, lost. There were a million and one things to do in Melbourne on a weekend. The trouble was she couldn't find the inclination to do any of them. She'd toyed with phoning Sam to see if she wanted to meet her out for coffee, but stopped herself. Sam was always busy with the twins and it wasn't fair to keep imposing on her.

Hannah was surprised to hear the doorbell chime, and got up to answer it.

She almost melted into Sam's embrace as she was flooded with relief at seeing her friend and being spared for at least the time being from finding ways to entertain herself.

'God, it's good to see you. Coffee?'

'And you. Yes, please. I'm escaping the boys. They're driving me nuts. So how are you doing? And it's me, Hann, so no censoring. Okay?'

'I'm lonely, Sam. I hate being on my own. And now I'm back at work I officially hate weekends.'

'It ...'

'Please don't say it'll get easier. I'm sick of all the clichés. Sorry, but I am. You know one of the sad things I've discovered?'

'What?'

'I have absolutely no interests. Tris was my whole world. And now he's gone I have nothing.'

'You have me and Rob and the boys and a tonne of other friends who love you, Hann.'

'I know, and it's lovely, but what I need is to keep busy, but to do that I need interests, things to occupy me on the weekends. I'm sorry, I'm just being a sad sack.'

'Well, you're allowed,' Sam said. 'What about gardening? I see a lawn and some weeds out there that'll need some attention soon.'

'Fun, Samantha, I want to enjoy myself. Well, at least try.'

'Fair enough. I couldn't think of anything worse, either. I wouldn't have the patience, but you love being neat and orderly. You could keep the garden neat and looking good, couldn't you?'

'Mmm. Probably.'

'How about golf? I'm sure Rob would love some company at the driving range. He seems to have gone right off it since losing Tris.'

'I think I'd rather garden.'

'You could take up flamenco dancing or yoga, or something. Hann, there're plenty of things you could do if you want to get out.'

'So says the one who dreams of being a recluse,' Hannah said, raising her eyebrows at Sam.

'It's weird, isn't it? You're yearning for activity, company and entertainment whereas I'd love nothing more than to be left alone in complete silence. So, I'm probably not the one to help you solve your problem. Sorry.'

'I wish I was creative and could lose myself in some project or other. Like you can,' Hannah said wistfully.

'Maybe you *are* creative. Have you ever actually tried?'

'I know I can't draw, for a start.'

'Being creative's not just about being able to draw. Perhaps you need to explore it a bit. Is there anything you're passionate about?'

'No. I was passionate about Tristan. He was my world. And now he's gone,' she said, looking down at the floor. 'I'm sorry, I'm just feeling sorry for myself. And dragging you down in the process.'

'What about going back and doing some study?'

'Maybe sometime, but right now I don't think I could focus enough. Anyway, I want to have some fun, not bog myself down further.'

'Hmm, fair enough. You know what I do when I'm searching for inspiration?'

'Visit art galleries, look at art?' Of course Hannah knew; it was her friend's favourite activity. She hadn't accompanied Sam much since she'd had the twins. Hannah had enjoyed their gallery trips, but for her it had been more about spending quality time with her friend than enjoying the art.

'Fancy coming along to an exhibition opening with me?'

'When?'

'This afternoon. Two o'clock.'

'Umm.'

'Please, Hann. You know how I hate going to these things on my own and I really want to go.'

'What about Rob?'

'He's home with the boys,' Sam said. 'I want to be able to study the art, not run around after two boys.'

'You're seriously getting back into it, aren't you?'

'Yes, I think I am. So, it's time I started mixing with the arty-farties.'

'That's fantastic.'

'So, will you come?'

'Okay.' Hannah knew she couldn't say no to Sam. Rarely could, but after all Sam and Rob had done for her, the least she could do was provide some moral support to her friend. And right now she'd probably agree to almost anything to escape the house and her loneliness.

*

The one thing Hannah hated about stepping into an art gallery – well, those with art for sale; public galleries were different – was the feeling of being scrutinised by the owner. Hannah thought about their silent stares and pursed lips while he or she tried to ascertain your net worth and if you could afford to buy and thus whether you were worth giving some attention to or not. She figured it didn't help that she didn't look in the slightest bit arty in her floral blouse and jeans.

Hannah picked up a pricelist from the pedestal and went over for a closer look at a series of brightly coloured abstracts on a nearby wall. To Hannah they looked like someone had simply thrown different colours of paint at a canvas, though she knew good art wasn't created that easily. And while they weren't to her taste, she suspected that these works were good, 'accomplished' – wasn't that the word? And of course being two and a half thousand dollars for a small square canvas told her as much. She liked the colour placement, which despite appearances was most likely very carefully considered. She'd once made the mistake many years ago of saying to Sam that a five-year-old child could splash paint around and do just as good a job. Sam had shot her down by saying she found abstract the hardest style to paint.

Hannah walked into the next room and gasped as she took in the colour of the wall – a stunning duck egg blue-green.

'Great, aren't they?' Sam said, coming up beside her.

'Huh? Oh, yes,' Hannah said, now looking at the black-and-white lino-cut prints. 'I was actually more interested in the wall colour, though. How do you think that would look in my house?'

'It's an incredible colour. Where were you thinking?'

'I don't know. I just love it,' she said with a laugh.

'It would look fantastic in your kitchen. Are you thinking of repainting?'

'I wasn't until I saw this. But maybe that's what I need to do – change the house a bit. Perhaps then I'll feel more settled.'

'Well, it would give you something to do.'

'Oh, I'd get someone in. I can't paint.'

'Of course you can paint.'

'But what about the edges? I don't think my hand is steady enough.'

'There are all sorts of gadgets at the hardware shops to help with that. I painted the nursery, remember?'

'Yes, but you're talented in that area.'

'But you've never tried, have you?'

'No.'

'Though, I don't think you should rush into anything. You don't want to be painting it over in six months when you're feeling different about life, or the colour makes you feel cold in winter.'

'Hmm,' Hannah said, thoughtfully.

'Hey, I know, why don't we go to some open houses and see what's popular in the area of interior design?'

'Oh. I guess that's one way to find out.' Hannah could feel the idea beginning to run away from her.

'You know, according to *The Block* judges, wallpaper is all the rage at the moment. Maybe you might want to look into that.'

'I hadn't thought about redecorating, I just saw this colour and liked it.'

'Fair enough. Now, *shh*, I need to study the art. How clever are these lino cuts?'

'Very,' Hannah said, peering at the small detailed images before finding herself drawn back to the walls behind. She'd love to know the name of the colour.

They made their way through each room of the double-fronted bluestone cottage. Hannah saw a lot of art she liked while Sam *oohed* and *ahed* and made notes beside her. They'd done a complete circuit and were just about to leave when Sam insisted on taking another look at the lino cuts.

From her body language of nibbling her lip and shuffling her feet, Hannah could tell her friend was desperate to whip out her credit card and get a red spot put beside one of the remaining unsold five pieces. While Rob earned a reasonable wage, she knew money was tight with Sam not working and the expense of twins to raise.

Hannah slipped out quietly and approached the desk with her pricelist.

'Can I buy number 39, please, the lino cut titled "Picnic",' she whispered, looking around as she thrust her credit card towards the gallery owner. 'It's for my friend as a surprise,' she added, feeling the need to explain her odd behaviour.

'Wonderful choice. And what a good friend you are,' the man cooed quietly, as he processed her payment.

'The exhibition ends on the thirtieth so you can collect it then,' he whispered, handing her card back.

'Thank you.'

'Thank *you*.'

'There you are,' Sam said, appearing at the desk beside Hannah.

'Yes, I was just waiting to ask about the wall colour behind the lino cuts,' she said with her eyebrows raised in question to the man behind the desk. 'Do you happen to know the name of it?'

'Well, actually, it doesn't have a name. It's a colour I concocted myself. I couldn't find the exact shade I wanted in the samples – for any of the rooms.'

'Oh. Okay. Thanks anyway.'

'All of your colours are fabulous,' Sam said. 'As is the art.'

'Thank you. Sorry I can't help with the colour,' he added with a warm smile. 'The exhibitions will be changed each month and we're all about fostering new local talent. We have many exciting works and artists coming up, so do please come back regularly.'

'Thank you. We certainly will,' Sam said, beaming back.

'Yes. Thank you. It's been lovely,' Hannah said.

'Now that wasn't so bad, was it?' Sam said when they were back in the car.

'Not at all. I enjoyed it.'

'It's a bit funny that you liked the paint on the wall more than any of the works of art, though.'

'I liked the art, too, but you have to admit that colour was pretty special. I wonder if it would be too much as a plain wall, or if it needs the pieces to break it up.'

'Only one way to find out.'

'I don't think I'd have the patience to mix paint colours. I'd have to just find one I liked.'

'And there's always wallpaper to consider. That colour with a design in silver over the top would be stunning.'

'Hmm. I'm starting to feel overwhelmed already,' Hannah said with a laugh.

'You'll stumble across the perfect thing when you're meant to. Just start by looking at magazines and open houses. God, I'd have loved one of those lino cuts,' Sam added wistfully. 'I thought I did very well to resist.'

'You certainly did. Well done,' Hannah said, laughing.

'Do you think the tax office would allow it as a deduction in the name of research?'

'I think you'd be pushing it. And you have to earn money to need a tax deduction.'

'Hmm, good point. Damn.'

'Are you doing lino cuts?'

'Thinking about it.'

'I'm so excited you're getting back into your art.'

'Well, it's early days. And I'm not sure I know what I'm doing anymore. I'm not sure I know anything anymore. Sorry, don't mind me. Seeing the work of talented people always makes me feel morose and inadequate – you know me. So, what do you fancy doing for lunch?'

'I think you're very talented, but you don't seem to believe me. Come on, let's get a sandwich or a pie or something and go and sit in the botanic gardens.'

'Good idea. I know just the bakery. It'll be nice to be able to sit without two children clambering over me or asking endless questions. Though I might need dessert since I won't be eating little people's leftovers – unless you're not going to eat your crusts,' she added, smiling.

'Oh, ha-ha.'

★

'Right, let's see if there are any flashy houses for us to look at for inspiration,' Sam said, opening up a newspaper that had been left on one of the tables in the bakery.

'Oh, I don't know …'

'It doesn't hurt to look. And, anyway, I still have two child-free hours left to make the most of,' Sam said, checking her watch. 'If there's nothing nearby fitting the bill, it's not meant to be. Okay?'

'You do realise there'll be hordes of people. There always is.'

'Come on, it'll be fun.'

'If you say so.'

'You know Peta and Sidney do this nearly every weekend – it's like a hobby for them.'

'What, wander through open houses – just for fun?'

'Apparently.'

'That's crazy. So, is there anything?' Hannah was feeling a little curious. She was keen to see what people were doing with colour.

'There's a viewing before an auction just over at Camberwell in half an hour. Looks nice. Estimate is nine hundred. What do you think?'

'I'm game if you are.'

'Right, just make sure I don't put my hand up and bid.'

'Same goes for me. I'm the unhinged one, remember.'

★

An hour later Hannah and Sam walked back to the car after the auction, feeling a little stunned. They'd been disappointed to find the house was not at all flashy. Neat and tidy, but far from being a candidate for a magazine spread. Clearly someone had used some very clever lighting for the photos or Photoshop was involved. They'd stayed to the end, unable to tear themselves away before finding out which of the many people who had gathered on the lawn out the front would be the new owners and how much they'd paid. A young Asian couple bought it for four hundred thousand dollars over the reserve.

'Wow,' they both said several times, looking over at each other with wide eyes.

'*And* it was beige,' Sam said.

'Yes, and it was beige,' Hannah said with a laugh.

*

Hannah remained standing on the path after waving Sam off. It had been a good afternoon and she didn't want her mood to change, which it would if she went inside where she had nothing to do. But it was too warm and the sun too fierce for a walk or run. She'd go later. So what could she do now? Looking around her didn't yield any inspiration so she reluctantly put her key in the door with a sigh. She'd defrost something for dinner.

After dumping her bag in the kitchen, Hannah found herself suddenly craving something fresh for dinner. She wasn't sure what, but not one of the reheated meals she'd been living on. They were lovely and homemade, but still not quite the same as eating fresh food. Suddenly she craved a grilled lamb chop with pumpkin and potato mash and peas. With a shock she realised she hadn't even been to the supermarket alone yet. Raelene had filled the pantry before she'd left and for milk and bread Hannah had been dropping by the Chans's store. *Yes, that's what I'll do.* Without a second thought she grabbed her car keys and handbag.

As soon as she dragged a trolley from the stack, Hannah wished she hadn't come. Nothing in the brightly lit supermarket, filled with row upon row of enticing packaging, felt familiar. She couldn't focus, couldn't remember where anything was. It was as if she'd stepped into a foreign country where she couldn't speak the language. It didn't help that she had left the house without a list. She'd never done that before. She'd thought she could do this, but it suddenly felt impossible. But she couldn't go straight back out, she'd have to make her way to the far end and go out through a checkout.

Just try, Hannah. Focus. You can do this. One step at a time. The voice in her head was kind and sounded a lot like Tristan's.

She wanted to sit on the floor and sob. But instead she took a deep breath and then, right in front of her, she spied potatoes and just beyond, pumpkin. She felt a glimmer of triumph. Now she just had to find the lamb and frozen peas and she was done. Was there already a bag in the freezer? She wasn't sure and didn't care – her meal wouldn't be complete without them. And she was determined now.

Despite feeling focussed, Hannah made her way around the store like a zombie. She tried to ignore feeling embarrassed at how she must look to all those people who were striding through the aisles. A few seemed to give her a wide berth, clearly thinking she had something contagious or she was a bit deranged. She tried to make the most of her trip and get other things as she moved down the aisles. She really didn't want to have to come back too soon. She suddenly didn't like being so close to this many people – some pushing past her, others bumping her trolley, rushing back and forth, reaching around her.

She found herself standing and staring dumbly at the shelf in front of her and then frowned. She usually picked up something from this aisle. She knew she did. But what was it? Her frustration turned to annoyance.

For god's sake, Hannah, you've done this every week – up and down, pluck, pluck, pluck. You can do this.

Hey, Hann, it doesn't matter. You can try another day.

Again the voice could have been Tristan's. Hannah bit the inside of her bottom lip hard. She hated the way her mind played these cruel tricks on her. *Oh, Tris, why aren't you here to help me?*

'Excuse me, do you mind if I just …' she heard a voice say and looked around.

'Oh, I'm sorry,' she said, stepping aside and nearly bumping into a small trolley where a prettily dressed but surly looking girl of around eight stood.

'Are you okay?' the young woman asked, peering at Hannah.

'Yes, fine, thanks.'

'Here,' the lady said, smiling sadly at Hannah and handing her a tissue. Hannah put a hand to her face and realised her cheeks were wet.

'Thank you. Just having a bad day,' she said, feeling the need to explain.

'Well, I'm sure tomorrow will be a better one.'

'Thanks, I hope so,' Hannah said, trying to smile.

'Come on, Lil, we've got to get Daddy's ice-cream,' the woman said brightly, and took off.

Hannah stared after the woman and then looked at the shelf she was standing beside. Tomato paste. That was always on her list. She picked up a bottle. What else was there?

Come on, Hann, you can do this and then you can get home to your safe haven.

★

Hannah didn't remember going through the checkout, handing over her credit card, leaving the store or driving home. But here she was, back in her kitchen, shopping bags beside her. *Tris, I did it. I did the groceries. All alone.* Hannah allowed herself to bask in her sense of accomplishment, ignoring the gloom trying to seep back in.

Chapter Sixteen

Hannah lingered over breakfast then laced up her runners. At the end of her street she paused. For the past week or so after work she'd stayed on the local streets and avoided crossing the road and running to the park. Could she go to the park where she and Tris had always gone? Of course she could *go* there – all it took was one foot in front of the other. But could she go alone and not dissolve into tears and make a spectacle of herself? That was the question.

She'd been doing all right. There hadn't been any major steps forward, but she was slowly coming to grips with her new life and there hadn't been any serious backward steps. She'd just have to see how she'd fare today, visiting one of her and Tristan's favourite haunts. She took a deep breath and looked left and right to cross the road.

The park was packed with people and dogs. Hannah focussed on striding purposefully around the main walking track in the opposite direction from the way she and Tris used to jog. It was strange how this one change made the track seem so foreign to her. She knew it wasn't only that, of course, but she couldn't let herself dwell on the other reason why it was so different or she might unravel.

She stood back from the pond and watched a couple sitting on the grass nearby who were tearing apart a loaf of bread. They were surrounded by ducks waiting to catch bits of the bread. There was something quite magical and relaxing about feeding the ducks. She'd loved doing it until she was horrified to learn that bread was bad for them. For years now she'd scattered shredded lettuce and various grains for the ducks and received strange looks from passers-by. She longed to tell these folk that what they were doing was wrong, but didn't want to get into an argument. The park was for peace and tranquillity.

Hannah had completely forgotten to bring anything from home – she'd been too focussed on just getting here. There was a bag of rolled oats in the cupboard and she definitely had some lettuce she could chop up. Perhaps next week.

She and Tristan had always completed a loop using the foot-bridges, but Hannah didn't feel like going any further. Instead she sat quietly and tried to get the feel of the place again – or a *new* feel for the place – try to soak up some of the happiness of those out enjoying the mild summer's day.

Dogs ran out in the dedicated open space, barking with excitement, darting this way and that, dodging, ducking and weaving around their owners, chasing balls, stopping to greet and sniff newcomers, pee.

She turned as a child squealed, and was ready to leap up and run to their aid. But it was okay, a group of children were all shrieking with delight at managing to catch Mum or Dad or their ball, or with excited fear as their parent let go of their bicycle. It was nice to see so many people having fun. But at the same time it deeply saddened her.

Now she would never have Tristan's child to bring to the park and teach to ride their bike or play with a ball or Frisbee or fly a kite or a remote-control plane when they were older.

Her heart thudded painfully, but she sat still, forcing herself to enjoy the sun on her back and soak up the positive energy from those around her.

She was concentrating so hard on looking across the open lawn and trying to force herself to think positively that she stopped seeing people passing on the path right in front of her. Suddenly she felt a bump to her knees. She was so startled she almost shouted and leapt up from the bench. But somehow she managed to keep her composure. A large German shepherd was standing in front of her. While she really didn't like dogs – was actually a little scared of them, especially big ones – she couldn't help but smile at the sight that greeted her.

As the dog sat, she noticed it had a tennis ball in its mouth. What wasn't quite so nice was how close to her lap the dog was – practically in it. The dog's thick tail brushed back and forth across the concrete slab under the bench. With its gaze locked on Hannah, the dog suddenly opened its mouth and deposited the ball onto her lap, the filthy, wet object was dripping with glistening, foamy saliva.

Hannah looked down and squirmed. Her stomach turned. The dog's tail stopped and it looked expectantly from her face down to the ball.

'Yuck. No, go away, I don't want to play with you.'

The dog cocked its head.

'He wants you to throw the ball,' a child of about seven yelled from several metres away. She thought she heard the word, 'Der' as well. She considered yelling back that she knew that but she didn't like dogs or soggy, chewed tennis balls and certainly did not want to touch said tennis ball or play with said dog and end up all smelly. But she wasn't about to get into this discussion with a child and spark a park-rage incident.

Hannah recoiled when the dog stood up. When it hopped up onto the bench beside her she was so taken aback she couldn't move. And then she was pinned to the spot as the dog settled its huge head in her lap.

Oh, god. She didn't know where to put her hands that had been in her lap and were now waving about above the dog. She didn't want to touch the creature. And she could feel the dampness from the tennis ball that had rolled back and was now being pushed deep into her crotch by the weight of the dog seeping through her track pants. *Bloody hell.* She carefully retrieved the ball with the tips of two fingers and tossed it.

The dog lifted its head, looked, and seemed to take in the direction of the ball but then relaxed into her lap again.

'I threw your damned ball,' she said. 'Go chase it and leave me alone. Go on. Go!'

But the dog stayed put. It lifted its head, looked up at her through long dark lashes, but then relaxed. She thought it might have whined or groaned softly, but couldn't be sure. There were so many people and so much noise around. She just wished someone would come and get their damned dog. The boy who'd spoken to her was nowhere to be seen. Clearly it wasn't his dog.

Hannah sat there pinned down by the large beast, trying not to touch it. She didn't want to try to get up or drag it off her in case it became aggressive. She really didn't know anything about dogs, except that they were scary and unpredictable and had lots of large sharp teeth, which could do serious damage.

Suddenly a loud voice cut in above the general noise. 'Charlie, come here. Now!'

The dog lifted its head and Hannah looked around for the owner of the stern voice. A fit-looking man in athletic gear was just metres away.

'God, I am so sorry. Charlie. Come on, leave the poor lady alone.'

The dog flapped its tail, but stayed put.

'I'm not sure what to do. I threw the ball,' Hannah said, shrugging and pointing towards the ball a little way away. 'But he seems to have changed his mind.'

'I'm really sorry. It's strange. He's normally very well-behaved and I've never seen him bother a stranger before, let alone sit on them,' he said, with an embarrassed laugh.

'He's a lovely dog,' Hannah said, and meant it.

'Thanks. But right now he's a naughty dog. Come on, Charlie, get down. *Now!*'

The dog got up and left the bench with what seemed to Hannah to be a deep, resigned sigh. Standing in front of her, his tail slowly moving from side to side, he leant forward and licked her hand. And then he sat again.

Hannah reached out and stroked his head and ears. 'Thank you, I like you too,' she said, surprising herself.

'Right, can we go now?' the man said.

As if to answer, Charlie walked over to the tennis ball, picked it up, and trotted off.

'Again, I am *so* sorry,' the man said with a wave and ran off, leaving Hannah to stare after them until they turned the corner. *What an odd encounter.*

She, and then she and Tristan, had been coming here for years and had never had anything so strange happen before. She felt dazed and a little discombobulated. But far from being frightened, she felt calmer than she had in weeks – since the accident, probably.

The breeze suddenly picked up, reminding her of her wet track pants. She cursed and instinctively sniffed her hands – gross. Time to go home and get cleaned up. She'd lost interest in the park now and she had a set of clothes to put in the wash to get rid of the dog smell and hair that seemed to be all over her.

As she walked back, she couldn't help thinking that apart from the smell and ick factor, her encounter with Charlie the dog had been quite nice.

*

The following Sunday Hannah fossicked through the fridge and put together a bag of withered vegetables, which she'd cut up, and some leftover cooked rice for the ducks at the park. She sat on the grass and began tossing the food. Slowly the ducks gravitated to her, coming closer and closer. A few times she was able to put out a hand and touch them. But amongst the group there were a few greedy grumps who chased the friendlier ducks away in the hope of securing more food. Despite the bag having been emptied, shaken out, balled up and placed in her pocket, Hannah had continued to sit. She was starting to enjoy being at the park. She'd come yesterday afternoon too and sat.

She felt relaxed and almost normal sitting there surrounded by a mass of friendly ducks or on a bench watching the people. She'd passed several hours here yesterday and wasn't ready to leave yet today. It was weird that being surrounded by strangers you had little or no interaction with could ease the loneliness.

Yesterday she'd been surprised to find herself scouring the newspaper and then heading out to a few open-house inspections again. While she'd hoped to get some ideas in case she did some work updating the house, it was the close proximity of people she'd actually found herself enjoying the most. It was strange. Ordinarily she hated crowds.

Hannah knew she probably should accept more invitations, be more sociable – it was, after all, still the summer party season. She'd gone out for after-work drinks on Friday, but had done a runner when someone bought a round of shots. A part of her had wondered if getting blotto might help her feel better or help her to sleep right through the night, but the more sensible part of her said not to go down that path. Though, perhaps if she made herself sick with booze she'd feel something real and different from empty, sad, lonely and confused.

Anyway, as much as she didn't want to be at home alone on a Saturday evening, or any evening, she still didn't think she could find the energy to consider what to wear let alone get dolled up. Heading out straight from work took care of that problem. She'd become very friendly with Caitlin and the sweet younger woman had become her rock at the office. But they didn't socialise together during weekends. Maybe she should try to change that.

She was really missing Auntie Beth. Suddenly she couldn't remember what day she'd be back. The memory she'd always been secretly proud of now leaked like a sieve. Thankfully her work brain still seemed relatively intact.

'Oh. Hello again,' Hannah exclaimed as the large dog bounded up to her, scattering the ducks. 'It's Charlie, isn't it?' she said a little nervously. She felt vulnerable sitting cross-legged on the grass with the dog practically standing over her. Again he deposited the chewed wet tennis ball into her lap.

'Oh, well, thank you very much.' Again she gingerly picked it up, touching it as little as she possibly could, and tossed it. But while the dog gazed after it, again Charlie chose to stay put. He lay down beside Hannah and rested his large head in her lap. He looked up at her before settling with a deep sigh. And again Hannah found herself stroking his soft fur and rubbing his ears.

'Oh, not again. Charlie!'

Hannah glanced up at hearing the familiar voice. Charlie looked up too, but didn't move. Hannah saw a figure silhouetted by the late afternoon sun.

'He's okay,' Hannah said, raising a hand to shield her eyes.

'Do you mind if I join you?'

'Not at all.' *You may as well since your dog has.*

'Nice to see you again.'

Hannah smiled and focussed on stroking the dog's fur so she didn't have to answer. She wasn't sure why she didn't want to talk to this friendly man.

'I know you won't believe this, but until last week, he seriously hadn't bothered anyone before. He always stays with me when I run. I guess he must have picked you out as a dog lover.'

'But I'm not. A dog lover, that is.' She cursed her honesty. *Why couldn't I have just nodded and smiled politely?*

'Oh. God, well, I'm doubly sorry, then. But you could have fooled me,' he said, nodding to her hand on his dog's head in her lap.

'I don't hate them, I just don't ...' Hannah gave up speaking and offered a shrug instead. She was starting to sound like not a very pleasant person. It wasn't the same as saying you didn't like snakes or spiders, was it?

'Fair enough, they're not for everyone.'

'So what do you do when you're not running around the park with Charlie?' Hannah asked, desperate to turn the attention away from herself.

'Oh. Well, I run most days. And when I'm not running I'm pretty much working. Yes, I'm a sad sack, but I love my job.'

Before Hannah had a chance to answer, she heard the sound of a muffled mobile chime.

'Sorry. Hang on. Oh, I've got to go,' the man said after checking it. 'An emergency has come in and I'm needed back at work,' he said, getting up. Charlie, clearly sensing the urgency, got up too. 'It was lovely to meet you.'

'It was nice to meet you, too,' Hannah said. 'Good luck with the emergency.'

'Thanks. I'll see you around.'

'Bye. See ya, Charlie, thanks for stopping by,' she said, giving the dog's ears a final ruffle.

She smiled after them, but continued to sit, unwilling to break the spell she felt herself in. It had been another strange but nice encounter.

★

When the sun went down behind the trees Hannah got up and slowly made her way home. As she walked she congratulated herself on having almost made it through another weekend.

'There you are!'

Hannah looked up, startled. She'd been ambling along, lost in her thoughts. There was Beth, standing by her front door.

'You're back!' Hannah cried, and hurried up the path.

'I'd nearly given up on you,' Beth said as they hugged tightly.

'I went to the park to feed the ducks. Come in and tell me all about your trip,' she said. 'Tea? Coffee?'

'I could murder a tea, thanks.'

'So, how was it?'

'Very enjoyable. I can't wait to tell Rob he was absolutely right about it being a floating retirement village. And, yes, wall-to-wall

Zimmer frames. Quite the funniest thing. It was fun. There were so many activities, I've come home for a rest! You could fill every moment of every day if you wanted to, or just sit and relax and read or watch the world go by. Although I didn't spend nearly enough time exercising – I've come back looking like a right roly-poly.'

'You look exactly the same to me.'

'Thanks.'

'So the food was good?'

'Well, you know me, it doesn't have to be particularly good for me to eat it,' Beth said. 'But, yes, everything was very tasty. And even better when you haven't had to prepare it yourself. Oh, I tell you, it really was the life. A few of us are even looking into planning our next one.'

'That's brilliant. I'm so pleased you enjoyed it.'

'So, enough about me, I'll bore you with the pictures and stories about who fell asleep playing bingo later. How are you? And no sugar coating.'

'God, I've missed you,' Hannah said.

'I've missed you too, dear,' she said, patting Hannah's hand. 'But, come on, no dodging the question.'

'I'm okay. I guess. I still spontaneously burst into tears.'

'That's normal.'

'But so bloody embarrassing,' Hannah said, shaking her head. 'And I hate being on my own.'

'Darling, it took me years to get used to that.'

'Great, just great.'

'You look better than when I left – you're a bit brighter and have a little more colour to your cheeks.'

'That's good. I've been running. Getting some exercise really helps.'

'Oh, Hannah, that's great. I'm so glad you're getting out and about. I've been worried you might have cooped yourself up.'

'I might have if I didn't hate being on my own so much,' Hannah said, managing a slight laugh. 'I've even started going to open-house inspections just so I don't have to be alone. Sam has been fantastic, but she can't spend all of her free time with me – what little she has.'

'Yes, it can be tricky. I remember making a roster when I lost my Elliot to make sure I didn't impose on one person too much. Though your parents could be very persuasive. They were my truest friends,' she said wistfully.

'I've realised Sam, Rob and you and one of my workmates are the only real friends I have. I thought I had a reasonably large social circle, but …'

'Well, it's times like these you find out who you can count on, not to mention who you truly value. There's no shame in letting go if someone is no longer your friend. If you haven't already, you'll one day realise it's about quality rather than quantity when it comes to friendships.'

'Hmm. Maybe you're right.'

'Try not to take it personally if a few people who you thought were good friends drop by the wayside. A lot of people don't know what to say to the bereaved and find it easier to avoid talking to them at all. They'll come back if they're meant to.'

'You're so wise.'

'Well, I don't know about that. So, what else have you been up to?'

'Working – that's been good. And I've managed to cook a few meals.'

'Oh, you're making great progress. I'm so proud of you.'

'Tristan and I always did the shopping together and now I can't seem to reprogram myself. You don't eat Nutella, do you?'

'No. Why?'

'Tristan loved it and I keep buying it. I think it's horrible. I even tried eating it to feel closer to him, how silly is that?'

'It doesn't sound silly at all,' Beth said kindly. 'I did the same with Elliot's sardines. I developed quite a taste for them for a while, trying to hold on. Can't stand them again now.'

'I can feel him slipping away, Auntie Beth. I'm forgetting everything. I can't remember the exact shade of his eyes or how he ran his hands through his hair when it was getting too long. He had a particular way and I loved watching him do that. I've tried, but I just can't picture it any more.'

'For me, some memories faded, but others came back stronger and stayed. Just try not to let it upset you.'

'I hate it, Auntie Beth, grief. It's the most unpredictable, chaotic thing I've ever had to deal with,' Hannah said. 'If it was simply a case of nutting it out or being organised – like setting up a new filing system – I'd be set. That's what I had thought people meant when they said the grief process was different for everyone.' But it wasn't like that at all, Hannah now realised. On top of everything else, she was having to face up to the fact that no amount of to-do lists in the world could help her deal with this – most of it was heart related and her heart was shattered.

'That it is, dear.'

'The other day I even found myself bargaining with God, and I'm not even remotely religious! As if some fictitious, mystical dude with a beard and a stack of old-fashioned ways of doing things was ever going to bring them back. Gah! I'm losing my mind.'

'It's quite natural to start searching for answers,' said Beth, 'questioning everything you believed in.'

'It's all so confusing. And hard.'

'Unfortunately what you're experiencing is not something you can logically and methodically work your way through, no matter how much you try,' Beth said, as if reading her mind. 'I wish it was like that, but it's not.'

'Never a truer word spoken, as Mum would have said.'

'Except, perhaps dealing with the paperwork and legalities,' Beth added thoughtfully. 'How are you getting on with the legal side of things?'

'I've tended to leave it all to the solicitor. He's been great, as has Mum and Dad's financial planner. I know it'll cost more, but I just can't seem to concentrate well enough to work out the serious stuff like that.'

'Yes, that is understandable.'

They sipped their teas in silence, lost in their own thoughts.

'Hey, Auntie Beth?' Hannah asked after a few moments.

'Yes, dear.'

'I've been left quite a lot of money. I feel weird, um, guilty, maybe. Do you think I should donate some to charity? And which ones?'

'Well, you did request donations to the organ donation place in lieu of flowers for the funeral.'

'That was what Adrian, Raelene and I decided, not because of anything in a will.'

'Oh. Right.'

'Their organs couldn't be donated because they were trapped in the car so long, so …'

'I see. Well, I think that was a lovely gesture.'

'But is it enough? And please don't say it's up to me.'

'But it is, dear, if everything has been left to you and there aren't any specific instructions. Your parents were generous people, but I don't remember them being big on any particular charity recently.'

'I didn't find any monthly withdrawals from their bank account that looked like it was going to a charity. They always gave a note to anyone rattling a tin they came across.'

'They were certainly generous.'

'Yes, which is why I feel I …' Hannah gave up. She didn't know what she felt, except guilty when it came to all the money.

'Darling, I think it's too soon for you to be thinking about this. And being left well provided for is not something you should feel guilty about. Your parents made that decision. *That* was their wish. And they raised you to be sensible with money, not to go handing it out willy nilly.'

'I guess.'

'If you want to make a donation down the track, then do so, but for now I think you need to concentrate on putting yourself and your needs first. You're young. You don't want to give it all away and then have something happen and find yourself short down the track. Sit tight for now, sweetheart,' she said, smiling. 'I think we're all still in shock. Just let the dust settle a bit.'

'What would I do without you?'

'And that's not something you need to worry about either. I'm as fit as a flea and not going anywhere. But I am hungry. So, we're going to order in a pizza and make pigs of ourselves.'

'That sounds perfect.'

Chapter Seventeen

'You can't use that excuse forever — that you'll drag the mood down. Anyway, you won't. Not that you ever would have — you've been amazing,' Caitlin said, becoming a little flustered.

If that's what you call managing to not have a bout of tears for three days, then, yes, I've been amazing, Hannah thought. The last episode had been the evening after a barbeque out in the park with friends to celebrate Australia Day. It had been her first true social outing since the funeral and without Sam. She'd managed to hold her emotions in and do a decent acting job, and had even enjoyed the day out with the large group of friends and friends of friends.

Quite a few who'd gone along were single so Hannah didn't have the feeling that she was a third wheel as she might have had in a more formal dinner-party situation. That's why she'd gone, really. And it had almost helped not to have Sam and Rob there to use as a crutch; she had to make conversation and fend for herself.

Going to the barbeque had made Hannah realise how much she was missing out on by declining invitations, and that people didn't seem to be dwelling on her situation as much as she'd thought they might be.

But while she had been all right at the time, it was still so hard to go out without Tristan by her side.

Hannah knew that telling Caitlin why she'd decided not to go out with the others would come back to haunt her. But it had been necessary. Oh well, at least this conversation was just between the two of them, quietly standing at the sink in the office kitchen. She really hoped Caitlin wouldn't tell anyone else. She was quite a bit younger than Hannah and while she had her silly moments, Caitlin was generally thoughtful and level headed. Although, what did it matter if people knew the truth?

'So, you're coming, aren't you? You have to, *everyone* is.'

'Um, well, I ...'

As Hannah focussed on stacking the dishwasher and avoided looking at Caitlin, she searched her mind for another excuse. It was the last Friday of the month and the office had a tradition that the whole floor headed out together to celebrate any birthdays that had occurred during that month.

The only people who didn't get shamed for not attending were those with a very good excuse – like a visit from their mother-in-law or that they had to go home to their kids. Though it seemed to Hannah that the people with children were often the keenest to lead the charge to the bar.

'Maybe a night out with friends is just what you need,' Caitlin prompted. 'Better than going home and being on your own. Come on, you know I'm right and you know you want to.'

'You're not going to give up, are you?' Hannah said with a laugh.

'Nope,' Caitlin said, and laughed too.

'All right, count me in,' she said. *It'll be fun. And no doubt they've practically forgotten what happened to me on Christmas Day.*

Thanks to so many years observing office gossip, Hannah understood how quickly her colleagues moved on to new subjects to talk about. And, as Caitlin had rightly pointed out, Hannah hadn't given them any signs to stop them moving on; no puffy eyes or tissues dabbing at tears.

'Come on, you two, we're off,' someone called and Hannah and Caitlin headed off in different directions to collect their things.

As they waited in the ground-floor foyer for the whole team to congregate, Hannah smiled and thought, not for the first time, how nice it was to be part of such a warm, loving group. Work was probably the only thing that had kept her sane these past weeks. If she didn't have that, she doubted she'd have found the energy and inclination to get out of bed at all.

Craig led the group along the street and up one of Melbourne's many laneways to a favourite haunt.

There were so many great venues near their office that they went to a different one each month, with those whose birthdays it was that month choosing between themselves. Other times, the one who suggested drinks tended to pick their current favourite. Tonight's choice was a moody bar with karaoke. While Hannah was determined to be sociable and enjoy herself, she was equally determined to be gone before the karaoke started.

As usual, the first round of beers and bottle of champagne – well, technically sparkling white – was on the very generous company they worked for. Seated around a few tables pulled together, they all hooted and cheered when Craig, accompanied by one of the bar staff, appeared with trays of bottles and glasses and bags of chips.

'Don't worry, folks, I've ordered some proper food as well,' Craig said.

The only alcohol Hannah had drunk in the past three weeks had been brandy in milk, which she'd upped from a dash to what was probably more like a double-shot – if she'd bothered to measure it. Quite often she had considered cracking open a bottle of white or red, but the words of Sam, who she trusted implicitly, warning that alcohol would only make things worse and that drinking alone was a no-no, always stopped her. She didn't need to feel any worse.

She accepted a glass of sparkling white wine and took a tentative sip. It was not the best she'd ever had, but certainly far from the worst. She took a deep slug. *Hmm, not bad, not bad at all*, she thought.

It took two decent swigs and about three minutes for Hannah to feel the warm glow and slightly numbing effects of the alcohol start to make its way through her.

Without thinking, she accepted a second glass, raised it and joined in with the jovial cry of 'Cheers' that ran around the tables.

It seemed like just minutes had passed and now the music was pumping, the bar had filled with crowds of office workers, and Caitlin was leading Hannah onto the small dance area.

A couple of times she felt so free she forgot herself and turned to look for Tristan among those still seated at the tables clapping and cheering. But she refused to be melancholy tonight. She managed to shake it off and keep dancing. She and Tristan had gone out separately to plenty of work functions so it wasn't too unusual that he mightn't be here. Of course, being more than a wee bit tipsy helped – she'd always been a happy drunk.

Suddenly the karaoke was being set up. In the interests of being sociable, Hannah decided she'd stay. Caitlin and her friend Chloe were always first up. Tonight Hannah thought she might even join them. She was enjoying feeling normal again and having too much fun to leave now.

For the first time in ages Hannah felt a part of things, really a part. And happy, genuinely happy, not just putting on an act for the comfort of the people around her.

She was shocked to notice as the strobe light flashed past that her watch read nine o'clock. No wonder she was feeling like she was. She'd guzzled too much too quickly. But, it had gone down so well. And no harm done. How many glasses had she had? Two or three? She couldn't remember. She'd better slow down. She'd had some of the chips, but that was hardly enough to be a decent sponge for the alcohol. Hopefully the bowls of wedges and sour cream and sweet chilli sauce or serves of pita bread and dips, which they usually ordered, would arrive soon. Her stomach grumbled in anticipation.

Next thing she knew, Hannah was being dragged onto the tiny stage by Caitlin and Chloe. There was barely enough room for the three of them, but despite Hannah's protests she joined them in an almost passable rendition of John Farnham's 'Pressure Down'.

Hannah felt exhilarated as they bowed to the enthusiastic crowd and stepped down to re-join their group. She would have been happy to stay up there and do another song, but not on her own. And Caitlin and Chloe said they needed a drink.

'That was awesome, you girls,' someone at the table said and everyone uttered agreement and another round of cheers.

Hannah's head was spinning when she sat down and picked up her glass again, which was half-full, room temperature, and no longer contained any bubbles. She really needed some water. And a wee. Hopefully when she got back some food will have arrived. As she stood up her legs felt weak and her stomach cramped.

'Where's the food?' someone called. 'I'm starving!'

'Me too,' Hannah chimed in with everyone else as she made her way from the table.

Inside the cubicle away from the noise and energy of the room, she pulled down her knickers and sat heavily on the toilet. Her head began to spin so she closed her eyes. But that made the vertigo so much worse and her whole body began to wobble. She opened her eyes and in order to steady herself she turned her gaze down to concentrate on the white tiles beneath her feet. But as she did, she noticed a dark red patch on her undies. Slowly she felt her soul constrict, the ball of ache reform in her chest and part of it break off and rise into her throat.

And then, without warning, something else inside her broke. A torrent of tears gushed down her cheeks, the likes of which she'd never experienced before and didn't know she had in her.

She leant forward and clutched her knees. But finding no comfort, pulled up her undies to hide the evidence. She felt herself sliding to the floor and couldn't do anything about it – didn't even want to. It was filthy, streaked with grime and goodness only knew what germs, but she didn't care – she just wanted to curl up and die. This was like losing Tristan all over again, maybe even worse because now she knew for certain she had no small living, breathing piece of him to hold onto into the future. She sobbed. What she wanted to do was wail, scream, and get angry. But it was sadness and disappointment that consumed her. And it was quiet. She gasped as the tiny pieces of her already shattered heart broke and the razor-sharp shards pierced her torn and broken soul – the soul that might have been starting to heal a little.

'Hannah, are you in here?' She heard Caitlin's voice. She didn't want attention. She wanted to be left alone.

'Yes. I'm fine.' Well, that's what she tried to say. But it came out more as a strangled gasp.

'Oh my god, have you had a fall? Are you okay?'

Suddenly Caitlin was on her knees and peering under the gap of the door. Something in Hannah came together and she registered just how embarrassing this scene was. She needed to get out of here. She tried to stand up, but couldn't get a grip on the tiles. She gasped as her elbow hit the hard floor.

'Hang on, I'm going to get some help.'

Hannah wanted to protest, but couldn't muster the energy for that either. If only she could just be left on her own. If only she'd been home and not out in a bar.

'Hann, it's Craig, what's going on?'

'She's only had a couple of drinks,' she heard Caitlin say. 'Something else must have happened.'

'I need you to move away from the door. I'm going to use a coin to open it. Okay?'

'Should I call an ambulance?' Caitlin said. 'Or maybe the fire brigade?'

'Just wait a sec and let's see what's going on first.'

Hannah wanted to help them, but couldn't make herself care enough to move. All she could think was she'd just lost everything all over again, and this time it felt a million times worse.

She began sobbing again when Caitlin's hand appeared under the divider from the next cubicle.

'Squeeze my hand,' Caitlin commanded.

Hannah squeezed.

There was a rattle and she looked up to see Craig's face peering at her in the gap of the partially open door. If she wasn't so upset she might have been mortified.

Hannah had no idea how he managed it, but Craig eased himself into the cubicle with her. He sat, his long legs folded in two on the other side of the toilet.

'You're not just drunk and disorderly, are you?' Now he could see she wasn't injured, he was trying to make light of the situation a little.

'I got my period,' Hannah whimpered. She knew she sounded pathetic. She *was* being pathetic.

'Oh. Right,' he said, a perplexed, slightly embarrassed look on his face.

How could anyone know the significance of what this means? Hannah thought. She was taken completely by surprise herself – it certainly wasn't rational.

Caitlin said, 'I'll get your bag,' gave Hannah's hand an extra squeeze and disappeared. She then heard the main door opening and closing.

'Tristan and I had been trying to have a baby,' she said.

'Ahh,' Craig said, nodding his head slowly. She accepted the checked handkerchief he held out and dabbed uselessly at her streaming face and dripping nose.

Gradually Hannah felt herself coming out of her stupor. She sat up and looked around as if seeing her surroundings for the first time. God, how embarrassing! She frowned and suddenly thought she couldn't remember coming in here. Everything was hazy. Her head now hummed.

'Come on, you can't stay here. Any second and all that champagne and lolly water will need somewhere to go,' he said, smiling sympathetically.

She nodded, clasped the hand he held out to her, and allowed herself to be eased up. A small part of her didn't want to leave. How the hell was she going to face everyone out there? The full impact started to hit Hannah. It was one thing to have a meltdown in the toilet cubicle of a bar, but another to go back out looking like she had.

She washed her hands and stood feeling helpless in front of the basins, trying to avoid the mirror. Craig stood beside her looking a little helpless. She began praying he wouldn't wrap his arms around her – she might never let go.

The door opened and Caitlin appeared clutching Hannah's handbag, her own slung over her shoulder.

'Here you are,' she said, handing it to Hannah.

'Thanks.'

'Right, we need to get you home,' Craig said.

'I can go in a taxi with her,' Caitlin offered.

'No, I'll take her in my car. We're not far from the office.'

'Okay. There's a back way out – I asked that lovely barman. Here, I'll show you.'

They helped Hannah out into a grimy narrow alley. She almost dry retched at the stench of decaying food and rubbish that hung in the air.

'Queen Street is that way.' Caitlin pointed.

'Thanks, Caitlin,' Craig said. 'Can you just go back to the group and convince them everything is okay. If you have to, tell them Hannah got a bit upset, but leave it at that. I'm sure they'll understand.'

Caitlin gave the dazed Hannah a quick hug, handed her bag to Craig, and disappeared behind the door she'd kept propped open with her hip.

Hannah nodded her thanks, but couldn't speak. She felt stunned and incoherent, just like when the police had visited on Christmas Day.

Chapter Eighteen

She stared out of the window of Craig's BMW, vaguely aware they were not driving towards her suburb. Then they pulled up in front of a house she didn't recognise and Craig was helping her out of the car.

He guided her to the front steps and put his key in the lock just as the door opened to the warm, friendly face of his wife Jasmine, dressed in a bathrobe. *Oh no, could it get more embarrassing?* Hannah didn't know Jasmine well even though they'd met several times over the years. She'd been at the funeral with Craig and the house afterwards, too, hadn't she?

'Oh. What's happened?'

'Hannah's upset. I didn't think it wise to take her home where she'd be on her own.'

'No, of course not. Bring her in, the poor thing.'

Hannah was still in a trance-like state as she was ushered into the house, down the hall, and into a bedroom. She heard hushed voices and activity in the hall. She sat down on the bed and caught her reflection in the mirror of the wardrobe and couldn't even bring herself to care that she looked a fright. Tears still streamed from her swollen eyes and down her raw, red cheeks.

Moments later she looked up to find Jasmine placing a pile of things, including a towel, a feminine hygiene package and tooth-paste and toothbrush on the bedside cupboard.

'There's an ensuite just through there,' Jasmine said, pointing to a door beside the wardrobe. 'Make yourself at home.'

Hannah nodded and opened her mouth to thank her. But instead of words, a gulp came out, followed by a fresh rush of tears. Jasmine patted her hand. 'I'll get you a cup of herbal tea to help you sleep.'

Jasmine soon returned with a glass of water in one hand and a cup of tea in the other.

'Here's some paracetamol in case you get a headache, if you haven't already got one. They might help you sleep, too,' she said, giving Hannah two tablets and the glass.

'Thank you.' Hannah swallowed the tablets, handed the glass back and then accepted the tea. She was still seated on the edge of the bed where she'd first sat down.

'We'll be just across the hall if you need anything. Hopefully you'll sleep well and things won't seem so bad in the morning.'

'I'm so sorry,' Hannah finally blurted as Jasmine was leaving the room. The woman turned.

'You really don't need to apologise. Would it help to talk about it?'

'I don't think I can.' Hannah whimpered like a child.

'And that's okay. You sleep well and I'll see you in the morning. We can talk then. Or not, it's entirely up to you.'

Hannah slipped in between the sheets. She'd used the bathroom, but hadn't got changed. She was exhausted and just wanted to curl up, go to sleep and never wake up.

★

Daylight filtered into the room, and Hannah woke, propped herself up and looked around. It took her a moment to remember where she was. Snippets of the night before came back to her. She'd been in the bar and then in the toilets. Craig had brought her home to his place. *God, how embarrassing. And now even more awkward.* How could she go into the kitchen and face them? She knew they were up because she could hear them down the hall and the sound of a coffee machine. She felt terrible and completely mortified. And then the reason for what had set her off seeped back in. She buried her face in the pillow.

A moment later there was a gentle knock on the door.

'Hannah, are you awake?'

'Yes,' she said quietly. She hoped Jasmine wouldn't hear her and would return to the kitchen, but to not answer would be too rude.

The door opened slowly. 'How are you doing?' Jasmine asked.

'I'm okay. Thank you so much for everything.'

'Don't mention it. I brought you a coffee. Craig thought you liked it white with one, so I hope I've got it right.'

'That's perfect.'

'Don't be mad at Craig for telling me, but he explained what upset you. I'm so sorry. That on top of everything else …'

'I feel ridiculous getting so upset. Being a single parent is not something I'd ever choose. I hadn't given a thought to being pregnant – it's too long since Tristan and I … well, you know …'

'The body reacts to stress in all sorts of ways,' Jasmine said, sitting down at the foot of the bed. 'Maybe subconsciously you'd hoped you were pregnant, even if you wouldn't want to raise children alone. To carry Tristan's baby would keep him with you in some sense and you wouldn't have to completely say goodbye. I get it. I think it's reasonable to be shocked and upset to find out you're not pregnant, even if it's something you didn't know you wanted. I imagine it will be like having to start your grieving all over again.'

Hannah caught the wistful tone in her voice and looked up. She could see her own sadness reflected in Jasmine's dark eyes staring back at her. She looked around and for the first time properly took in her surroundings. The room was a nursery. The walls were painted in lavender with a mural of Beatrix Potter animals. There was a white cupboard with a change-table on top, matching cot, bookshelves with stuffed toys and children's books, and beside it, near the window, was a rocking chair. Hannah's heart went out to the sad woman sitting beside her.

'How many babies have you lost?' she asked in a whisper.

'Two. I'm hoping for third time lucky,' she said, smiling sadly.

'Oh, Jasmine. I'm so sorry. I had no idea.'

'Thank you. We've kept it to ourselves. But it's nothing compared to what you've been through, and are going through. I have so much else – my health, a good life, a wonderful husband, beautiful home … If it's meant to be, it'll happen. I think that if you don't have hope and faith in at least *something* you don't really have anything.'

'I still can't believe how upset I was last night,' Hannah said a few moments later.

'I can.' Jasmine took hold of Hannah's hand and squeezed it. 'How are you feeling now?'

'A bit better, I guess. Though I can't imagine ever not feeling damaged and sad. I'm beginning to think you actually can die from a broken heart, and that it's a very slow, painful death.'

Jasmine nodded and gave Hannah's hand another squeeze.

'How do you ...?' she began to ask, but at that moment a large dog rushed into the room and startled Hannah by hopping onto the bed beside her.

Hannah tried not to recoil.

'This great lump helps,' Jasmine said, giving the happy looking dog's ears a rub. 'Though he is very naughty, aren't you, Dougal? But, honestly, there have been days when if I didn't have him needing me to feed him or let him out I would have never got out of bed.'

Craig appeared in the doorway. 'Dougal, come on out of there. Darling, Hannah doesn't like dogs.'

'Oh. I'm sorry. I didn't know.'

Hannah opened her mouth to protest, but what could she say? It was the truth. And here she was being practically pinned down by a large, hairy beast. And it was drooling. Urgh! What was it with dogs trying to befriend her?

'How are you doing?' Craig asked.

'Okay. A bit better. Thanks so much for everything. I'm so sorry to ...'

Craig held up a hand. 'Hannah, it's fine. I may be your boss, but I hope you count Jasmine and me as friends too. Now, do you think you're up for some breakfast, because I don't have too long before I head off to golf.'

Hannah had a quick shower before making her way down to the kitchen where she was greeted with the sizzle and aroma of a fry-up. She'd remembered how she'd once yearned so much for a hot, greasy breakfast she practically ached. She'd always enjoyed good food and thankfully managed to keep within a healthy weight range. But since the accident she could barely find the energy to eat, let alone with any enthusiasm. These days she really just ate out of habit. She braced herself to put on a decent acting job as Jasmine invited her to sit down.

'How much time do you want to take off from work?' Craig asked. 'Whatever you need.'

'I don't want to take any time off.'

The thought of being at home alone all day with nothing to do terrified Hannah.

'At least take the week off,' Craig said, as he tucked into his bacon and eggs.

'But ...'

'No need to get a medical certificate, I'll clear it with HR,' he said.

'Please don't make me,' Hannah said, shocked that she'd uttered the words aloud. 'I'm really sorry I had a meltdown, but I'm fine. I *have* been fine, haven't I? It hasn't affected my work. Please, I need my job. It's all I've got.'

Craig stared at her. 'Hannah, I'm not firing you. I just think you need to take some time off.'

'No, I need to keep busy. If you think I'm not pulling my weight ...'

'Of course not. You're brilliant and I'd be lost without you. I'm just trying to help.' He rubbed a hand across his face. She knew the mannerism well. He was out of his depth.

'All of my friends are still away on holiday or back at work. What would I do on my own all day?'

'Visit art galleries, shop, window shop, go and see movies ...' Jasmine said, lighting up. 'You could do a short course of some sort. I'm doing interior decorating two afternoons a week.'

'Jas has also been known to paint rooms and pull carpet up while I've been at work.'

'I did the nursery, but next time I'll get someone in who knows what they're doing and has all the right tools.'

'Yes, it's one thing to keep busy, but overdoing things isn't good,' Craig said. 'Though it didn't help that Jas changed her mind about the colour and ended up painting it twice.'

'I rushed in, desperate to be in charge of *something, anything.* Grief is so unpredictable and all-consuming that I think when you can finally breathe a little and think beyond the sadness for a few moments you become desperate for some semblance of normal. That's how it is for me,' she added with a gentle shrug.

Hannah looked at Jasmine. She liked that Jasmine seemed genuinely kind and caring but pulled no punches.

'You should be a counsellor,' she said.

'That's what I keep telling her, but she wants to be paid to shop,' Craig said.

'Oh ha-ha,' Jasmine said, and threw a tea towel at Craig's head.

'Well, I appreciate your advice,' Hannah said. 'I was actually thinking about doing some painting, changing the look of the place a bit. But now I think I'll hold off.'

'Obviously it's entirely up to you, but I'd recommend sitting on your colour choice – or whatever else you have in mind – for a few weeks, months even, to make sure you love it. And, seriously, get someone in to do it, if you can afford to. Now is not the time to add more stress to your life. No matter how easy these things seem in the beginning, it tends to never end up that way. I blame those reality TV shows!'

'I don't think I've ever watched one.'

'Well, don't start, they lure you into a false sense of security and that never ends well. You know,' Jasmine went on thoughtfully, 'there's another way to keep your mind occupied without turning the house upside down and taking on a large project.'

'Oh? What's that?'

'Travel. Ooh, I love going away. Lounging around in four and five star hotels …'

'But it wouldn't be any fun travelling alone. And I've actually never even been on a plane.'

'Really? Wow. Well, you don't have to fly to travel. Even just a night or two in a swish hotel. I love travelling on my own. No one to answer to. Sorry, darling.'

'I think that's my cue to leave,' Craig said, pushing his chair back from the table and taking his plate to the sink. 'Do you want a ride home, Hannah? Your place is pretty much on my way, so it'd be no trouble.'

'Oh, well …' She was enjoying Jasmine's company too much.

'No, stay. I can take you home later, if you like – I've got nothing on.'

'Okay. Thanks. I'd like to stay for a bit, if that's all right. And when you drop me off you can tell me what you think of the paint colour I'm considering.'

'Brilliant. Have a good round, darling,' Jasmine said as Craig kissed her on the cheek.

'See you Monday unless I hear otherwise, Hannah. Let me know if you change your mind. Take care and don't let her corrupt you,' he said, pointing at Jasmine.

Hannah smiled after him while trying to ignore her feelings of envy at seeing their affection towards each other. Oh, she'd give her right arm for another hug from Tris.

'You know, travelling on your own is not nearly as scary as you'd think,' Jasmine said. 'It's really not a whole lot different to normal life – all the other things we do on our own; going to work, getting groceries … And there are tour groups you can join that pair you up with someone.'

'I really don't do much on my own. I love movies and I go quite a bit, but I've never been to one on my own.'

'Yes, it can be confronting at first. I often go to the movies on Saturdays when Craig's off playing golf. I'm a little older than you and the trouble with being my age is all my friends have kids or teenagers they're driving around over the weekend. I've got used to doing things on my own. And I was single for years before meeting Craig so had it all down to a fine art. It can actually be quite liberating once you get over society's view that if you're alone you're automatically a loser. But it does take time. What else do you enjoy?'

'I can't remember what I used to do on weekends, um, before. It reminds me of them and how much everything has changed. And that hurts too much.'

'I can imagine. It's good to think about happy times, but I understand if it's still too painful or you don't want to talk about it with me.'

Hannah felt bad. Jasmine had been so nice she didn't want her to feel as if she didn't want her as a friend. She'd have to make an effort.

'We always seemed to be busy,' Hannah said, thoughtfully. 'Friday nights we often went out to drinks with people from work. Sometimes we'd go to dinner afterwards or just head home with takeaway. We both love – loved – Indian curry and Thai.'

'Craig and I do too. What else?'

'Saturday mornings we'd do a fry-up at home or head out for breakfast and then go grocery shopping. We enjoyed going to the markets and wandering around. Sometimes we'd invite people over for dinner.

'Tristan played golf most Saturdays too, and while he did I'd often hang out with Mum and Dad, take them to do their groceries, or go out with Mum shopping or with girlfriends. Or I'd stay home and get the washing done or clean the house. God, we sound like a middle-aged couple, don't we?'

'It doesn't matter how you sound. And your weekends don't sound much different to ours.'

'What if we were really boring? What if *I* was, *am*, boring and too much like my parents? What if Tristan wanted to do more and I held him back?'

'He was a grown man, Hannah, if he wanted to do something else, he would have, or at least he would have talked to you about it. Perhaps he was simply content. Did he ever say you were boring?'

'No.'

'He wouldn't have married you if he thought that. Hannah, there's nothing wrong with contentment. Perhaps your predictability and stability is what Tristan loved most about you. From what Craig has said, he was really easy going too.'

'He was, except sometimes when it came to golf – he'd get in such a rage when his slice kicked in he'd become a different person.'

'Ha, don't they all? It brings out the monster in Craig all too often.'

'I really don't get the appeal of golf.'

'Me neither. I went out and walked around with Craig to show an interest when we first got together, but it was too boring for me.'

'I did too. So did my friend Sam.'

'Suckers, all of us,' Jasmine said, grinning.

'Yep,' Hannah agreed.

They lapsed into silence.

'Food was our thing – it was a huge part of our life. And entertaining. We made a great team,' Hannah said wistfully.

'That's lovely.'

'It's so hard to think about the good times. I get sad, though.'

'It will get easier. And it's much better to be sad remembering the good things than getting frustrated at the what ifs. Now, come on, let's head out. There's a fun looking movie just out that I'd like to see and we could go to some shops first. I'd love the company, if you want to join me.'

★

'Honestly, it really is a gorgeous house just as it is,' Jasmine said as they hugged goodbye. 'So don't get all gung-ho about painting. And if you do get the urge, call me first so I can talk you out of it.'

Hannah didn't think she would paint now; Jasmine had pointed out all the pieces of the jigsaw puzzle that she would need to consider – just as Beth had, but more precisely. If she wanted to do it properly – and one of Hannah's mantras was If it's worth doing, it's worth doing well – there was a lot more to a decent makeover than slapping on a coat of paint.

She could see now how being unsettled in one part of your life – well, her whole life had been torn apart really – could make you want to change other parts that were actually fine as they were. Jasmine was right when she'd said it was all about trying to wrest some sort of control. Thank goodness she had good friends to look out for her and guide her. And she felt she and Jasmine had become firm friends.

Chapter Nineteen

'Happy birthday!' Hannah said, opening her front door and wrapping her arms around Sam. It had been a tough day full of reminders of the many times she and her mother had worked together in this very kitchen with these same recipes. But, like everything else that kept cropping up, she'd managed to keep going long enough to put together a decent meal.

Now seeing Sam's face, she was pleased with herself for having insisted on carrying on their tradition of cooking for each other on their birthdays.

'Thanks. But, god, Hann, I'm feeling old. And tired.'

'Twins'll do that. And, yes, it's too late to send them back.' It was an ongoing joke between them that hadn't had a run since Christmas Day.

'I'm so sorry I haven't been in touch much these last few weeks. After we came back from the holiday, I've been in creative mode and you know how I get,' Sam said.

'You don't need to apologise. It's great you're creating again. Auntie Beth has been keeping an eye on me and I've really just been going to work and coming home. Come in.'

'Hi, Hannah, good of you to have us,' Rob said, pecking her on the cheek. 'I was going to mow your lawns, but I see they've already been done.'

'Oh, that's very good of you. Have they, though? Gosh, how terrible am I? I haven't even noticed.'

'I'll check the back, but the front and the edges have definitely been done recently. Is there anything else I can do while I'm here?'

'You came for dinner, not to be put to work.'

'I don't mind. Is there something that needs doing?'

'Well, actually, yes, the light under the back verandah blew. I'm still working up the nerve to get out the ladder.'

'Consider it done. Is the ladder in the garage?'

'Yes. There's a globe on the kitchen bench. I got that far. Thanks so much.'

'No worries. It won't take long. I'll be back in a minute.'

'Hi, Auntie Hann,' Oliver and Ethan said in unison, throwing themselves at Hannah and almost winding her.

'Hello there, my favourite five-year-old twin boys. Sorry I missed your birthdays while you were away.' Hannah felt a little guilty, but was relieved she hadn't had to deal with buying gifts and celebrating on top of everything else.

'That's okay. And we're the *only* five-year-old twins you know,' Ethan said. 'Mum said.'

'You'll have to excuse him, Auntie Hann. He's in a *mood*,' Oliver said. Hannah smiled. She loved how grown-up the boys often sounded. They really were old souls and were so good at mimicking adult mannerisms and conversations.

'And why is that, Oliver?'

'Mum wouldn't let him keep Jasper,' Oliver said.

'Who's Jasper?' Hannah asked.

'A daddy long legs spider he found. He wanted to put it in a jar and keep it. How would Ethan like it if someone did that to him?' Oliver said.

'They don't make jars that big, stupido,' Ethan said, folding his arms.

'I'm sure Jasper is happier roaming free,' Hannah said.

'See, Ethan. I tried to tell him, Auntie Hann. He wouldn't listen, as usual.'

'Mum, Oliver's teasing me,' Ethan said, and disappeared into the kitchen.

'How are you feeling, Auntie Hann? Are you still really sad for Uncle Tris and Granny Daph and Grandad Dan?' Oliver asked quietly as he put his hand in Hannah's.

'I am, sweetie, but I'm really glad to see you. How are you? What have you been up to?' she asked.

'I'm okay, thanks. I've been a bit sad, too. I miss them and Dad said it's going to take a long time until we're not sad anymore.'

'I think you're right, Oliver,' Hannah said, matching his sage tone. The dear, precious little boy.

'Can I please have a cuddle?' he asked, holding his arms up.

'Of course you can,' she said, bending down to pick him up. She drank in his sweet smelling hair and as she did tried to conjure up Tristan's scent. Nothing. She felt panic begin to surge. She was forgetting everything about him.

'Thank you. That's enough now,' Oliver said, squirming out of Hannah's clutches.

'Can you tell your mum and dad I'll be there in a minute? There's something I have to do.'

'Okay.'

Hannah bolted down the hall and into the bathroom where on the shelf she kept Tristan's aftershave – along with the bottle of her father's and one of her mother's perfumes, which she'd brought back from their villa. She picked it up and sniffed. It smelled nothing like him – all she detected was the original manufactured scent, which had smelt completely different on Tristan's skin. Her heart sank. She tried her father's aftershave and then her mother's perfume. Again, nothing. She had to accept that they were slipping further and further away from her. No matter how hard she tried to hold onto them in her memories, she was losing them. She knew it was part of the process, but had hoped it wouldn't happen so soon. She was disappointed, but couldn't say she was surprised.

She carried the small bottles through to her bedroom and sat down heavily on her bed. Had she ever really been able to remember their individual scents? Probably not. Thankfully her eyes remained dry as she sat staring ahead at nothing in particular.

'Are you okay?' Hannah looked up to see Sam standing in the doorway.

'I've forgotten what they smell like. All of them.'

'Oh, sweetie,' Sam said, sitting down next to Hannah and putting her arm around her shoulder.

'I'm okay. It just came as a bit of a shock. I don't know why when it's part of the process and I knew it would happen.'

'Don't be so hard on yourself.'

'Oh, Sammy, I wish I could fast-forward to a year from now and have all the firsts over and done with. One day I think I'm doing okay and then, bang, something else crops up and I'm back where I started.'

'Well, for the record, I think you're doing amazingly well. I'd be a basket case by now – I *am* a basket case. This is a big thing and, look, you're not even in tears. You're getting stronger.'

'But I'm not, though, Sammy. Last week I completely freaked out because I got my period. That's just plain irrational.'

'Nothing's irrational when it comes to grief, Hannah. And I can see why, you and Tris were planning on having kids. So getting your period would completely turn you upside down again. Why didn't you call me?'

'You were away. It was when you were off with the Carringtons.'

'Oh. I'm sorry I wasn't here for you.'

'Sam, stop apologising. You have your own life. You're my best friend and I love you, but you're not responsible for me. You've already done so much. Unfortunately, as awful as all this is, apparently it's my lot in life at the moment.'

'Well, as I said, I think you're doing incredibly well.'

'Thanks. I don't feel like it. I feel like I'm barely hanging on.'

'I know it doesn't help, but I am sure it will get easier.'

'I hope you're right. And, yeah, it doesn't help,' Hannah said, forcing out a tight smile before hugging her friend. The truth was, Hannah feared the sadness that was consuming her would be with her forever. And a part of her hoped she would always feel this way because if she didn't, would it mean that she'd left her loved ones behind too easily?

'Should I take Rob and the boys home? It's fine if you'd rather not have guests after all.'

'No way! I've made you a chocolate sponge with lots of whipped cream and strawberries.'

'Goody.'

'Though it might be a wee bit salty – there are quite a few tears in the mix as well,' she said with a grin.

'I'm sure it'll be perfect. Shall we get this first milestone out of the way then?' Sam said with a gentle smile. She stood and offered a hand to Hannah.

'Yes, let's.'

'Just be kind to yourself, sweetie, and don't rush it,' Sam said as they made their way back down the hall.

'I hope you boys are hungry for lasagne,' Hannah called as she walked into the kitchen.

'Are we ever!' Oliver declared.

'Yes please,' said Ethan. Hannah smiled at seeing them sitting beside each other companionably, their earlier disagreement clearly forgotten.

'But make sure you save room for chocolate cake,' Sam warned.

'Yum,' Oliver said.

'Yes, we love your food, Auntie Hannah,' Ethan said.

'Gee, thanks a lot. You can't be mean to me, it's my birthday,' Sam said, pouting.

'Sorry,' Oliver and Ethan said quietly one after the other, suitably contrite.

'Speaking of being the birthday girl,' Hannah said, pulling the gift-wrapped artwork from where it was resting beside the end of the bench and handing it to Sam.

'But we don't do birthday presents,' Sam said. 'We've never done birthday presents.'

'Well, call it a thank-you-for-everything-and-being-my-best-friend present, then, if it makes you feel better. I saw it and couldn't resist. But if you don't want it ...'

'Of course I want it,' Sam said, reaching out, grinning. She read the card with tears in her eyes and hugged Hannah.

'Don't go getting all mopey – just open it!' Hannah said.

Sam tore off the wrapping and stared at the framed piece of art.

'Oh, wow, I love it. Rob, look.'

'That'd be right,' Rob said.

'What?' Hannah asked.

'The one time she can tell me exactly what she wants for her birthday and you go and get in first,' he said, laughing.

'Sorry.'

'How did you know which one I really loved out of all of them?'

'Well, it wasn't hard, it was the one you stood in front of for the longest. You were practically drooling.'

'Ew, gross. Ethan does that when he sleeps in the car,' Oliver said.

'I do not.'

'Do too.'

'Enough, you two,' Rob said.

'Right, sounds like we all need some food,' Hannah said. 'Thanks so much for doing the light.'

'No problem at all. I'll do the smoke detectors when daylight saving ends. If you think of anything else, let me know.'

'You're a gem.'

'Thanks again, Hann, it's gorgeous,' Sam said, putting her arm around Hannah while they were at the oven retrieving the garlic bread and lasagne. 'But you really shouldn't have.'

'I should have given it to you on a random day, but I couldn't keep it to myself any longer. So, I don't want you thinking for a second I want us to start giving presents after all these years. But I saw how much you liked it and I saw it as an opportunity to say thanks for everything. And if I've learned one thing this year, it's not to put things off.'

Chapter Twenty

By April, Hannah was growing used to the renewed sadness and setbacks that accompanied major milestones such as birthdays and other anniversaries. She'd made some progress, though. One big step forward was mowing her own lawns and trimming the edges. Rob had come over to show her how to fill the lawn mower and whipper snipper with fuel and to get them started. At first she'd found it all quite terrifying, but when she got used to it, she felt empowered. Once she'd mastered the basics of the gardening she'd gone around to her nearest neighbours to try to talk them out of taking such good care of her. They had been wonderful to step in and look after her garden for so long – especially when most of them were her parents' age – but she was now mentally strong enough and physically able to do it herself. She had felt great saying, 'Thank you, but I can do my own lawns and edges now.' She'd taken along baskets of muffins and cakes she'd made and gave them vouchers to the movies, but there was no way she'd ever be able to adequately express her appreciation.

She was even starting to feel more at ease with being alone, helped by Jasmine over regular lunches while Craig played golf. Her friend gave her pep talks about all the things she'd enjoyed when she was single. As she listened, Hannah wondered if Jasmine was missing single life a little too much.

Hannah had wrapped up Tristan's and her parents' estates a couple of weeks ago. She'd even taken on most of the paperwork under the guidance of the family solicitor, with some help from the financial adviser. It had kept her busy and her mind occupied for months, and now she almost missed it. While it had been confronting, she'd managed to approach it academically and work her way through each step. Thankfully she and Tristan had been completely open with their passwords, bank accounts, and other personal details. That had certainly made the process much easier. More than once she'd sat shaking her head and marvelling at how much harder it would be to navigate without having the list of passwords that had been attached to his will. Thank goodness for an on-the-ball solicitor, and a husband and parents who were conservative and sensible with their finances.

For a thirty-something, she'd ended up quite wealthy. If she was really smart with her money, she might never have to work full-time again. Though she loved her job and the thought of all those extra hours by herself was still quite terrifying. She was stalling discussing her own situation with the financial adviser. While he'd been helpful and seemed nice enough from the few dealings she'd had, and had had the good grace not to do a sales pitch to her, she felt uncomfortable about her windfall. It had been hard enough discussing Tristan's and her parents' finances with a stranger.

It had come as a bit of a shock to Hannah to learn that her parents had been well-off. Of course she knew she was born into the lower end of middle class. After all, she lived in a decent suburb not far from the city, but only her father had worked and as far as she'd seen he hadn't progressed beyond middle-management. If only they were here for her to say how proud she was of them. But of course, she wouldn't even if they were still alive.

Hannah hadn't told anyone exactly how much she'd ended up with. She was still struggling to come to terms with the figures involved and the circumstances. She'd paid off the mortgage and put the rest of the money in the highest interest account she could find while she gathered the necessary courage to book in to see the financial adviser or one of the others recommended by friends. Rob and Sam and Raelene and Adrian had all echoed Beth's sentiments about taking care of her own financial needs first and not making any life-changing decisions – financial or otherwise – for at least twelve months.

Her parents had raised her to be careful with money and she'd married a man with the same values. She'd never be a reckless spender. The only things she'd bought that she'd consider to be big-ticket items were a new electric mower and whipper snipper so she didn't have to deal with the smelly fuel anymore and so much noise. She was secretly a little proud of herself for going off to the shop alone and making her purchases. It was probably run of the mill for most people, but not Hannah, who had come to realise what a sheltered life she'd led – and in some ways would continue to lead thanks to the financial legacy.

But with all the milestones she'd faced and pushed on through, one stopped her in her tracks.

It was Saturday morning and she was just finishing breakfast when her phone rang with an unfamiliar number on the display.

'Hello, Hannah speaking,' she said.

'Is that Mrs Hannah Ainsley, wife of Tristan Ainsley and daughter of Daniel and Daphne White?'

'Yes.'

'This is Constable Smith at Brunswick Police Station. I have available for collection the belongings that were in the car, your, um, relatives were travelling in, when it, um, crashed. The investigation has now been completed.'

'Oh. Right.'

'Please come to the reception desk and talk to the officer on duty. You'll need identification. There are two boxes for collection.' The policeman seemed to let out a relieved sigh. She felt for him. He was probably the most junior on that day and had drawn the short straw.

'Okay. Thank you.'

'After fourteen days they'll be sent down to lost property and you'll have to …'

'It's all right. I'll come and get them now.'

Hannah's heart began to race. She hadn't heard anything about the investigation. Tristan's parents had agreed to be the go-between with police, and she'd made it clear to them she didn't want to know any of the details. Like Raelene and Adrian had said – and pretty much everyone, except Sam who admitted to being nosey by nature – whatever she found out wouldn't bring them back from the dead, so there was no point knowing. Hannah had quickly formed the same view. It was odd that the constable had called her to collect the things. Perhaps it was because Raelene and Adrian were interstate. Perhaps it was a case of two departments in the police service not communicating with each other. But it didn't really matter, did it? The fact was she'd received the call.

Her first instinct was to call Rob to ask if he'd go on her behalf. But then she reminded herself how much stronger she'd become. No, she really needed to do this herself. And, anyway, they'd said she had to bring ID.

I can do this. I can and I will. Hannah grabbed her handbag and keys. She glanced at her attire of track pants, t-shirt and runners in the hall mirror. Not ideal, but it would have to do. If she went and got changed now she might lose her nerve.

★

Hannah felt tense and apprehensive as she walked through the automatic glass doors and up to the desk. Her hands shook as she plucked her driver's licence from her wallet and placed it on the counter.

'Hello, how can I help you?' the uniformed officer behind the desk asked. Hannah recognised the voice. And his nametag confirmed this was Constable Smith.

'Hello, Constable Smith. You called me a little while ago. I'm Hannah Ainsley. I've come to collect my, um, deceased husband's and parents' belongings from …'

'Ah, yes. They're just here,' he said. He reached down and brought up one cardboard archive box and then another.

Hannah looked at them wondering how she was going to get both to the car in one trip.

'Sorry, I can't offer to carry them for you – I'm not allowed to leave the desk,' Constable Smith said, sounding genuinely apologetic.

'It's okay. I'm just parked around the corner. How heavy are they?'

'Not very, probably just a bit awkward.'

'I might have to make two trips.'

'That's fine.'

Hannah checked the weight of each box.

'Actually, I think I can manage. You're right, they're not too bad.'

She put the heavier of the two on the floor and the other on top and then gripped the cut-out handles of the bottom one and hoisted the boxes up.

'Thank you,' she said to the officer as she turned to leave.

'You're welcome. All the best.'

Parked back in her driveway, Hannah found she couldn't get out of the car. It was a cold day and she was enjoying the warmth of the sun streaming through the windows. She also felt as if she'd used all her energy to make the journey to the police station and back – and all her courage. Now she was afraid of the boxes sitting on the floor and seat beside her. While she had a certain level of curiosity about their contents, she was also afraid of them upsetting the little equilibrium she'd managed to achieve.

She looked up, slightly startled, when she heard a tap on the window. Her heart surged at seeing Beth.

'Sorry, I was just taking a moment,' she said, opening the door and getting out of the car.

'Are you okay? Has something happened?'

'I've just been to the police station to pick up everything that was in Tristan's car when it, um, you know …' She pointed to the boxes.

'Oh, darling. You didn't need to do that alone. You should have called me.'

'I thought I was fine to do it. I am fine, really, it just took more out of me than I'd expected.' Though, the longer Hannah stood there, the worse she was feeling. Her legs were even beginning to shake.

'Well, you are looking a bit pale. You've clearly had a shock,' Beth said. 'Come on, it's cold out here, let's get you inside. Can I manage one of those, do you think?'

'That would be good, thanks. They're not heavy at all,' Hannah said, handing Beth the lightest of the two boxes.

Hannah walked inside and through to the lounge in a slight daze. Seated, she stared at the boxes now in front of her on the floor as Beth fossicked around in the kitchen. Soon she came in with a glass of milk – which Hannah hoped contained a decent dose of brandy – and a cup of tea that most likely had two teaspoons of sugar. She accepted the milk, in which she immediately detected the subtle smell of brandy, and drank it.

'Thanks. You don't need to look so worried, I'm okay. Really. As you said, it was just a bit of a shock, that's all. I thought the police had given Raelene and Adrian all of their personal effects and they'd passed them onto me just after it happened. You know, jewellery, wallets, Mum's handbag.'

'So what's in these then?'

'They said they're things from the car. I'm guessing whatever was in the boot and the police only found them when they started investigating and then they were kept somewhere as evidence. It's most likely Tristan's first-aid kit, a couple of bottles of water and maybe some jumper leads – that sort of thing.'

'Aren't you going to look? Check there's nothing important?'

'I guess. Though it's been nearly four months, I doubt there's anything important.' She took the lid off of the closest box and peered inside.

'Oh!' she exclaimed.

'What is it?'

'Christmas presents,' she said, bringing out a colourfully wrapped box. Her heart clenched and the all too familiar lump rose into her throat at seeing 'Dearest Hann. Lots of love from Dad xxx' written in her father's rough scrawl on the gift tag.

'Oh, Hannah, darling,' Beth said, putting her arm around her.

Hannah's chin wobbled as she stared at the battered parcel for a moment before putting it aside and pulling out the next one.

While she could concentrate on how much she had loved Christmas her whole life and opening presents, Hannah could forget for a moment the tragic truth behind these. And the fact that most likely in the bottom of one of these boxes was a small pile of carefully folded and pressed tea towels and aprons that might just have the faintest trace of her mother's scent on them. While Hannah desperately wanted to experience that again, she just as strongly didn't want to. Not right now, anyway.

One by one she tore the wrapping from each of the six presents she'd lined up on the floor at her feet – three from her father and three from her mother. First was a box containing a pair of expensive-looking Merrell hiking boots. *Odd*, Hannah thought, and moved onto the next parcel, which contained two pairs of thick, charcoal-coloured wool and possum socks.

'Were you planning a hiking tour somewhere?' Beth asked.

'Not that I know of. This is weird.'

The final parcel to her from her dad contained two finely knitted wool tops – one black and one pink – and a pair of black leggings. She handed them to Beth.

'These look like thermals to me,' Beth offered after close inspection.

'I'm a born and bred Melbournian. I have all the winter wear I need. And I've never needed thermals. What's this all about?'

'No idea, sweetie,' Beth replied. 'Perhaps there's an explanation in one of those other parcels.'

'Oh, look,' Hannah said, her eyes filling with tears as she pulled from the torn wrapping a hand-knitted beanie in the softest, most gorgeous dark pink and grey wool, and then a matching scarf and gloves. The knot in her heart pulled tighter and tighter as each piece was revealed. She held the garments to her tightly before bringing them up to her nose. She breathed – could she detect the slightest trace of her mother's perfume on them? Her rose-scented hand cream, maybe? If Hannah had been alone, she'd have given into a bout of weeping. 'I didn't even know she'd been knitting,' she said with a gulp.

'I think that's rather the point, dear, it was meant to be a surprise,' Beth said.

'But I don't understand. Mum and Dad gave up buying me clothes years ago.'

'There's definitely a theme here. Perhaps Tristan was planning on taking you to the snow.'

'We went to Mount Hotham the other year and I nearly froze.'

'Well maybe he was planning on taking you back and you *not* nearly freezing. Or perhaps a holiday overseas to beat the summer heat here, then?'

'Tristan had a fear of flying, he was practically phobic, and I've never been on a plane. I can't imagine him deciding on a long-haul flight without at least discussing it.'

'I had no idea. Golly. Really?'

'Yes. Before I met him I never had the need to fly anywhere. Then when we were married we always did road trips back to South Australia to visit his mum and dad so we'd have the car. Any travelling we've done has only been local. We briefly discussed seeing if he could be hypnotised or something so we could go overseas for our honeymoon, but we changed our minds. Our priority has always been saving to buy the house and paying it off as quickly as possible.'

'Very sensible. Perhaps the clue is in those other presents – the ones from Daniel to Daphne and vice versa. Maybe Tristan had got help with his phobia and thought it was time to treat yourselves.'

Hannah felt unsettled at the possibility of Tristan keeping something so big back from her. She thought they'd always been open with each other and never had any secrets.

She picked up another parcel. 'It doesn't feel right to open a present addressed to someone else.'

'No. It's entirely up to you – if you want to know or not.'

'Oh well, here goes.'

From her mother to her father was another set of warm knitted garments – this time in navy blue. Hannah bit her lip in an effort not to cry as she pictured him in them. And she almost smiled at how her father would have feigned surprise upon opening them because no doubt Daphne had sat on the chair beside him for months knitting his Christmas present.

Her father had given Hannah's mother a pair of lovely warm-looking wool-lined leather gloves, socks, and hiking boots very similar to those Hannah had been given. God, they'd spent a fortune. They'd always given thoughtful, meaningful but generally inexpensive gifts. They'd certainly gone all out this year.

Hannah looked at Beth with raised eyebrows.

'Definitely looks like a family holiday to me. And to somewhere cold.'

'Mum must have been knitting all year to get these done.'

Hannah continued unwrapping. There was another set of knitted pieces to Tristan from her parents – this time in charcoal grey. There was also a wallet from Daniel to Tristan.

'Golly, even I wouldn't dare give Tris a wallet – it's such a personal choice. Dad was game.' There were no more presents to unwrap, and still no definite clues. It was all very strange.

'Hang on,' Hannah said. 'I've just remembered something. I'll be back in a sec.'

She went into the garage and stared at the bag of wrapped presents she'd been avoiding for the past few months, just beside the boxed tree and decorations.

As she fossicked through the gifts, she was surprised to find some marked from Tristan to each of her parents. That was weird – she and Tristan had always chosen their gifts together, or at least discussed what Hannah was going to buy for her parents. Finally she plucked out the gifts from Tristan to her – the ones she hadn't opened after finding the ladybird charm. Now even more puzzled, she went back inside, unloaded the presents onto the floor in front of a startled Auntie Beth, and sat down to begin unwrapping.

'I couldn't bring myself to open them before,' she explained.

'Are you sure you're able to now?'

'No. I haven't been sure of anything since Christmas Day and probably won't be ever again, Auntie Beth, but I think I need to do this.'

'Fair enough.'

Tears filled her eyes again as she drew out a puffy down-filled coat in the most beautiful purple colour.

'It's gorgeous, but we're not supposed to spend that much,' she said.

'Lovely. He was definitely planning on taking you somewhere cold,' Beth said thoughtfully, as if to herself.

'The fact that this is from Tristan to my dad is weird in itself, but look,' she said, holding up a wallet very similar to the one from Daniel to Tristan.

'Still no notes of explanation. And this is the last one – from Tris to Mum. It's all too strange. And I've no idea why he'd take the risk of choosing a handbag for her,' she said, holding it up.

'Maybe she chose it and told him which one she wanted.'

'But I thought she only liked leather. This isn't her at all, is it? It's very plain,' Hannah said, handing the black bag to Beth to examine. As soon as the words left her mouth Hannah felt terrible for being critical. It was as bad as speaking ill of the dead, wasn't it? But she was so confused. And sad all over again. Damn these setbacks.

'Oh,' Beth said, sounding a little excited. 'I know what that is. It's for travelling. Look, it's got special pockets for protecting your credit cards from people skimming or whatever it's called when they walk past and steal your information and money electronically. And look, this strap has a cable in it so it can't be slashed and stolen. Rosemary had one similar on the cruise. See, it's all here on the tag. Clearly Tristan and your parents were planning a family getaway somewhere cold and overseas,' Beth said triumphantly.

'But I would have found details in the paperwork – I've been through everything and there's no travel agent or big credit-card expenses.'

'As you've pointed out, Tristan wasn't the sort of fellow who would go too far with planning something so big without discussing it with you.'

'I wonder where he wanted to go.'

'Not a Caribbean cruise, I'm guessing,' Beth said, with a knowing smile.

'Yes, well done, Sherlock,' Hannah said, grinning despite herself.

'London, the USA?'

'I don't know. But surely he wouldn't take me anywhere cold, I struggle with Melbourne's winter as it is.'

'You wouldn't feel cold decked out in all this lot, which I gather was the idea. Perhaps he was looking at the off-season so it's not as expensive. And skating in Central Park looks so romantic in all the movies. Maybe he was thinking of a white Christmas.'

'But we always have — had — Christmas together with Mum and Dad.'

'You're forgetting the matching sets of woollies, dear. Perhaps you were all meant to go.'

'Hmm. So typical of Mum to sort out everyone else first and put herself last. I wonder if she was planning to knit a set for herself. I didn't find any with her things.'

'Sadly, sweetie, we'll probably never know. Nor what the actual plans were. Please don't dwell on it.'

'Mum always wanted to go to London,' Hannah said sadly. 'I bet Tris was trying to make that happen — that's the sort of sweet thing he'd have done. God, I miss them.'

'I know.' Beth wrapped her arms around Hannah who crumpled into her ample chest.

Chapter Twenty-one

Hannah's phone rang.

'Hi, Jasmine. How are you?'

'Did you know there are reporters outside your house?'

'What? No.' Hannah went to the lounge room window and peered through the gap in the curtains. She was shocked to see three people carrying notepads and microphones and three more standing behind large cameras on tripods. 'What would they want with me?'

'You know the media, they like to put faces to tragedies – bad news selling and all that.'

'It's been over nine months. Why now?'

'Well, I did see a small piece in the paper the other day about the trial starting soon for the trucking company because the driver's claiming poor maintenance was at fault, not his driving. I would have mentioned it, but I thought you preferred not to know.'

'Thanks. And, yes, I don't want to know anything about it. I'm going to damn well go out and give them a piece of my mind. How the hell do they know where I live, anyway?'

'Hang on a sec. Don't engage with them. You've been doing so well, you don't want a crazed version of your lovely face splashed across the TV tonight or newspapers tomorrow. And you know what the media can be like with twisting words or taking things out of context. Just grab your handbag and let's go and enjoy our lunch – smile politely, thank them for their interest, but say you have no comment.'

'God, I'm shaking. I don't know if I'm scared or angry,' she said.

'Repeat after me: Thank you, I have no comment.'

'Ever!'

'Say it.'

Hannah did.

'Good. Now grab your handbag, lock the door behind you and come out and get in the car. We're already a bit late.'

Hannah hesitated with her hand on the door when the three reporters called to her as they ambled up the driveway. She almost laughed at how much it wasn't like what appeared on movies or TV – the rush, jostling for position and microphones being thrust in people's faces. But they did all call her name at once and ask a flurry of questions.

'Mrs Ainsley, do you hope the driver goes to jail?'

'Mrs Ainsley, what punishment do you think the trucking company deserves?'

'Mrs Ainsley, Hannah, how do you feel about knowing the accident that killed your loved ones was preventable?'

Hannah locked the screen door behind her and then stood on the porch for a moment, torn between racing to Jasmine's car parked at the kerb and responding to the reporters' questions. She wanted to ask them why they were interested in her and why they thought it was okay to disrupt her life further. And she wanted to tell the cameramen to watch where they were putting their bloody feet – they were close to trampling on her mother's roses. She hoped they got pricked by the thorns. But as she stared at the reporters inching closer she realised they looked to be barely out of school. Most likely it was hard enough for them to be there without Hannah tearing strips off them.

'I have no comment at this time. Thank you,' she said, ducked past them, walked quickly down the path, and got into Jasmine's car.

Normally she and Jasmine hugged in greeting. Today Jasmine checked her mirrors and pulled away from the kerb quickly without a word as soon as Hannah had shut the car door.

'Well, that was interesting,' Jasmine finally said after they'd navigated the winding, narrow streets of the suburb and were on a main road.

'Yes, just bloody brilliant.'

★

'Looks like they've given up on you,' Jasmine said when they returned. They'd lingered over their lunch, which Hannah had been too distracted to fully enjoy, had wandered through a couple of stunning interior-design shops and then had stopped by the supermarket on their way back. It was now dark – still Hannah's least favourite part of the day.

'Good,' Hannah said, letting out a small sigh of relief. She wasn't sure how she'd feel knowing strangers were lurking outside her house while she tried to sleep. She reminded herself this wasn't Hollywood. And these were media, not paparazzi.

'Do you want me to come in with you?'

'Thanks, but I'll be fine.' The truth was Hannah would love nothing more than for Jasmine to come in and never leave. While she was getting used to being on her own and was no longer afraid, she couldn't say she enjoyed it. 'I'm really sorry I was such bad company.'

'You weren't. A little distracted at times, maybe, but it's okay – and totally understandable. You just call if you need anything. I can send big, burly Craig around if they come back and start giving you grief.'

'Thanks, I'll let you know. You're the best,' she said, hugging her friend.

As she waved Jasmine off and walked up the path, Hannah found herself imagining the media misconstruing Craig's presence and painting her as the widow who'd moved on too quickly. She shook her head at the absurdity of her thoughts and then almost snorted. She wouldn't put anything past them. She hadn't thought for a second they'd turn up here, but they had. She shouldn't be so cynical, but it was hard not to be. The whole world knew that negative and sensationalist news sold. They'd probably left her alone for so long so they wouldn't look too bad.

Hannah had just finished putting her few groceries away when the home phone rang.

'Hello.'

'Hi, Hannah, it's Raelene. How's things?'

Hannah immediately tensed a little. Tristan's parents were creatures of habit. They only ever rang on a Sunday evening. Today was Saturday.

'Pretty good, thanks.' It was Hannah's standard answer. People didn't really want to know how you actually felt, even family. It was only a figure of speech and it wasn't fair to lay the catalogue of your woes at their feet.

'Look, we just wanted to call and warn you. We've had the media here trying to question us.'

'Me too. They were here this morning. I found it a little confronting, to be honest.'

'That's understandable.'

'Apparently legal proceedings are starting. Did you know?'

'Yes. I thought you didn't want to know any of the details. That's why we ...'

'I don't. It just came as a bit of a shock.'

'Sorry about that.'

'There's no need for you to apologise. Why are they interested in us, anyway?' Hannah asked.

'A few of them came to the house after the funeral. We sent them away.'

'Oh. Thank you. I had no idea.'

'That was the point, dear,' Raelene said.

'So why are they back now?'

'I think with the trucking company in the frame it's going to become a pretty big story,' Raelene said. 'They always like some human emotion to colour the technical details and evidence. So be prepared.'

'Were you interviewed, um, last time?'

'Yes. And it was clearly a slow news week because they pestered us. Sat at the gate until we said something. I got really annoyed with them, which of course got reported. There was the most dreadful picture of me in the paper – I looked like a crazy woman. I can laugh about it now – well, almost ...'

'I was polite, but I told them I have no comment.' Hannah sent a silent blessing to Jasmine for her wisdom.

'As you have every right to. But I'm sure they'll be back. And don't burn the bridge, because one day you might just want to tell your story.'

'I have no story.'

'Well, you do as far as the media is concerned. You're a ...'

'Please don't say victim,' Hannah said with a groan.

'All right. But, sweetheart, you are a casualty in all this. It's changed your whole life. And you're doing really well. It's entirely up to you if you speak to them or not. Whatever you decide, we'll support you.'

'I don't have anything to say to them.'

'That's okay. And you can always change your mind later. As we've said a million times, you have to do what you feel is right for *you*, not anyone else. Look, I'm sure you're exhausted from having to think about all this. I know we are. I'll leave you now. And if you need us, just call.'

'Thanks so much. Having your support means the world,' Hannah said, choking up.

'And you mean the world to us. If you want to escape, you're welcome to visit. We're in beautifully warm, sunny Townsville at the moment. I hear Melbourne still hasn't got into the swing of spring yet.'

'Okay, don't rub it in. It was a maximum of fifteen degrees here today,' she said with a laugh, grateful for the opportunity to talk about lighter topics. If she didn't have to work on Monday, she might seriously consider it. The lingering cold weather wasn't really bothering her, she was gloomy enough as it was, but perhaps a change of scenery would help. 'Have you seen anything interesting this week?'

'Lots of sunshine!' There was a voice in the background. 'And Adrian says more bloody flowers,' Raelene said, laughing.

Hannah smiled. Adrian was always ribbing Raelene good-naturedly about how all she wanted to see everywhere they went were gardens and Raelene was always ribbing him about him only wanting to see museums.

'I'd better let you go before it turns into a domestic,' Hannah said.

'Good idea.'

'Thanks so much for the call.'

'You're welcome. And just remember, like with everything you've been through this year, there is no right or wrong. You just do what feels right to you. Nothing you say can change what's happened.'

'Thanks. I will.'

★

In the morning, Hannah woke feeling groggy and headachy, but with an idea. During her tossing and turning throughout the night she'd decided that perhaps a change of scenery *was* what she needed. When she thought about it, she and Tristan would have had at least two weekends away by now – for their anniversary and his birthday. She wasn't sure she could quite muster the courage to take a week off work and not have that security anchor, but she could stay in a city hotel for a few nights for a change.

The more she considered it the more excited she became. She and Tristan had spent a couple of weekends playing tourists in their own city. They'd had a great time. It wouldn't be the same without him, but she could at least try. A little voice inside her said she owed it to him – and her parents – to move on. Begin to live again. She could almost hear them all lecturing her: *Enough is enough, Hann. You need to get back out there and learn to smell the roses again.*

She stretched, responding to the strange feeling of awakening spreading through her. She got out her laptop, brought up the hotel booking site and put in today's date for check-in. She hesitated over the check-out date. Was a week in a nice hotel over the top? Most of them were more than two hundred dollars a night. She'd never splurged like this in her life. Should she spend so much? At this stage it was only a date, a number – it could be changed. At least it was a starting point.

The masses of options that turned up were almost overwhelming. There were pages of lovely hotels for great prices. How could she choose? And then she remembered Jasmine saying she always used the surprise hotel feature if it was available. She'd explained that that way she couldn't be disappointed with her choice – because she hadn't actually chosen. Why the hell not? And why not a week? *I can afford it*, Hannah thought, in a wave of bravado, and clicked on the option.

She felt pleased with herself as she printed out the booking sheet, but also sad that she'd be staying at The Hotel Windsor without Tristan. They'd stayed there on their wedding night. Again she found herself wondering what Sam would make of this coincidence. Even Hannah had to admit it was a little spooky that the surprise hotel turned out to be The Windsor – it was like drawing a name out of a hat.

She was relieved to see there was no media waiting outside her house when she made her way with her suitcase to the yellow taxi waiting at the kerb. She knew she'd probably packed far too much for just a week, only a few suburbs from home, but didn't think it would matter.

'Hello. The Windsor Hotel, thank you.'

Chapter Twenty-two

Hannah was prepared to drop her bag off and go exploring, but was pleasantly surprised to find her room was ready early and she could head on up. Walking along the long corridor from the lift, past the sweeping staircase with its landing of beautiful old tessellated tiles, she was again saddened at remembering her last visit with Tristan. But she also felt comforted at finding everything just the same. And while the grand old hotel had all the modern conveniences, it also had a lovely warmth and ambiance that you didn't tend to find in the modern four- and five-star hotels.

She slid the card into the reader and opened the door to her room. As she took in the patterned carpet and matching curtains with their swag and tails, she let out a contented sigh. It was exactly as she remembered from five years ago.

She put her case in the small walk-in robe, tucked her key away in her handbag and left. If she sat on the bed and allowed herself to think too much she might become mopey and never leave.

★

She returned the doorman's friendly greeting and stood on the footpath for a moment as she decided whether to turn left or right. To her left, the free city-circle tram was approaching on its clockwise lap. She checked for cars and raced across to the stop. She hadn't caught this tram for years and had never done a full lap. But today she was pretending to be a tourist and was happy to step up into the old rattler.

She settled into the last available seat amongst people talking in different languages and snapping away with their cameras and taking selfies with their mobile phones.

Hannah didn't do selfies and hadn't been on Facebook for months. After using it to contact people en masse for the funeral and wake – which Sam had taken charge of anyway – she'd only logged in a couple of times. She'd found it too sad and depressing to see everyone posting the same news and everything going on as usual, regardless of what she'd lost and how much her life had changed. A couple of times she'd even considered closing down her account, but it was a good link to people she wasn't in contact with day to day. And now that she was starting to get out more, perhaps there might actually be events posted she'd be interested in going to.

Hannah resisted getting off and walking down Flinders Lane to check out the many art galleries for Sam. She didn't want a mission, just wanted to wander and see what she found. Perhaps she'd go there next Saturday.

The biggest change Hannah saw was at the west end of the city, which had been densely developed with tall apartment blocks since she'd last been there. There were also restaurants and a shopping precinct. Hannah wondered what it would be like to live in a high-rise city apartment in the Docklands area.

While she didn't really enjoy tending to her large garden, she did enjoy sitting out in the backyard. Here there were outdoor communal areas for residents, but while Hannah thought that was all good in theory, she wondered how many people really wanted to sit with strangers. She wouldn't mind betting, not many.

The other thing she realised she liked about having a yard was sleeping in sheets that had been hung outside in the sun to dry. She smiled at conjuring up the smell of warmed linen. It was one of her favourites. Did they smell the same out of a dryer?

The tram rattled on, stopping and starting, people getting on and off. Hannah found the movement, the noise, and the commentary mesmerising and the sun streaming in the window was making her sleepy.

She didn't think she'd actually fallen asleep, but was surprised to realise she was nearing the end of her lap. She got off one stop before where she'd got on and, after overcoming the shock of the icy blast of air that hit her, headed down La Trobe Street and then towards the Queen Victoria Market, which she hadn't been to in years.

The stalls weren't as interesting as she remembered, but she found some Italian coffee and pastries.

Realising she hadn't checked her phone for hours, she began digging for it in the bottom of her bag. Just as she turned it on it began to ring. 'Jasmine mobile' was brightly lit on the screen.

'Hi, Jas. How's things?'

'Good. Are you okay? It's just I've tried calling a couple of times. I was worried after yesterday so I popped around, too.'

'God, sorry. I've had it turned off in case the media might have somehow got the number. I'm fine. I'm actually in the city playing tourist.'

'Oh, what fun.'

'Yes. I decided to be brave and book myself into The Windsor for a few nights.'

'Good for you. Well done. Ooh, I'm jealous, though, I've always wanted to try their high tea.'

'Would you fancy doing that with me next Saturday?'

'I'd absolutely love to, but I'm afraid next Saturday's out for me. Anyway, I don't like your chances – they've been known to be booked out for months.'

'Oh, well, another time. Hey, sorry about not letting you know I was away.'

'Don't be silly – you're a grown woman, Hannah, you can do exactly as you wish. So, what have you seen and done?'

'Nothing special, just checking out the usual sights, really. But I'm having fun being in a different environment.'

'Listen to you being so adventurous.'

'I'm not sure wandering the streets of Melbourne counts as an adventure, but I am enjoying myself. And, you know, it's not as bad doing it on my own as I thought it would be.'

'That's wonderful to hear. I'm proud of you. So, tell me where you are and what you're doing right now – other than talking to me.'

'I'm actually standing outside a real-estate agent's office reading the ad for a fabulous looking warehouse conversion.'

'God, you Melbournians and your obsession with real estate!'

'I bet it's the same in Sydney. Anyway, you're one of us now, don't forget!'

'Haha, you're probably right about that. And, yes, yes I am!'

'Don't worry, I'm not signing up for anything.'

'It's brilliant to hear you sounding so upbeat, especially after yesterday. I'll let you go. Enjoy apartment hunting.'

'Hang on, aren't you one of the many telling me not to make any major decisions in the first twelve months?'

'It doesn't hurt to look. And I'm not about to let you sell your gorgeous house without some serious grilling. I'd better go. We're heading out for a curry.'

'Enjoy. Thanks for the call. And, s ...'

'Don't you dare apologise again, Hannah. As long as I know you're okay and having fun, I'm happy. Enjoy!'

'Thanks. Speak soon.'

Hannah hung up feeling good. She took a snap of the advertisement of the warehouse with her phone before moving off on a lighter step. There was so much to see in the city – she hadn't even visited any of the interesting laneways yet. She was almost disappointed that she'd be back at work tomorrow.

When she returned to her room, Hannah was exhausted. She toyed with getting into her pyjamas and ordering room service for dinner and staying in, even though it was only a quarter to six. The meals on the menu sounded divine. But she told herself that this trip – if she could call it that – was about pushing at least a little beyond her comfort zone. She decided that if she braved the hotel restaurant on her own for dinner she was allowed to eat in her room every other night that week if she wanted to.

★

Having showered and changed, Hannah waited at the restaurant's reception desk, feeling nervous and self-conscious. The room was practically empty. She wasn't sure what was worse – to sit alone in a full restaurant or an empty one.

'Table for one?' the smiling young woman asked.

'Yes, please.'

'Do you have a reservation?'

'No. Is that okay?'

'It's fine. No problem at all. Come this way.'

Hannah noticed a man sitting alone at a small table as she was led to another small table in front of him. She stopped short when he spoke.

'Excuse me. If you're dining alone, would you like to join me?' He stood up and laid his white linen napkin on the table.

'Oh. Well. I …'

He raised his hands as if in a gesture of surrender. 'Please don't think I'm hitting on you. I can see you're married. It's just that I prefer not to eat alone, if it can be helped,' he said, smiling kindly at her.

As Hannah looked down at her wedding ring a jolt ran through her.

'It's entirely up to you. And there would be no hard feelings if you'd rather not …'

She took in his appearance: wedding ring, late thirties to early forties, dark hair beginning to grey, brown eyes, average height, well-cut suit, nice blue and white shirt in large check, no tie. He didn't seem like a serial killer. And she was in a public place.

'Thank you. Some company would be good. I'll sit here, if that's okay,' she said to the waitress.

'Great. Welcome. Brad Thomas,' he said, holding out his hand.

'Hannah Ainsley,' she said, accepting his grasp.

As she sat, Hannah felt a surge of gratitude to this man for his forwardness. He was much braver than her. She hoped his wife wouldn't mind if she knew.

'Lovely to meet you. So, Hannah, what brings you to Melbourne?'

'I actually live here. Well, a few suburbs out. I've treated myself to a bit of a break.'

'Brilliant. Well, you couldn't have chosen a more charming hotel. And the food's great, too.'

'I agree. My husband and I stayed here on our wedding night five years ago.'

Hannah cursed the question, 'So where is he?' that was left hanging in the air. She was relieved when the waitress returned with the menu and bread rolls. It was a well-timed distraction.

'Would you like to share a bottle of wine?' Brad asked.

'Thanks, but I don't think I'll drink.'

'Fair enough. Do you mind if I have a glass?'

Why would I mind? Better yet, why would I tell you if I did? I don't even know you. 'Not at all.' Her puzzlement must have shown.

'I don't want to make you feel uncomfortable if you're a recovering alcoholic or something,' Brad explained.

'Oh, right. No, nothing like that. I've just been through a lot and ...'

'It has something to do with your husband not being here, doesn't it?'

'Yes. He was killed in a car accident along with my parents last Christmas.' Hannah was a little surprised at how matter-of-fact her words sounded. But she felt guilty at seeing his expression, which she was having trouble reading. He was slightly flushed.

'God, how awful.'

'Sorry, I didn't mean to make you feel uncomfortable.'

'I'm the one who should apologise – for being so damned nosey. Hazard of the job, I'm afraid.'

'Oh? What is it you do?'

'Journalist.'

Hannah stiffened and a chill ran the length of her spine. Had he been here when she'd arrived, followed her all day?

'Are you okay?'

'I think I should eat alone, after all,' she said. She wanted to get up, but was gripped with an even greater desire to not make a scene. She looked around the restaurant that was now quite full. If the waitress came over, she'd tell her she was leaving and would eat in her room. But she was at the other side of the room with her back to Hannah.

'I'm not sure how, but clearly I've touched a nerve. Or my profession has. Please don't go. Come on, we're not all bad. I'm a freelancer, anyway, if that helps.'

There was something disarming about his smile. And he had kind eyes. Hannah would put money on him being good at his job and getting information out of people who were initially reluctant to give it.

'I mainly write about business and the economy,' he added.

Hannah softened. She was overreacting. He hadn't been outside her house yesterday morning. And he was either a very good actor or he hadn't known who she was at all.

Suddenly the waitress appeared to take their orders. Hannah ordered the pork belly and plain water and settled back into her seat.

'Sorry. Yes, you did touch a nerve,' she said when the waitress had taken Brad's order of steak and glass of Shiraz, and left them.

'Do you want to talk about it? Obviously off the record.'

'Does that even mean anything: "off the record"?' She barely stopped herself from scoffing at him.

'It does to me. So, I take it you've recently had a run-in with a journalist. Is this to do with your family's car accident?' Hannah nodded. She sighed to herself. She couldn't really close the box now it was so far open without appearing rude, could she?

'Yesterday journalists turned up at my house. Apparently a court case is about to start, but I haven't kept up with any of the details – I haven't wanted to know. Anyway, it came as a bit of a shock. It's coming up to ten months, for goodness sake! Anyway, a truck was involved and apparently now the trucking company is being charged over faulty maintenance, or something. As I said, I don't really know anything about it, and I don't want to.'

'I hate to tell you this, but court cases can drag on for years. And the media always wants to show the human impact of these things. So, I'm afraid, unless you're planning on moving in here permanently, you might have to put up with the odd journalist turning up on your doorstep now and then, and asking questions.'

'Well, aren't you a ray of sunshine?'

'Maybe if you gave an interview – an exclusive – they'd leave you alone.'

'You mean with you? I thought you wrote about business and economics.'

'I do. But I'm freelance, so I'm not locked in to any one subject or publication. And, yes, if you felt comfortable with me.'

'But I don't want to be seen as a victim.'

'Whether you like it or not, you are, to some extent. And maybe you can help other people with what they're going through by speaking out.'

I'm no crusader and I certainly have no desire to become famous for this! Hannah thought. She'd seen it happen so often on TV and in the papers – a victim or their family speaking to the media and then becoming a household name.

'God, the last thing I want is to become a spokesperson.' Hannah noticed a few people look up. She'd raised her voice without realising. And, again, she was overreacting. 'Sorry.'

'I wasn't saying that at all. Look, no one is telling you to *do* or *be* anything. I'm certainly not – I don't know you. But hiding from what you've been through – whether it be physically, here in a hotel, or mentally or emotionally, or however, might not help you in the long run. If that's what you're doing. Just saying. Maybe talking about it can help you heal. Here, take my card for if you ever change your mind and decide you do want to tell your story.'

'Thanks. I'll think about it,' she said, accepting the card and feeling the need to be kinder. And polite. He really did seem like a nice man.

'And, now, I'm not going to say another word about it and we're going to enjoy our meals together. Cheers,' he said, raising his glass and smiling at her.

'Cheers,' she said, raising her glass. 'Nice to meet you.'

'Even if I am a journalist?'

'Yes.'

'So, what is it you do?'

★

Hannah was surprised to check her watch and find it was closing in on ten o'clock. The restaurant was almost empty again. They'd chattered through their meals, which both had agreed were wonderful, and then shared a chocolate pudding dessert and cheese platter as neither of them could decide between the two.

She'd initially felt a little odd sharing food with a stranger, but then reminded herself she was meant to be stepping outside of her comfort zone, no matter how small those steps. And, anyway, in the last few hours they'd basically covered their life stories. Hannah really hoped he stayed true to his word about their conversation being off the record.

Thankfully an awkward moment over the bill was avoided by the on-the-ball maître d' presenting them each with an account. Hannah had been prepared to pay it all, but had been concerned about revealing her room number. While Brad seemed honest that was a step too far. She might be a novice traveller, but she wasn't naïve.

They walked to the lift together and stepped in.

'Right. I'm on level four. Which one are you?' Brad asked, his finger hovering near the buttons.

'I'm on four as well.'

They rode up in silence.

'I'm this way,' Brad said, pointing to the left.

'I'm that way,' Hannah said, indicating to the right with a slight wave of relief going through her at again not having to disclose her room number. They stood both looking a little awkward.

'Well, I'd better get going. I've got a big day ahead,' Brad said.

'Me too.'

'Thank you so much for keeping me company,' he said.

'Thank you for asking.'

'I have something else to ask,' he said, a little shyly.

'Yes?'

'Would you mind terribly if I hugged you? Just a hug, I promise.'

'Actually, I'd like that.'

Hannah sank into his strong chest and arms. He was the perfect height and he smelled divine – a mixture of manliness, faded after-shave and linen. She'd had plenty of hugs from friends – including men – but they were different. Even Rob, who she thought gave her the best big brotherly type hugs, didn't feel as good as this. She didn't want Brad to let go. And it had nothing to do with sex. He wasn't trying to kiss her; he wasn't stroking her hair. It was just an amazing, comforting bear hug.

Hannah had a lump in her throat when they parted.

'Thank you. I needed that,' she said.

'I thought you might,' he said.

'Good luck with your billionaire tomorrow. And safe travels back to Sydney.'

'Thanks. And you keep on being brave. I'm sure you're a lot more capable than you think. And if there's anything I can do, let me know.'

Chapter Twenty-three

Hannah walked through the city to work thinking about how nice it was to have had breakfast cooked for her, and that she'd be coming back that evening to a cleaned room – all without having to lift a finger. And she didn't have to think about dinner, shop for ingredients or cook and wash up.

Ah, this is the life. And oh how easy would it be to get used to. Though the lack of space might get on her nerves once the novelty wore off. And laundry was expensive to have done in-house. Brad had said people who didn't travel always thought flying and staying at hotels was glamorous.

She'd smiled when she went to bed last night, thinking about him. Meeting him really had had an effect on her. She just wasn't quite sure how, or why. Sam had always said there was a reason for a person entering your life, and leaving it. Hannah didn't want to think about it too much.

Her step was light and she enjoyed the walk, even though the morning air was cold and the frosty wind was whipping about her face. As she waited at each set of lights to cross with the other commuters, she took in her surroundings. Would she like to live right in the city? Maybe a change would be good? But was she brave enough to make such a change?

'Hey, Hannah,' Caitlin said, stepping into the lift.

'Hi Cait, good weekend?'

'Not bad. God, how cold is it out there?'

'Icy,' Hannah agreed.

'I wonder where spring has got to. Wish it would get a move on, I'm so over this weather.'

'Hmm.'

'Hey, I saw you on the news the other night. How was it having the media turn up to your house?'

'A shock.'

'Right. It must be horrible to have it keep coming up when you probably just want to get on with your life.'

'Yeah.'

'What you've been through is bad enough without that — it's not fair,' Caitlin said.

And there's that look, Hannah thought, *the look of concern verging on pity. God, I hate that expression.*

'Thanks.'

They wished each other a good day before heading to their areas on opposite sides of the building. Caitlin's comments left Hannah feeling deflated, but she tried to buoy herself as she hung up her coat and put her handbag away.

As she sat down, for the first time in years she felt she didn't really want to be here. *Just the Monday blues*, she told herself. It would be better when the office filled up and the chatter started. A tremble of fear snuck through her. Unless the chatter was about her and the court case. Should she ask Craig for the week off? She shook it aside. She couldn't let it get to her. It would pass and until it did she'd put on a brave face and answer any questions – not that she had any answers. The looks she got could never be as bad as those she'd received right after the accident.

'Good morning, Hannah,' Craig called, as he went into his office and turned on the lights.

'Morning. Good weekend?'

'Yes thanks. Can you come in here for a sec?'

'Sure,' she said, getting up.

Craig closed the door behind her. 'Take a seat.'

Hannah raised her eyebrows but sat. In the eight years she'd been working for him, Hannah could probably count on two hands the number of times Craig had closed the door behind her and asked her to sit down.

'What's up?'

'Jas tells me you're staying at The Windsor for a few days.'

'Yes, that's right.'

'She also told me about the journalists turning up. I'm sorry you had to go through that.'

'You don't need to be sorry. It's my own fault for not keeping up with that side of things – if I had I wouldn't have got such a fright. But I just didn't want to know. Still don't, really.'

'I can imagine it's pretty confronting.'

'Apparently court cases can go on for years,' she said, for something to say. Craig was looking a little awkward – probably as awkward as she was beginning to feel.

'Look, are you sure you're doing the right thing burying your head in the sand about it?'

Hannah raised her eyebrows again.

'Sorry, I'm making a real hash of this,' he said, rubbing his face. 'I'm talking to you as your friend, not your boss.'

'Okay. Say what you want to say. We've known each other long enough, Craig.'

'Do you think maybe watching the proceedings might help you get some closure?'

'No, I don't. I'm fine.' *I think having my whole family wiped out by a truck was decent enough closure, actually.*

'Right. Well. All right then. So you don't want to take some time off to go along?'

'No thanks. Do *you* think I should be going to court?'

'I honestly don't know, Hannah. And I really couldn't say what I'd do in your position. I just want to make sure you've thought it through.'

'I have, and I do know that attending court won't bring my family back,' Hannah said. 'All it would do is make me a sitting duck for the press.'

'They're not all bad, you know. Maybe it would help to speak to them, tell your side of the story,' he said with a shrug.

'No, thanks.'

'Fair enough. But – and I know you've got plenty of support – but if you'd like to go and you'd like some company, then I'm putting my hand up,' he said.

'Thanks. I really appreciate the offer. But I'm fine. And I'm not going.' Hannah went to get up.

'There's one other thing. I have a favour to ask.'

'Okay.'

'Could you spend Saturday with Jas?'

'Hang on. I suggested we go for high tea on Saturday but she said she's already got something on.'

'Not any more. She was supposed to be with me, but I've been called into an off-site partners meeting in Ballarat.'

'Oh no. I haven't seen it on your calendar or been asked to make any bookings.'

'No, it's last minute and Toby took care of everything direct. But, anyway, it means I won't be able to have lunch or dinner with Jas for her birthday. I know how close you've become and how much she values your friendship and enjoys your company. She doesn't have many other friends in Melbourne. It really would mean a lot to me – and her – if you'd have lunch with her. On me.'

'Does she know I'd be taking your place?'

'I've broken the news I won't be around to take her out. She was naturally disappointed. Please. Do I have to beg?'

'Don't you dare. I'd love to have lunch with Jas. I had no idea it was her birthday soon.'

'No buying presents – she'd be embarrassed.'

'We actually could do high tea at The Windsor, well, more like lunch, really. I checked this morning and they've had two rare cancellations for their noon session. I hadn't decided who else to ask.'

'That's perfect. It's clearly meant to be. So you'll do it?'

'Of course.'

'You're a lifesaver,' he said with obvious relief.

'Having lunch with your wife, who's been very supportive and has become a dear, treasured friend, is hardly an imposition, Craig.'

'Regardless, I owe you one.'

'If you say so.'

'Maybe you can get manicures, or something, too?'

'I'm sure we'll find plenty to do to entertain ourselves for the day. Now, was there anything else?'

'No. And, thanks again. Oh, except can you call Jas and tee up the finer details?'

'No worries.' Hannah returned to her desk to phone Jasmine before starting her work.

*

Hannah had spent most of the day deflecting comments and questions from her colleagues about the court case, and was weary and tense when she headed back to The Windsor. She wondered how she'd cope if it really did go on for years. For ages she'd been counting on things being so different – so much better – after the twelve-month anniversary that was Christmas.

She perked up a bit when she focussed on where she was going and how little effort a delicious meal that night would require. Although, maybe she'd head out to a restaurant if she felt like it, after a shower. If she was feeling brave. There was, after all, a whole city full of great dining to be explored and she was supposed to be playing tourist.

Chapter Twenty-four

'I love this place,' Jasmine said, looking around the foyer of The Windsor after she and Hannah had hugged. 'And I'm so excited about finally having high tea here.'

'Me too. Come on, let's go make pigs of ourselves.'

'Oh, yes please!'

'Thanks so much for this,' Jasmine said when they'd been seated at their table. 'I have to admit I was really disappointed when Craig had to cancel. I know birthdays shouldn't be a big deal at my age, but they kind of are to me – not the presents, of course, but marking it as a special day. Or perhaps I just need an opportunity to try to get Craig to do something romantic for a change. I don't know. Sorry, here's me wittering on and I'm sure birthdays – and every other occasion – are quite awful for you now.'

Pretty much. 'Please don't apologise, Jas, one of the things I like about you is you don't give me that look of pity so many people do, so please don't start now. It is what it is. Don't let me bring down your special day. Cheers,' she said, raising a glass of champagne.

'Cheers. Oh, what fun,' Jasmine said, looking around her at their elegant surroundings. 'So, have you ventured down for dinner or stayed in your room?'

'I ate in last night, but I braved having dinner down here on Sunday.'

'Well done, you. And it wasn't too terrifying?'

'No. I came armed with my book – thanks so much for that tip, by the way. But you'll never guess what.'

'What?'

'There was a man eating alone and he asked me to join him – which I did.'

'Wow.'

'He was nice and, thankfully, he didn't try to flirt with me. Anyway, he's married and just wanted the company. We had a lovely time. You know, it was really nice to talk to a man, and one who didn't know my history. Of course I had to tell him and of course I had to endure the sympathy. But it wasn't too bad. It can't have been – we sat here until almost ten o'clock. I couldn't believe it. And then when we said goodbye he gave me the biggest, nicest, lingering hug. I know it sounds creepy, but it wasn't. The thing is, Jas, I didn't realise how much I've been missing touch. You know, not in the way girlfriends hug. I can't really explain it.'

'I think I know what you mean. So has it awakened a yearning in you?'

'Not for sex, if that's what you mean. God, no. I can't imagine ever wanting to do it with anyone else, let alone actually doing it. It was like Brad blew on a tiny warm coal in my heart that I didn't know was there. But it's left me aching – a different sort of ache – a longing for more. Not more of Brad – well, maybe more hugs. Anyway, he lives in Sydney.'

'Well, I think if you're starting to feel something good deep within it means you're healing.'

'I suppose. But what do I do about it? It's like an itch that needs to be scratched.'

'Er, find a way to scratch it,' Jasmine suggested. 'What about joining an online dating service?'

'And, what, putting on my profile "No sex, just wants to spoon and hug"? Yeah, right.' Hannah looked at Jasmine with raised eyebrows.

'How about: "Fragile widow seeks an affectionate man for friendship and outings"?'

'Wouldn't that be weird?'

'It's your profile. It's entirely up to you what you say you're looking for. That's the point. It can be like a shopping list.'

'How romantic,' Hannah said, rolling her eyes as she lifted her glass to her lips again. 'Anyway, aren't those websites full of desperados and creeps?'

'Don't tell anyone, but Craig and I met online.'

'Oh. I'm so sorry, I didn't mean to ...' Hannah's eyes were wide with wonder.

'It's okay. And you're almost right, there were a lot of creeps to sift through. I went on some pretty ordinary dates, I can tell you. That was years ago, so it might have changed now. Don't you dare let Craig know I told you. Look at me, half a glass of bubbles and I'm spilling all our secrets.'

'I won't tell anyone.' *You have no idea the secrets I'm holding as PA – I'm a veritable vault.*

'The thought of meeting a stranger in a restaurant is terrifying. Far too scary,' Hannah said, taking another sip of champagne. 'Oh, my god, this is amazing,' she said, sighing.

'Don't try to change the subject. And yet, just a few nights ago that's exactly what you did, Hann,' Jasmine said.

'God, I did too. But only by accident.'

'It still counts. Promise you'll tell me if you ever do feel ready, and I'll help.'

'I still can't believe that's how you and Craig met,' Hannah said, shaking her head.

'Well, he's not a bar type of guy and wouldn't have wanted to meet that sort of person, and I'm the same.'

'Weren't there any decent guys in Sydney, though? Moving cities is a pretty big move and a risk.'

'I was ready for a change.'

They watched with wonder as a waiter placed a three-tiered plate stand laden with delicacies on the table between them.

'Thank you,' they both said.

'How beautiful is this? It looks almost too good to eat. Almost,' Hannah said.

'Yes, it's a real work of art. And I bet everything will taste divine,' Jasmine said.

'The question is, where does one start?'

'At the top, with the scones while they're still hot. The instructions on their website say one is meant to start at the top and work one's way down,' Jasmine added, putting on a prim voice.

'Instructions? That's too funny. But helpful.'

'Yes, heaven forbid we do the wrong thing – like touch the sides of the cup with your spoon when stirring.'

'That's a rule? Seriously?'

'Apparently. It was on their video. And no pinkies sticking out.'

'Right. Got it. Clever you, I didn't even think to check how to do it all properly.'

'Well, you probably don't need to.'

'I don't know about that – I was ready to tuck into the sandwiches, being savoury, and then working onto desserts, which I now know is wrong, don't forget.'

'Come on, let's dig in,' Jasmine said, taking one of the scones.

'I'm not sure "dig in" is the appropriate term to use at a high tea, but yes, let's,' Hannah said, grinning and following suit. 'We have to decide what sort of tea we want, too – there's a menu.'

'Oh, decisions, decisions,' Jasmine said.

'Yes, it's a tough life.'

'These are amazing,' Jasmine said, after taking a large bite of her scone covered with thick layers of jam and cream.

'Mmm, incredible.'

★

'What beautiful warm weather,' Jasmine said as they walked out of the hotel and into the sunshine. They'd spent two hours devouring everything on the three tiers and a pot of tea each. 'Are you happy to go for a look down Flinders Lane? There are a few galleries I want to check out.'

'It's your birthday, so we'll do whatever you want to do.' Hannah had been secretly pleased when Jasmine had turned down the suggestion of going and having their nails done, or any other type of pampering.

They were about to walk down the steps into a basement gallery when Hannah was startled to see Sam, with a twin on either side, coming towards her.

'Sam!' she cried, pulling her friend into a hug.

'Hello, Auntie Hann,' Oliver said.

'Hello, boys.'

'Can we have a hug too, please?' Ethan asked.

'Can you ever,' she said, squatting down and wrapping an arm around each of the boys. They seemed to have grown a lot taller.

'Sorry, Jasmine,' she said, releasing the boys. 'Sam, you remember Craig's wife, Jasmine, don't you? She was at the, um …' *Funeral.* Hannah couldn't bear to say the word aloud.

'Yes. Hello. Lovely to see you again,' Sam said, holding out her hand.

'Oliver and Ethan, this is my friend Jasmine,' Hannah said.

'Hello. Nice to meet you,' they both said, holding out a hand.

'So what brings you guys into the city?' Hannah said, looking from the boys to Sam.

'We're having a cultural experience,' Oliver said.

'Yes. And we're being very good and not touching everything. We're allowed to have another ice-cream soon,' Ethan said.

'*Another* one, you're a bit lucky,' Jasmine said.

'Well, we are being *very* good,' Oliver said, indignantly.

'I bet you are.'

Hannah almost laughed at picturing the poor gallery owners' faces when they saw two small boys entering their precious spaces.

'Are you having fun?' Hannah asked.

'Yes, I saw a blue poo,' Ethan said.

'I think it was actually meant to be a glass paperweight,' Sam explained.

Hannah tried not to laugh.

'And what about you, Oliver, are you having fun?'

'Yes. I had an ice-cream with sparkles and a donut for breakfast.'

'Please don't call human services,' Sam said, shaking her head with consternation.

'And then he farted,' Ethan said, and giggled.

'So did you, stupid head.'

'Enough. What are the rules?'

'Seen and not heard,' they said.

'Exactly.'

'Impressive,' Hannah said, grinning.

'Yes, well, we're about to call it a day. I'm not sure what I was thinking bringing them along. I had an urge to get out and the sun was shining.'

'You're an artist, aren't you?' Jasmine asked. 'What are you working on?'

'Well, I try. I'm just getting back into it semi-seriously after having the boys. One day I'd love to actually make some money with my art.'

'She's being far too modest,' Hannah said. 'Sam's very talented.'

Sam shrugged. 'What is it you do, Jasmine?'

'I'm studying interior design. Like you, I hope one day to earn a living from it. What medium do you work with?'

'All sorts. That's the problem, I can't seem to settle on just one thing. I'm all over the place. I came to the galleries today to get some inspiration and see what's selling.'

'A stall at one of the decent art and design markets would be good for building your profile,' Jasmine said. 'I have a friend who sells her photographs at the Sunday Arts Centre Market at Southbank and does really well. I think she's on the committee, too. Maybe she can help, or at least give you some tips. I could give her a call, if you like.'

'Oh, um, er, okay. Thanks very much. So, what are you up to, anyway, Hann?'

'It's Jasmine's birthday and ...'

'Happy birthday.'

'Thanks.'

'We've just had high tea at The Windsor – for lunch.'

'You lucky things. I hope it lived up to all the hype.'

'It certainly did,' Jasmine said.

'Yes, it was incredible,' Hannah said.

'It's so good to see you, I'm sorry I've been so out of touch lately. I'm a bit scatty when I'm in creative mode. Though I fear I've been even worse than usual. Poor Hann knows to just drop the odd text and not expect an instant reply,' Sam explained to Jasmine.

'It's fine. Really. I would have called if I needed you or Rob.' *It's probably actually been good for me to be forced to be more independent, anyway.* 'How is he?'

'He's good. No, actually, he's a bit stressed. Something's going on at work, but I'm not exactly sure what it is. I'm not a very good listener at the moment,' Sam said. 'Anyway, it was great to see you both. I'd better get the little munchkins home while they're still able to walk.'

Hannah's heart nearly melted when she looked at the two boys sitting quietly, side by side on the top step with their hands clasped in their laps.

'Hey, speaking of birthdays, Hann, what are you going to do for yours? Do you still want to come for a quiet evening? You and Craig would be welcome too, Jasmine.'

'Sam, it's months away. You've got to get through the Spring Racing Carnival first.'

'Yes, don't remind me.'

'I've been meaning to ask you, Hannah, if you do anything special for The Cup,' Jasmine asked. 'And what about you, Sam? What do you do on Cup day?'

'Avoiding it like the plague while I pray for the horses and jockeys,' Sam said.

'Sorry?' said Jasmine.

'We're pretty much anti-horse racing, generally, and Sam's quite involved with the campaigns to end the use of whips and jumps events,' Hannah explained.

'Oh. Right.'

'Best you don't get me started. I'm a bit vocal about it.'

'Okay. Fair enough.'

'We went to one of the races while we were at uni and a horse broke its leg and had to be put down right in front of us,' Hannah explained. 'It scarred me for life. I can't bear to watch a horse race now – even on TV.'

'I can't even watch the highlights on the news, even when I know it all ends okay,' Sam said.

'God, I'm not surprised. How awful,' Jasmine said. 'Sounds like watching the interest rate announcement is a much better bet,' she added, clearly trying to lighten the mood.

'Yes, much. I can see we're going to get along just fine, Jasmine,' Sam said, smiling. 'Now, I'm changing the subject. So, Hannah, about your birthday. It's in six weeks – a Saturday this year.'

'Since when do you think that far ahead?'

'When I have two little boys I have to remember to get off to school next year and who need uniforms and goodness knows what else bought for them first.'

'Oh. Right. Well, don't worry about me.' The truth was, Hannah had been trying hard not to think about her first birthday without Tristan and her parents. *Please just let it go.* 'I'm hoping you might still be madly creating. I wouldn't want to impose.'

'Darling, you're not getting out of having a birthday, if that's what you think you're up to,' she said.

'Well ...' Hannah said.

'We know it's going to be hard, but you can't spend it alone, hiding away. I'm talking the usual low-key approach, maybe even as low as spaghetti on toast if you want.'

'Oh, how can I resist?' Hannah said.

'Could I maybe do something?' Jasmine offered. 'If you're busy, Sam, and it wouldn't be intruding?'

'Hey, I know,' Hannah said. 'Since you're both clearly not going to let this go and I've become so brave and can stay at a hotel on my own, why don't *I* do it. A proper dinner party perhaps. Or maybe a high tea. Just for the girls. I could invite Joanne from Mum and Dad's village – she's been wonderful …' The idea was taking shape in her mind and Hannah was becoming excited. She could do this. It was time to get herself back out there. Putting on a nice lunch would be a great start. And perhaps a good distraction from her actual birthday.

'It's your birthday. But do you think you're up to doing all that?' Sam asked.

'You know, I think it's time I learnt to be.'

'Well, if you find you're not, we can always relocate or I can take over,' Jasmine offered kindly.

'Thanks. So, it's on – December third. I'll send invitations and do it all properly. It will be fun,' Hannah added.

'Can we come too?' a little voice said.

'Yes, can we?' said another little voice.

'Um.' Hannah hesitated. What she had in mind was a ladies' luncheon, but how could she disappoint the two angelic faces staring up at her?

'You won't like it. There won't be any other little boys there,' Sam said.

'But Auntie Hannah will be there.'

'Yes, and we love Auntie Hannah.'

'Thanks, boys. And I love you too, oh so much. We'll see. I might need some dashing young waiters.'

'Careful,' Sam whispered.

'Can we go now please, Mummy? I'm tired,' Oliver said.

'Yes, please, I'm tired too,' Ethan said.

'Too tired even for ice-cream?'

'I think I am, actually,' Oliver said.

'Yes, probably,' Ethan said.

Hannah smiled. When the twins were being precocious, which they often were, they sounded so much older than five, and so very cute.

'Oh, dear. We'd better have ice-cream at home with Daddy, then, hadn't we?'

'That's a very good idea, Mummy.'

'Yes, please.'

'That's my cue – I'd better get these darlings home before they turn feral. See you soon,' she said to Hannah and hugged her tightly. 'So lovely to see you again Jasmine. Happy birthday.'

'Thank you. I'd love to see some of your work sometime – no pressure, when you're ready to share it,' Jasmine said.

'Okay. I'll let you know. It's a little too soon yet.'

'I understand.'

Hannah and Jasmine watched as Sam made her way along Flinders Lane with the two boys in tow. Then they walked down into the gallery.

Chapter Twenty-five

Back at home, Hannah was in a spin. Sebastian, the real-estate agent, would be here any moment to give her house a quick once-over and she couldn't stop thinking about the city warehouse apartment she'd viewed – twice.

On her way back to The Windsor from work on Wednesday she had noticed that it was open for inspection and she had ventured into the alley to take a look. Purely out of curiosity. It had been so beautifully done and so quirky – nothing like the house where she'd always lived – that she hadn't been able to resist. She'd liked it so much she'd gone again yesterday morning before meeting Jasmine for lunch.

'Ooh, back again, Hannah, that's a good sign,' the real-estate agent said.

'Oh, no, I'm just looking. I'm not a serious buyer.' She'd wanted to make it clear that he shouldn't waste his time on her, but he wasn't having it. His raised eyebrows and knowing expression said, 'Yet, here you are.'

He'd disarmed her and she'd begun babbling.

'I think it would be too big an adjustment for me to live in the middle of the city.'

'Oh, and where is it you live at the moment?'

'Hawthorn.'

'Lovely.'

'Are you in an apartment, townhouse, freestanding home?'

'A bungalow, actually.'

'My favourite,' Sebastian said and began rubbing his hands together. 'I must see it.'

'Oh. But I'm quite sure I'm not interested in selling.'

'I do sense you are curious though, Hannah. Am I right?'

'I suppose.'

'It's always good to know the value of one's investment. There's absolutely no obligation. I can pop by for a quick visit tomorrow morning, if you like. Say, ten o'clock?'

'Oh. Okay.' And just like that she'd been talked into this morning's visit.

'Wonderful, I'll see you then,' he'd said with a beaming smile, handed her his card, and then abruptly but without appearing overly rude he'd turned to talk to another woman who was viewing the property. Hannah was left feeling annoyed at being so easily manipulated but impressed with his deftness. If she were ever to sell her house, he'd probably be the agent to have. She'd put money on him being very successful.

*

Hannah was pacing the house, double-checking all was in order as she'd been doing for the past half hour, when the doorbell rang.

'Ah, Hannah. Wonderful to see you. And what a gorgeous house on a very lovely street.'

'Thank you.'

'Right, let me see what we're about,' he said. 'Bedrooms, this way?' he asked, pointing to the hall.

'Um, yes.'

Sebastian strode through the house in a matter of minutes, opening and closing every built-in cupboard, and walking around the front and back gardens and down each side of the house, with Hannah trailing behind. By the time they returned to the kitchen, Hannah felt as if she'd run around the block.

'Well, Hannah, I think I could get you just over the two million line. I have several buyers looking for a property of this calibre. And of course if we went to auction ... Well, anything could happen,' he said, waving an arm theatrically. Then he rattled off some of the prices houses in the suburb had recently achieved. She was pleased to hear that the property had appreciated significantly since her parents' generous terms to help them buy it five years ago. Her curiosity had been satisfied, not that she'd take Sebastian's word on actual numbers. He was just trying to lure her in – it was how agents worked, she decided. Anything could happen, either way, when the time came to sell a property.

'I'd urge you to act quickly,' Sebastian said. 'Spring is the perfect time to sell – especially now the weather has got its act together. Oh, and there has been some serious interest on the warehouse you're looking at. So, what are you thinking?'

'As I said, I was really just being curious. I don't think I'm ready to make any decisions or take it any further right now.'

'Okay then. You have my details if you change your mind. All the best.'

Then he shook her hand firmly and abruptly, and left, leaving decidedly cooler air in his wake than when he'd arrived.

An hour later Hannah was still feeling unsettled from the brief but intense encounter with Sebastian. Her tea sat beside her untouched as she alternated between drumming her fingers and doodling on the pad in front of her as she tried to process what had gone on and how she felt about it. Confused – that was it.

What had she been thinking organising for an appraisal? She still couldn't believe she'd been talked into his visit. In her job she was the gatekeeper for Craig, for goodness sake. And a damned good one! She was at ease firmly saying thanks but no thanks. What was it about the city apartment and Sebastian Rowe that had her so discombobulated?

She looked around. It really was a lovely home. But was it time to move on? Or was it too soon? All change is scary, is that where her concerns lay? Did she need to move house to deal with the pain and to get on with this new stage in her life? Or would it feel like a betrayal to her parents and Tristan? She cursed the shadow of sadness closing in on her. She'd been doing so well recently. God, how she hated this unpredictable, debilitating rollercoaster that was grief.

No, you're not dragging me back down. I'm fighting you! Hannah grabbed her keys and hurried out of the house, praying as she went that her dear, wise Auntie Beth would be home to welcome her with open arms and offer some sound advice.

Thankfully the old lady was on the porch watering her pot plants.

'Darling, I'm so glad to see you,' Beth said, wrapping her arms around Hannah. 'I was just finishing this and then I was going to pop over.'

Hannah felt herself begin to relax as she followed Beth inside and through to the kitchen.

'Sit, sit. Tea?'

'Yes, please.'

'So, tell me, is the high tea at The Windsor all it's cracked up to be?'

'Oh yes, and more. I loved it. In fact, it's inspired me to put on a lunch for my birthday. I'm doing formal invitations, but keep the date of Saturday third December free. I hope you'll be able to make it.'

'Are you sure you want an old biddy like me cluttering up the place? Honestly, I won't be offended if you keep to your age group.'

'Nonsense, don't be silly, Auntie Beth. I'm inviting those people who've helped me so much through this year as a thank you, as well as being my birthday. Just the girls. You've been my rock – of course you're invited!'

'Oh, aren't you the sweetest? Thank you. It means a lot to this old duck,' she said, smiling at Hannah. 'You know, your mum and dad, and Tristan for that matter, would be so proud of you and the way you're coping,' Beth said.

'Please don't, Auntie Beth, you'll set me off.'

'Right. Well, your high tea sounds wonderful. Count me in. And if there's anything I can do to help, you know where I am.'

'No, you are off duty for this one.'

'So, other than the high tea, was staying at The Windsor as fabulous as I imagine it to be?'

'Yes, I can certainly see why the rich and famous live in hotels. Oh, to not have to think about meals and cleaning ...'

'That's what I loved most about the cruise, and it's the only reason I'd voluntarily move into an aged-care facility.'

'Auntie Beth, did you ever consider moving after you lost Uncle Elliott?'

'That was a real-estate agent in the flashy blue car, wasn't it?'

'Yes.' *You don't miss much, do you?*

'I thought it might have been – he had that look about him – but I didn't want to pry. And to answer your question – yes.'

'And?'

'And, as you can see, I'm still here.'

'Why?'

'Why did I think about it or why didn't I move?'

'Both. I've seen the most gorgeous apartment in the city that I think I can afford and I can't get it out of my mind. I wasn't even seriously looking at property.'

'Oh. Right. Well. Do you want to live smack bang in the city?'

'I don't know, but oh it's gorgeous …'

'And time is of the essence with these properties, right?'

'Exactly.'

'Sweetheart, only you can know what is right for you.'

'But how did you know?'

'I had your mother and father as the voices of reason. They made me see that wanting to move was a response to feeling that my life had completely turned upside down. I was trying to make some sense of it and gather back some control.'

'Do you think that's what I'm doing?'

'I don't know, dear, but it might be. Other than being in the same job and having the same friends, your life is nothing like what it was this time last year, and not in a good way. You're a smart, organised person, so I think it's entirely natural for you to want to fix things. And right now, selling the house and buying the apartment might seem like the only thing you can fix. And maybe the opportunity to move away from some of the reminders is appealing too.'

'So, what do I do?'

'It's not for me to say, darling.'

'But if you were me. And you've been here before.'

'I'd do nothing.'

'Nothing?'

'Nothing. Just sit tight. I know that's hard for people like you and me – and I see some similarities between us – but if the apartment is meant to be, it will be there when you're ready. You could always rent for a while in the city and see if you like it. You might hate being that close to so many people after a few weeks, and the squeak and squeal of the trams. That would drive me batty.'

'Hmm.'

'Then again, you might love it. And maybe there's an even better city apartment still to come onto the market.'

'It's really lovely.'

'I'm sure it is. But do you want to deal with packing up everything and moving at the moment? I couldn't think of anything worse.'

'God, I hadn't thought of that.' She remembered Tristan's clothes in the wardrobe, which she still hadn't found the strength to go through. She wouldn't have a choice if she went down this path.

'Tell me if I'm overstepping the mark here, but I think you've been through enough without adding moving house to your pile. You do know that along with losing a loved one and divorce, it's in the top three of life's most stressful events, don't you?'

But maybe moving would be easier after all I've been through? Hannah wondered.

'Just because you've had a few good days doesn't mean you're home and hosed. The grief might come back and leave you feeling like you haven't got anywhere.'

Ain't that the truth?

'Really, dear, now's not the time to put yourself under more pressure. Focus on having more good days and being kind and gentle with yourself. To be honest, the first anniversary hit me for a complete six and I didn't have the added complication of Christmas, like you have.'

Bloody Christmas! I hate it!

'Obviously it's entirely up to you how you live your life, but for now, why don't you focus on using the planning of your birthday party as an escape instead. That will be stressful enough.'

Hannah wanted to scoff and say that she could organise the party with her eyes closed, and couldn't see how she could possibly stretch the planning out over six weeks, but stayed silent. Maybe Auntie Beth had a point – several, in fact. She took a deep breath and let it out.

'Sorry,' Beth said, clearly misreading Hannah. 'I've probably said too much and been too bossy, but, Hannah, darling, I care about you so much.' She gripped both of Hannah's hands in hers before continuing. 'You can tell me to butt out, but I know your mum would want me to help guide you like she did me. The truth is I nearly did sell this place – anything to escape the pain and take back some control of my life – but I know now that I would have regretted leaving this wonderful street where everything I need is close at hand or easy to get to, including some of my dearest friends. It's clearly not sitting quite right with you, either, otherwise we wouldn't be having this conversation and you wouldn't be looking so conflicted. So just sit tight for a bit, eh?'

'Hmm. You're probably right – you usually are,' Hannah said. She felt a wave of disappointment at saying goodbye to the apartment, but also slight relief at having made the decision.

'Well, I don't know about that, but I am terribly sensible,' she said, smiling and clearly trying to lighten the mood.

'I'm so glad you didn't move, Auntie Beth,' Hannah said, thinking about the support Beth had given her these past ten or so months.

'Me too, dear,' Beth said. 'Now, come on, you haven't told me what you had for your high tea.'

'I'm taking you for your next birthday. My treat.'

'You don't have to do that.'

'I want to.'

'All right, it's a date. But in the meantime, I want details – every little crumb of a detail – pun intended – including the rest of your stay.'

'We're going to need another pot of tea for that, Auntie Beth.'

Chapter Twenty-six

On the Tuesday morning the week before her party, Hannah was surprised to see Craig pacing back and forth in his small office when she arrived at work. Something was going on with the partners. They'd had their off-site powwow weeks ago and had retreated into the boardroom for several other meetings. Whatever was going on was a big deal and more confidential than usual. Craig usually trusted her with information that was meant for partners only.

'Good morning,' she called brightly.

He turned. 'Hannah. Good, can you come in, please?' His voice was practically a bark.

With slightly raised eyebrows, Hannah did as she was told.

'Sit. Sorry. *Please* take a seat,' Craig said more gently, but remained standing.

'What's going on?' She tried to sit still, remain calm, but found her hands twisting together in her lap.

'Unfortunately the firm is having to tighten its belt and ...'

A sharp pain gripped Hannah and her heart began to race. *Oh, god, no, please don't take my job away. It might be the only thing keeping me sane.* She forced herself to take a slow, deep breath. Getting ahead of things wouldn't help.

'Oh, god, you're not ...?'

'It's okay, just let me finish,' he said, holding up placating hands. 'Right. So the firm needs people to take their leave and stop accumulating it.'

Oh, is that all? Hannah relaxed slightly. The partners griped about this every couple of years.

'I've told you, you all need to be meaner bosses and stop putting on good coffee and biscuits. Then people will take their leave quick smart.'

'They're serious this time, Hannah,' Craig said, sitting down. 'It's become too much of a liability for everyone to be comfortable with. And there's noise starting to be made about long service, not just annual leave.'

'Okay. So you need me to write letters to everyone telling them how much they've got and when they need to take it by, or something, right?'

'Yes. The letters need to come from the lead partner, not HR. Here's all the info you need,' he said, passing her a folder. 'We drew names out of a hat to allocate the dates. I'm sorry, I tried to put a case forward for you. The other partners were sympathetic, but they didn't think it fair for you to be treated differently.'

She opened the folder and saw her own name staring up at her.

'Oh.' She looked up at him.

'Yes, I'm afraid you're first cab off the rank. I'm really sorry. I did try.'

'It's okay, Craig. Rules are rules. I understand.' She didn't want to make him feel any worse than he already did. In fact, one of Hannah's biggest fears in life was making someone else feel embarrassed or awkward. Poor Craig. Bless him. If he didn't think her so fragile, he would just have given her the information and she would have got to it.

As it was, she was beginning to feel decidedly anxious. What was she going to do with herself for six weeks? The thought of taking leave when the office was closed over Christmas had been bad enough. The last thing she needed was to be at a loose end while everyone was Christmas shopping and getting merry. And afterwards, when they'd all returned to work …

'You don't need to worry about me, Craig. I'll be fine. I actually thought for a minute I might be losing my job so this isn't too bad.' She tried to sound nonchalant but she suspected she might actually look as downcast as she felt.

'Right. Is there anything else or should I get on with this?' she said, forcing herself back to work-mode. *For God's sake, I'm being ordered to take leave, it's not something to be upset about!* she told herself sternly. *Plenty of people don't even have a job.*

'As long as you're all right.'

'I'm fine, Craig. Really. I'll give you the letters to sign as soon as possible.'

Back at her desk, Hannah felt stunned for a moment then gave herself a pep talk. She was being ridiculous and needed to pull herself together.

She noticed Craig was on the phone so picked up her own. She toyed with dialling Sam – the one person who would understand what she was feeling without her having to spell it out – but didn't want to distract her from her own work. She was staring blankly at the phone when it started to ring. She felt a huge weight lift as she answered it.

'Hey, Sam, how's things?'

'Sorry to call you at work. Do you have a moment?'

'Yes, it's fine, go ahead.'

'You're never going to believe what's happened.'

'What?'

'Your friend Jasmine's friend – you know, the one she was talking about with the stall at the Sunday Arts Centre Market?'

'Yes.'

'I've just got off the phone with her and she has to go away early in the New Year to take care of her mum who's having an operation. She's offered me her stall.'

'That's fantastic news. So why aren't you sounding like it is?' Hannah asked.

'I'm terrified, Hann. I've realised it'll mean dealing with people.'

'Yes, you goose, selling usually *does* involve dealing with people,' Hannah said, grinning.

'God, Hann, I'll smack someone over the head with a sculpture for sure if they say they're too expensive. Or, heaven forbid, ask what it's meant to be.'

'It'll be good training for when you're snapped up by one of Australia's most prestigious galleries. You'll be fine. I'll come and help you.'

'Oh, would you? That'd be fantastic. Look, I'd better let you go since I've called you at work. And I've got to pull my finger out and make some more stuff to sell.'

'It'll all work out, Sammy, you'll see. You've got a whole month to get organised.'

'Yeah, to become a nervous wreck, you mean. Sorry, enough about me – you're right, I'm being ridiculous. It's a great opportunity. Deep breaths. How are you, anyway? I'm really excited about your party.'

'You'd better still be able to make it.'

'Of course. I wouldn't miss it for the world. Hey, are you okay? Do I detect something up with you, too?'

'Yes, I'm having a little freak-out of my own here, actually.'

'What's happened?'

'The partners have put their feet down about the amount of unused annual leave and are forcing everyone to take it. I'm on annual leave for six weeks as of Monday. I've just found out.'

'But that's not so bad, is it?'

'Sam, this place is my lifeline.'

'Well, I'd say the universe has decided you don't need it anymore.'

'But I *do*. What will I do with myself after the party's done?'

'You can start with coming around and helping me sort out what's crap and what's suitable to sell, and for how much. But seriously, you should do whatever you want – read, cook, garden, or nothing at all. Maybe what you really need is to just spend some quiet time,' Sam said. 'Hey, why don't you travel – go away somewhere?'

'Hmm. I'll think about it. Meanwhile, at least I'll be free to do any last minute racing around for the party.'

'That's the spirit. Hannah, being forced to take annual leave is not something to be afraid of. Look at all you've got through this year. I know we all keep saying it, but you are a lot stronger than you think. Just remember that. And start believing it.'

'Thanks, Sammy. Perhaps you should listen to your own advice too.'

'Okay, smartarse. Touché.'

Hannah smiled. 'I'd better go. I've got a stack of work to do.'

She'd just hung up when she received a text from Jasmine:

Craig told me about the forced leave. Hope you're okay. Won't call as sure you're busy, but here if you need me. J xx

She responded with:

Bit of a shock, but am fine. Appreciate you checking on me. Thanks very much. Speak soon. H xx

*

It took Hannah a couple of days to get used to not going to work, but by Wednesday she had started to appreciate having the time off. She wasn't sure how she'd have done everything for the party if she'd been working full-time. Though, she also accepted that she was usually even more organised when she had a lot to do, rather than a little. Preparing for the arrival of Tristan's parents from Darwin had been another great distraction.

'Oh, it's so good to see you both,' Hannah cried, hugging first Adrian and then Raelene tightly when she opened the door to them. 'I still can't believe you came all the way down for my little party.'

'I wouldn't have missed it. And you're not to feel badly about not inviting Adrian,' Raelene said.

'No, absolutely not,' Adrian said, 'it was my choice to come when I knew it was only for the ladies. I'll make myself scarce while the party's on. I've got Federation Square and the National Gallery and two movies earmarked. I'm looking forward to my day.'

Chapter Twenty-seven

Hannah woke on the morning of her birthday to a strange mixture of emotions. Her parents and then Tristan had always celebrated her birthday with gusto and she didn't know how she would get through the day without them.

What had she been thinking putting on a party? Why couldn't she have let it slip by and stayed in bed? But she did feel a glimmer of excitement at the thought that she'd have her dearest friends around her. And, of course, the icing on the cake was having Tristan's parents here with her as well.

There was rattling coming from the kitchen. She'd better be a decent host and go and tend to them.

'Happy birthday!' Adrian and Raelene cried as Hannah appeared in the doorway.

'We're cooking you a celebratory breakfast,' Adrian said, smiling at her from the cooktop where he stood at the sizzling frypan, spatula in hand.

Hannah cursed the lump forming in her throat. But she was determined not to cry today, especially this early – even if they were tears of joy and gratitude. Oh, bless them. She knew Tristan's family had never made much of a fuss over birthdays.

'That's so lovely of you both. Thank you. But you really didn't need to ...'

'Nonsense. It's your birthday. And you've been so good having us stay. Come on, come and sit down. I have freshly squeezed orange juice,' Raelene said, putting an arm around Hannah and squeezing her shoulders before ushering her to the bench.

Watching Tristan's parents rushing around her kitchen almost caused Hannah to weep. She wanted to give in and let the emotions out, but instead forced them back and focussed on the smell of cooking bacon. Yum. It really might just be her second favourite scent after sun-dried linen.

'Oh, that was so good. And just what I needed,' she said, taking her breakfast plate to the sink. 'You guys are being far too good to me.'

'It's our absolute pleasure,' said Raelene.

'It certainly is,' said Adrian. 'If you can't be pampered on your birthday, when can you?' Hannah sensed they might have needed this small celebration as much as she had.

'And here's a little something for you, with our love,' Raelene said, handing Hannah a tiny parcel wrapped in purple with silver curling ribbon.

'Oh, wow, you shouldn't have. But thank you,' she said, carefully untying the ribbon. Hannah drew a jewellery pouch out of the paper and undid the gold drawstring. 'Oh, it's beautiful,' she said, holding up a pearl pendant necklace. 'Thank you so much.'

'You can put the pendant part onto your bracelet if you'd prefer,' Raelene explained.

'No way, it's perfect just as it is.'

'It's a Darwin pearl,' Adrian explained. 'I had no idea there was a thriving pearl industry there – you only tend to hear about Broome.'

'Can you help me put it on?' she asked, turning her back to Raelene and holding out the two ends.

'There. Go and look in the mirror, it looks lovely on you.'

'I've never owned a pearl before. It's absolutely gorgeous. Thank you so much,' Hannah said, drawing them both into a hug before going into the hall. The glossy sphere did look stunning and the chain was just the right length.

'We hope it will bring you good luck and serve as a reminder that the world is your oyster,' Adrian said solemnly.

Hannah hugged them again while she blinked back the gathering tears.

'Now, I have time for one more coffee before I get organised to make myself scarce for the day,' he added.

After they said goodbye to Adrian Raelene and Hannah set the dining table then worked together, making the delicacies Hannah had chosen to serve at her high tea.

★

Four hours had seemed plenty of time, but as soon as they finished the preparations, and got ready themselves, Raelene and Hannah only had a few minutes to sit down before the guests arrived, starting with Beth. Everyone was right on time and soon they had all been introduced, and Hannah, Raelene, Beth, Sam, Joanne, Jasmine and Caitlin were sipping on champagne with strawberries floating in it. Hannah was so relieved everyone had followed her instruction to not bring anything and definitely no presents.

'This looks amazing,' they'd all said when they'd gone through to the dining room.

'Wow, printed menus, just like The Windsor,' Jasmine exclaimed. 'And it looks like what we ate there too. How exciting and clever of you.'

'Well, I doubt it will be quite up to the same standard. And I certainly couldn't have got it all done without Raelene's help,' Hannah said, putting an arm around her mother-in-law's waist. 'Thank goodness you're here. I think I may have bitten off more than I could chew.'

'You've got a new necklace,' Sam said. 'It's lovely.'

'Yes,' Hannah said, putting her hand up to it. 'Raelene and Adrian gave it to me. It's a pearl from Darwin.'

'Absolutely stunning,' Sam said and everyone agreed. Hannah felt Raelene beaming beside her and was pleased for Tristan's mum. And so grateful to her for making the effort to be there. The day just wouldn't have been the same without her.

'Excuse me for a sec while I put the scones on. No, you sit, Raelene, you've done so much already today,' she said when Raelene made a move to stand up.

Hannah was grateful when Beth came into the kitchen just when she was constructing the three-tiered cake stands she'd hired.

'I wanted to say what an incredible job I think you've done, Hannah.'

'Thanks, but not so incredible that I figured out how to carry in all these plates with only two hands,' Hannah said with a laugh. 'Bless you for always being right where I need you, when I need you!'

'Ach, child, you would have simply made two quick trips, and you know it,' Beth said. 'But, thank you, anyway.'

'Before we tuck in, I just want to say a few words,' Hannah said after arranging the tiered stands on the table. 'I want to thank you all so much for being here. You've each been invited because you've been a really special friend during what has been a terribly difficult time for me. You might think you've done nothing extraordinary, but you have. Just by being on the end of the phone has meant the world, and you've each done so much more. And now, before I cry, please tuck in. And enjoy! Scones first while they're hot.'

There was a round of applause and then murmurs of ecstasy as the guests bit into hot scones spread with liberal amounts of jam and cream.

'Oh, and the correct way to do it is work your way down from the top, right, Jas? And there are two pieces of everything for everyone, so no fighting!' she added, which caused a ripple of laughter.

Hannah beamed. The meal was off to a perfect start.

★

They had just finished the plates of food when the doorbell rang.

'Excuse me,' Hannah said as she got up and laid her linen napkin on the table. She opened the door to two beaming school girls. *God, please no cookies!*

'Hello, there,' Hannah said.

'Hello. Would you like to buy a Christmas wreath,' one girl said while the other held up a wreath.

Hannah felt the blood drain from her face. 'Um.' She wanted to shut the door on them and their Christmas joy.

'They're thirty dollars and you'd be helping the orphans in ...'

'Okay. Hang on.' Hannah dragged her wallet from her handbag just behind her in the hall. She handed over the money and accepted the wreath.

'Would you like a receipt?'

'No, that's fine. Thanks.'

'Thank you for supporting the orphans. Have a merry Christmas,' the girls chanted.

'You too,' Hannah said as she retreated into the house.

'Who was that?' Beth asked as Hannah walked back into the dining room.

There was a collective, 'Oh,' as Hannah held up the wreath.

'I hate Christmas. I wish I didn't, but I do,' she said, sitting down with a sigh. She stared at the wreath she was still holding.

'That's quite understandable,' Raelene said.

'The fact you were so polite *and* bought a wreath says a lot about how far you've come, Hannah,' Joanne said. 'I hope you can see that.'

'Thanks, Joanne.'

'You don't have to thank me, it's the truth.'

'I agree. You're doing incredibly well,' Raelene said.

'Yes, look at you, no tears even,' Sam said. 'Well done, sweetie.'

'Maybe I've finally run out.'

At that moment the muffled but unmistakeable tune of 'Rudolf the Red Nosed Reindeer' could be heard.

'Oh, shit,' Caitlin said, blushing as she opened her handbag. 'God, I am *so* sorry.' She brought out her phone and turned it off.

'Don't worry about it, Cait,' Hannah said. 'Really. And, Sammy, it's okay, you can laugh,' she said, noticing her best friend folding her lips in on each other. She knew that expression well.

'I'm really sorry. I must be overtired and delirious, but I'm finding the irony a little bit funny,' Sam said.

'It is a bit,' Hannah agreed. 'Well, the elephant has well and truly left the building now,' she said in an attempt to lighten the mood.

She thought she heard a collective exhaling of breath. And just like that, the slight tension she'd been feeling all around her dissipated.

'It wasn't my imagination, was it?' she said. 'You've been trying hard all day to avoid any mention of Christmas, haven't you?'

'Guilty as charged,' Joanne said.

'Ah-huh,' a still flushed Caitlin said.

'Because we love you so much,' Jasmine said, putting an arm around Hannah's shoulders.

'Yes, and it's damned hard when it's absolutely everywhere!' Beth said with a laugh.

'And I love you all too and really appreciate your efforts, but you can stop now,' she said. 'Come on, let's go into the lounge room. I'll decide what to do with this later,' she said, putting the wreath on the table and standing up.

Hannah had originally thought about inviting her guests to play some old-fashioned parlour games after lunch – she'd found the instructions online and printed them out. Then she'd settled on charades and had bought the game. But now, she realised that instead of entertaining them, she needed their help. Because suddenly, Hannah knew she didn't want to be in Melbourne for Christmas. She couldn't really explain why, it was just a feeling that was consuming her thoughts. But where could she go? She knew she had a standing invitation with Tristan's parents. But they had already mentioned that they were moving on across the top of Australia. They'd be miles away from an airport. Of course they would wait around if they knew she wanted to join them, but she couldn't upset their plans. She didn't like to impose on anyone – ever.

'So, what's everyone doing for Christmas?' she asked. One by one the women gave their answer and asked her to join them.

'Oh, no, I wasn't fishing for an invitation. I'm going away.'

'Where?' Beth asked.

'No idea,' Hannah said with a laugh, 'you guys are going to help me decide. Any suggestions?'

'How about somewhere cool,' Caitlin said. 'Europe, New York, London?'

'It depends. What do you want to see and do?' Jasmine said.

'No idea,' Hannah said.

'Don't think you'll find anywhere to escape the Christmas frenzy, unless it's a place you shouldn't or don't want to travel to,' Sam said.

'Yes,' Caitlin said. 'Christmas was even in Dubai when I had a stopover there a couple of years ago. Who would have thought?'

'That's the good thing about travel being so easy and the world getting so small, or the trouble with it – depends on how you look at it,' Jasmine said. 'New Zealand is one of my favourite places, especially Queenstown. I'll never go bungee jumping, but I did go skiing there once years ago.'

'There's always cruising,' Beth chimed in. 'I wish I'd discovered it years ago. You can come with me. I'm leaving on the morning of Christmas eve.'

'Thanks. I'll think about it.'

'Cruises are fine for singles,' Beth chimed in.

How can I tell her I don't want to be with anyone I know without hurting her feelings?

'You could throw a dart to choose. I've done that before,' Joanne said.

'Oh, where did you go?' Hannah asked.

'It landed on Australia,' Joanne said, rolling her eyes.

'I'd have thrown it again,' Sam said.

'Did you, Jo?' Hannah asked.

'No, I took it as an omen and did a road trip around Tasmania. It was wonderful, but I wasn't on my own. I don't think it would be as fun alone.'

Nothing's as fun alone, Hannah thought, but kept it to herself.

'The Greek Isles might be interesting and would be cheap,' Raelene said.

'Go to Paris, I'm sure they'd welcome you with open arms and it should be safe enough with security being extra tight,' Caitlin said. *The city of love? Alone? I don't think so.*

'I'd love to go and wander through all the major art galleries one day,' Sam said. 'But I know you'd be bored after five. Perhaps if you can't decide it's a sign you should stay in Australia and come with us to Rob's brother's place. Hang on, you could have trouble getting a passport at such late notice. You might have to stay here, anyway.'

'I might never have been on a plane, but I do have a passport,' Hannah said. 'I got it when we were thinking of going overseas for our honeymoon.'

'Oh, well, the world *is* your oyster, then. I'd love to travel the world and stay a night in each of the hotels of a famous chain – like the Ritz,' Jasmine said dreamily. That sounded to Hannah like an awful waste of money.

'Was there anywhere you and Tristan seriously dreamt about going one day?' Joanne asked.

'Not really, we always focussed on buying a house and paying off the mortgage.' It was the first excuse that came to her. She didn't want to tell everyone about Tristan's fear of flying. Of course she'd dreamt of travelling the world, who hadn't? But it wouldn't have been fair to Tristan to talk about going here and there and making him feel worse than he already did about his phobia. At least he'd considered trying to conquer it; that's when they applied for their passports. Everyone was right – she could go anywhere. That was the problem.

'Visit London. After our own country, I think that's the place all us Australians should visit at least once,' Beth said. 'I hope I'll get there one day.'

'I thought the Londoners would have been friendlier than the New Yorkers, but nope,' Caitlin said. 'And they didn't seem to understand the concept of personal space at all. I got completely squashed in the tube and nearly freaked out.'

'You lot are really no help at all,' Hannah said. She tried to laugh lightly, but suspected it didn't quite come out as she'd hoped.

'Maybe you're meant to be around supportive people, not running away and hiding amongst strangers,' Sam said. Hannah sensed her friend was a little miffed.

It was probably cowardly and most likely could be considered running away, but Hannah also tried to tell herself it was about drawing a line in the sand. She hoped that if she went away things would be different and better when she returned, after the terrible first anniversary had passed.

A little voice inside reminded her that nothing else had changed with each passing milestone during the year so why would going away make any difference?

On the other side of her brain another voice suggested that perhaps this was what she needed, and what harm would it do to give it a try?

If only she could think of somewhere to go. She had her lovely puffy jacket and other warm accessories – perhaps she should focus on somewhere cold. Maybe then she'd start to *feel* again.

It was something she couldn't explain to anyone even if she tried – and it didn't even make sense to herself. Of course she could *feel*, her senses just didn't seem to feel the way they used to. She was always heading out with a cardigan when she didn't need it or without one when she did. People were often asking her, 'Aren't you cold?' or 'Aren't you hot?' It would be good to feel temperature properly again – *feel* anything in the normal way again, for that matter.

'Hmm. Definitely somewhere cold. I wish I knew what Mum and Dad and Tris were up to with those presents,' Hannah said. She hadn't given the gifts much thought since unwrapping them and making use of the gloves and scarf during winter. She'd tried the puffer jacket twice, but found it too warm.

'Oh! I'd completely forgotten about them. Of course. Yes, if you go, it has to be to somewhere cold,' Beth said, clapping her hands.

'What are you talking about?' Sam asked.

'Oh, didn't I tell you? It was a few months ago. Anyway, I got a call from the police to collect the stuff that was in the boot of Tristan's car and it was mainly wrapped Christmas presents. Mum had knitted a pile of winter woollies and there were thermals and a purple puffer jacket.'

'I can't believe you didn't tell me,' Sam said.

'I must have forgotten. Anyway, the three of them had clearly planned for us to go somewhere cold together, but I have no idea where or when.' She shrugged.

'I love a mystery,' Caitlin chimed in, clasping her hands together on her lap. 'Are there any other clues? Were there any other Christmas presents?'

'Just this ladybird charm,' Hannah said, holding out her arm.

'Yes, I've been admiring it all year. It's gorgeous.' She inspected it more closely. 'Oh,' she said.

'What?' Hannah asked.

'I could be completely wrong and it might just be a coincidence, but I don't think that's just any old ladybird – it's a nine-spotted ladybug. We call them ladybirds, but they call them ladybugs. And, see, yours has nine spots?' she added, pointing out nine black spots.

'Yes?' Hannah said.

'Tristan was in finance, right?' said Caitlin. 'If this is a clue, I think he meant to take you to New York – most likely to see the Wall Street Stock Exchange. Maybe he was buttering you up for moving there for a job or something.'

'Sorry, I'm not following,' Sam said. 'What's New York and Wall Street got to do with the number of spots on a ladybird, ladybug, whatever you call them?'

Good question, Hannah thought, but she was stuck a step behind even that – on trying to work out if Tristan would be so cryptic. They'd always just sat down and discussed things.

'Since nineteen eighty-nine the nine-spotted ladybug has been an animal symbol of New York. I could be completely wrong about your ladybird being a clue, it could just be a coincidence.'

'Wow,' said Sam.

'I'm not sure what to think,' Hannah said.

'How could you possibly know that?' Joanne said with a laugh.

'I have a memory for random, often totally useless facts,' Caitlin said. 'Even if I'm wrong with the connection, it would at least give you somewhere to visit. If it isn't a clue, make it one! I can't just go "the world is my oyster, where shall I go?" I need a purpose – like old buildings, famous landmarks or art galleries, train trips.'

'Hmm. You know, I think I might just do it. Is it safe to book flights and accommodation online or should I go through a travel agent?'

The older members of the group said they preferred to use a travel agent whereas Caitlin and Jasmine said they'd never had a problem with online bookings.

'Thanks, everyone. Well, I might be off to New York for Christmas!' Hannah said. She just hoped Sam wouldn't be too upset with her no longer being available to help with preparing for the market stall in the New Year. That was probably why she was a little miffed.

'Meanwhile, enough about me – who fancies playing charades?'

Chapter Twenty-eight

Hannah settled back into her seat against the plane's window for the first leg of her trip and let out a sigh of relief. She could now see why travelling was considered so stressful. But it was also a bit exciting.

She was organised, had gone through everything dozens of times, had read and followed all the instructions and tips on the airline's and government's travel information sites, scrolled through a heap of forums for advice and had left home feeling prepared – a little on edge, but okay.

She stared out the tiny window and watched the suitcases being tossed from a trolley onto a conveyer belt and then disappear, glad Jasmine had warned her how little care would be taken and to wrap any liquid toiletries in plastic bags in case of breakage. She took a deep breath, trying to still her nerves, and looked across when she felt movement next to her.

'Hello,' an older woman dressed head to toe in hot pink said brightly.

'Hi.' Hannah tried to smile, but it was more of a grimace. 'Sorry, I'm a bit nervous. I've never been on a plane before,' she explained.

'Never? Not one?'

Hannah shook her head.

'Well, I'll be. Don't worry, there's nothing to fear,' the woman said. 'Qantas has the best safety record of any airline. We'll be fine,' she added, plucking a magazine from the seat pocket.

Hannah took it as a sign their conversation was over. She looked out again to see if she could find her bag with its bright purple and white spotted ribbon on the trolley.

There it is! At least she now knew her luggage would make it as far as Sydney. She'd discovered that was her greatest fear about travelling – ending up somewhere in a different climate with no luggage. Also thanks to Jasmine's advice, she had packed some thermals and winter woollies and her necessary toiletries into the bag she carried on with her, in case the worst happened.

Jasmine had been a wealth of information and it was only thanks to her that Hannah was as calm as she was. There had been so much to look into and organise, though she'd been grateful for this new, exciting project. And in true Hannah style she'd planned it all to a point only just on the healthy side of obsessive, fully encouraged by Jasmine.

If there's anything I've forgotten I'll buy it, she'd told herself. It was another piece of advice from Jasmine to stop herself going through everything over and over in her mind. She could buy anything she needed in New York. Now she was seated she was free to look forward to this adventure.

Wow, I'm really doing it. I'm really going to New York!

She felt like shouting it to all the passengers filing in around her. She was starting to understand why people pushed themselves out of their comfort zone – it was exhilarating. But she'd better calm down – she had hours of sitting ahead of her. After all the rushing around and thinking she'd had to do, she was even looking forward to not having anything to do but sit, watch movies and read for hours on end. Hannah regularly marvelled at what a lifeline reading had become for her since Sam had given her that battered old novel on New Year's Day. Hannah was now a confirmed bookworm and rarely went anywhere without a book in her handbag. If she hadn't tried it, she'd never have believed just how therapeutic it could be to lose herself in the pages of someone else's story for a few hours and forget about the harsh realities of her own life and circumstances.

She felt weary looking back over the last year at all she'd lost and been through. But she was determined to stay upbeat and not give into any sadness – well, not in public, anyway.

Alone, but not lonely, she reminded herself. It was something Joanne had said that had really struck a chord with Hannah and become another mantra for her. She had a group of wonderful friends just an email or phone call away if she needed a pick-me-up. She often wondered how she'd cope if she didn't have her little tribe around her.

Now she was starting to feel herself living again, not just surviving.

★

Settling into her seat for the long leg to New York, after a short stopover, Hannah decided she liked taking off and landing the best. She didn't find it frightening at all – she enjoyed the feeling of power beneath her, of being thrown back in her seat and then, eventually, the roar of the engines slowing the plane down. It was incredible how quickly the beast came back to an amble on the tarmac too. What was even more astonishing was that the machine got up and stayed in the air at all, but she didn't want to think about it too much.

★

Outside it was completely black except for the blinking light on the end of the wing behind her. There was a collective gasp as the plane seemed to turn and then rise steeply. Hannah longed to ask the flight attendants what was happening, but didn't want to be a nuisance. Anyway, she'd heard the announcement telling them to be seated for landing. But that was ages ago. What was going on?

'Shit,' she said, grabbing the armrest as the plane leapt. 'Sorry,' she said to her companion as he glanced at her, 'I'm new to flying.'

'Don't worry, it'll be fine,' he said, flashing her a warm smile. 'I fly a lot and have always arrived safely. There's probably a snow-storm and we can't land because of poor visibility or delays with another plane on our runway, or something. It happens all the time. Be grateful they're keeping us safely in the air and not taking risks,' he said with another smile, and returned to the folder of pages on his lap.

'Okay. Thanks,' she said. She now felt bad she hadn't spoken to him for the past nineteen hours except to say, 'Excuse me' each time she'd needed to stretch her legs or get up for the bathroom.

'Apologies, folks, there's been a snowstorm, which has caused some delays on the ground. We'll have you landed as soon as possible. Meanwhile, please stay in your seats with your seatbelts fastened.'

It seemed only moments later that they had touched down and were making their way towards the terminal. Now she knew she was safe, Hannah felt a little thrill at seeing the snow piled up around them, lit by the many floodlights.

'See, safe and sound,' her companion said as he passed her bag to her from the overhead locker.

'Thanks. Yes. Thank goodness.'

Hannah felt like she'd been standing for ages waiting for her suitcase to arrive on the carousel. She was worried about keeping her private transfer driver waiting. Jasmine had assured her that the driver would keep an eye on her plane's arrival time and be across any delays. Nonetheless, panic was just starting to rise within her when the bag appeared. She had to stop herself whooping with joy.

'Welcome to the United States. Enjoy your stay,' the uniformed man behind the immigration desk said curtly after handing back her stamped passport.

'Thank you. I'm sure I will,' she said and offered him a warm smile.

Now Hannah had to find the driver. *Please still be here waiting for me.*

She walked out into the crowded meeting area and scanned the sea of names printed on signs. Her heart began to race. And then out of the corner of her eye she noticed a man rushing from the other end of the hall, then holding up a small whiteboard with her name scrawled across it. She fought the overwhelming urge to throw herself into his arms and weep.

'Hello. I'm Frankie,' he said, taking her suitcase. 'This way please.'

As they left the terminal a blast of dry, icy wind hit Hannah's face and made her gasp. She hurried on after Frankie across a car park, over and through small mounds of snow, feeling grateful for wearing waterproof hiking boots.

'Here,' he said, sliding open the door to a black people-mover. She really hoped he was a good driver in icy conditions.

She was starting to feel calmer, but knew she wouldn't feel at ease until she was safely checked into her hotel. Fingers crossed they hadn't mucked up her booking. God, when had she become so damned pessimistic?

It's an exciting adventure. You're so lucky to be able to do this, she told herself. *Thousands of people would swap places with you. You're just tired.* Everything would be brighter in the morning after a decent night's sleep, and then she'd enjoy exploring.

Out of sheer nervousness, she itched to engage Frankie in conversation, but didn't want to distract him. It was snowing and the road was chock full of traffic.

Suddenly he was turning off the eight-lane road and then took a series of turns. The city loomed large, office towers brightly lit around them. Everything seemed so much bigger and taller and busier than Melbourne. And Melbourne didn't have all the flashing neon signs, nor did it ever have snow heaped up on side-walks. It was all very different, but at the same time a little familiar thanks to the American movies and TV shows she'd seen.

'Good place to eat,' Frankie said, pointing left just before making another turn. 'I bring my family here.'

'Great. Thanks. I'll check it out,' she said, taking note of the lit sign announcing Jerry's Diner. She was just wondering how far it was from her hotel when she realised Frankie had pulled to a stop — the diner was just around the corner. Frankie helped her with her bag and Hannah checked in the van three times to make sure she hadn't forgotten anything.

The entrance to the hotel looked dark and nondescript. She'd have had trouble finding it on her own. She pressed a twenty dollar note — twice as much as she'd originally intended as a tip — into Frankie's hand and thanked him profusely. Again, she desperately wanted to throw her arms around him, but resisted. With a friendly wave he hopped back in his van and drove off.

A doorman in the foyer ushered her into the lift and took her up to the reception level.

Hannah felt revived after a long, hot shower. She'd hoped she'd feel like going to bed, but she was now wide awake and hungry. Dare she venture out on her own to the diner or into Times Square? She peered out of her twenty-fourth floor window. In the glow of the streetlights she could see people the size of ants hurrying along the sidewalks, picking their way between mounds of snow.

She got rugged up, and headed out, clutching her folded map with the hotel circled in red, to try a burger from a genuine American diner.

Chapter Twenty-nine

No wonder it's nicknamed the city that never sleeps, Hannah thought, standing on a corner in the middle of Times Square surrounded by bright lights flashing and changing colour. She found herself drawn here every night to watch as people bustled all about her – even at almost midnight – all rugged up like the Michelin Man against the cold. And it seemed they weren't just rushing to get home, but shopping and heading to dinner or a show. There was so much to see that at times she found herself standing and staring in awe and wonder at it all – especially the magnificent Christmas tree.

She loved how free and safe she felt. Despite being a born and bred Melbournian, she would never be in the city alone late at night wandering aimlessly, as she was doing in New York.

One of the things about travelling alone that Hannah didn't like was that you couldn't get great photos of yourself. She hadn't really got the hang of selfies, and anyway, that wasn't quite the same. But she did have a few of herself in Times Square surrounded by the lights and with Cookie Monster and Elmo from *Sesame Street*. There was a whole collection of people dressed up as characters from various shows. She'd been reluctant to hand over her mobile phone to one of the characters to take photos, but everyone else seemed to be doing it. She felt silly when she'd thanked them and walked away only to be curtly told by the woman inside the Cookie Monster suit that they were doing it for tips.

'Oh, I'm so sorry, I didn't realise,' she said as she put a couple of dollars into the outstretched paws. She'd thought it was a promotion and they were paid actors. Hannah didn't mind – they'd been nice and had taken a couple of photos of her with each of them.

'Ah, Aussie, where you from?' the woman asked.

'Melbourne.'

'Ah, Melbourne. Good. Enjoy New York.'

'Thanks very much. I am.' And then they were off with a wave of their colourful paws.

Hannah headed back to her hotel with a smile on her face. *What fun!*

The following morning she did a hop-on hop-off bus tour of Manhattan and got a great sense of the scale of the city. One of her favourite sights was the triangular Flatiron building. It was called that, the bubbly tour guide explained in his wonderful New York drawl, because from the air it looked like the underside of a clothes iron.

'Am-I-right?' he said, as if it was just one word. Hannah wasn't sure if it was a common New York saying or just his trademark. Regardless, she could have listened to his dulcet tones all day and he seemed to know everything about this city he so obviously loved. Hannah showed her appreciation with a decent tip at the end of the tour, as requested. *What fun!* was becoming Hannah's new catchcry.

Over the next few days, with her map and metro ticket, Hannah went back over much of the route of the tourist bus to enjoy the sights at her own pace. She also visited the must-sees from Jasmine and Caitlin's lists and generally explored the city while hunting for the perfect souvenirs. It really was a great city to walk around, just as Caitlin and Jasmine said it would be – although she had to be careful because the ice on the sidewalks was very slippery. The trick was to not rush or change direction quickly.

Hannah found the subway brilliant too, though she often struggled with the directions of trains going up and down town, and then which exit to take from the station. Sometimes when this confusion mixed with tiredness and strong emotions, tears rose to the surface. One day she'd embarrassed herself by bursting into tears when a woman stopped to offer help. It was made worse because this older woman reminded Hannah of Auntie Beth. Thank goodness the lady hadn't put her arm around her, she'd have dissolved for sure.

'Oh, dear, are you okay?' she asked, offering Hannah a tissue from her handbag.

'Yes. Thank you. I think the jetlag is catching up with me.'

'Ah. I'm prone to getting a little teary too when I get over-tired,' she said.

'Thank you,' Hannah said, pulling herself together.

'Now, where is it you're trying to get to? Can I help?'

'I'm trying to go here,' Hannah said, pointing on her hotel circled on the map, 'but I can't for the life of me figure out which exit to take to get out of here.'

'I'll show you.'

Up on the street the woman pointed and said, 'You need to go that way. Okay?'

'Yes. Thank you so much.'

'You're very welcome.'

Hannah was surprised when the woman turned around and disappeared back down the stairs the way they'd come. She'd come all the way up two flights just to show Hannah the way. She almost began weeping out of sheer gratitude. Instead she focussed on making her way to the pizza place she'd walked past the other night on her way back to the hotel. *I'm going to have myself a slice*, she said in her head, complete with a New Yorker's accent.

The following morning, Hannah left her room feeling tired. If only she could sleep properly. She briefly considered staying in, but didn't want to be there when the house-keeping staff came. And, anyway, she was determined that this would be the day she'd find the perfect souvenir – a ladybird of some description – to take back to each of her dear friends.

'Good morning, Miss Australia,' said the hotel doorman, grinning and nodding to Hannah as she exited.

'Good morning,' she called back, smiling warmly. Her day had turned considerably brighter. She'd only had to say 'Thank you' a few times when he'd held the door for her and the doorman had picked her accent. 'Have a great day.'

She could see why New York was a much-loved city. There was so much to see, it was easy to get around and, despite the frigid weather – which she was finding she didn't mind – it was warm and friendly. Well, except, it seemed the older men of the city. Those running the diner she'd visited on her first night had been particularly brusque, and the guy in the pizza place was the same. But the pizza had been incredible.

Hannah went into the Metropolitan Museum of Art on Fifth Avenue but decided against joining the long queue waiting to buy entry tickets. She'd come back later. But she noticed the gift shop was almost empty so went in. She was becoming quite the shopaholic. It didn't help that clothes were incredibly cheap here, even with the exchange rate. She'd bought the cutest puffy jackets for the twins.

She left the shop feeling thrilled with her purchases – a puzzle each for the boys, a lovely bookmark with the museum's logo on it, and a necktie and clip for Rob. Back outside she bought a hotdog from one of the many food stands on the sidewalk. *Oh, yum*, she thought, biting into it. She ambled along the forecourt taking note of the other cuisines on offer and on towards Central Park.

Hannah stopped to finish her snack at the frozen lake in the park. She was watching the skaters for a few moments when her heart started to ache so badly she couldn't swallow the next bite. Lovers were holding hands, skating across the ice, and when a guy got down on one knee, presumably to propose, she had to turn away. If the hotel had been closer she might have retreated, but instead she walked a little further to a bench, brushed the light dusting of snow off one end and sat down. She stared at her half-eaten hotdog with tears running down her face.

Suddenly a dapper looking man with a German shepherd on a lead stopped in front of her. She'd only seen Charlie those two times, but oh how she suddenly missed him. Every time she'd been to the park at home she'd kept an eye out. She'd have given anything to wrap her arms around Charlie's neck now. *What a strange thing to think.*

'Excuse me. Are you all right?' It was a very British accent. 'Can I be of some assistance?'

'Thank you, but I'm just having a moment,' Hannah said, offering him a sad smile before swiping at her nose with the paper napkin that had come with the hotdog. 'My husband died and I ...' She lifted her hand awkwardly and tried to point to the lake before dropping it again and shrugging. *Why am I telling a complete stranger?*

'Ah. I see,' the man said, swiping the snow off the bench and sitting down beside her. 'Yes, I can understand that setting you off. Is that an Australian accent I detect?'

'Yes, it is.'

'Are you visiting or living here?'

'Just visiting.'

'On your own?'

'Yes.'

'You're very brave.'

'Thanks. Though I certainly don't feel remotely brave at the moment,' she said, with another sad smile. 'Can I give him the last of my hotdog? I've lost my appetite.' She nodded to the dog.

'Go ahead, he loves the damned things.'

'He's a beautiful dog,' she said.

'That he is. His name's Kip, and he's kept me sane since I lost my wife Margaret. Haven't you, boy?' He patted the dog's head as he gazed adoringly up at his master.

'Oh, I'm sorry.'

'It was several years ago. I'm adjusting. Probably always will be. That's the thing, isn't it? There's the sadness, but it's the getting used to everything being the same but also being completely different that still threatens to bring me undone sometimes. That doesn't make sense, does it?'

'It does to me.'

'I'm sorry, I was meant to be cheering you up. And here I am getting morose.'

'No, I'm sorry. It's my fault. I'm the one sitting here crying in public.'

'Let's just agree to stop apologising. I'm David, by the way,' he said, putting out a hand.

'I'm Hannah,' she said, accepting it. 'Thank you so much for stopping. I feel better now. I really do.'

'That's good.'

'I think I might be homesick, too.'

'Do you know the best thing about being alone – and travelling on your own?'

'What's that?'

'Being able to do exactly as you please and when. If you're homesick, go home, Hannah. You have nothing to prove to anyone.'

'Oh, well, I ...' Hannah wasn't sure what to think.

'And on that note, I'd better get myself and Kip here home and out of this cold wind. Goodbye, Hannah. It was a pleasure to meet you. All the very best,' he said, getting up.

'Thank you, David, and you, Kip. It was lovely to meet you both.'

David put a finger to his head as if in a salute, smiled, nodded and left.

Hannah watched after them until they turned the corner and then wiped away the remainder of her tears and got up. *I'm okay. I'm enjoying being here. I'm having fun. Aren't I?*

She thought about the other afternoon at a diner she'd found nearby, when she'd been served by singing waiters and waitresses. She'd passed it several times, but at regular meal times there had always been long queues outside. Until the other day at four p.m. She'd been hungry and as it seemed quiet, she'd ventured in. She'd initially cringed at discovering its unique selling feature – singing and dancing waiters who would spontaneously erupt into loud, lively performances – but she'd had an absolute ball. She'd found herself clapping along and boogying in her seat to the rock'n'roll as waiters danced around her, leaping up onto tables nearby. It was wonderful, and the one place she'd eaten in so far where she'd felt completely comfortable being a lone diner. Everywhere else had been welcoming enough, apart from the grumpy old men, but at this place they really looked after her. Tom, her personal waiter, was very attentive and put her at ease from the moment he greeted her at the door. She worked her way through the most amazing crispy chicken wings, coleslaw and garlic bread, and then New York cheesecake whilst soaking up the exuberant atmosphere. Having left an extra-large tip for Tom – who would never know just how much she'd appreciated his attention and warmth – she'd returned to her hotel feeling full and happy.

Hannah now smiled at the memory.

The one thing Hannah hadn't found yet was the perfect souvenir for each of the girls.

She'd visited stores full of pens, hats, t-shirts and sculptures of apples and landmarks in all shapes and sizes, but not found one ladybug beetle – let alone a nine-spotted version. Did no one know it was one of their city's emblems?

Hannah left the latest store feeling tired and a little dejected. And her feet were killing her. There was no way she could get back to the hotel without a fortifying cup of hot chocolate. She'd given up on coffee – she hadn't had a decent cup yet and couldn't for the life of her see what the appeal of Starbucks was other than the free Wi-Fi. She had coffee with her cooked breakfast each morning, but that was more as a necessity to get her going than out of any great enjoyment.

Hannah looked around and saw a diner on the next corner. There seemed to be somewhere casual and cheap to eat every fifty metres. She walked in and smiled back to the waitress, who introduced herself as Chelsea.

'Coffee?' Chelsea asked.

'No, thank you. Could I please get a hot chocolate and the warm apple pie?'

'Sure thing. Won't be a minute.'

With the warmth of the staff and the sugar hit, Hannah left feeling much better. It took her several blocks to realise she'd taken a wrong turn and that the street names were going away from her hotel rather than towards it. And suddenly it was snowing heavily. She looked around for a shop to duck into and spied a small art gallery. She stared at a display of gorgeous cuff links in the window and felt sad. She should have been shopping for Tristan for Christmas. Swallowing down the rising emotion, she ventured in.

'Hello,' a lady called from behind a glass counter in the middle of the store.

'Hi.'

'Let me know if I can help you.'

'Thanks very much. I'm just having a look.'

'Oh, you're Australian,' the woman said, beaming.

'Yes. I'm visiting from Melbourne for a couple of weeks.'

'I hope you're enjoying your visit.'

'I am, very much, thank you. Except I've taken a wrong turn and apparently I'm heading downtown instead of up.' She'd meant to be light-hearted, but just sounded weary. She was annoyed to suddenly find tears filling her eyes again.

'Oh, my dear, you poor thing. Come over here and sit down,' the lady said, pulling out a chair from near the counter.

'I'm sorry. I'm fine, just a bit tired.' But Hannah sat down anyway.

'I think it's more than that. Your aura's not looking so great,' the lady said, frowning down at her.

'Pardon?'

'Sorry, I should keep my thoughts to myself,' she said. 'I'll get you a cup of tea.'

Before Hannah could object, the woman had gone. She looked around at the lovely objects and paintings.

'Here you are. I'm Brenda, by the way,' the lady said, returning with two cups of milky tea and handing one to Hannah before taking a seat just behind the counter.

'I'm Hannah. Thanks very much. I'm not sure what's come over me,' she said, taking a sip.

'You've been through a lot.'

'Everyone says travel is exhausting, now I know it's true,' Hannah said, smiling. 'And today I've spent a frustrating day looking for the perfect souvenirs for my friends, and failed.'

'You can only outrun things for so long.'

'It's fine, it's only souvenirs.' Hannah was starting to feel a little uneasy. Brenda was looking at her strangely – frowning and intense – as if she wasn't quite looking at her. She was looking past her or through her. And then she seemed to shake her head and be all smiles and brightness again. *Maybe she's tired too*, Hannah thought.

'Is there something in particular you're looking for?'

'Well, I want to find a ladybug beetle – perhaps as a small enamel sculpture or a brooch. Glass even, and preferably made in America, not in China like so many of the souvenirs I've seen.'

'Oh. No, sorry, we have nothing like that.'

'I've found plenty of apples and of course souvenirs depicting the important buildings and landmarks – though made in China – but no ladybugs. I thought it would be the perfect gift – given their association with luck and New York.'

'New York?'

'It – the nine-spotted ladybug in particular – was made a state symbol in nineteen eighty-nine.'

'Oh. I had no idea. How terrible of me.'

'Don't worry, you're clearly not the only one who missed the memo.'

'We do have some lovely timber puzzle boxes in the design of an apple – made by a local craftsman. Would you like to see one?'

'Yes, please.'

'Here we are.'

'Oh, it's gorgeous!' It would indeed make the perfect gift, though a little on the expensive side. But, then, she'd be buying something genuinely American and not a tacky object made in a sweat factory in China. 'The only problem is I need seven. Do you have that many?' She wanted to buy the same gift for all her friends who had been at her birthday lunch, so there were no misunderstandings. And she wanted one for herself too.

'Hmm. I doubt it. I'll check out the back. Excuse me a moment.'

Feeling a little better, Hannah got up and took a stroll around the shop. A glass bowl in stunning shades of pink, purple and green – her three favourite colours – caught her attention. But she thought it would be impossible to get it home safely. Though it would be a lovely reminder of the trip.

'I found two more.'

'Oh,' Hannah said, feeling deflated.

'But we have another store so I'll just phone and check.'

'That would be good, thank you.'

Hannah tried not to get her hopes up when she heard Brenda say, 'That's great. Hang on, I'll just check.'

'There are only two more at our store on Fifth Avenue – but that's still only five. There's a courier there right now so I can have them here in less than half an hour.'

'Oh. Okay. Um, yes please.' With Brenda standing with her hand over the receiver, Hannah felt pressured. Once she'd been good at making these sorts of decisions quickly.

'It's all right. There's no obligation. If we get them here and you don't like them, it's no problem at all.'

'Okay. Yes, please have them sent over. I'm sure they'll be perfect.' *Only five. Damn. I can live without one – I've bought plenty of stuff – but that means I'm still one down.*

'Would you like another cup of tea while we wait?'

'That would be lovely, thank you.'

As they sat drinking tea, Hannah tried not to look at the bowl in the window. It kept catching her eye and she was beginning to fear she would not be able to walk away from it. She tried to calculate how much it would weigh and how she could rearrange her luggage to accommodate it. She'd have to see how big and heavy the parcel of wooden apple puzzle boxes turned out to be.

Hannah noticed Brenda looking thoughtful, as if she were deliberating over whether to say something or not.

'I'm right, aren't I – that you've been through a lot?'

'I must be looking haggard or like an unkempt backpacker,' she said, smiling and smoothing her hands down her jeans. 'But, yes, I have been through a bit,' she said with a sigh. She didn't really want to elaborate and risk crying.

'I'm sorry for your loss. Your husband and parents loved you very much,' Brenda said. She had that strange look on her face again.

Hannah's eyes opened wide.

'I don't mean to pry. And please don't be alarmed, but I have some psychic abilities – I see things,' Brenda said. 'There are times when I wish I didn't, but it's not something I can control.'

'Oh. Wow. Really?' Hannah had the strange thought that Sam would love this. She was confused and not sure what to think – or where to look. The strangest thing for Hannah was that instead of feeling frightened, a sort of warm, peaceful feeling flooded through her.

'I shouldn't be saying anything. My boss would fire me.'

'I won't tell,' Hannah found herself saying. 'What can you see?' she said, curiosity getting the better of her. *Oh if only Sammy were here.*

'Are you sure?'

'Yes, go on.' *Can you see I'm not a believer? And I'm not, am I?* 'You said something about not outrunning things.'

'Yes.'

'I thought I'd been facing up to things quite well, actually,' she said, unable to keep the annoyed tone completely out of her voice.

'Yes, but you're here in New York, aren't you, instead of being home and facing up to Christmas?'

'Guilty as charged,' she said a little sheepishly. 'What?' she asked as Brenda's warm, sympathetic smile became a deep frown.

'I think you'll feel better when you get home.'

'Yes, I think I'm starting to get a little homesick,' Hannah said. 'Can you be more specific?'

'No, unfortunately my visions are rarely precise. I'm just the interpreter and medium passing them on. I'm seeing darkness, dark clouds gathering over you and your home. It could be symbolic or literal. But there's also bright light behind the clouds. It tells me that good things, *new* things are coming. Yes, that's it.' She relaxed.

'When?'

'Soon. I think. Yes, very soon.'

'When?' *Days, weeks, months?*

'Please don't worry, Hannah, the dark clouds are clearing.'

'Do you think I should cut my trip short and go home? Honestly?'

'Oh, well, that's really not for me to say. I couldn't possibly advise you to do one thing or another. I'm just telling you what I've seen and I shouldn't even have done that. I'm sorry if I've caused you concern. I need to learn to keep my big mouth shut,' she added in a mutter as if to herself.

At that moment the door opened and Hannah looked up to see a person bustling in wearing Lycra and a bike helmet.

'Hi Brenda. I have two wooden apples for you.' The young man took off his helmet and placed his backpack on the counter and began unclipping it. Brenda brought the other three over and lined them up. There were now five wooden puzzle boxes a little larger than the size of her palm complete with stalk and worm inside. They really were very cleverly made.

'Perfect. I'll take them.'

'To Australia? Are you an Aussie with that accent?' the courier asked.

'Yes. Melbourne.'

'One of the top ten liveable cities, if I'm not mistaken.'

'It most certainly is.'

'So what are you doing here in New York?' he asked.

'Just a holiday for Christmas.'

'Surely not on your own, a gorgeous thing like you?'

'I'm on my own, yes.'

'Would you like a personal tour guide?' he asked, moving closer. Hannah found herself feeling both amused and a little chuffed at his attention.

'Benjamin, leave Hannah alone. She's a strong, independent woman and she doesn't need you fawning all over her,' Brenda scolded, causing Hannah to smile. 'I'll just bubble-wrap these carefully for you. They aren't too fragile ...'

'Well they won't be when Brenda's finished with them.'

'... but you'll need to pack them where they're easily accessible as I believe your quarantine people will want to check they're safe to bring in or if they need treating first.'

'Oh, I hadn't thought about that. I think they're very strict with wood.' *Am I making a mistake buying these?* 'Though, I think if there's a concern they just charge you and spray them with something,' Hannah said. She remembered seeing it on the TV shows.

Hannah paid then took a final look at the glass bowl. It wasn't cheap at four hundred dollars and she'd already spent that on the puzzle boxes. She'd sleep on it and come back tomorrow if she changed her mind.

'So, how long are you in our fine city?' the courier asked.

'Oh, another week.'

'What are you doing for Christmas?'

'Er, I um, haven't decided yet.'

'Benjamin! In the storeroom there's a package for you to take back to Angela. Up on the top shelf. Now, please,' Brenda added as Benjamin stood his ground. He let out a frustrated *harrumph* and walked away.

'It's calling to you, isn't it?' Brenda said, following Hannah's gaze and nodding at the bowl. A beam of sunlight – one of the few Hannah had seen during her time here – suddenly shone through it, highlighting the already stunning colours.

'Yes, it is.'

'She who hesitates can be lost,' Brenda said, startling Hannah so much that she spun around to face her. It was the exact phrase her mother had used many times when they'd shopped together. One her mother had modified from the original of '*He* who hesitates *is* lost.' Was she imagining it or did Brenda have a knowing expression on her face?

'Oh, all right, why not,' Hannah said, trying to shift the strange feeling of discomfort surging through her. How could this person know these things? Was it just coincidence?

Around eight hundred US dollars all up. Just in this shop. Eek! Oh, what the hell, she thought as she accepted the handles of the large carry bag. It was quite heavy. She hoped the airline staff wouldn't tell her off.

'Now, don't forget your map. And you know which way it is back to your hotel?' Brenda asked, nodding at Hannah's map still sitting on the countertop.

'Oh. Yes, I need to turn right when I leave here,' she said.

'And, please, forget about what I said.'

'Okay.' Hannah had struggled to think of anything else.

'I can lead you back to your hotel.' Benjamin said, reappearing.

'Off you go, Benjamin,' Brenda said, thrusting his helmet into his chest. 'I need you to take that parcel back to Angela. Now!'

'Okay, I'm going. But remember, it's the festive season, so you should be being extra nice to me,' he said, taking his helmet. 'Enjoy the rest of your stay. Maybe I'll see you in your city one day,' Benjamin added, smiling at Hannah as he left the shop.

'It was nice to meet you, Benjamin. Enjoy your Christmas,' Hannah called. 'Thank you so much for the tea and the gorgeous souvenirs, Brenda. I'm sure my friends will love them as much as I do.'

'Take care. Good things are around the corner for you.'

As she walked out, Hannah's feeling of confusion gave way to bemusement.

What a crock. Absolute rubbish.

But she did know who I'd lost. And she used Mum's saying just as she did – and she knew it. I know she did. How else could she know these things if she isn't psychic? And she was definitely holding something back.

The encounter with Brenda continued to nag at her. Back in her hotel room she paced back and forth then she sat on the bed and checked online for the time in Melbourne. It was four a.m. – far too early to call anyone and see if there was anything going on she should know about. Next she brought up her favourite news site on her phone. Under Breaking News were severe weather and flood warnings for Melbourne and suburbs. Hannah nibbled on her lip. Maybe that was the black cloud Brenda had been referring to. Perhaps she *could* see things.

What was the first thing she'd said? Something about outrunning things? Hannah tapped her lip, trying to think. *Ah, yes, that you can only outrun things for so long – or something like that.* Is that what she'd been doing with her life, with Christmas? Would it be better if she went home and faced it? What was she really avoiding anyway,

Christmas was all around her here and she was fine with it. Her mind went back to what the nice man with the dog, David, had said to her. He was absolutely right; she had nothing to prove. To anyone. Not any more. She'd proven she could be independent, could survive alone, and perhaps even thrive if she counted being here. *Good things are around the corner.*

Hannah felt her heart rate slow and a calmness take over. *I need to go home, don't I?* she asked the silent room. But then she felt a little sad. For the most part she'd really enjoyed her time here and still hadn't been to see a show on Broadway, the Statue of Liberty or had a close look at the Macy's Christmas windows.

Okay. If I can change my transfer to be picked up in half an hour I'll go. If not, I'll stay.

She wasn't sure where half an hour had come from, but it had, so that was the deal. The fact her fingers weren't shaking when she dialled the number and someone answered straight away told her she was doing the right thing. Yes, a car was doing a drop off not far away and could pick her up outside her hotel in half an hour. Hannah suddenly wasn't sure if she was pleased or disappointed.

She bundled everything into her suitcase, surprising herself by remembering to put her change of light summer clothes into her carry-on. Stuff trying to fit her shopping in, she decided, she'd damn well take two carry-on bags like everyone else did.

While she waited for the lift, Hannah took one last look out of the huge windows on the twenty-fourth floor. She had a view across the city to the Hudson River in the distance.

Several times she'd found herself pausing on her way to and from her room and wondering if she was looking right at the point where the airline pilot, now nicknamed Captain Sully, had made his famous river landing. She liked to think so. She loved that story of incredible courage and composure.

The lift arrived, pulling Hannah back from her reverie.

'Goodbye, New York. Thank you,' she whispered to the view, and stepped through the open doors.

There was no one waiting at the hotel's reception desk, which she took as another good omen. When she'd checked in there had been three lines five people deep. She quickly explained that no, she wasn't unhappy with her room or stay but that there had been an emergency back at home in Melbourne and she had to go. A white lie was easier than explaining further.

She had just emerged into the cold wind outside when a black people-mover pulled up.

'Mrs Ainsley.'

'Yes. Hi, Frankie.'

'You get in.'

'Thank you.'

'You leave New York early?' he said.

'Yes.'

''Tis okay,' he said, nodding, as if trying to convince himself.

'Yes, it's okay,' she said, smiling and catching his eye in the rear-vision mirror. 'I've had a lovely time, but I have to get home.'

Frankie replied with a shrug.

And as he navigated the traffic Hannah sat back and thought that that about summed it up.

At least she had some nice souvenirs, she thought, pulling her shopping carry bag closer to her. She really did feel sad to be leaving New York so abruptly but also happy to be going home – provided she could get on a flight …

Chapter Thirty

After a worrying wait in the check-in line, which seemed to take an age but was actually only a few minutes, Hannah was disappointed to learn she could only change her flight over the phone. Shaking, beginning to sweat and coming close to freaking out, she thanked the woman who seemed genuinely sorry she couldn't help, got herself out of the way and dug out the number to call amongst her travel documents. Damn, she could have – should have – done this while sitting in the car.

But Hannah received another buoying sign of good luck when she managed to get connected right away to a particularly efficient customer service representative and was able to get a seat on the six o'clock flight to Sydney, which she just had time to check in for. Even better, it was a cheaper fare so she received a small refund rather than being further out of pocket – even with the hefty fees for changing at such short notice.

She let out a big sigh of relief as she left the check-in counter clutching her boarding pass. *Now to get through security in time to catch it*, she thought, joining the massive queue. Thankfully a lot of check-points were open and it moved reasonably quickly. She checked her watch. She had an hour before boarding – just long enough to check out the shops and buy another book to read.

When she looked around for which direction to find her gate, Hannah noticed that right in front of her was a Metropolitan Museum of Art store. She'd enjoyed visiting their Fifth Avenue location, so she wandered over for a browse.

'Hello,' the assistant said, as she entered the store. 'Let me know if I can help you with something.'

'Thanks. I'm just looking,' she said. She walked around the compact space and recognised pretty much everything from the other store. She moved to the front display counter. And then she saw it. A ladybug just like she'd imagined – bright, glossy enamel. Absolutely stunning!

'Oh! A ladybug. Oh wow.'

'Yes. Isn't it beautiful? Would you like a closer look?'

'Yes, please.' Her chest was aflutter with excitement and she was surprised to find she could speak. She suspected she was gulping like a fish.

'Oh my,' she said, looking at the object sitting neatly in the centre of her palm. *I've found it. I really have. Oh, Sammy, you're going to love this.* Hannah was starting to feel so overwhelmed – this time in a good way – tears began to fill her eyes.

'It's very good quality.'

'Yes, I can see that.'

'It actually comes apart – see, you could hide a few rings or earrings in it.'

'It's perfect,' Hannah said a little breathily. 'I'll take it.'

'Brilliant. I'll just get one that's already in a box. I think that's all we have left, so it's your lucky day,' he said brightly.

Oh, you have no idea.

'Um, could I also take this one that's been on display?' Suddenly it felt important to Hannah that she and Sam have matching souvenirs.

'Oh. Okay. If you're sure?' The guy was nice, but he was being quite slow. Hannah checked her watch. She wasn't sure how long it would take her to get to the gate. She'd come this far, she couldn't miss her flight now. She also wanted to get a new book to read.

'Yes, quite sure. I'd actually better get going – I have a flight to catch,' she said, handing over her credit card.

'Okay. I'll give you a twenty-five percent discount for the one that was on display.'

'Thanks very much. That's great.' *Please just hurry up.*

Hannah rushed towards her gate. She wouldn't completely relax until she was there. She was relieved to see she still had twenty minutes until her flight began boarding and that there was a bookshop nearby. Everything was working out beautifully.

*

Picking up her Sydney to Melbourne connection had been seamless and the quarantine officers had approved her timber pieces without any issue, too.

She was now sitting in a cab, rushing past the Melbourne suburbs that were a wet, distorted blur. The driver wasn't up for chatting, but she had managed to discover from him that the rain had started at five that morning – five hours ago. So, it seemed the forecasters had got it right for once. Hannah hoped they were wrong about the extensive flooding.

She had several missed calls from Sam to return, but she felt the need to be quiet right now and take it all in – what, she wasn't actually sure. But she felt different in some way. No, she revised, not *different*. Shifting. She felt a strange sense that she was in the middle of something. She almost laughed and shook her head at herself. She was being silly. She was clearly overtired.

As she pulled into her street her heart swelled at the familiarity. She loved this place, had done so her whole life. How could she have contemplated moving, even for just a second? Thank goodness for Beth's sensible advice.

Everything looked lovely and shiny with the rain. But the gutters were full, with water surging and lapping at driveways – at any moment these refreshing summer rains could become devastating.

She sat in the cab for a moment staring at the front of her home, a strange and strong reluctance to not get out and return to normal life coursing through her. Here, right now, despite her tiredness, she felt a peacefulness the likes of which she hadn't felt in ages, if ever. It didn't even bother her that it was Christmas Day and she would be spending it home alone.

'Miss?' the driver said, snapping her out of her reverie.

'Sorry. Here. On savings, thanks,' she said, leaning forward and passing her key card through the gap between the seats.

'Thanks very much. Enjoy the rest of your day,' she said after the driver had placed her suitcase on the end of the brick path. 'Oh, and merry Christmas,' she added.

'Thanks. And same to you.'

Hannah longed to stand there and hold onto the last shreds of her strange but nicely altered state. And there was something particularly lovely about experiencing rain when the temperature was so mild. But when the gently falling drops turned into a downpour she let out a gasp, picked up her suitcase and raced to the front door.

She sat at the kitchen bench feeling a little lost for a moment, listening to the rain beating forcefully on the roof before snapping to attention. She'd better make sure the stormwater drains around her house weren't overflowing and causing damage in the downpour.

With an umbrella and wearing a light rainproof coat, Hannah checked outside all around her yard for any signs that water may be getting into places it shouldn't. Satisfying herself that everything was well, she walked across the street to Beth's and let herself in the side gate. She knew Beth had a drain at ground level out by her garage that had become blocked a couple of times over the years and had caused her laundry to become flooded. Hannah was almost pleased to find it clogged and with water rising around it – her return home early was vindicated. Perhaps this was what Brenda had been referring to, she thought as she squatted and cleared the leaves, dirt and debris away with her hands and then waited for the water to begin flowing freely again.

★

Hannah had just finished putting on a load of washing after taking a long hot shower, and was walking down the hall when she heard a strange sound. It was a squealing squawk, but didn't sound like any of the birds in the area. Anyway, they'd be off somewhere sheltering from the rain, wouldn't they?

Needing to satisfy her curiosity, she went to the front door, opened it and looked out. She glanced left and right along both sides of the street. Another squeak, sounding very close this time, caused her to look down. There on her porch was a wet, dishevelled grey tabby cat. It was looking up at her with big, pleading eyes.

It meowed again – a mere throaty squawk this time.

'No, I'm not feeding you. And I'm not a cat person. Go away,' Hannah said, and closed the door.

She set about making a cup of tea. But when she sat to drink it she couldn't settle. And there it was again, damn it. She wasn't going to feed the cat – that was one sure way of encouraging every stray cat in the suburb to flock to her yard and call it home and make a mess with bins and kill off any birdlife or small native animals. But she probably should at least give it something to drink. She ignored the little voice that told her there was water rushing about everywhere – there was no way the cat could be thirsty. But she felt she should do *something*. She'd never had a cat turn up before.

She took a breakfast bowl from the cupboard, filled it with water and went outside. The cat sniffed at it, looked at her, and then back down to the bowl.

'Be grateful you've got water. I am not feeding you,' she said, and went inside without a second glance. She sat back down in the kitchen and tried to ignore the uneasy feeling growing inside her that the cat was lost and needed help. It had seemed frightened, but hadn't hissed or spat at her so it might be someone's well-loved pet that had got lost or perhaps swept away with the water.

'Okay, I'll put out a towel for you to sit on and get dry, but that's it.'

She opened the door, looked down, and gasped.

There sitting in front of the cat was a tiny tabby kitten with white paws. Another one dangled from the mother cat's mouth. 'Oh,' she said. For the first time Hannah realised just how tiny the mother cat was – barely more than a kitten herself. And so thin that Hannah could see her ribs. Hannah's heart stretched tightly. *Now what am I meant to do?*

She tried to think if she had a box to put out for them and uselessly looked around her. She raced into the garage and tipped the Christmas decorations out onto the floor and placed the towel inside the box. She hoped they would still be there when she got back.

Now the mother cat was sprawled out limp on the tessellated tiles panting, with the kittens searching her belly for sustenance. Hannah didn't know much about cats but shouldn't the mother be nudging the kittens into position? And then the cat let out a moan.

Without a second thought, Hannah scooped her up, placed her carefully in the box, put the kittens in beside her and took them inside. *I can't just leave them there. It's Christmas, after all.*

She opened a can of tuna and placed some on a plate and put it under the mother cat's nose. But while the cat appeared interested, she didn't seem to have the energy to get up out of the box. Hannah sat cross-legged on the floor and took a sliver of tuna from the spoon with her fingers and held it near the cat's tongue.

After shrinking back in fear and then taking a sniff, and then after a few moments' hesitation, the cat carefully took the first sliver from her, and the second, and then the third …

Up close, Hannah saw the terrified look in the mother cat's eyes, the way it tried to shrink warily from her. She felt sure now that it was a stray or feral, but was dealing with her fear of humans in order to save her babies. Her two remaining babies. Hannah didn't know anything about kittens, but wasn't two a very small litter? The poor thing. *Bless her*, she thought, choking back the lump in her throat. No doubt they'd been safely hidden in one of the drains before the rain had come. The dear little things. The poor cat had most likely lost several kittens and then used the last of its nine lives to save her remaining babies. The thought struck Hannah forcefully.

And to think I almost ignored you.

She was careful not to feed the cat too much too quickly – she'd offer her some more again a little later. She put out another bowl of water, spread out a few layers of newspaper in the far corner of the kitchen, added some from the shredder in the office for a makeshift litter area, lay a towel over half the box, and then reluctantly left the room. She wanted to sit and keep watch, but knew the cats needed their rest.

She probably should have put them in a room where they could be confined, but they were there now and had been through enough of an ordeal to be moved again. The laundry was the obvious choice, but it wasn't quiet and calm with the washing machine churning away – and there was still another load to do.

She'd just put on the last of washing and was carrying the clothes rack up the hall to the lounge room to hang the first lot up to dry when she heard a voice at the screen door. She'd left the main door open so the house could air after being shut up for a week.

'Hello? Anyone there?' It was Sam.

'Sam! Merry Christmas,' she said, careful to keep her voice low. She opened the door to her friend.

'Merry Christmas. What the hell are you doing here?'

'I could ask you the same question.'

'I just popped by to make sure your houses weren't getting flooded …'

'That's so lovely of you. I wasn't sure if I should ring Beth or not. I didn't want to worry her. I've checked the drain and cleared it, and will again before dark. All's fine here, too.'

'But you're meant to be in New York.'

'I came back early.'

'I can see that. I'm just waiting for the explanation. And why are we whispering?'

'I've taken in a cat with kittens. They're in the kitchen resting.'

'You've done what?'

'You heard.'

'Yes, but since when does Hannah Ainsley have pets inside the house?'

'Since now, apparently. They turned up at the door and I took pity on them – as it's Christmas. I know, I'm as stunned as you are. But you should have seen their sad little faces. And the weather's so bad. They were drenched.'

'I need to sit down.'

'Sorry, come through to the lounge – I don't want to disturb them.'

'You've lost your mind.'

'You could be right.'

'Come on, I'm dying to know why you're back a week early. Didn't you enjoy it?'

'It's not that, I did. It was great. I really enjoyed it. And I think just what I needed.'

'That's wonderful, but stop dodging the question.'

★

'Wow,' was all Sam said when Hannah had finished telling her about the trip, the lovely, random strangers she'd met along the way, and how she came to be back early.

'It's weird that I had to go all that way to find out that I need to be here.'

'It makes sense to me. It's the forest for the trees factor – sometimes you can't see what's right in front of you and you have to take a step back before you can. I'm so glad you're home. And I bet mamma-cat in there is too.'

'Yeah.'

'At least I guess travel insurance will take care of the accommodation you didn't use. You did take out travel insurance, didn't you?'

'Of course. But no, it doesn't cover me for changing my mind. Don't worry, before I left Jasmine suggested I book directly with the hotel and spend a bit extra on having a refundable room. She really should be writing a blog on travel tips or something ... But, hang on, shouldn't you be off at Rob's brother's recovering from stuffing yourself too full of Christmas fare? What's going on?'

'I told you, I just popped by to check yours and Beth's places were okay. I'd better get back. Do you want to come with me?'

'Thanks, but I'm exhausted and, anyway, I need to keep an eye on the cats and deal with all the washing and unpacking. Speaking of which, I got you something – a souvenir.'

'You didn't need to do that.'

'Of course I did – I know how you love presents. Just wait there.'

Hannah raced to her bedroom.

'Now, close your eyes and hold out your hand,' she said when she'd returned with the gift hidden behind her back.

Sam grinned expectantly as she did as requested.

'Okay. You can open them now.'

Sam opened the box and unwrapped the tissue paper to reveal the lady beetle.

'Oh my god, I love it! It's gorgeous, the most beautiful thing I've ever seen. Oh wow, Hann. Thank you so much. I'll treasure it always,' she said.

Hannah beamed at her friend.

'I got one for me too, I couldn't resist.'

'I'm not surprised. It's incredible, and really is the perfect souvenir. You know, though, it could be said that two ladybugs are officially the start of a collection,' she said with a laugh, nodding at Hannah's charm bracelet.

'Haha. I hadn't thought about that, but you might be right. So, what do you think of these? This is what I got for the girls – all the same so there'll be no fighting. Each is a little different, though, because they're handmade. They're puzzle boxes.'

'I can see that. They're gorgeous,' Sam said, picking the first one up and examining it.

'They're meant to depict New York as the big apple.'

'I got that too. I love the little worms.'

'Yes, aren't they cute? I had so much trouble finding something that wasn't tacky.'

'I love them, but I love my ladybug more. Thank you so much,' she said, pulling Hannah to her.

'I'm glad. And it's my pleasure. I have presents for Rob and the boys, too, but they are still packed up. I had so much fun shopping. Went a little overboard, but, hey, it's not every day you go to New York,' she said. 'God, it's so good to see you,' she said, hugging Sam.

'I missed you too – though goodness knows why when you were emailing nearly every day,' she said, laughing. 'I'd better go back and then get the boys home and into bed.'

'Yes, and I'd better hang the washing up before it goes mouldy.'

'Good idea. Hopefully the worst of this weather's over. Now, before I leave, I have to take a little peek at your new friends.'

'Okay. Just a quick one.'

Hannah felt like a proud mother herself carefully pulling back the towel to reveal the cat and her kittens, who were all snoozing soundly. The mother cat stirred and looked at them warily before laying back down again.

'Oh, the poor little things. They're *all* tiny. And she's so thin. I wonder if she's lost some kittens. What have you got to feed her?'

'Tinned tuna. And I'll defrost some steak and chicken. Is that okay, do you think? Should I just take them to a vet?'

'A vet will cost a fortune on Christmas Day. No, I think just try and feed the mother up for a few days. She'll take care of the kittens. Fresh meat should be okay and I'm sure the corner shop will have some tinned food. Don't give her store-bought dry food, though, I've read some terrible things about it online. Don't forget you're also going to need some proper cat litter and a tray and scoop. If you're not sure of anything, just Google. Welcome to the world of pet ownership!'

'She's just visiting, Sam. And only because it's Christmas. I still don't do pets.'

'Yeah, right, famous last words. She looks pretty settled to me. And calm about being inside for a stray. You'd better take her to a vet in a few days, anyway, and make sure she isn't microchipped – and not full of fleas and worms.'

'They'll do all that when I deliver her to a shelter when she's a bit stronger.'

'Whatever you say, Hann. I'd really better go. Thanks so much again for my ladybird – I'll treasure it always,' she said.

They walked out together.

'And, again, merry Christmas,' Sam said, pausing before she got in her car.

'Thanks, you too. You know, I never thought it would be again, but, yes, it is a merry Christmas,' Hannah said.

Chapter Thirty-one

Hannah set about defrosting a piece of steak and a chicken thigh fillet to share with the mother cat. She was standing beside the microwave waiting, when she was startled to feel something brush against her leg. She looked down to find the mother cat rubbing against her.

'Hello. I'm getting us some dinner,' Hannah said. 'We have chicken and beef and of course there's still some of the tuna. You can have some of each, if you like.'

The cat let out the cutest squeaky meow, which Hannah took to be approval and thanks, before sitting on her bottom and wrapping her tail around herself neatly.

'Look at you, sitting down to wait patiently. What a good kitty.' Hannah squatted down to stroke the cat who began purring and rubbing against her hand. 'You really are a little sweetie, aren't you?'

Without thinking Hannah tentatively picked the cat up and held her to her chest. She didn't struggle and didn't seem particularly afraid. Hannah felt her heart swell when the cat climbed a little higher and snuggled into her shoulder. She could feel the gentle vibrations of the cat's purring against her chest through her t-shirt.

'Oh, darling thing,' she murmured as she let out a long breath. *Is that possibly the most comforting, relaxing feeling in the world?* Hannah knew at that moment that Sam had been right. She was hooked. The cats – all of them – would be staying. There was now no way she could send the mother cat away or part her from her kittens.

'What do you think about staying?'

The cat snuggled in closer.

'And how do you feel about being called Holly – since it's Christmas? Oh, you like that, do you,' she said and giggled as the cat licked her ear.

The microwave dinged and Hannah reluctantly put Holly the cat down and got up.

*

Hannah lay in bed unable to get to sleep. Her body clock was all over the place. She itched to get up and check on Holly and the kittens, but resisted. As lovely as they were, they needed to be left alone to rest. It was early morning. Hannah knew she could get up and go for a walk or make herself a coffee, but she didn't want to disturb her new family. Despite knowing she was being completely ridiculous, she stayed in bed, keeping quiet and listening out for them. It was actually nice to feel needed, to have such a worthwhile responsibility.

She found her gaze drawn to the wardrobe that was still full of Tristan's things. *Should I? Could I?* Her heart rate picked up slightly. She got up and went over. Taking a few deep breaths, she opened the door. Tristan's scent was still there – not as strongly as before, but still detectable. Or was her mind playing tricks on her? She took a deep whiff.

Oh Tris. But she was surprised to find herself remaining calm and her eyes dry. *I'm okay. I can do this. Or at least try*, she thought, pulling a plastic bag from the roll she'd left in the wardrobe and shaking it open.

She carefully eased the first of his suit jackets from its hanger and checked its pockets. She wasn't expecting to find anything – he'd always been careful to empty his pockets.

Next she moved onto the pants and then the second suit. She paused when she'd finished his work clothes and took stock of how she was feeling. A few tears fell as an answer. She was disappointed at the depth of pain gripping her. She cursed being brought down when she'd finally been feeling so positive. She buried her head in her hands and let the tears fall.

Hannah was surprised to hear a little squeaky meow. She looked up to find Holly sitting in front of her, peering up at her. She couldn't help but smile when the cat pushed her way into Hannah's lap.

'Oh, Holly, girl, bless you,' she said, gently gathering the cat to her. She loved the feeling of the cat's purring against her chest. 'I thought I could, but I can't do it,' she said. The cat responded by wriggling free with a little *harrumph*, lay on the carpet nearby and began licking her paws and then cleaning her face. Hannah found herself smiling.

'Is that your get-on-with-it-I'll-wait-right-here pose?' Hannah said to the cat. 'Great, so you're ignoring me already. I've heard cats are contrary creatures. But I don't mind, I think you're lovely,' she said, reaching over and scratching Holly under the chin. The cat answered with a lick to her hand and then continued her ablutions.

Hannah wiped her eyes and gritted her teeth. *I can* do this. *It's* time, she told herself firmly and returned to the task, the little cat toiling away quietly beside her.

★

Placing the bag of socks and jocks into the rubbish – no one wanted used underwear, did they? – and then seeing the five bulging garbage bags lined up in the hall threatened to bring Hannah undone again. But she was distracted by Holly who always seemed to appear just at the right time. A cuddle with the cat was a great distraction and made her feel better. When she put the cat back down, Hannah felt a little more detached from the bags beside her. *I have my memories, holding onto his things would be selfish.* She liked the thought that someone who was having a hard time might get a job and turn their life around wearing one of Tristan's lovely suits.

When she returned to the kitchen to get Holly some breakfast, she found herself feeling almost exhilarated at having got through such a big task without falling apart. Something she'd put off for a whole year. It was a major milestone. *I'm so much stronger, I really am.* It crossed her mind to phone and tell Sam, or send a text, but she thought better of it. *I've done it. I'm proud of myself, end of story. I don't need anyone else's praise.*

★

Hannah felt bad about bundling the cats up for a trip to the vet for a check-up, but knew it was the right thing to do. She was decidedly anxious about what would happen when the vet passed a scanner over Holly's neck. Though, she kept telling herself, if the cat had another family then she would be consoled by knowing she'd done a good thing taking her in when she needed help, and she'd bring relief and joy to a family who had been devastated at the loss of their pet. Perhaps they might let her keep the kittens. Only time would tell.

It was out of her hands now, she told herself as she pushed open the glass door to the vet practice and carried in the cats in their new carry box. She had chatted to them quietly the whole way there in the car, trying to reassure them and herself that all would be fine. She felt jittery – she'd always hated medical waiting rooms and this place was just like those for humans.

'Hello,' the receptionist said. 'Who do we have here?'

'Hi, we have an appointment for three – at three. This is Holly, Lucky and Squeak.' After getting to know the kittens a little better, Hannah had decided on these names. Not very original, but accurate nonetheless.

'Lovely. Thanks, Mrs Ainsley. Take a seat and Doctor Walker will be with you shortly.'

Hannah had just sat, placed the carry box on the chair beside her and picked up a magazine to read when she was startled to suddenly find a large German shepherd standing in front of her. It was staring up at her and wagging its tail. She recognised him straight away as Charlie, the dog from the park all those months ago.

'Oh. Hello there,' Hannah said, and was rewarded with a lick to her hand.

At least you're showing some restraint and manners and not trying to clamber into my lap this time, she thought with a smile. Now she was a pet person, she was better equipped to deal with such behaviour. Perhaps he detected this change in her.

'Charlie. Please don't harass the clients. Oh.'

Fiona McCallum

That voice was familiar, too. Hannah looked up.

'Hello.' She found herself blushing slightly.

'Thank goodness you're here,' the handsome man said.

Hannah frowned. 'Sorry?' *I'm not late for my appointment, am I?* She stood up and was about to pick up the cats when she was stunned to find herself being pulled into his chest. *No wonder Charlie the dog's a little too forward.*

'I thought we'd lost you.' Hannah frowned again as she tried to figure out what he was talking about.

'You look well,' he said, holding her back and scrutinising her. She blushed a little more.

'I think you have the wrong person,' she said. 'I'm Hannah Ainsley – we have met a couple of times, with your dog, but …'

'At the park. Yes, I know. Though, I didn't know your name. Hannah, that's nice.'

'Er, thanks.' *What the hell is going on here?* 'I'm here for a check-up. Well, not me exactly. Are you Doctor Walker?' she said, lost for something else to say.

'No, that's my colleague. I'm Doctor Shaw, Pete,' he said, holding out his hand for her to shake. 'Sorry, you must think I'm really weird,' he said as if he'd just noticed her perplexed expression. *He's really quite cute*, she was startled to find herself thinking.

'Let me explain.' *Oh please do.*

'We've discovered Charlie here seems to have a knack for detecting people suffering from terminal cancer – reacting just like he did with you those two times. So, you see, I was really worried for you.'

'I'm fine. And not suffering from cancer – terminal or otherwise,' she said brightly.

'That's great to hear. He must have just taken a shine to you for some reason, then.' He frowned slightly as if thinking that was odd.

'Maybe he gravitates towards non-animal people too.'

'That's right, I remember you saying you're not an animal person. So what are you doing at a vet clinic? And if I'm not mistaken, that's the sound of a cat and kittens,' he said with a laugh, pointing at the carry box that was now emitting various squeaks and meows.

'Yes, well, I'm new at all this. I've never owned a pet before in my life and have never wanted to. They turned up looking wet and miserable and I took pity on them because it was Christmas Day.'

'And after two days you couldn't think of your home and life without them in it, right?'

'Yes, I've been well and truly suckered in,' she said with a laugh.

'Lucky kitties, and I'm sure you'll have lots of fun and happy times together. Thank goodness Charlie got it wrong and you're okay.'

'You know, maybe he didn't – well, not completely. At the time I did feel like I was dying – from grief,' Hannah said quietly, sitting down again. 'Perhaps he was picking up on my sadness.'

'Oh?' Pete sat down next to her.

'I had recently lost my husband and both parents in a car accident.'

'God, that's terrible. Um, not the accident involving the truck? On Christmas Day last year?'

'Yes. That's the one.'

'I'm so sorry.'

'Thanks. It took quite a while to pick myself up, but I'm doing much better now,' she said. 'And these guys are certainly helping by giving me a new focus.'

'Yes, there's nothing like needing to care for someone else to drag you up out of the doldrums. I lost my wife six months before you lost your family – cancer.'

'I'm so sorry.' *God, she must have been very young.*

'Thanks. You learn to muddle through, don't you?'

'Yes.'

'I have a patient to see now, and I have no idea if it's too soon for you, or if you'd even be interested, but I'd really like to get to know you a little better, Hannah. Would it be okay with you if I got your details off the system and gave you a call sometime? Perhaps we could go out for a coffee, or a drink, or a meal. Sorry, I'm clearly terrible at this. It's been a long time since I ...' he said, wringing his hands together.

'I know what you mean. Me too. And, okay, yes, since I've already had your dog slobbering all over me, it would be nice to get to know you too,' Hannah said, smiling at him.

'Great. Brilliant.'

The next moment they were interrupted by the sound of a door opening and then a female voice.

'Holly and Lucky and Squeak?'

'Yes,' Hannah said, getting up. 'I look forward to seeing you again,' she said to Pete, gave him another beaming smile, touched his arm and rubbed Charlie's ears briefly before picking up the box and walking towards where Doctor Walker stood waiting for her.

Hannah couldn't wipe the grin from her face and the warm feeling from her heart. Though she also felt a little jittery as she waited to find out if there was any formal record of Holly's existence.

She held her breath as the scanner was passed over the perfectly well-behaved cat, and then her day became even better when she learned there was no microchip implanted. Hannah was free to keep her, along with her kittens – discovered to be both little boys. Even better, all three were declared fit and healthy.

Pete was nowhere in sight when Hannah paid the bill for the consult and bags and tins of cat and kitten food and a few cat toys and booked Holly in to be de-sexed in a few weeks when the kittens were weaned. The little boys had to wait a bit longer for the snip. She'd taken her time, but couldn't hover any longer without it looking odd, so she left. She was just in her car and about to turn her key in the ignition when her mobile dinged. The number was unfamiliar. She read the text.

Hi Hannah. Really looking forward to catching up again sometime. Let me know when suits. Cheers, Pete (& Charlie)

'Oh,' Hannah said, staring at the message. 'What do we think about this, Holly girl?'

Hannah sat staring at the phone trying to think of how to reply. *Thanks, I'll let you know*, didn't seem at all adequate. But it was what came to mind. She sat for a few moments longer. And then a strange feeling came over her.

'Sorry, guys, change of plans.' She stuffed her phone back in her handbag and threw it over her shoulder as she got out. She collected the carry box from the passenger side and went back inside the vet clinic.

Pete was standing at the reception desk looking at something on the computer. He glanced up.

'Hannah. Hi.'

'Do you have a minute?' she said, beginning to blush under his gaze.

'Sure, come on back here,' he said, standing aside. 'Have a seat,' he said when she was in what looked like the staff tea room. Hannah was glad to, suddenly her legs were beginning to shake. He closed the door and sat with his hands loosely in his lap. 'Is everything okay?'

'Yes. Good. Sorry, I'm getting flustered.'

'I sent you a text.'

'Thanks, yes, I saw it.'

'And …?'

'Well, the thing is … God, this is really hard.'

'It's okay, Hannah, take your time. Just tell me what's on your mind,' he said kindly.

'I'm not going to be calling or texting you to catch up. I've changed my mind and I wanted to tell you in person.' *Shit, too harsh, Hannah.* She took a deep breath. 'You see, the thing is, I'm not ready to start dating. You seem nice, you really do and it's lovely to have met you, but … Sorry.'

'You don't have to be sorry, Hannah. If you're not ready, you're not ready. Only you can know. But, I'd be happy to take things slow, get to know each other as friends and see where it leads. There wouldn't be any pressure.'

'But I think there would be. As you said, you're that bit further along than me. Every time we met you'd be wondering if I'm ready or when things are going to change between us. God, I'm rambling like an idiot. The truth is, and I never thought I'd hear myself say this in a million years, but I need more time on my own. It just hit me, really. Anyway, I wanted to tell you in person,' she added with a shrug and got up. 'I'm sorry.'

'It's okay, Hannah, really,' he said, standing up too. 'I admire your strength. It took some serious guts to come in here and tell me to my face. I appreciate that.'

'Thanks. I wish you all the best. I really do.' Hannah was surprised to find herself leaning in and giving him a kiss on the cheek.

'The same goes from me. I hope one day we'll meet again, Hannah, and you'll feel differently. But I promise I won't be sitting around hoping or waiting for your call,' he said, smiling at her.

'Great. Thanks.' Hannah smiled at him and went to leave. She knew she'd done the right thing, but still she ached a little with disappointment.

'Um, Hannah? I think you've forgotten something,' Pete said. She froze and turned back. He had his eyebrows raised and was smirking and pointing at the carry box sitting on the floor.

'Oh my god. Fine pet owner I am!' she said with a laugh and blushed furiously. 'Sorry, kitties,' she said sheepishly to the box as she reached down and grabbed the handle. 'Bye, Pete.'

Chapter Thirty-two

Hannah's doorbell rang at eight o'clock on New Year's Eve.

'Auntie Beth, it's so good to see you,' she said. 'How was the trip?'

'Wonderful, but very similar to the last one. One cruise is very much like another – good, but still … More to the point, how were your travels?'

'Great. I really enjoyed it. I'll tell you all about it, but first you'll never guess what has happened. Come in.'

'Is everything okay? I got your note on my door asking me to come over. I'm sorry I'm so late – the ship was delayed coming into port and then a few of us went out for a bite to eat before heading home. I hope I haven't held you up.'

'No, not at all. I'm still talking myself into going out to Caitlin's party, actually. Anyway, come through. Cup of tea? I've just boiled the kettle.'

'Oh, yes, please.'

'I'm not sure if you've caught up with how much rain we've had. Sam came by and checked we weren't being flooded and

I've been keeping a close eye on everything,' Hannah said as she organised the tea.

'That's very thoughtful of you both, and very much appreciated. Did my outside drain hold up okay?'

'It was blocked when I first checked, but it's been fine since.'

'Thank goodness for that.'

'Here we are,' Hannah said, putting down the mugs of tea. 'I also have some melting moment biscuits if you'd like one.'

'Oh, that would hit the spot. It's wonderful to see you so chipper, dear. And you're practically glowing. Now, what is it you're so keen to tell me. But do please sit, you're making my head spin.'

'Sorry,' Hannah said, and settled on a stool. 'You'll never guess what happened here on Christmas morning. I got back to find ...'

'Hang on, you were meant to be in New York for Christmas.'

'I came home early. I'll tell you all about *that* in a bit, but the thing is ...'

Right at that moment Holly walked in and went straight over to Beth and rubbed on her leg.

'Oh. Hello there.'

'Auntie Beth, this is Holly,' Hannah said, getting off her stool and picking up the cat.

'Hello, Holly,' the old lady said, reaching over and stroking the cat. 'Aren't you just lovely?'

'She is – and so are her two darling little kittens.'

'Don't tell me you've agreed to do some pet sitting.'

'No. You're looking at a newly crowned pet owner.'

'Golly. Really?'

'Yes. Don't look so startled.'

'Well, it is quite a turn up for the books.'

'I've been reformed, thanks to Holly. She appeared at the door completely soaked through and bedraggled, and with two of the tiniest kittens in tow. You should have seen the state they were in. I just couldn't say no.'

'Good for you, darling,' Beth said. 'Yes, it's very hard to resist when they choose you.'

'I understand that now – I never did before. But it's such a powerful force. This really was meant to be. She's a huge comfort and has given me such a boost. You know, I think she's done more for me in a few days than I could ever do in a lifetime for her.'

'You really have seen the light, haven't you?'

'Yep. Scary cat lady in one fell swoop,' Hannah said with a laugh.

'I think you're far from that, dear. At least she's small. Can I have a hold?'

'Of course. You don't mind, do you, Holly?' Hannah kissed the cat on the head and handed her over.

'Aren't you just the sweetest thing?' Beth said as Holly snuggled into her chest. 'Oh, I've so missed having a pet.'

'I know you have. Auntie Beth?'

'Yes.'

'You know how you've said before that you can't get another dog because you'd hate for it to be taken away if something happened to you?'

'I couldn't bear it. At my age, there's every likelihood a pet will outlive me or I might end up having to move somewhere I can't have one. Sadly, these are the realities of old age, my dear,' she said with a sigh.

'If you want to get another dog, Auntie Beth, I promise it will have a home forever here with me if anything happens.'

Beth peered at Hannah.

'I mean it.'

'That's a very generous offer.'

'And a genuine one. I'm serious, Auntie Beth.'

'But a dog would mean picking up poo in public, Hannah.'

'I know. I never thought I'd be cleaning out a litter box either, but I do now. And I haven't gagged once!'

'You have a lovely purr, Holly,' Beth said.

'Auntie Beth, the offer is there.'

'Thank you, darling. I have to admit I have been pining quite of late for a furry companion. You know, maybe I'll go to the RSPCA tomorrow if they're open and see what they have. But right now, Holly, you have to show me your kittens – I just know they're gorgeous. Maybe you'll turn me into a cat person too.'

'My offer would still stand. Come on, then,' Hannah said, getting up and leading the way.

'Oh, I think my heart just melted,' Beth said, bending down to look at the kittens nestled in the box as Holly rubbed against her legs. 'I don't think I can leave them. They're just so darned cute.'

'Exactly. Why do you think I'm still here and not off at Caitlin's fancy dress party?' Hannah laughed.

'Oh. Yes. That's right. I forgot about it being New Year's Eve there for a moment. You go. I'll stay and babysit.'

'Would you? I know it's silly of me to be so attached to them.'

'Darling, it's quite all right. And the pleasure would be mine.'

'It would only be for a few hours – just long enough to see the New Year in. I really would like to go, actually.'

'Well, that's settled, then. Do you have something to wear? I hope you're going to dress up.'

'What do you think about me going as a black cat? Black leggings, black t-shirt and ballet flats, with a tail and ears that I've made.'

'Perfect.'

'I'll wait and pin the tail on when I get there – it would be too uncomfortable to wear while I'm driving – but can you help with my ears?'

'Of course. And you're going to need a black nose and some whiskers. I can do that for you with eyeliner, but we'd better get cracking. Oh, what fun!'

'You know, Auntie Beth,' Hannah said, looking at the old lady in the bathroom mirror, 'I think I'm going to be okay. I didn't think so there for a while, but now I'm sure.'

'I *know* you're going to be okay. You *are* okay. You've survived, now you're going to thrive,' Beth said. 'Oh, darling, I'm so proud of you.'

'I'm even a little excited to see what the future holds.'

Acknowledgements

Many thanks to Sue, Annabel, Adam, Cristina, Michelle, James, and everyone at Harlequin Australia for turning my manuscripts into beautiful books and for continuing to make my dreams come true. Huge thanks also to editor Bernadette Foley for her kindness, valuable insights and guiding hand to bring out the best in my writing and Hannah's story.

Thank you to the media outlets, bloggers, reviewers, librarians, booksellers, and readers for all the amazing support. It really does mean so much to me to hear of people enjoying my stories and connecting with my characters.

Many thanks to the members of the South Australia and Victoria police forces who very patiently answered my many questions and helped make procedural aspects as authentic as possible. Any errors are my own or down to taking creative liberties.

Finally, huge thanks to Carole and Ken Wetherby, Mel Sabeeney, NEL, and WTC for continuing to provide so much love and encouragement, and for being the best friends a person could ever hope to have. I am truly blessed.

talk about it

Let's talk about books.

Join the conversation:

 on facebook.com/harlequinaustralia

 on Twitter @harlequinaus

www.harlequinbooks.com.au

If you love reading and want to know about our
authors and titles, then let's talk about it.